SMOKE,
LIES, AND
GRIMOIRES

Nia Rose

A Poisoned Apple book
Poisoned Apple Publishing, L.L.C.

Copyright © Nia Rose 2020

Smoke, Lies, and Grimoires (Coven Chronicles, Book 5)

Book design by Poisoned Apple Publishing
Editing by Poisoned Apple Publishing

Published by Poisoned Apple Publishing, L.L.C.
www.poisonedapplepublishing.com

ISBN: 978-1-7348272-6-2

Printed in the United States of America

Coven Chronicles series by

Nia Rose & Octavia J. Riley

SPELLBOUND & HELLHOUNDS
SECRETS OF THE SANCTUARY
SPIRITS OF THE BLACK FOREST
SAND DUNES & BLOOD MOONS
SMOKE, LIES, AND GRIMOIRES

Stand Alone Novels by
Nia Rose
SONS OF STARS
KING OF CROWS

Dedication:

To my Tante Tigger.
Your home was a place of fantasy and magic. Around every corner there was something new to entangle me and pull me deeper into a place full of mystical, beautiful wonders. Thank you for being a light in my life.

DESERT
TEMPLE
HEAVEN'S HAND
DRAGON'S MOUTH
HELL'S F
MOUN
TEM
GAYGHA
PESHTPENHVET I
ESTVETSYT' AYNNIRUV
RED TIPPED
MOUNTAINS
THE GOLDEN SEA
SILVER THREAD
TOLVAI
BANSHEE
BOG
LORV
TEMPLE RUIN
JEWELED CA

FOREST TEMPLE

SATVIRIYA

THE CURSED
MIRROR

THE BLACK
FOREST

HALF HEART
BAY

KEMBERE LAKE

THE GENTLE TITAN

THE DEVIL'S PITCHFORK

O LAKE

ANOPY

AERISTRIA

 *Chapter 1:*

"I'm who?" Vanessa questioned, feeling both lost and confused.

"I feel as though we are missing a rather big something," Bobo added.

"I don't think I am capable of handling any extra surprises," Lyx admitted in exasperation.

"Okay. There are so many questions that I have right now," Leon added.

"Wait!" Ell cried out. Her hands flew up and were held out as if to ward off the barrage of questions that were to soon follow. As if controlled by unknown sorcery, there was silence from the group surrounding her.

Ell scanned over all the party members as they blinked curiously at her and Raven. Instantly, her gaze darted to the flustered and lively Coven lobby. Without wasting another moment, she scrambled over to her desk and tapped on the counter. "Pristine. Pristine! You lazy feline. Come manage the desk while I handle something."

From under the desk, the exotic white cat leaped up to the top of the counter and yawned while stretching. Her paws kneaded the counter as her claws scraped over it lightly. Pristine's tail floated languidly behind her as she slowly licked the hair of her paw flat. "I'm here, I'm here. No need to shout. You're welcome for me taking on this burden for you. Now, be on your way then, human," Pristine purred proudly.

Turning back to the group, Ell tried to appear more commanding and less rattled, but the panic swimming in her blue eyes gave away every emotion she was trying to hide. "You," she stated with a pointed look to Raven, and then she spun in a circle. Her frantic orbs landed on all the beings in the party. Every single body they landed on seemed to make the poor receptionist's eyes bulge out a bit more.

"One, two, three, four, five. Oh ... oh, goddess, help me." She fumbled over what to say and sighed loudly. Motioning for them to follow, she said, "*All* of you follow me." Quickly, she headed for the closest library door and headed down while the others followed.

"I do say. This is all rather unexpected. Is everything all right, my dear?" Bobo questioned in a concerned manner.

Shaking her head, Ell shook up a vial and it started to glow, illuminating the darkened halls of the endless rows of books, scrolls, and shelving. "I'll explain when we get somewhere more private," she whispered loud enough for the ogre to hear.

"What? What did she say?" Leon asked.

"Still waiting to know who I am ..." Vanessa griped with a heated glare over her shoulder at Raven.

"She said she'll explain when we are more secluded," Bobo informed.

Collectively, they all nodded.

Except Raven.

Since Ell's strange outburst, she had remained lost in thought and avoided making eye contact while she nibbled on her lips nervously. The worry was scrolled all over the Dark Elf's face. Vanessa didn't know what to think or feel when she looked at the woman. If asked a few moments earlier, she would have told that being that she trusted Raven with her life. Because she had been put into situations with the elf where her life was on the line and she had protected it. But now ... now the Spellweaver was wondering what secrets were being kept from her, and how on Raen Ell was tied into the whole mess.

A gentle brush of fingers on the back of her hand made Vanessa jump. Quickly, she noted the wizard that was lacing his fingers with her own. "You'll get your answers, Vanessa," he said softly.

Would she?

That was why she was upset, wasn't it? Because she was worried that answers would, somehow, elude her once more in her life. She was upset over the fact that there had been secrets kept from her. It was hard not to admit that there was a sting of pain over the fact that Ell held a portion of her life, a life she knew nothing of, and had made the choice to keep it from her. That is what was both frustrating and painful. How could Ell do that? *Why* would Ell do that? The more that she probed the methods and motives, the more that she realized the answer to the mounting questions could very well scare her more than anything she had ever witnessed.

Leon's hand squeezed hers, and Vanessa jolted from the unexpected action. Her wide eyes snapped to him as she broke out of her daze. "There is a good reason. I'm sure of it. I'm here with you. Bobo is here with you. We all are. You're not *alone* in this," he assured. And, as silly as the simple words were, they brought comfort to her.

She smiled and nodded. Squeezing his hand in return, she took a deep breath and tried to exhale all the negative thoughts that were taking root in her mind. She honestly wanted to hear everyone out, and she wouldn't give them a fair chance if she went in angry, guarded, and so fixed on her own emotions that she would shut out whatever they had to say. This was a chance to learn something about herself. She wasn't going to let pride or emotions get in the way of that.

They made their way through the library following Ell as she scurried through the massive shelving lining the corridor. They stopped momentarily in front of an old door—half hidden with boxes of scrolls and boards and a thick layer of smut that turned the once brown of the wood into a gray that matched the stone walls it was nestled into. The frazzled blonde started to remove a few of the boxes from in front of the door while Bobo and Raven went to aid with moving the heavier items out of the way.

Turning to face Vanessa, Ell wrung her fingers as she fidgeted relentlessly. "I always knew that there would come a day that you would find out about all this. I think I got more attached to you as I watched you grow up." She drew her lips into her mouth and nodded a lot as her eyes traced the bookshelves hugging their sides. "I suppose I thought I had a few more years before I'd need to tell you. I-I," she sighed and pushed a stray strand of hair behind her ear. It didn't stay in place, but the receptionist carried on as if it hadn't defied her. "I thought I had more time to prepare everything ..." Her eyes misted, and she shook her head. If the young lady was going to say anything more, she chose not to. Reaching into her pocket, Ell pulled out an iron key and fitted it into the lock behind her.

A turn of a key had never sounded more daunting than that key in that lock in that moment. The world seemed to stop for a fraction of a second as Ell pushed on the door, and it *creaked* open wide. Without a word, the receptionist walked into the darkened room.

The space was small and packed to the brim with boxes, items, and spare shelving. A metal bucket rested on the far side of the wall with a mop plunged inside, lost and forgotten. Resting on the rim of it were the handles to a few brooms, all of them sporting more cobwebs than they had probably ever swept up in their lifetime. There were a few pieces of furniture covered in white sheets, and the eerie, red moonlight spilling in from the small window high up gave enough light to show that there wasn't much to the room except for a monumental amount of clutter and enough filth to indicate years of neglect. Bobo removed his handkerchief and held it up to his nose as they all walked into the small storage area.

"Is Ell working part-time as the janitor, too? I know the girl works a lot, but this is a bit much," Lyx whispered to the party.

Bobo gave a quick upturn of his lips before clearing his throat and leaning toward the succubus saying, "I don't think this is about her occupation, my dear."

"Oooh," the she-demon whispered with a slow nod.

The small blonde fussed with a few sheets. Lifting them off their perch caused a flow of debris to circle her. Dust bathed the stale air and forced the poor woman to cough and sneeze relentlessly. Naturally, Bobo was there to save the day, offering his handkerchief to Ell.

"The air is rather dreadful in here, my dear. Might I inquire as to what has inspired you to bring us here?" the ogre asked. His concern for her was as great as his desire to leave the run-down, abandoned janitor room.

Ell sniffled after blowing her nose and smiled up at the gentleman-beast. "Thank you," she stated quietly. A heavy sigh escaped her as she gathered the courage to look Vanessa in the eyes. "I—I've held onto it for several years now. All the while, I tried to practice ways to tell you. The goddess seems to be forcing your fate today, and I can no longer keep it from you ..." The receptionist stepped forward, clutching her fists close to her chest. Her mouth held hints of a warm smile. "You were so little when you first came here," she started with a far off look in her eyes. "Couldn't hold you enough, and you were such a good baby. So quiet. So happy." The more she spoke, the more nervous she seemed.

The young woman wrung her hand that protectively held onto ... something. Ell's eyes peered down and nodded to herself before closing the distance between her and Vanessa. Her hand slowly opened to reveal the contents therein. It was a locket. A silver ball with two wings pressed down on the sides like clamps, and it shimmered in the dim light as the young woman's hands opened.

"It was your mother's," Raven said, her voice sounding distant and full of pain at the same time.

Vanessa spun to look the elven woman over and then scrunched her brow in deep thought. Slowly, she faced Ell and asked. "You-you both knew my mother?" It took everything in her to not process every shred of emotion that begged to take her over in that moment. Happiness, sadness, excitement, curiosity, and ... betrayal. Raven had no idea who Vanessa was when they met, but Ell? Ell had been her friend for years and her guide when she first arrived at the Coven. How could she keep such an important secret from her for all these years? The questions that she wanted to ask were all shadowed by that one, important detail.

Both of the women shared a look and then sympathetically looked to the young witch before nodding simultaneously. A lump grew in Vanessa's throat, and she was sure she would choke on it before she would be able to get a full breath of air in her lungs that didn't feel like it was a bucket of salty tears. Her chest burned as she willed herself not to breakdown right there.

"What was she—" Vanessa started to ask.

"Strong," Raven said, cutting the Spellweaver short. "She was a strong woman. And an even stronger Dark Elf."

Vanessa whirled around so fast her tangled hair whipped her in the face. "A-a-a Dark Elf? But I don't—"

Again, Raven cut her short by pointing to her ebony locks. "You're hair."

"My ears, though," she stated, touching each one on the side of her head as if they might have sprouted pointy tips in the last few minutes.

"Your father was human," Ell informed softly and then held out the locket she cupped in her hands. Her eyes held so many emotions that Vanessa felt like she was drowning in the receptionist's gaze. "He was fair, just, and kind," she listed as she reached out with one hand and gently grabbed the young witch's appendage. Turning it, Ell dropped the ball locket into the Spellweaver's palm. "They were a match that could rival the armies of Heaven and Hell, but, sadly, they could not withstand the hate of the wolves."

The words sank deep into Vanessa like one of the giant beasts had come to haunt her and sunk its taunting teeth into her skin. The wolves had killed her parents. She stumbled back and landed rump first on a rickety box. She felt dizzy, and her mouth felt dry.

"Vanessa, my dear, are you all right? You look a bit pale." Bobo's concerned voice surrounded her like a warm, familiar blanket. She nodded, but the action did nothing for her and the thoughts spinning in her mind.

Was she all right?

Raven's black, starlit eyes were in her view, and she followed the woman like she was mesmerized. The Dark Elf crouched down in front of the witch. "They were very dear to me. And very close. I took care of you often for them, and we would venture out into the woods together to gather flowers and herbs. You loved our long walks together, even though you were just a babe back then. But when everyone was being targeted by the wolves, our people became scared …" She trailed off, not sure how to continue.

Ell added, "My family has long since been the head of a secret society." She paused to let everyone soak in what she was saying.

Well, that was a surprise. If it hadn't been for the fact that they had been through so much in the past few days, they might have sputtered and gasped. However, they had been through a lot. It still didn't take away from the fact that not only had Ell been hiding things about Vanessa's past from her, but also the fact that the receptionist was part of a secret society. Oh, wait ... Ell's family was the head of it too?

Their heads spun, but they all remained quiet for a long moment. For one, they wanted to let Vanessa speak first. Ell held the keys to information about her family, and no one was going to take that away from her.

"Y—" what she was attempting to say fell from her being. A hand held her clammy forehead, and she felt lightheaded for a moment. This was too much, and her nerves were singing a chaotic melody as she attempted to take it all in. She almost looked annoyed about the information.

One more secret.

One more thing kept from you.

Vanessa shook off the feeling that was settling in her chest and drew in a deep breath to calm herself. What was she going to ask? Where did she start? As interesting as a secret society was, the fact that she could know more about her past seemed a smidgen more important to her presently. But where did she start when she felt like she was navigating a sea of lies and deceit.

Bobo spoke up first, "But why tell us this? Forgive me for saying this, but isn't the whole point of a ..." he searched around the room and then dropped his voice a bit as he continued in a whisper, "... Secret society is that it remains a secret?"

The ogre had long ago had his suspicions that not all was as it seemed. There was always something amiss during a mission or information that had conveniently been tucked away, forgotten, or lost. It happened too often to be filed incorrectly. His less-than-amused features spoke in volumes of how he portrayed the whole ordeal.

"You were going to need to know about it before we head out," Ell began.

Lyx's face contorted with concern. Her bright, golden hues were fixed on the young witch that was still steadily trying to absorb everything she had been told. It was clear that she wanted nothing more than scoop the Spellweaver up in a tight embrace. The succubus tried to step closer to comfort Vanessa, but paused when her inhuman ears heard something the rest hadn't. Looking torn for a moment, the demoness rushed over to the entrance.

The sound of the door shutting caused everyone to jump. Lyx cringed and forced a smile. "Sorry. Thought it would be best to shut and spell it with a privacy spell." She eyed over the room. "This is ... something I'm assuming needs to stay a secret."

Leon nodded, mumbling, "I think I've reached my quota for surprising bits of information for the year." He walked over to the door to spell it while Ell returned her attention to Vanessa.

"There had been burn notes sent between the hidden elves that had made a small village within the Black Forest and the secret society. They were requesting aid after the yearly blizzard. I had been frequenting with my parents to drop off provisions for those that had chosen to settle outside of the elven city. That year's snowstorm had frozen much of their stock, and, because of the newly melting snow, they had lost a lot of their grains and stored up items. It didn't help that they also lacked essential supplies like medicines and clothing along with the food shortage. I had met your parents that day, Larissanna and Charles, and I had seen you for the first time. A few short months passed with long visits and joyful meetings between us all. Until the reaping." She looked away and frowned hard.

The room was silent. Painfully silent. Vanessa clutched the necklace in her hand and gathered the courage to ask, "What was the reaping?"

Raven cast her eyes to the floor and whispered like every word she spoke was haunting her. "It was the night that the wolves attacked the town. The place where we had all settled and called home had been safe for years. As long as we did not stray too far into the woods, and as long as we stayed clear of the warded city, the wolves left us be. We were such a small and peaceful village. We weren't a threat to anyone." She shook her head. "They didn't think so. They took so many ... there was ... there was so much blood." She swallowed hard, squeezed her eyes shut, and clenched her hands into fists. "I had been out gathering what little food I could find with a scavenging party. We arrived not long after the wolves had attacked." She paused and slowly licked her lips. A shaky breath was drawn, and she released it with a slight shiver. "As the massacre took place, I ran to your parent's home, and they rushed out to meet me. Throwing a cloth bag over my shoulder and thrusting you into my arms, they spun me around and yelled at me to run." She hung her head low. "I took one look at your face as you cried and did as they told. I didn't even turn back to say goodbye. My heart had never felt as heavy as it did that day."

Laying a hand on Raven's shoulder, Ell continued while the Dark Elf collected herself. "I was in my last year at the academy. The night that Raven stumbled into town was a night I have never been able to forget. I had just gotten out of my night classes. Magic casting had always been a dream of mine, but I lacked the natural ability to do more than a crystal ball call. I thought extra studying would awaken some long-lost powers in me," she quietly laughed at herself before she continued. "I bumped into Raven holding you in the center of the bridge near the Adalith district. She—she looked so frantic. After explaining everything to me, I decided that I would take you to the safest place that I knew."

"The orphanage," Leon whispered.

Ell and Raven both nodded, but it was done too slowly and lacked both of the women's usual luster.

"Agatha was more than happy to take you in, but she knew that we had to keep what you were a secret. We didn't know how far the wolves were willing to go to kill off the Dark Elves," Ell admitted.

Vanessa looked confused and then snapped her gaze to Raven. "But you didn't stay." As she spoke, the Spellweaver realized why. "You went back to check on my parents and ..." She covered her mouth.

The shame in Raven's eyes couldn't be masked by their endless inkwell depths or glittering star shine. "I was too late," she breathed the reply. "To keep you safe, and all of those that I could save within the forest, I stayed behind and went underground, vowing that I would protect any that I could from the jaws of those fiends."

Climbing down from her seat and inching toward Raven, Vanessa gradually came to kneel in front of the woman before wrapping her arms around her neck in a tight hug. "I'm so sorry," she said softly.

The sadness ebbed from Raven's eyes, and a warm smile glided over the Dark Elf's mouth. She wrapped the Spellweaver in a lovingly embrace. "I saved you. For that, I am thankful."

"Thank you," Vanessa whispered.

Patting her back, Raven nuzzled into the young witch's hair and said, "I'd do it all over again if I could. I'd always pick to save you. Always."

There were trailing voices of two Coven members entering the library that brought them all to a dead silence. They went still, like the privacy spell had never been cast. Hearing the members seemed to jog Vanessa's memory. She turned on her knees, stood, and gasped at Leon. "The tablet!"

"Oh, imp poo," Lyx hissed.

Leon waved the thought away. "Don't worry about it. I'll take Lyx and handle all the Coven based stuff. You take care of what you need to. Head home, crystal ball message me that you got there, and I'll see you in the morning after we all get some much needed rest."

"Thank the goddess," Lyx purred. After being up for days on end, the thought of a warm, cozy bed was all the demoness needed to spur her and Leon out the door. "Be safe, darling!" she chirped, hugging the young witch before heading for the exit. Suddenly, the succubus stopped, turned, and gave a bright smile to the ogre. "You be safe too, Booboo," she said with a wink. Before anyone could reply, the two were out the door and heading to turn in the tablet.

Ell cleared her throat. "There is one more thing," the young lady said.

Blinking, Vanessa asked, not thinking that there could be anything crazier than finding out that you're half-elf, "What would that be?"

🎻 10

Raven pulled the young witch to her feet while grinning proudly. "Your grimoire."

 *Chapter 2:*

"I have a grimoire?" Vanessa screeched. She didn't know if she was happy or baffled, but it was safe to say it was probably a healthy dose of the two.

Nodding with a giggle, Ell chortled as she replied, "Yes. You do, but we need to hurry and head out so you can get it."

"I-I mean. Okay, yeah! Let's go!" Vanessa's enthusiasm over getting her very own grimoire silenced many of her questions and negative thoughts. Already, she had quelled her doubts over why Ell had kept the secret from her. She wasn't happy about it, but she could understand why it would have been hard to explain her origins. She was silently thankful that the receptionist had waited until they had emerged from the Black Forest. Until after she'd experienced all of the secrets that the dreaded place offered.

"Oh, by the goddess, not that place again," Raven whispered.

"It isn't that bad," Ell corrected with a pointed look to the Dark Elf.

Pausing with her hand on the knob, Vanessa turned from the door and asked, "Is there something I should be worried about?"

"No," Ell replied quickly.

"Yes," Raven grumbled.

Both of the women shared a look. But the narrowed gaze of Ell burrowed deep into Raven, and the elf turned away. Waving her hand like she was shoeing away a fly, the elven woman stated in a flat tone, "*Nun, nun.*"

"I am merely guessing that she is saying *no* and I, myself, doubt the honesty of her words," Bobo muttered.

With a hard slap to the elf's shoulder, Ell raced over excitedly to Vanessa's side at the door while Raven groaned in pain and massaged the spot that had been hit. "Come on," Ell chirped. "Let's go get this witch her grimoire!"

The four of them made their way back up to the main floor as they followed behind the receptionist. Hailing a pixie at the front entrance, Ell quickly asked them to collect any forms turned in with Pristine and file them away while she was gone. The request was happily obliged, and they all headed out.

As they headed for Star Child Orphanage, Vanessa ignored the wave of memories she was sure to be drowning under within the next several minutes by inspecting the jewelry that Ell had given her back in the Coven library. The soft, orange light from the lamps lining the streets glinted over the slick, chrome orb that hung from its silver chain. From the top of the metal orb, two curved wing-shaped clasps hugged the locket together, keeping it from spilling open. Vanessa turned it in her hands as she inspected the seam, curious of what might lay inside. But … also afraid.

For so long she had her past shrouded in mystery and only vague answers to her pressing questions. Now that she was receiving them, she didn't know what to think. In her earlier years, there had been a comfort in her lack of knowledge. Now, she was caught between the desire to know the answers to questions that had kept her up at night and the fear of what those answers could bring to her. For she knew all too well that not all answers brought peace of mind. Sometimes, answers caused just as much damage as the silence. She had managed to find solace in being alone for so long that she felt conflicted with all the information that was being handed to her.

And then there was the locket. That locket in the hands of someone like Vanessa was like a ticker spell. Any minute it would explode, and the damage could be catastrophic or so precise that there was no hope for her heart's salvation. Did she dare to open it?

Her fingers fumbled with the intricately designed clasps that seemed to be stuck fast. Ell's soft voice caused the young witch to jolt from the unexpected sound.

"There it is," the receptionist whispered.

And there it was …

In all of its shabby glory, the Star Child Orphanage stood proudly near the streets that overlooked the Silver Thread River. The structure was a mesh of brick and wood that was sun-washed and weather-worn. The steps leading to the front doors were lopsided, and the bell tower that was bathed in black soot on one side (from the chimney stacks nestled next to it) was crooked. The shingles on the rooftop were patchy and the smooth, wooden sign with the faded name of the building creaked slightly from side to side as the spring breeze played over it. It was just as she remembered. If not a bit better off than she last saw. The Coven had given a nice sum of money to help with the cost of repairs for the building as well as food and clothing for the children that resided therein.

The frown on her face was as deep as her sorrow for the state of the building's appearance. She needed to donate to them this month. Help them more. After all, they had raised her. As her eyes traced the orphanage, she could feel every memory when she lived there. Every experience that she had in or on that property threatened to come out of the building and override every single one of her senses. She took in a breath, and it sounded like she was on the verge of tears. A large, warm hand tenderly rested on Vanessa's shoulder. Slowly, she faced the gentleman-beast at her side. She and the ogre shared a silent moment as they stared at each other and then looked to the building before them.

Patting his hand, the young witch expressed, "I'm all right," in a soft, reassuring manner.

Whether he believed her or not, the gentleman-beast said nothing, but he did nod in reply as he gestured for her to walk up to the large, rickety home. It was hard not to take notice of the fact that Raven, Ell, and Bobo were all watching her with a mix of emotions scrolled all over their faces. The Spellweaver turned her attention back to the orphanage and took in another breath, held it in place, and marched for the front steps. Desperately, she attempted to get the drumming of her heart to match the slow, rhythmic beat of her footwork.

It wasn't working. Not unless she wanted to run.

As she scaled the steps, she tried to swallow, but it felt like her throat was tightening. Could they come back another day? The grimoire would be there tomorrow, right? She looked over her shoulder and forced a wry smile before facing the forward and grimacing with a deep groan.

Bobo knocked on the door and, with puffed cheeks and blazing red coloring her features, she glowered at the ogre. Her disgruntled, twisted visage bothered the demon not. He simply tugged at the worn lapels of his jacket, straightening out the tattered garment, and then fussed with his dulled-with-dirt cufflinks. After clearing his throat, he mumbled, "We were going to be here all night, and I would rather get on with the show, make it home to a warm bath, have a good cup of soothing tea, and lay down in the comforts of my own bed before I wind up seeing the sunrise."

The witch rolled her eyes. "I wasn't going to procrastinate," she lied. "I was about to knock."

"Mhmm," the ogre hummed, unbelieving.

On the other side of the barrier, there was the click of high-heeled boots over the worn, wooden floors as they neared the entrance. A few seconds later, the locks could be heard shifting about before the knob turned, and the door eerily cracked open.

Agatha Regina Martell, or Miss Tell—to most—was a woman of short stature that exuded nothing but patience. She had tight, natural, spiral-curled hair that was a rich, burnt apricot color, and it tickled the tops of her shoulders as she peered out through the sliver of an opening. She wore a forest green dress with creamy lace trim, and a bright, white apron was tied around her waist. A small spell pouch was knotted to a thin, black belt that also bore a large iron keyring decorated with several old keys. Although her age was teetering in the midsection of her sixties, her hazel hues had yet to lose their luster, her skin was still soft and supple, and the aged lines made her seem more refined rather than 'old.' The apples of her cheeks became more predominant as the smile claimed her thinly drawn mouth. "Bless the stars, it's you!" She reached out and took hold of Vanessa's hands and gripped them tightly. However, it was the locket brushing over the woman's palm that stole the caretaker's vision from Vanessa's.

Looking down, blinking, Agatha noted the object and flicked her gaze back up to the young witch. "Oh. Oh! I-I see," she fumbled faintly. "I thought we had more time," she whispered and started to withdraw her hands.

"Me too," Ell admitted, while Raven nodded in agreement at her side.

Vanessa squeezed the tips of Miss Tell's fingers before they slipped completely from her grip. Their eyes collided, and Vanessa curled her lips into the saddest and most genuine smile that she could offer at that moment. Agatha smiled back and lightly petted the Spellweaver's hand. "Come in. No use in talking about things of this length and …" Her eyes swept the quiet streets. "Well, it's best to come in either way. Our district was never the best for evening chattering," she stated and stepped back inside, widening the gap of the door so that the others could enter. "I just started the kettle for tea," she announced with a grin.

"A woman of grace and beauty after my own heart," Bobo said with a wink.

The woman pressed a hand to the side of her face and chortled. "Don't tease me, young man. I'm single and old and don't care for the games. I'll have you take a knee if you wink at me like that again," she warned as she closed the door behind them.

The ogre chuckled. "My dear, I think you and I will get along swimmingly."

"Of course, we will. A fine specimen such as yourself and a gifted crone like me? My, my, the world is not prepared for a pair like us."

"I couldn't agree more, my dear," Bobo stated while offering the crook of his arm to the caretaker.

Agatha gave a faint smile as she hooked her arm around the demon's and gathered her skirt with her free hand. "To the kitchen, my good sir. Down the hall just past the drawing-room and to the left. If you get lost, just follow the whistle of the kettle."

Leading the way, the gentleman-beast replied with, "As you wish."

The five of them headed for the kitchen and, just as they passed the drawing-room, the whistle of the kettle started to build

🕯 16

further within the large home. Vanessa, knowing the layout and that the children were all in bed already, sped ahead to remove the pot from the flames and poured the hot water into the teapot waiting on the small table fixed in the center of the room. It was more of a small seating area and extra food prepping space rather than a table to eat at. The actual dining table was in the main dining hall outside the kitchen. Vanessa stared at it in the joining room as Miss Tell picked a nice blend of tea from the slanted cabinets. Once upon a time, that table had seemed as large as a runeball field to the young witch. Now, it resembled a joy she forgot that this place had provided her with. It had been a home filled with laughter. She remembered passing food down the long stretch of the table while everyone took turns talking about their day and shouted out their dreams to anyone that was listening. It was things she now lacked. There was a time in her life— not so long ago—that she thought leaving this place would be equal to gaining a home and finding her place in this world. But the truth was she was constantly reminded of everything she didn't have. She was always pestered with the reality of all that she had lost during the long and quiet nights that followed her joining the Coven.

"Vanessa, my dear, are you all right?" It was the second time that Bobo had asked her that, and, this time, Ell was curiously waiting next to him for her reply.

"Hmmm?" she played it off like she hadn't lost herself for a moment. "Oh, I'm fine," she said with a wave of her hand.

Agatha clasped her hands together and held them against her aproned waist. "Vanessa, child, could I ask if you've opened your locket yet?"

Looking down at her hand as she opened it and looked at the item in question over, she shook her head and answered with, "No. I think it's been closed for too long. I can't seem to get the clasps to lift."

The older woman nodded, understanding. "Oh, it will open." She enthusiastically motioned for the Spellweaver to come closer. "Come. I'll show you."

A bit hesitant at first, Vanessa inched closer and dropped the locket in Agatha's waiting hand. The caretaker inspected the silver orb with soft features, almost like she was remembering something as she held the piece of jewelry within her grasp. Her thumb thoughtfully rolled over the small, smooth surface of the orb, and Miss Tell sighed. "I remember that you had this clutched in your tiny fist when you came here," she remarked with a faraway look in her eyes. "I didn't want to take it away from you." As she spoke, her eyes misted. With a quick sniff and a light clearing of her throat, Agatha shook off whatever sadness was trying to claim her. "Well, this isn't a day about me, is it?" she stated with a short laugh. "Come, come. Let me put it on you."

Ebony locks were lifted and pulled to the side to enable the caretaker the ability to put the necklace on the young witch. Gingerly, the older woman turned Vanessa around to face her. There was a strange presence of pride in her dewy gaze as she smiled warmly at the girl in front of her. "It's bound with a spell that your parents placed on it. You'll need to say the words in elvish."

With that, Agatha nodded toward Raven who came closer and said, "*Deghlu les fum.* Reveal to me."

Vanessa nodded as she tried to mentally recite the words the Dark Elf had just effortlessly spouted. "Degh-lu les … foam?"

"*Nun.* Goddess, help you. *Deghlu les fum. Fum,*" Raven repeated, annoyed with the Spellweaver's inability to learn a second language at the drop of a pointed hat.

As Raven gradually shook her head from side to side, Vanessa lifted the orbed locket and held it in her fingers. She spoke in a low tone, almost like she was treating the silver ball like it was a being she was trying to coax out from a hiding place. "*Deghlu les fum.*"

There was a faint *pop* as the seam of the locket opened, and the wings on either side rose. Slowly, the opening widened, and faint music started to play. The tune was like a forgotten music box, the melody distant in sound and soft in nature as it encased Vanessa. Milky mist sparkled like pixie dust as it poured out like water and pooled in mid-air. The cloud grew around her. Surrounding her like a blanket on a harsh winter's night. It was a barrier of memories to fight off the bitterness of the cold and lonely heart. Encompassed in the magic of the necklace, Vanessa saw shadows play across the glittering smoke.

"Charles. Charles," a feminine voice called happily before a short giggle erupted from the shadowy female form. *"Hurry. The spell is rolling!"* she called with hints of laughter lacing her words.

Gradually, the picture became something more.

"Frol tue, Larissanna! I'm coming," a man replied excitedly.

The images swirled, the darkness started to take on a more defined shape. A tall, mahogany-skinned elven woman with long, flowing, black hair and eyes that looked like the night sky of heaven had been spun within her sockets waved someone closer. Vanessa bit the side of her cheeks as she noted the baby bundled in a soft, peach blanket within the woman's arms. *"Quickly, she's getting fussy,"* she urged with a smile and cooed at the infant in her embrace. *"Shhh ... Shhh, Vanessa. Just wait a moment longer,"* Larissanna whispered to the baby. Vanessa's throat tightened, and she bit down on her cheeks harder as she watched.

A slightly shorter male jogged over and stood next to his wife. His bright, hazel eyes shined as he looked down at his daughter with pride. *"Give her here, div zalan. She might just want some time with daddy,"* Charles stated with a tender smile and picked up the child. Instantly, giggles poured out from the baby girl. *"That's right. Daddy's got you."* The child's arms reached out and tried to grab at her father's chestnut curls.

Vanessa's eyes burned, the welling tears blurring her vision. She wiped them away and tried to blink past them as she watched the bittersweet moment unfold before her.

Larissa motioned to the orb recording the memory with her chin. *"Look at the crystal ball, little one,"* Larissanna ordered sweetly. Charles lifted the baby to an angle where her face could be seen. The couple pressed in close and nuzzled into either cheek of the infant Vanessa. The child erupting in laughter, attacking the Spellweaver's heart in a way she didn't know it could be. Happiness and sadness soaked her being and dragged her down.

"That's daddy's girl," Charles chuckled.

Covering her mouth, the young witch felt the first, uncontrollable wail claw up her throat. Tears were spilling down her cheeks violently as she sniffled. "Mom ..." she tried to speak, but the word came out choppy like it was being torn out from her throat. "...

Dad," she breathed out because her voice couldn't rise beyond that of a faint whisper. The lump she had tried to swallow past broke into a thousand shards and cut up her body from the inside out as she watched the infant hand of her younger self latch onto each parent and tug at them. The hand around her mouth slid down and clutched at the cloth around her chest. Her grasp tried to loosen the clothing around the area like the garments were too tight and making it harder to breathe. She hiccupped and sobbed as the memory played on.

"*Raven!*" Larissanna coaxed someone beyond the orb. Vanessa's mother lifted a hand and waved the other being over. "*Come, come! You get in here too.*"

Vanessa watched as a younger version of Raven raced over and picked up the child in Charles' grasp. "*Vertia is here, little shadow. Vertia is here.*"

Charles chuckled and patted the top of Raven's head. "*You're going to have to take care of your aunt here. She gets into a lot of trouble.*"

"*You're no better,*" Larissanna stated with a deadpan expression toward her husband.

Nervously, Charles gave a throaty laugh and diverted everyone's attention. "*Look at the crystal ball, Vanessa. Mommy wants a happy memory!*"

As Raven started to laugh out loud, Larissanna tugged on a lock of Charles's hair. Her father yelped with wide eyes. The infant chipperly cooed. The memory slowed and went still. The stilled image was a mix of emotions captured in time.

As the fog dissipated, Vanessa could see Raven turning her head. A streak of black trailed down her deeply tanned cheek. "They loved you like family," the witch managed to say, threads of sorrow still woven into her voice.

The Dark Elf nodded. "They did," she stated softly, a hand brushing away the tear.

Without warning, Vanessa dove across the distance separating them and crashed into Raven. Her arms wrapped around the stunned woman as she squeezed the elf tightly. "We are family!" Vanessa bellowed, and her voice cracked like an old tree in a powerful storm. "We're family," she whispered, and new tears spilled out.

Tearing out of the girl's embrace, Raven grabbed the sides of the witch's face and searched her eyes. Softly, she said, "You were never alone. You always had a family. You always will. You have so much love surrounding you, little shadow." She quickly drew her in and hugged the Spellweaver like she was going to fly away.

All around her Vanessa could feel it, the people that had always been there, and the newly acquired friends that had entered her life. All the love and sense of family she had pined over and felt that she had somehow lacked. She could feel it all around her. And it was painfully beautiful.

 *Chapter 3:*

Stepping out of the washroom, Vanessa took a deep breath and felt like herself again. Just a different version. It was like she had shattered her taped up heart and remade it. There was still pain aching within her chest, but there was understanding and beauty and closure that came with what that locket had gifted her.

Everyone was still in the kitchen. Bobo was washing the tea set while Agatha wiped down the table. When the young witch reentered the room, Miss Tell's content face went a touch somber. "Feeling better?" the old caretaker inquired.

Nodding, Vanessa replied softly, "Yeah. I'm fine."

Turning off the water, Bobo dried his hands on a dishrag that Ell handed to him. "Glad to hear it, my dear."

Sighing, Miss Tell brushed the wrinkles from her apron and fussed with threading stray strands of hair behind her ears. "Well, I know that I'd love to sit here and talk to you all night, but there is one more pressing issue we must tend to."

"What's that?" Vanessa asked, feeling lost.

"Your grimoire," Ell reminded as she closed the silverware drawer.

Recollection cleared the bent brow and confused features from Vanessa's face. "Oh, yeah." She looked around the kitchen. "Where is it?"

Raven mumbled something, but Miss Tell's voice was louder and drowned out whatever the elf was grumbling about. "It's not here. It was put into safekeeping. I suggest we go ahead and get a move on before it gets too much later." Putting away the sugar and cream, she continued, "Let me just get nurse Glenda to watch over the kids while I'm occupied."

"How is she doing?" Vanessa asked excitedly.

"You know that ol' dog. She keeps the house free of evil beings, spirits, and thieves, and she's as spry as ever," Miss Tell said with a smile.

"Who?" Ell asked.

Agatha winked to the young blonde. "Oh, you'll see."

The caretaker dipped a hand into a small pouch next to the iron keyring dangling at her hip. The gold dust therein was mixed with lavender, and Agatha pinched a small portion between her fingers before withdrawing them from the pouch. When the woman held the dust in front of her face, she spoke in a soothing voice as she recited, "Ring like the bell of a prayer house." As soon as she finished the spell, the caretaker snapped her fingers. But instead of the usual sound of a crisp snap breaking through the still air, it was the sound of a large bell ringing.

Dong.

Dong.

Dong.

Its deep song resonated through the candlelit room. The deep melody ebbed before quiet descended in the kitchen. Bobo opened his mouth to speak, but, instead of his question, there was a howl. The gentleman-beast instantly shut his mouth and looked about the space. "I'm not the only one that heard that, right?" he whispered.

Ell shook her head, Raven mirrored the receptionist, but when they all looked to Vanessa, she knelt down and whistled with a faint smile claiming her lips. "Glenda, girl." She clicked her tongue over her teeth a few times and then there was a louder and much closer howl followed by the ticking claws scratching over the orphanage's floors.

Bounding out of mist and shadows, a giant dog with black, shaggy fur leaped through a swirling dimension that manifested out of thin air. The animal crashed into Vanessa who promptly landed on her back with a thunderous *Thwack!* Laughter immediately erupted from the young witch instead of a painful cry or a string of choice words.

"Shh, you two," Agatha warned.

"I missed you too, girl," Vanessa giggled as she tried, and failed, to dodge the massive lapping tongue that assaulted her with loving kisses. An excited yip escaped the dog, and it wagged its tail while towering over the Spellweaver.

Ell whispered, "Big puppy," with wide eyes and hands that itched to pet the animal all over.

"Have some sense, you foolish beast," Agatha ordered the dog.

Raven's mouth unhinged. "Is that a—"

Bobo finished for the flabbergasted female with an answer. "It's a … Church Grim."

Pulling on the pup's ruby red collar, Agatha strained as she tried to pry the animal off of Vanessa. Breathlessly, she answered the awestruck group. "Yes. When the prayer house next door had been knocked down to make room for more local businesses, they built a new prayer house in the Adalith district, but it was too far for Glenda to protect. Because we were so close to her grave, we claimed the graveyard area, and Glenda became our watchdog."

The canine whined and turned, and Agatha almost fell over when the beast was no longer fighting against her tugs. The shaggy dog nudged into the caretaker and lapped its tongue over Miss Tell's hand before rising on its hind legs and trying to lick at her face.

"Oh, you." Agatha tried to sound angry, but tiny peals of laughter crept out of her mouth. She gave up the unhappy ruse halfway in and petted the dog ferociously. "I just can't stay mad at you," she admitted in a high-pitched voice.

Bobo gave Miss Tell a look as he cleared his throat and then looked to Vanessa, who didn't seem to mind the extra wait.

After a short session of baby-talk and lovingly petting Glenda, Agatha straightened up and sniffed as she brushed off the front of her dress. "Right. Back to business." She propped her hands upon her hips and stared the Church Grim down with a serious look scrolled over her face. "Sit," she commanded. The shaggy beast plopped its rump down on the kitchen floor without hesitation. "I need you to watch the little ones while I'm out," she informed. "No funny business, and no visitors. You know the drill."

The dog barked once and nodded its head diligently. Miss Tell scratched the happy hound behind her ear. "I'll be back soon, Glenda. Mind the house and see that the little ones are well protected." With a fading howl, the spirit animal complied and vanished from sight.

"My word. I must say, that was my first time seeing a Church Grim. She is a splendid specimen," Bobo said.

Agatha smiled proudly, "And she calls this place home and will guard it as such." Motioning for the rest to follow, everyone fell in line, Raven taking up the rear as she chewed on the edge of her pointer finger. Vanessa wanted to ask what had the elf so worked up, but Bobo had come to her side and started up a quiet conversation.

"So, this is where you grew up?" he remarked awkwardly.

Nodding, the young witch replied, "Yeah. A lot of good memories came from this place." Her eyes trailed the hall covered in the same old wallpaper. It was a dingy, pale yellow stamped with a tight design of deeply shaded mahogany manticores.

He bobbed his head while his eyes walked through the narrow corridor. "We could all see the locket memory," he stated, finally.

She almost locked up in place but managed to keep her feet moving, following Miss Tell and Ell down into the basement. As she watched the receptionist aid her old caretaker down the stairs, she drew in a slow breath and released it even slower. "It was nice," she said finally.

He exhaled loudly, "Yes. I could tell that it meant a lot for you to witness such a moment." There was a short pause before he added, "You know you look like her, your mother, Larissanna ...? She was quite beautiful."

That was not what she expected him to say. There was no controlling the smile that was claiming her lips. "You think so?"

He chuckled a bit, "Yes, my dear. I really do."

"Thanks," she whispered and reached for his hand as they walked and gave his gargantuan paw a light squeeze.

"Mind your head and careful of the cobwebs. I've not tended to this space in a number of years," Miss Tell warned the group.

"I'd rather deal with the spiders than what we're about—" Raven started to grumble in the back.

Loudly, Agatha made a high-pitched sound and exclaimed, "Ooh. There it is!"

Vanessa didn't know if she should ask what Raven was talking about or not. But even if she wanted to, Miss Tell had called to the young witch. "Child, come here. I'll need you to assist me. My magic isn't what it used to be, and I'm a bit tired from my long and arduous day. Keeping those children in line is like herding wild griffins."

"Coming," Vanessa announced and quickly went to the caretaker's side. "What do you need of me?"

Ell was quick to fill the Spellweaver in. "She's going to do a revealing spell, but there will be remnants of a veil. She needs someone to help her conjure the double spell."

"Double spell?" Vanessa asked, confusion scrolled all over her face. "Why are we using such complicated magic, Miss Tell?"

The older woman fussed with lighting a smudge stick. Making sure there were no impurities or magic with ill intent or even cloaked beings close by, Agatha made sure to sweep the room thoroughly with the cleansing smoke as she spoke to everyone. "A long time ago, before you were born, the Celestial came to me and asked me to guard something for her. She had asked me to guard an entrance that none could know about. A few years later, Raven and Ell came to my door holding you. It was late at night then, too." She smiled as she recalled the memory. "You were such a tiny thing." Agatha sniffled and was promptly presented with a clean handkerchief from Bobo. "Thank you, dearie."

"My pleasure," the gentleman-beast replied.

After dabbing at her eyes, she continued. "There were two items with them," she stated while looking at both Ell and Raven before locking her gaze with Vanessa. "Aside from you in their possession, they had a locket and a grimoire." She took in a long, thoughtful breath and released it slowly. "I knew why I had been safeguarding the entrance. That night was the first night that I had ever cast the revealing spell and stepped through the opening," she admitted.

Vanessa scrunched her brow while thinking. "So, my grimoire is on the other side of this spell?"

"Along with so much more," Ell whispered. "But we must hurry. The spell to open it is not easy to cast, and we need to ensure that no one outside of us knows of this place." Her face went cold, and her eyes lost their shine. "Upon pain of death, none can know what is beneath this orphanage." The blonde's voice had become something that Vanessa and the others could only refer to as scary. They all nodded, and Ell turned her attention to Raven. "Guard the basement door."

The look of pure, elated relief washed over the Dark Elf's features. "With pleasure. Rather be stuck with cobwebs, sleeping babes, and skittering spiders than a labyrinth full of giant—"

"Have some respect!" Agatha shot out at Raven, who instantly shut her mouth and twitched her lips off to the side.

Ell nodded in agreement with the caretaker. "Should be careful of what you compare beings to. You of all beings should understand the pain that comes with close-minded judgments."

With a sigh, Raven lifted her hands and motioned for everyone to calm down. "All right. You win. I get it. But I'd rather stay here and watch the basement door just the same. You all run off before it gets too late."

"Right. I agree with the young lady. If time is of the essence, I suggest that we get this spell over with and venture therein to gather Vanessa's grimoire and return home. We still have quite the detailed report to make back at the Coven in the morning," Bobo added.

Agatha looked flustered for a moment. "My dear. Goodness me, I don't want to take any more of your time. You need your rest." Turning, the caretaker snuffed out the smudge stick and spoke hurriedly to Vanessa. "I want you to feed your magic to the spell to sustain the unveiling. While you do that, I will use an incantation to open the portal. Once both spells are successfully cast, you will have one hour to retrieve your grimoire and return here."

"There are other ways in and out of the heart of … this place we are about to travel to, but they are more difficult to open. Only the outskirts of this area have easier access points," Ell added.

Bobo turned to the young blonde. "Why not use one of those then?"

"Her book is held in a very specific place. All of the grimoires in their possession are," the receptionist informed while Miss Tell lit candles on a small oak table.

"Their?" Vanessa chimed in with a questioning tone.

Raven sighed. "She'll explain on the other side. Get on with the spell already!"

"Such a fussy elf," Bobo grumbled in a hardly audible tone.

Agatha reached for the young witch's hand and squeezed it lightly. "You've waited so long for answers, and you're finally getting them. But there is a world within the world that you live in, Vanessa. Take it in a little bit at a time. You cannot reveal a whole world in a single moment. Don't rush for the knowledge. Whether it is a fight or seeking an answer, be patient, my dear child. Be patient."

With that, the caretaker guided the Spellweaver over to a small altar near the wall. At first glance, it looked like a normal wall, but as Agatha began to recite the incantation, white chalk lines appeared over the concrete surface. The design mirrored the runes back at Coven headquarters above the underground library. These, however, seemed like they were akin to them but more ancient and drawn in a language that Vanessa was not familiar with.

Whispers filled the basement. Not the sort that was incredibly noticeable, but the kind that could be confused with the wind playing over the windowpane or the water rushing through the pipes weaving and looping overhead. Everyone could feel an energy play over their skin.

"Now, Vanessa. Hurry," Agatha reminded Vanessa of her task.

The witch instantly reached out and grabbed the caretaker's awaiting hands. Vanessa pulled at her inner being and called forth the flow of magic from within. She called to it, asking it to ride the spiritual current and collect within the other practitioner. She could feel it, that door that had lost its chains and bindings and could now be coaxed open at will. She could still hear the voice of the quilin speaking to her, mentioning the gift that it had left her with. She reached for the door and pulled it open, unafraid of the power lying on the other side and no longer hindered by her insecurities. A rush of golden light enveloped the two as the power rushed out and doused them both.

Agatha opened her eyes with a gasp and stared at Vanessa in wonder before a warm smile curled her lips. A mighty laugh left the older woman, and she nodded approvingly. Silently, she showed the girl she had helped to raise that she was proud of her. Continuing on, Miss Tell started the second half of the spell.

"On this moonlit night, within pallid light, let the shadow veil rise from ethereal lies." As Agatha spoke the last word of the incantation, the chalk lines on the wall rippled like the cement had turned into a pond, and they had thrown a pebble into the placid waters.

The faintest current of air could be felt grazing over them all, carrying with it the thick scent of old, damp air and sewage water. Instinctively, Vanessa crinkled her nose and jerked back from the smell as it assaulted her nostrils. Cupping a hand over her nose and mouth, she asked, "What is that smell?"

"The least of your worries, I assure you," Raven announced from the safety of the steps.

"There isn't much time. Hurry. Go," Agatha urged as Ell pushed the young witch from behind.

"But—" Vanessa tried to speak, but she was shooed once more by the caretaker.

"Hurry!" Agatha commanded in a hoarse tone.

Reluctantly, she walked through the spelled wall. Bobo quickly slipped through the portal after the young witch. Once on the other side, the image of Raven, Agatha, and the basement faded from view, and all they saw was the brick walls of the underground sewers ripple chaotically as they walked away.

 *Chapter 4:*

Dim lighting caressed the rough walls of the wide tunnel. The soft trickles of churning water could be heard rolling its way through the channel that ran through the middle of the sewers. It was actually a delightful sound, and it was followed by the rhythmic clicks from the soles of their boots as they traversed deeper into the passageway. The smell, however, had burned Vanessa's nose hairs clean off. She was sure of it. Bobo was at no risk, as his trusty handkerchief was stuck to his face like it was an added feature. Gathering up the edge of her cloak, Vanessa covered her mouth and nose and felt some of the tension in her body ease up now that she could breathe a bit more freely.

"Why is my grimoire in the sewer?" She didn't mean to sound like she was complaining, but none in the party could fault the witch for it.

"I must admit, my dear, that this seems like an awfully horrible place to hide a book of this caliber." His eyes trailed the dark, damp walls and slick-with-slime stones lining their path. "Or any book, for that matter," he mumbled.

Ell didn't answer them right away. Her eyes were darting all about as if searching for something that was hidden within bricks themselves. "Your grimoire isn't hidden in the sewers. It's hidden in a place that is hidden in the sewers," the blonde corrected.

Vanessa blinked and then looked to Bobo as she whispered to him, "Was that a riddle? I'm horrible with riddles." Prodding her pet with her staff, the Spellweaver urged him quietly, "You answer it."

The disappointment scrolled all over the ogre's face should have been a dead giveaway of how wrong his master was. However, she wasn't paying attention to the demon. Her sights were fixed upon the squirrelly receptionist that darted about in front of them while her hands glided over the smooth, wet surfaces of the bulbous rocks that made up the passageway. Vanessa quietly called out to Ell, "What are you looking for? A hole or a box, perhaps?"

"Your common sense. Your manners. Oh," Bobo paused and snapped his fingers together. "I know. Your intelligence."

Vanessa stopped dead in her tracks and spun around to face the monstrosity that was her partner. "I'm starting to think she was actually looking for your—"

There was a soft, short spell recited before Ell's voice erupted from in front of them. "I found it!"

"The best news I've heard all day," Vanessa announced.

"I've never agreed more in my life," Bobo added.

The pair turned around just as they saw the ruffle of Ell's skirt disappear inside a wall. A second later, the receptionist poked her head out with a mad grin and pointed energetically at the wall. "It's over here. Come on!"

Bending her brow, the young witch turned her head to face Bobo. "Another spelled wall?"

"Most peculiar," the gentleman-beast whispered.

Indeed, it was peculiar. Hidden doorways and secrets were all abound. Just what were they getting themselves into? If you asked the demon at her side, he would tell you, *"Trouble with a capital 'T. Without a doubt."* Reluctantly, they both stepped forward and stopped in front of the wall. Vanessa reached forward and paused. "You go fir—"

Her words were cut short by Bobo saying, "Ladies first, my dear," before promptly being shoved forward.

Instead of being met with a slimy, stone wall, the young witch stumbled through the unexpected opening and whirled around as she tried to catch her footing in a strange dance of awkwardness. Fussing with cufflinks that were hanging on by mere threads and dusting at a dirt stain that refused to budge from Bobo's buttoned-up shirt, the beast strolled through the opening with style and grace. Even in his battered attire, the ogre looked properly dashing.

"You're a horrible pet," she seethed.

"You're words hurt, Vanessa. I was merely attempting to aid you in overcoming any silly fear that you might have. After all, what harm could there be, hmmm? Ell had walked through but a moment before you."

He wasn't wrong, and as soon as that reminder was uttered, the Spellweaver looked confused and turned to try and locate the missing young lady in question. When she spun around, however, she was not prepared for what she saw.

The ceiling rose overhead to a height that was both impressive and unexpected. Within the domed structure were a thousand glittering lights like the excited flickers of countless candles swaying in the gentlest of breezes. Their illumination glowed over the polished bronze decorations and plating that adorned the walls. Underfoot was a mesh of baby blue and warm brown tiles that flowed into the surrounding marble flooring. The sconces on the walls held flames that burned in cool blues and cast their light throughout the deep opening that stretched on beyond where they stood. Lush, green ferns sat in the corners, drinking in the bloodshot moonlight that spilled in from a few skylights. Around the base of them were bioluminescent mushrooms that hugged the damp soil beneath the lush, bushy plant. Intricate swirls of bronze patterns decorated the walls in pleasing, large, flowered patterns as they etched their way down the hall. The foul, bitter smell that had once drenched their surroundings was gone. A sweet, cool air that was lightly perfumed with delightful hints of flowery fragrances swirled about them. There was no way that this was the same sewer that they had entered only moments ago.

"Ookaay, I'm officially confused," Vanessa whispered.

"For once, I agree with you," Bobo replied.

"Follow me," Ell ordered, grabbing an unlit torch from the wall.

"Where are we?" Vanessa asked.

Ignoring them, the receptionist sprinkled Tinker Bell's Spirit over the tip of the torch. The blonde then whispered a small lighting spell. A warm, enchanting glow grew around them all, and Ell smiled over her shoulder at the other two. "Welcome to Allahlav, hidden city of the Skrittish." She then turned and headed further into the halls.

Bobo blinked unsure of what to say, but Vanessa had him covered. "The who? Where are we again?"

Ell giggled softly. "We are in the underground city of Allahlav, home to the Skrittish."

The ogre righted himself and said, "You mean the refuse collectors?"

The blonde nodded happily. "Yes. They are also grand alchemists, philosophers, and beings."

Vanessa was still trying to grasp everything. "I didn't know that they would have such a vast and clean city," she stated slowly as her eyes walked the halls and glossed over every detail of the neighboring walls.

Swiping the torch from side to side as they came to an intersection, Ell quietly eyed over each tunnel before turning to the left. "Most don't. This city stretches far beyond the borders of Tolvade itself and has been here longer than any other known being of Aeristria."

Speechless, Bobo and Vanessa followed after Ell as they processed everything as quickly as they could. Conversation dwindled as they hurriedly pressed on through the weaving path. Eventually, the tight tunnel turned more spacious. Pillars ten times the size of Bobo lined the sides of the walkway, and the wall melted away to reveal a great cavern beyond the safety of where they stood. Underneath them, water could be heard churning, and, after glancing over the edge of the stone bridge, Vanessa spotted the white fabric of ship sails. The channel was no longer small, but a massive river that cut its way through the core of what she had expected to be miles of sewers. The sides were more like the faces of mountains rather than underground walls, and within them were tiny, carved-out holes where candles glowed and movement was seen within the shadows. Fearing what she might see within those darkened corners, she turned her eyes up overhead. There she found chandeliers with a yellow light that washed over the breathtaking mosaics that made up the ceilings. Within the artwork, elementals were dancing in meadows, dragons were flying over mountaintops, unicorns were playing in streams, manticores lay next to lambs in a lush valley, and Giants roamed through the jeweled canopy of the jungle as fairies encircled around vibrant fields of flowers. Colored glass, polished tiles, and shiny stones that made up the ornate art glittered in the light of the elaborate chandeliers.

"This is the most splendid thing I've ever seen," Bobo whispered, spinning as he tried to keep the pace and drink in all the sights around him.

They came to a sharp turn ahead. It opened even wider as Ell asked, "Are you sure about that?"

Beyond, there was a small port where ships were unloading barrels of wine, and shipments were documented by cloaked figures with scrolls. A little further downstream were trash barges where more giant cloaked beings spelled the heaps of garbage, condensing them into small cubes, and a line of the beings magically waved the trash through an opening that lead into hidden alchemy stations. Along the channel were carved out openings with arched doorways and small docking areas for boats. Giant bowls with burning blue flames lined the edges of the streets and paths. A small waterfall came spewing out next to the port and dumped into the main flow of water.

Vanessa followed the waterfall upstream and saw two, massive, robed women holding giant orbs on their shoulders. One orb was depicted as the sun and the other the moon. Behind these towering structures was a massive phoenix made of gold. It mirrored what was on the Coven emblem. The mythical bird's beak was open and pointed upward, wings outstretched, and a deep ditch surrounded the bird along the stone base. Inside, it glowed with bright, lapping blue flames. From this perch, water was gushing out and down to become the waterfall.

"That is the water sanitation area," Ell informed.

They passed by a massive stone carving of a Cerberus chained to the wall. "My word," Bobo gasped. "How could we not know such glorious wonders lay beneath our feet?"

To that, Ell laughed. "Because it's a secret, silly. Besides, no one really tries to get to know the Skrittish."

Guiding them further into Allahlav, they passed by small markets and meat vendors and stalls where pottery, jewelry, fabrics, and an assortment of treats or knickknacks were sold. But there was a hush over the bustling area. Instead of a hundred voices blending into a seamless song of a cheerful throng of beings, there was a calming quiet. The normalcy of the scene was disturbed by the lack of chatter and faces hidden behind hooded robes and cloaks added an unsettling air to the image before them. But Ell didn't seem to mind it at all. It was as if the event didn't bother her in the slightest.

Vanessa fell in stride with her pet and was practically hip to hip with the gentleman-beast. "Say not a word, my dear, for I find this place just as blissfully beautiful as I do unsettlingly strange," he murmured to his master. The young witch only nodded relentlessly in reply.

There was no time for lengthy explanations, and Ell wasn't keen on trading many words. Her fast-paced footwork and darting eyes spoke in volumes to the urgency of staying within the time limits that Agatha had warned them about.

As they rushed through the cloaked beings, Vanessa tried to steal a glance here and there, but every time the hooded being turned their head, their visage was just out of sight. Hidden either by fabric or shadow. But she was sure she saw whiskers. Soon, they were down a narrow ally before she could attempt to see anything more.

"All right, it's right up ahead. Stay with me," Ell advised, then put out the torch and rested it beside the steps leading up to the front entrance of a building. She rapped lightly on the wooden door.

An enchanting jingle softly sounded from the barrier. "I seek a family's hidden secret, I search for a tome, let us inside, to a world most have never known." The lock clicked, and the knob jiggled before the door slowly opened.

Stepping in, one by one, they entered the home.

 *Chapter 5:*

Inside, the bioluminescent glow of countless growing mushrooms and plant life paired with the light of fairies darting about as they were engrossed in their work, giving the space a magical and ethereal light. From behind a thick tapestry that divided the main room, a giant being emerged. Much like the many that walked about in the city itself, this creature wore a hooded robe. Standing at an intimidating eight feet, the being loomed—easily—over everyone present. The forest green garbs were traced in looping, silver embroidery, and it hung from the being like it was a drying rack, giving no shape or indication of what may lay beneath the folds of fabric. The dim lighting aided them very little in seeing beyond the shadowed depths of the cowl. But slowly, as their eyes adjusted to the minimal lighting, Vanessa could see what peered back at them from the confines of the hood.

A pointed snout covered in whiskers and equipped with two, long front teeth poked out from the hood before it was lowered from the being's head. Long, round ears protruded from the side of the creature's skull. What was once hidden in the depths of the hood was a head full of short, coarse, finely combed fur, and two yellow eyes that stared back at Vanessa and the others. A long, peachy-pink tail slithered out from behind the robes and coiled around the creature's feet. Cloth-wrapped hands baring sharp, needle-like claws emerged from the long robes and motioned toward them.

The voice that pierced Vanessa's mind was calm and caring. *"Why have you come here?"*

Ell was quick to answer with, "We seek her family's grimoire."

The being turned, and a series of clicking sounds rolled from under the cowl before the kind voice spoke through all of their minds once more. *"What is the child's name?"*

Looking back to the Spellweaver, the blonde thought for a moment before she turned back to face the Skrite and said, "Vanessa Peterson. Daughter of Charles Peterson and Larissanna Dah'Ruellun."

The Skrite watched her intently, its yellow eyes penetrating through them all deeper than what lay upon the surface. It chilled her to the bone as she felt like it could see insecurities that she had tried to hide for years. A pixie softly excused itself as it fluttered by and dusted off a nearby shelf.

After a long, quiet pause, the being spoke to them telepathically once more. "*Follow me.*" Without waiting for a reply, the Skrite turned and disappeared behind the tapestry.

They didn't question the being and quickly followed after it. On the other side of the tapestry, the room was not much larger, but it was brighter. A few oil lamps drenched the neighboring fabrics that were hanging on racks to dry from recent dyeing, and countless, rolled up cloths of varying color and patterns were stored in cubby spaces lining the walls. While spindles spun, a large loom on the far side of the room slowly toiled away on its work with the aid of magic and nearby pixies. Needle and thread were bobbing about the air as delicate embellishments were embroidered on pieces of clothing draped over large, headless mannequins.

"*Try not to touch anything. The oil from your hands could ruin the fabrics before they can be properly treated to repel such grime,*" the Skrite stated as they passed through the room and came to a door that looked a foot smaller than the being.

Vanessa turned away from the workers and asked, "Do you have a name?"

The pause from the creature that followed her question was unnatural. It was the kind of stillness that you'd expect from a vampire or any other ancient being. It was the type of creature that could school its features into a neutral expression without trying and could go motionless with the blink of an eye. It was unnerving to say the least. After a moment, the being spoke to her, "*Kishnar.*"

The young witch repeated the name to herself before she said, "Thank you, Kishnar."

The being turned just enough to face her fully as its clawed, cloth hand remained holding onto the handle of the door. *"For?"* it asked, curiously.

She met those beady eyes without fear or disgust as she said, "For keeping my grimoire safe."

The slight curl of its lips could be seen, and then it gave a slight bow. *"You are most welcome, but it is merely my job."*

After that, the door to the next room was opened, and they were ushered through, silently.

The corridor that they went through was tight quarters. Poor Bobo's shoulders practically brushed the stones that made up the wall on either side of him. But the being assured that it wouldn't last for long. And, as promised, it didn't. They came to a door, and the Skrite twitched its nose in thought. A second later, it shook its fuzzy head and headed further down the hall. Each time they came to another entrance, the creature would stop, inspect the door and shake its head before moving on. However, around the fourth time they paused, there was a series of clattering clicks trickling out from the Skrite's mouth.

"Ah, here we are." A keyring was manifested from thin air, and the giant iron lock was undone. *"Your grimoire is in here."* The aged hinges protested to being opened, and the room inside was more than what Vanessa had expected.

Floating flames were surrounded by topaz jewels, and the lights centered themselves around the middle of the room. A desk was fixed in the corner. Atop it was an inkwell, a few calligraphy brushes, a quill pen, and a rather large hourglass. An out of control ivy plant slithered and snaked its way over the surface and had wrapped its thin green fingers over the thick, cherry red legs of the furniture. Over to the other side of the room, a ladder was resting over the built-in bookcases that went, at least, twenty feet high. Everywhere the stones of the wall should have been visible, a bookcase devoured it. Worn spines of varying sizes became a dusty, muted rainbow of color that adorned the shelves surrounding the room. Not a space went unused, and they were packed to the point of almost overflowing as each shelf had not an inch to spare. There were windows, but the light that poured in through their spotless surface didn't seem natural at all, and it held hints of the same blue that surrounded the bioluminescent plant life that Vanessa had seen littered throughout the city since their arrival.

The Skrite informed warmly, *"The demon may enter here. This is not part of the library."*

"What is this place?" Vanessa asked in wonderment.

"One of the grimoire archives. Every known witch or wizard that needs their family tome safeguarded can bring it to various drops for us to gather. But most of these are from lineages that no longer exist or have been lost," Ell answered.

Bobo couldn't stop his jaw from unhinging. "My word. This … this is magnificent."

"Which one is mine?" Vanessa could hardly hold back her excitement.

The Skrite motioned its hands to the many bookcases in the room as it telepathically replied, *"You will have to find it. Rest your hand upon the spine, but if you do not feel the magic accepting you, do not open it."*

"Oh!" Ell announced. "I need to pick up a few scrolls while I'm here. We are rather pressed for time, so if we could hurry ..."

"I believe the robes you requested to be made are ready as well. I'll assist you to gather them." The Skrite turned and reminded Vanessa in a grave tone, *"If the magic does not accept you, do not open the book."*

"I got it. Don't open if the magic doesn't accept me," she stated as she got on the ladder.

Bobo did a double-take from the Skrite and Ell rapidly making their way down the hall to Vanessa already gliding her hand across the first line of tomes. "Oh, dear. I'm the side character that gets left with the main character that never listens, aren't I?"

"What are you going on about, Bobo?"

"Your inability to listen in dire situations, that's all, dear."

"Oh, stop your bellyaching. I'm trying to find a book. What could possibly go wrong?"

"I implore that you don't ask that question."

Vanessa shook her head and laughed. "Oh, please. Nothing bad is going to happen, you cynical demon!"

"Realist, my dear. I'm a realist," Bobo muttered as he pulled on the corner of one of the nearby grimoires and glanced over the front of it. "What do you suppose your book would look like?"

"Double-dip a candlestick. I should have asked Ell before she ran off. It would make finding this thing a lot easier." Vanessa sighed and pulled one of the books out halfway. She looked at it hopefully and reached deep for the magic inside her. She needed just enough to have the book react to her. She closed her eyes as she swam through the known space of her being. The gate that had been locked for so long, the power that she could now freely tap into, she called to it. Beckoning for it to come forth. The warmth of her power prickled over her skin as it climbed up her arm and spun down through her hand.

ZAP!

There was a short crackle, and her arm involuntarily pulled away from the book with such force that it almost sent her flying off the ladder. She caught herself on the smooth rod of the ladder with her free hand as her body dropped and her legs slammed against the wooden edges. She grimaced as she looked down at the unforgiving stone floor below. "Suppose that isn't the one," she grunted while hoisting herself back up. A dull pain throbbed in her shins that she tried to avoid as she looked over the sea of grimoires.

"You think?" Bobo asked. Vanessa could only grin in reply. Rolling his eyes, the ogre put away his glasses and pushed back the most recent book he had been inspecting. "Let me get a description of the confounded thing before you hurt yourself." He paused and narrowed his eyes at the young witch as she curiously tugged at another book. "Or worse," he grumbled and rushed to find Ell.

"It's just books," Vanessa complained as she let a smaller burst of power worm up through her arm and down through her fingertips. This time, there was heat so scalding permeating from the book that she clamped her mouth shut and gripped the side of the ladder to stop herself from shrieking out in pain. Quickly, the young witch yanked her hand away. She sucked on the pads of her throbbing digits and scowled at the book responsible for the pain.

"Hex it all. A simple no would work just fine. You don't need to burn me," she complained to the item and pressed on with her search. Two rows later and Vanessa had been zapped three times, burned twice, almost had her hand frozen to the binding of one, and had a gust of wind slammed into her. Risking the chances of having a repeat of the listed events happen or something equally unpleasant occur, she reached forward toward the spine of a worn, leathery tome. Only this time she had a newfound respect for the objects. Caressing her aching fingers over the edge, she let the faintest brush of magic merge with the tome.

There was no pain, no freezing, no heat, nothing. There was only the faint cry of a crow that made her look all around the room for a sign of a possible bird flying about. But the space was free of anything aside from herself. Snapping back to the book, she raised a brow questionably toward the object. Could this be it? Was this her grimoire? It hadn't rejected her like the rest. It had to be.

Right?

A little more apprehensively than she had expected to, she drew the book from betwixt the thick line of volumes and stepped down the ladder with it cradled against her chest. Once her feet were firmly planted on the ground, she looked the cover over. Leather stampings of birds encircling a twisting tree and an imprint dusted faintly in gold stared back at her. She bent her brow and took in a deep breath. Turning it in her hands, her thumbs found the side and cracked the book open right down the middle.

Instantly, she looked down at paper teeming with words and small drawn pictures for reference. Her eyes rapidly tried to drink in the first spell.

Birds of a Feather Vision.
You will need:
Gold dust
Three crow feathers (Raven feathers are fine to use as a substitute)
Will powder
Eye of newt (herb not organ)

One spectral rune
One clean piece of parchment
One piece of charcoal

Invoke the ability to see (short term) through the eyes of a summoned murder...

As she read the page, a blot of ink near the picture of the herb required for the spell started to bleed out more. The black stain on the page inched its way at such a slow rate that Vanessa pulled the book close enough to the parchment that her nose practically touched the dry surface. Just then, the ink ... gurgled? A large bit of black rose up from the page and splattered itself further out. Charred blobs of ink saturated the book as the writing itself swirled and sizzled as if it were boiling water in a kettle. More bubbles rose and popped, now at a faster pace, to the point that there was more ink than there was paper. The sound of something wet hitting the floor drew her attention away from the book as she noticed the night-shaded liquid pouring over the edge of the tome and splashing all over the floor. She took a few steps back to avoid the growing puddle.

"What in the name of magic?" she breathed the question, and an ear-splitting caw snatched her gaze from the ink splattered stones underfoot. Snapping up from the book was a sloppy, wet blob that vaguely held the form of a bird. Its inky feathers slapped over one side of the book in Vanessa's hands while the other poorly formed wing limply fell over the edge. Its beak opened, and a raspy noise escaped as it inhaled, the sound gurgled as the air passed through dripping ink. Another sharp caw clambered out from the messy beak, splattering murky liquid from its open jaws as it cried out. The young witch reeled back from the thing. It flopped around like an oil-drenched fish out of water as it attempted to climb from the pitch that now made up the grimoire in Vanessa's hands. The crow tried to take flight, but only splattered more ink everywhere, and the droplets of ink slapped cold and unwelcoming across the Spellweaver's face. Revolted, she tried to wipe the gunk from her face with the sleeve of her tunic, but only managed to smear it, instantly making matters worse. She could *feel* the magic that the ink was submerged in, and it was nasty. It wanted to devour her. It wanted every drop of her magic, and then it wanted to leave her bleeding on the library floor. She gasped and dropped the book as two more birds were birthed from the growing black puddle. Sickening caws filled the air. That was when she noticed the droplets at her feet had turned into little crows as well, and they were already flapping up into the air. A melody of unnerving cries erupted as the alarming scene unfolded to her horror.

This was not her grimoire.

Upon that very obvious realization, Vanessa scrambled to pick up the book as the tiny birds darted through the air, swirling about her in a vicious whirlwind of razor-sharp beaks, talons, and unforgiving wings that slashed at any visible skin leaving paper cuts behind. She slammed the book shut and whispered a prayer of apology. Right before her eyes, she watched the ink collect into puddles that then streamed rapidly back into the book.

She was noting the fact that not a drop of ink had been left behind on or around her when Bobo came rushing through the entrance. He suspiciously eyed over the room and then his master. "I don't know if I should be disappointed or proud. You and the room are both in one piece," he announced and then furrowed his brow as he noticed the cuts on her face and hands. "My word, you really are hopeless, aren't you?"

"Hmmm?" was all she could muster as she was still trying to calm the chaotic beating of her heart.

"Did no one show you how to read, my dear? You-you're covered in paper cuts," he announced.

Rubbing her arm nervously, she changed the subject. "Did you get the information from Ell?"

"Uh … ah, yes," he stated while reaching for his crystal ball pouch. "I wrote it all down." Fishing the glass orb out of his pouch, he scrolled over the surface until he found what he was looking for. "Here it is," he announced chipperly.

"Tell me," she urged eagerly, the excitement mounting in her once more.

"It is black leather with gold etchings along the spine and a large labradorite gemstone fixed in the dead center of the front cover," he informed with a grin. "I should surmise that finding it will be done quite easily with this information."

And right the demon was, for only about twenty of the texts nestled in the bookcases had the matching description of the spine and binding listed. But only one had a labradorite stone fixed on the front of it. She tested, just in case, with her power. The power was like a ribbon being dragged over a bare arm, it was so faint. But the moment that it connected with the book, it was like she had been slammed in the chest. She gasped and coughed as she felt the power connect with her and embrace her. The sensation was like that of a bear hug. She felt like it was difficult to breathe but refused to relinquish her hold on the grimoire. She could feel it, with each passing moment, binding itself to her.

The wave of power died down, and she smiled, laughing lightly to herself. "This is it," she confirmed.

"And good that it is because we are on a schedule, missy. Time to go," Bobo announced, putting the other books back on the shelf in their respective spots, and he gave the room a quick once over before they headed for the main room.

Halfway down the hall, they ran into Ell and Kishnar. "Oh," the blonde looked surprised. "I was just about to come help you," she admitted.

"No need," Vanessa informed. "I found it." She stopped to lift the book into the air and then went back to hugging it to her chest.

Ell beamed. "Well, I suppose we are done here, then." She turned to Kishnar and asked, "Could you give us a portal spell to the main entrance? We are in a bit of a rush."

The being nodded before it wordlessly turned down the hall. They all followed quietly after. Ell had a newly acquired pack fixed to her person. Surely it was full of the items mentioned before they had left Vanessa to search for her grimoire. The witch stole a glance down at the book in her hands and traced the gemstone with her fingers. The colors shifted brilliantly under the lamplight. It was mesmerizing. Just holding the object felt right. Like a piece of her had always been missing and now she had found it.

"Have you opened it yet?" Ell asked.

Vanessa shook her head 'no.'

The receptionist smiled warmly at her. "It's all right. Don't want to overdo it after everything you've been through. Best save that for tomorrow, right?"

"She makes a valid point," Bobo said as they came to a new door, and the Skrite unlocked it like he had the archive room.

"I know," Vanessa stated happily as her hand played over the cover as if she were soothing a small child to sleep in her arms.

Bobo blinked, taken aback for a moment. "I do say. She is tired! No fight and no fuss. Quickly, I need to get her in a bed before she changes her mind," he demanded playfully.

Ell giggled. "Be nice, Botobolbilian."

The gentleman-beast chuckled as Kishnar walked over to a table that looked like it had been carved out of blue apatite stone. Littering its top was an assortment of bottles, flasks, and jars. Each filled with a liquid or (in some) a smoky substance and fitted with a cork stopper. The Skrite used a claw to tip a glass container here and there until it spotted what it was looking for. Pulling away from the throng of potions, he came over to a shallow hole that had been worn into the floor. Removing the stopper, the creature then tipped the bottle and let the contents drain to the floor. The empty container disappeared into the being's robes before the cloth-bound hands reached out over the puddle.

The concoction smelled vaguely of flowers and spice, and Vanessa could feel its perfume dancing on her tongue as she breathed in. Kishnar whirled his hands over the worn spot on the floor and made humming sounds. But instead of calming, they were baritone in nature, and the tune thrummed with command. From the middle of the potion resting in the dip in the floor, a ripple formed, and then another, and another until it appeared as if the ground were shaking. But only the liquid moved. Slowly, it rose up from the shallow pit and swirled vertically, mirroring the movements of the Skrite's hands. The center of the vortex shifted and became still as glass while the edges continued to swirl.

"*This will take you to the spelled area just outside the sewers, friends. Be safe on your journey,*" Kishnar spoke gently to them.

Ell stepped through the portal first with Bobo following close behind, leaving Vanessa to walk through last. "I know it was your job, but, thank you again for keeping my grimoire safe, Kishnar," she said, and then put one foot through the portal.

"*You're welcome, daughter of Saellah,*" he replied.

Vanessa gasped. Did he know what that meant? She had heard it so many times. She turned to try and ask, but the spell sucked her through. "Wait!" she called back, her hand outstretched as if to grab the Skrite and pull herself back through but it was too late.

She landed on the other side and turned around in place with a frown. The portal was gone, and she couldn't ask Kishnar what being a daughter of Saellah meant.

"Is everything all right, my dear?" Bobo inquired.

Vanessa looked back to where the portal should have been and shook her head. "No. I had a question, but I don't think I am meant to know the answer right now," she said in a soft voice.

"You're scaring me, Vanessa. You sound…insightful and wise." Bobo was fussing with the clasps of his ax as he spoke.

The Spellweaver shook it off and felt a soft smile tug at the corner of her lips. "Come on. I'm tired. Let's go home."

"That's more like it," the ogre announced relieved.

Ell motioned for them to follow after poking her head out from the wall portal that lead out into the sewers. "All's clear. Let's hurry. We still have a bit of time, but I don't want poor Agatha holding open the doorway any longer than she needs to."

With that, the trio headed through the sewer with more speed than their tired limbs would have liked. Soon enough, they all reached the basement of the orphanage in record time.

 *Chapter 6:*

"Glad I was on basement door duty," Raven announced as the others sealed up the wall again. The Dark Elf shivered and gave a look that said she'd rather be caught with an arm tied behind her back and stuck with the wolves in the Black Forest than in the middle of the underground Skrittish city.

"Been there before?" Vanessa asked.

Raven nodded once. "And it was enough for me. I assure you." She shivered again.

Bobo harrumphed. "I don't see what the big problem is. It was a rather delightf—"

His words were cut short with a blood-curdling scream that erupted from the Dark Elf like she was auditioning for a horror play. Her bulbous eyes were staring down the far side of the basement, and she held her bone ax out in front of her like it would keep the assailant at bay.

The assailant was nothing more than a small rodent with glistening, beady, black eyes. Its gray mass could be seen scurrying up the edge of a bit of cloth that was draped over a grain barrel. Tracing the floor back to the panic-stricken Raven, it became abundantly clear why the woman didn't want to be caught in Allahlav. Curling her lips between her teeth, Vanessa attempted to hide any and all proof that she was about to laugh to the point of gasping for air.

"I suppose everyone has their fears. I'm aware of yours now." The ogre looked the woman over and sighed as he stood between Raven and the tiny monster. "Shoo. Go now. Be on your way. Shoo," he ordered the mouse. The tiny thing skittered away and into a hole in the wall.

"Should get me a fat cat to guard this basement," Agatha thought out loud.

"I'll buy you two," Raven whispered like she was hexing someone.

Raven was going to stay at Ell's for a few days. The receptionist insisted that they catch up, and the prospect of a spare room only sweetened the deal for the Dark Elf. "Crystal ball call me when you are free. I want to spend as much time as I can with you," Raven said as she hugged Vanessa.

"What about Raka?" Vanessa asked.

Raven could only give a burst of nasally laughter. "What about him?"

Vanessa pulled back to inspect the elf's features with a questionable glare. She was met with a smile and then drawn in for a second, briefer, hug. "I can use my scrying mirror to speak with him later on. You are family, I'd like to catch up with you too, little shadow."

Vanessa felt a new wave of tears threatening her vision as her eyes misted. She squeezed Raven's hands as they parted and nodded as she spoke. "I'll call you as soon as I get up."

"Are you sure that you don't want to head to the Coven's infirmary? You all could use some tending to," Ell pressed.

Vanessa shook her head with a faint smile. "I'm fine. I'd rather just go home, perform a few light healing spells and get some rest. I'll go to the Coven infirmary tomorrow," she assured.

"For once, I agree with the girl," Bobo added.

"If you insist, but … do hurry home. You've been through enough."

"I will," the Spellweaver replied softly.

The group dispersed and each headed to their respected residences. Vanessa could feel the sunrise stirring, even though the horizon remained colorless and drenched in the unrelenting embrace of the night. The fading stars guided their weary body's home, where Bobo entered through the front door of the apartment like a famous hero returning from a victorious quest. Not that it was far from the truth.

"Ah. How our humble home has been missed. May your comforts not be taken for granted again, my sweet!" he announced, crashing into the wall and caressing it like a long-lost lover.

Shutting the door, the young witch yawned and stretched, feeling sleep tug at her bones. "Go wash up and get out of those rags. I'll brew and steep you your favorite tea. After that, I'll be in my room."

"As much as I would like to question your kind gesture, my worn spirit yearns for a good soaking and clean attire. I shall away," he boomed and raced for his room to gather his things.

She giggled to herself as she made sure the front door was locked and dragged her throbbing feet toward the kitchen. Carefully, Vanessa placed her grimoire on the breakfast bar as she went to work. The stove was lit, the kettle was heating, the tea set was pulled out, and the tea selected. The witch yawned again as she leaned against the wall. Her eyes continuously landed upon the leathery tome not a moment after she looked away. It was as if it were talking to her, coaxing her to gather it up in her arms once more, open it, and spend the whole night reading it.

The sound of the kettle whistling brought her out of her daze. Quickly, she removed it from the fire and poured the boiling water into the teapot. Steam curled out through the top until the lid was gently placed on, and she called out to Bobo who was still soaking in the tub in the main hall. "Tea is steeping."

"Will you be having a cup tonight?"

"No." As she said it, she held her stomach. She didn't think she could handle a cup of soothing tea tonight. She felt off and tired. All she wanted to do was sleep.

"Very well." A low groan rumbled behind the bathroom door. "It'll take another bath to get this filth to leave me," the ogre whined.

She laughed as she put the tray on the breakfast bar for him. "It'll be a nice way to wake up," she suggested the idea of a morning bath.

Already, she could hear the gentleman-beast agree. "True."

With that, Vanessa's job was done. On the way to the hall, she gathered up her grimoire and headed for her room. The door opened, and she turned on the light. The brilliant overhead light shined over every comfort that she had missed in recent days. The door was slowly shut. Behind the safety of her closed door, she put the book next to the bed on the nightstand and shed off her clothing. Mud, bits of leaves, things from the forest that had followed her like a second layer of sweat collected all around her as she disrobed and tossed her garbs into the hamper with a crinkled nose. The memories flooded her as she stared at the rip in her cloak, the bloodstains on her tunic, and the slashed fabric of her trousers. What followed after each horrific event that she had faced in the past few days was the first sting of hurt. The image of the ghost blade gliding through a short distance before slamming into Denmarius's gut made her gasp, cover her mouth, and screw her eyes shut like she could escape the torment of her mind. She could hear her voice, even as she whispered for it to stop. It echoed that memory she wanted nothing more than to forget.

"*One.*" A word that now carried the weight of a broken heart.

Opening her eyes, she snapped her vision to her hands, and the memory assaulted her again as Denmarius coughed blood up in her face. Instantly, her appendages went to her cheeks, and she bit her lip as the burning tears built up. Slowly, her arms went to wrap around her naked body.

One. A number that would forever haunt her.

The desire to take a shower was undeniable. Though her body wanted nothing more than to lay down in the comfort of her bed, her mind needed the satisfaction of a decent bar of soap, loads of hot water, and a good, long scrubbing.

But, in the shower, Vanessa found herself battling against a truth she couldn't accept. Blood could visibly wash away from the skin, but the life she had taken had been done by her own hands, and that would never wash away. Feeling weighted, she finished cleaning up and mangled her hair with her comb, breaking a few of the teeth in an attempt to destroy the persistent knots that had made a home in her ebony strands.

Feeling cleaner, but slightly ill, the young witch put on a nightgown, cut off her light, and climbed into her bed. But even with her covers snuggly drawn up to her chin and her head nestled deep into the soft pillow, she couldn't stop her mind from racing. She tossed and turned as comfort eluded her. Until, finally, she was facing her nightstand and the spine of her grimoire.

Sitting up, Vanessa groaned to herself and lit a match to bring a nearby candle to life. The orange glow washed over the book, making the gemstone look more mysterious. She reached out and brushed over the smooth face of the embellishment with the tips of her fingers. "Just a peak," she whispered with a mad grin.

Sliding the book over, Vanessa wormed the worn book her way as the excitement bubbled in her belly. The book was gently placed in her lap, and she looked it over proudly. Her hand brushed over the smooth stone and hard leather. She drew in a breath, held it, and opened the book to the very first page.

Vanessa carefully inspected every inch. Even though this was her grimoire, she didn't want what had transpired back at the archives to be reenacted in her bedroom. But, the first picture in the book set her mind at ease. A massive, gnarled tree with branches holding large, oversized leaves fixed at the end of them stared back at her. Each limb and leaf held a head of the house's name in curling letters.

Her eyes traced over every letter and detail. This was her family tree. *Her family.* She giggled to herself and curled up, bringing the tome closer to her as her knees were drawn in. A leaf, near the top and nestled into a collection of bare and nameless leaves, shivered on the limb. The branch wiggled. Vanessa's eyes grew wide. The branch shook again, and, before her eyes, grew across the paper, and stopped just short of her mother and father's names. Gradually, letter by letter, her name appeared on the leaf in the same writing as the rest of the tree. If that alone wasn't grandly amazing as it was strange, there came a distant jingling sound. The young witch's eyes floated up from the book and circled her bedroom before she realized where the sound was coming from. The bell-like ringing was coming from the page!

The leaf with her mother's name shook, like the wind of a storm was rustling through that singular part of the tree, and an item fell from behind the foliage. But instead of it being a drawing and falling to the grass surrounding the trunk of the family tree, it fell right out of the book and into Vanessa's lap.

"*Oop!*" She jolted as the hag stone plopped onto her stomach. She closed the book and set it on the nightstand as she scooted upright and picked up the stone. Inspecting it in the candlelight, she could see a smooth gray stone with tiny, blue flecks of mineral deposits swirled around the surface. A large hole made the item look like a flat, rocky donut. She flipped it over in her hand and then held it up to her eye.

"A hag stone, a grimoire, a family, and a precious memory, all in one day," she muttered to herself. Another yawn overtook her, and she smiled at her newly obtained objects. Placing the hag stone next to her grimoire, she found herself sleepier than she had moments ago. Her eyes drooped as they longed to close, and her body demanded the comforts of a good night's rest.

Right when her lips were puckered to blow out the candle, there was a gentle knock on her door. "Vanessa, my dear?" Bobo called to her from the other side.

"Yes?"

"We haven't done a mending spell yet and … well … I mean we've both been through a lot. I just wanted to make sure that you weren't going to be too sore to sleep soundly tonight."

"I can wait until the morning," she admitted. "What about you? Will you be fine to sleep or do you want a mending spell before bed?"

There was a pause before he answered. "If you are well, Vanessa, then I am well. We can mend over breakfast. My treat."

She perked up to that. "Promise?"

A deep, throaty chuckle escaped the ogre. "On my word as a scholar and an ogre."

She pouted. "You're not a scholar."

"Oh, but I could be," Bobo mused.

They both laughed.

"You better make breakfast," she said, settling back down into her bed.

"Consider it payment for the healing," he assured.

"Thank you."

The candle was blown out, and the two rested soundly throughout the night.

 *Chapter 7:*

The next day, she didn't wake up until well past noon. And only because of a pesky crystal ball call. The orb's pouch was hanging on the hook next to her bed, and the incessant chimes of an incoming call roused a very reluctant witch from her peaceful slumber. "Banish a banshee, I'll send them all to the underworld," she grumbled in a groggy voice.

"Answer the confounded contraption, Vanessa or, so help me, I'll march in there myself and crush it," Bobo threatened from the kitchen.

A wild hand slammed down in various spots and swatted around the open air as the Spellweaver blindly attempted to find her crystal ball. "If that ogre didn't make one hex of an omelet, I'd throw the thing right at his head," she muttered indistinctly. With success, she found the satchel, dug inside, and removed the item. The ringing, that caused her great vexation, got louder.

Lifting her head from her pillow, she fought the unruly curtain of untamed black hair and skimmed her fingers over the surface as she answered the call. "Yeah?" she announced while peering through one bloodshot eye and fighting past her longing for more sleep. A moment passed before the cloudy haze dispersed enough to reveal the caller.

"Just woke up I take it, Spellweaver Peterson?" A Coven member with short, deep brown hair and blazing blue eyes asked. His tanned skin told her he loved long days in the sun, and his smirk on his lips told her he had a mischievous spirit. But it was his gold insignia staring back at her that prompted Vanessa to sit up and frantically smooth out her more disobedient strands of hair.

The man waited for Vanessa to finish fussing with her appearance before he waved at her to calm down. Second Chosen David was one of the newly appointed Second Chosens to take the position after the battle of the blue cloaks. "I heard you had quite the adventure recently," he stated plainly.

Double-dip a candlestick! She forgot to submit her report. Resisting the urge to palm her face while on the crystal ball call, she forced a sleepy smile and replied with, "Yes. I will be in later to fill out a complete, detailed report."

The throaty chuckle that escaped him made her jump and almost lose connection of the call. "Don't worry about it. Leon submitted his report last night. We just need your signature on the forms," Second Chosen David informed.

She visibly lost the tension in her shoulders and gave an audible sigh of relief. "I can manage that later on this afternoon, sir."

"Good. Now, on to other matters. The High Priest Council is going over some finer details of a rather important issue. Once they have come to a consensus, they will summon you for a highly classified mission scroll."

She perked up. *Highly classified?* "Oh?" That was all she could muster while blinking the sleep from her eyes.

"Yes," he continued. "In light of the situation and your most recent findings and difficulties on your last mission, the Council has decided that you take a three-day reprieve from all missions. After your rest, you will be summoned."

She must have looked as disgruntled as she felt about taking a break from all missions because Second Chosen David perked a brow over one eye. "Is there something the matter, Spellweaver Peterson?"

The witch pouted despite her better judgment, "No missions at all?"

Again he laughed and shook his head. "You really are something, you know that? I've heard the rumors, but …" He trailed off with a smile and a sigh. "How about I put you on standby for information retrieval missions? The High Priest Council wants you well-rested for the next mission scroll, and I have to agree with them. But I see no harm in information gathering."

It was better than nothing.

"Honestly, that would be great," she admitted.

"It's settled then. I'll make the proper arrangements. For now, rest up, Peterson. You've done the whole city a great service many times over, now. Take the day off. You've earned it."

She nodded. "Yes sir."

The connection dissipated, and she sluggishly rose from her bed and dropped the crystal ball back into its pouch before she trudged out into the hall and to the breakfast bar. Bunching up her nightgown to one side, she slid up onto one of the barstool chairs along the counter and promptly plopped her face down on the bar top with a muffled whine. Her feet could be heard kicking about as she threw a (somewhat) silent fit.

"Tell me your troubles and woes," Bobo sighed as he checked on the sizzling peppers, onions, and meat in a separate pan and placed a lid over the top of the cooking omelet.

Tiny whimpers trickled out of her before she lifted her head and let him hear the annoyance in her voice as she complained about the recent call. "The Council wants me to take a few days off," she muttered.

The ogre looked over his shoulder and inspected his keeper. "Oh? You make it sound like such a terrible thing. I hardly see what the big deal is. We are long overdue for a decent vacation."

She groaned. "I knooow, but I just can't sit still after everything that has happened recently. I just … I want to help in every way that I can, Bobo."

"You have a kind heart and a longing to stay active, but that can bring you down quickly if you're not careful." He gave her a stern look. "And you are far from careful, my dear."

"Ha, ha." She sighed again and swirled a digit over the top of the breakfast bar. "I just don't want to deal with a lot of downtime right now," she said softly. She didn't want to be haunted by her memories. She wanted to be distracted for a little bit.

The demon went about cooking as he spoke, "I take it they caved and gave you light work then?"

"Yeah."

"I see. Then I fail to see the problem. You still get some time to rest, you still get to stay on active duty, and you have plenty of time to look through your grimoire. Honestly, Vanessa, you have your plate full enough."

She drew in a deep breath, and the ogre pointed at her. "Don't you dare sigh again."

She let out the air and couldn't help but laugh halfway through the action. "Sorry, it's just really frustrating. I really don't want any downtime right now. My mind can't take it," she admitted and sounded as defeated as she felt.

"Come now. There should be something that you could do over the next few days to keep you busy."

"Well …" She stopped suddenly and looked away.

"Yes?"

"Nothing, it's silly," she said.

Bobo plated her breakfast and started to place it in front of the young witch. When her hands were just about to receive the meal, he pulled the plate away and said, "Out with it."

She pouted and slumped in her chair as she crossed her arms over her chest.

"Vanessaaaa," he said her name like he was warning her of a nasty fate.

"Ugh!" She sat up and rapidly whispered quietly, "I've always wanted to learn how to bake."

The gentleman-beast didn't know if he should be surprised or dumbfounded, so, he settled for both and just stared blankly at the girl.

The Spellweaver wiggled awkwardly under his unwavering gaze. After a long moment, she shot up from the seat. "Never mind, I told you it was stupid."

"Not in the slightest!" Bobo barked out before she could retreat. "I was just trying to see who would be best suited for the job."

Vanessa turned to face the demon as he put the plate down in front of her previous seating place. The utensils were then laid out as he patted the counter and motioned her over.

"Come now. Before it gets cold. I suggest we eat and heal up because you, young lady, have a new craft to learn." His joyous smile was so pleasantly warm that Vanessa could only give a goofy grin of her own as she slipped back up onto her seat and dove into her breakfast.

After breakfast, Bobo and Vanessa healed up using a small healing incantation, drinking a minor revitalizing potion, and using a quick sweep of a quartz crystal. It was a lot of tedious work, but it was cheaper than visiting a healer, and Bobo refused to let Vanessa step a foot into the Coven even if it was to visit the medical wing.

Before the dangers of the kitchen were tackled, they went into town for a few supplies, to go grocery shopping, and then made a pit stop by the runesmith to get the sun etching magically replaced onto the rune Leon had let her borrow before. It was the least she could do. While there, she made sure she had a full set herself and replaced any missing runes.

The duo hadn't made a step out of the runesmith when she received a crystal ball call from Raven. Since they were out, they all met up in town near a small restaurant and had lunch together.

"How's your visit been?" Vanessa asked.

"Lots of story trading, that is for sure," Raven said with a yawn. "I didn't get a lick of sleep last night between Ell and I chatting and me checking in with Raka."

"I say, is he faring well?" Bobo questioned.

She nodded. "Yeah. That sly Crix was more aid to me than the other way around. I'm not worried about him. Especially since the wolves took such a beating recently."

Vanessa tried to act like she wasn't battling horrific images of past events when she changed the subject. "Bobo's going to teach me how to bake!"

"I hope you bake better than your mother," Raven said with a cringe.

"Oh, dear. It might be a family curse," the ogre mumbled to himself.

"She couldn't bake?" Vanessa looked blown away.

Shaking her head, the Dark Elf said, "No. Charles, your father, he was the chef of the house. I miss his cooking."

"A sliver of hope," Bobo whispered.

"Some of his recipes should be hidden about somewhere. I'll ask Raka to look around the house for them," Raven added.

"I'd love that!"

The rest of lunch was spent chatting over stories of what Charles and Larissanna were like. Vanessa would occasionally toss in a tale from her childhood, but most—when uttered aloud—sounded lonely and lacked a happier tone. She opted for more recent tales from her Coven days where Bobo could slide in a comment here or there, even if they were making fun of her. She still laughed with the rest of them. After a couple hours, Raven parted ways saying she needed to run a few errands and attempt to stay awake for the remainder of the day. They hugged each other, promising to call later on, and parted ways. Then Bobo and Vanessa headed back home to unload.

As soon as they walked through the door, Bobo set the grocery bags down on the kitchen counter and then headed straight for the candles in his room. "What are you doing?" Vanessa called to him as she put everything away.

"I'm going to need my calming vanilla candles. I have a feeling my nerves will be tested along with that poor oven," the ogre yelled back.

Vanessa rolled her eyes. "The sassiest ogre I know," she snapped under her breath.

While waiting on her demonic partner, she skimmed through the baking book. Earlier, while they were out, Bobo stated that she should start simple and easy and opted for the young witch to start with learning how to make chocolate chip cookies. She read over the recipe again and again, trying to memorize the ingredients and steps like she was preparing for a ritual.

"Put this on," Bobo commanded, tossing a green apron that reminded Vanessa of pollen-congested swamp waters during a spring afternoon. The item landed on the counter in front of her.

She eyed over it with a sneer and snatched it up. As she turned to face him she said, "I'm not putting on this silly—" Her statement was snatched clean out of her mouth by the image before her.

Bobo wore a chalky, onyx apron with a fuchsia bow pinned to his left breast, and there was a black and white, checkered pattern decorating the ruffled fabric along the hem that was three layers thick. Draped over his shoulder was a kitchen rag, and he was fixing his glasses that were now fastened with a thin, jewelry-like necklace. She blinked, unsure of what to say.

"What?" he inquired, coming to reach for the cookbook.

Instantly, she shook her head. "Nothing," she swiftly replied. All of the sudden, the pale green apron didn't seem so bad. "What is the first step?" she asked while tying her apron tightly around her waist.

Clearing his throat, Bobo read over the directions as he pointed to the refrigerator, "Eggs, butter, and sugar."

 *Chapter 8:*

Her braid was speckled in cookie batter, her face was smeared with flour, and her hands were a sticky mess. The once pale green apron was now hidden under a thick layer of powdery white. Vanessa's face was inches from the oven window as she watched the seventh batch of treats bake.

"You'll burn your nose if you get any closer," Bobo hummed while reading a book and he leaning against the counter.

"I'm not burning this batch," she whispered like if she spoke too loudly the cookies would explode into flames.

"Trust the timer, Vanessa. Baking is an art. You won't get it right the first few times you try."

She sighed. "Magic is easier."

"And yet you manage to mess that up," he reminded as he turned another page.

The look that Vanessa shot him was far from kind. But as she silently tried to burn a hole through his precious book with her glowering stare, he sniffed unaffected and calmly stated, "Do you smell something burning?" To which the Spellweaver whipped her vision back to the oven window and inspected her baking cookies in a panic. The ogre sighed heavily and closed his novel before laying it on the counter. "Seriously, my dear, you need to just calm down. A few more moments and you'll be able to taste the fruits of your labor."

Rising from the floor, Vanessa sighed and walked over to lean against the counter next to Bobo. All the while, the twitchy witch kept peering over at the oven. She was fully prepared to dash over and retrieve the baked goods in a flash if necessary.

"So, do you want to talk about your riverbank lip-lock with Leon, or are we going to pretend that it didn't happen?" Bobo casually dropped the statement and Vanessa almost fell over as if the words had weights tied to them. But the ogre's eyes did not waver from their mark. They remained transfixed on the girl as she searched the kitchen with shifty eyes.

"I … Uh …" She floundered for a proper response. Her heartbeat slightly picked up in tempo. Slowly, she straightened up and fussed with the hem of her simple tunic. "It was unexpected," she answered finally.

"I'll say," Bobo muttered. "Though, I cannot say that it was entirely unexpected. I had assumed that there were blossoming affections growing between the two of you for some time. I, however, had not foreseen the two of you …" He grimaced and lifted his index fingers and then pressed them firmly together to reenact the moment like a finger puppet show.

Vanessa felt her body instantly flare with heat. She gasped and made Bobo part his fingers and then slapped him over the shoulder. "You did it! I was merely reminding, my dear," he shot out defensively.

"I care a lot for him," she shot out. "I wanted to talk about everything, plan it out …" she trailed off and looked away.

The gentleman-beast nodded to himself. "Ah, I see. But, Vanessa, you cannot plan matters of the heart like that. There are times in this life that emotions will prevail over reason."

"Just like when you hugged Lyx?" Vanessa asked, a wild grin curling her lips.

Bobo's eyes widened in surprise. "Well, I mean, that was just me trying to comfort the distraught thing. What sort of gentleman would I be if I had let her remain in such a sad state?"

Vanessa laughed then. "If you say so, big guy. But the way you held her seemed like it was just as much for you as it was for her."

"How absurd," Bobo whispered.

The timer went off behind them. "Time to check the cookies," Vanessa chirped gaily and skipped off toward the oven.

Bobo narrowed his eyes at her. "Banish a banshee. You are a most vile thing."

The Spellweaver could only giggle as she retrieved the chocolate chip cookies from the oven. One by one they were placed on the cooling rack. Snagging a cookie, she hissed as she blew at the piping hot treat before taking a bite. She turned and gave a thumbs up with a half-smile. "It's edible," she declared before rushing off for a glass of milk. "But, I think I added too much salt," she admitted.

"Then, let us try again. This time, follow the directions. Honestly, how can someone mess up so many times on such a simple recipe?" Bobo wondered out loud.

The night went on in a similar fashion before Vanessa and Bobo passed out, only to wake up the next day and try again. They had lost count of how many batches of batter had been mixed, but they had used up all of the flour they had purchased. The eggs were gone, too.

"I hope they turn out okay this time," Vanessa whispered as she lay with her head on the counter. A moment passed, and she yawned.

"I'm sure they will be fine," Bobo replied.

She turned her head to face him. "You said that a lot today."

"And I meant it every time, my dear."

She sighed, and the ogre patted her head. The last of the sand trickled through the hourglass, and the soft—yet annoying—chiming of unseen bells rung throughout the apartment. Vanessa bolted from her seat, ignored the timer, and dashed over to the oven. While she managed the cookies, Bobo placed a ribbon within the battered pages of his book before closing it and came to turn off the device. The smell of melted chocolate swirled within the apartment.

"Well, my dear, what is the verdict?"

She beamed as she placed them on the cooling rack. "The best ones yet," she murmured.

"And you'll get better with every mistake and attempt," Bobo assured.

Happy with her triumph, she dusted her hands off on her apron before she hastily untied it and tossed it onto the kitchen counter. "I'm going to go change," she announced.

"Oh?" the ogre questioned as he approached the cooling cookies. "Have some plans?"

The young witch was practically bounding out of the kitchen and down the hall as she yelled back to her pet, "I think these cookies need a cup of coffee from the Grim Bean."

As his master fussed over an outfit, Bobo took it upon himself to steal a cookie off the cooling rack. "Best when fresh out of the oven," he stated, nibbling on the edge of the treat. He paused and shivered. "Not as deadly as the previous batches," he muttered, looking over its flattened surface. She had used way too much vanilla and an excessive amount of butter, but they weren't completely *horrible*. He chuckled to himself and called out to Vanessa. "If we are heading out, I shall change my tie into something more presentable. An afternoon out on our day off sounds like a marvelous idea."

"Okay!" she elatedly replied from behind her bedroom door.

Moments later, Bobo returned fastening his gold cufflinks to his brown, plaid, three-piece suit and adjusted his deep red tie. A silk handkerchief (matching his tie in color) was removed from his breast pocket, and he inspected his appearance in the hall mirror before shining up his horns. With a sniff and a dashing grin, the ogre tucked the hanky safely away.

"I thought you were only changing your tie," Vanessa teased.

The gentleman-beast chuckled and brushed unseen dirt from his sleeve. "I very well couldn't remain in a suit dusted with flour, now, could I? Besides, an outing that isn't us parading around as undercover Coven members is a rarity, my dear. I desired sporting a suit that seldom sees the world outside of my closet due to our dreaded schedule."

His eyes walked a line toward the living room where Vanessa stood holding the tin full of her cookies. She wore a deep purple, high-low skirt with midnight blue ruffles, the colors so close in shade that they melted into one another. She had a silver shirt with an opening along the shoulders and belled sleeves. It shimmered in the sunlight pouring in through the windows. The dark purple waist cinch matched the shade of her skirt, and it was lined in silver fastenings. The thin, plum-colored cloak that she had her silver insignia proudly pinned to gleamed brightly in the sunlight. He looked down at her brown, ankle-high boots and then back up to the young witch.

"I see that you've decided to dress up. What's the occasion? Do you plan on running into anyone in particular, Vanessa?"

His inquiry was enough to make her look away to hide any expression she might have been suddenly gifted with in that moment. "No," she muttered softly. "Are you ready?"

"Of course," he stated while motioning to the door and letting her lead the way.

The two of them stepped outside, locked the door, and headed down the hall to the flat. The air was warmer today. Though there was plenty of wind, it hadn't made it unbearably cold outside, and the thin cloak would provide her with enough shield from the strong breezes.

"Any other plans for the day since we are out?" Bobo inquired curiously. "I mean, our coin purses are full, and we have the day off. I say we enjoy it."

Vanessa laughed. "And the truth is revealed. You just wanted to play dress up and get out of the house!"

He grunted. "Says the witch in fancy attire."

She pressed her lips together and clutched the tin of cookies a little harder. She held her breath for a moment and puffed out her cheeks in a playful huff. "I rarely get a day off and, besides, it is really difficult to fight in something like this. Even spell casting is hard while wearing it," she half-whined. "I just wanted to feel pretty," she whispered finally.

"Preposterous," Bobo loudly blurted out.

Vanessa stiffened as they waited for the flat to arrive at the end of the hall. She didn't say anything. She just stared straight ahead as she tried to pretend the comment didn't hurt.

"You always look lovely, my dear. Scuffed up boots, worn leather pants, or your casual robes all look stunning on you. Don't let anyone tell you different, or they'll hear from me and my ax." He tapped his weapon at his hip for good measure.

Instantly, Vanessa turned to face her pet. She was met with a sincere smile. She felt all the rising tension and doubt in her melt away. She gave a curl of her lips as she let the words sink in.

"Thank you," she muttered and leaned against his side. "That means a lot coming from the most dashing demon in all of Aeristria."

The ogre patted her head with a soft chuckle, "You deserve to hear it, my dear."

 *Chapter 9:*

"I knew it. I knew you couldn't stay away from that place for a whole day," Bobo grumbled, disgruntled with his master's slight (and most undesired) change in plans.

"Why is it such a big deal?"

"We are so close. We can just breeze right on by like it isn't even there."

"Oh, come on. What is the big fuss all about, Bobo? Coven HQ is on the way. I just want to see if there are any information retrieval missions. I won't take any on. I just want—"

"Yes. Yes. I know." Bobo sighed heavily. "We shall inquire if there are any bland, sensible missions to sate your hunger for work and trouble."

"I don't like getting into trouble," she whined defensively.

"No one believes that, my dear. No one."

Vanessa only shook her head and pressed on the few extra blocks to the Coven while dragging a reluctant ogre in tow. The crisp air was accompanied by clear blue skies and thin wispy clouds. Drifting scents of stewing soups, roasting meats, and fried pastry dishes mingled and wafted in the spring breeze as they walked through the thicker parts of the market.

Bobo licked his lips as his eyes strayed from the sidewalk they traipsed down. "I do say, Vanessa, dear, I hope that we can make this visit rather short. I fear these street vendors have awoken a hungry beast in me," he announced while trying to hold back a fit of drool.

"All right. I hear you loud and clear," Vanessa replied as she quickened her pace and looked down at the tin in her grasp. A wild grin overtook her lips while she drew in a prideful breath as the Coven building came into view.

Her body felt like it was all a flutter with excitement. Walking through the main entrance, she stood in the front lobby. Her eyes scanned about, looking for a clear path to the third floor where Second Chosen David's office was located. A collection of members parted as they approached desks, halls, and communal crystal balls.

"I still don't understand why we couldn't just send a message via crystal ball," Bobo griped.

"I'll be quick. Promise," Vanessa assured while Bobo grumbled a few choice words under his breath.

They had barely made it to the steps when they heard a familiar voice call out to them.

"Vanessa?" Leon yelled from across the lobby. Quickly, the Summoner wrapped up his conversation with his group of friends and trotted over to the Spellweaver and ogre. His eyes trailed over her slowly, and his positively wicked smile spoke in volumes of what he thought of Vanessa's outfit. "You never called. What are you doing here today? I thought that missions are on hold for you right now."

Sheepishly, she rolled her lips into her mouth and pressed down as she darted her eyes around from side to side. "Oh," Bobo started. "Not going to tell him why you're here?"

She started to turn red in the cheeks, and it slowly seeped over the cuffs of her ears. "I had a lot happen and I forgot. Yesterday morning I had spoken with Second Chosen David about taking on information retrieval missions. I was just going to stop in on my way to the Grim Bean after looking to see if there was anything available," she spouted, and then gave a confident nod to her pet.

The ogre rolled his eyes with a groan.

"The Grim Bean, huh? I could use a cup of coffee, and my break's coming up. Mind if I tag along?" Leon asked with slight hesitance.

Vanessa shook her head *no*. "I don't mind," she admitted.

"Great. I'll grab Lyx and meet you at the front gates in fifteen then?"

"Sure!" she exclaimed.

A dashing smile swept over Leon's lips, and he winked as he backed away. "See you in fifteen then," he stated before turning and heading for the summoning practice grounds.

"You really should apologize for being so forgetful." The gentleman-beast shook his head. "Well, come on then. Let's get this over with," Bobo sighed the words and sluggishly made way for the second floor.

Vanessa watched Leon disappear from her sight and blinked out of her daze. "Hmmm? Oh, yeah, right."

Following behind the ogre, the young witch made way for the third floor. The hike up the staircase was, for the first time, not such a daunting task.

Once on the third floor, the black walls and white baseboards were washed in the usual orange glow of the oil lamps lining the narrow hallway. Countless corridors endlessly branched out from the main hall, making Vanessa feel as though she were a rat plopped down in the center of a maze and expected to find the morsel of cheese hidden at the center.

"This is your endeavor, my dear. Lead the way," Bobo demanded in a grumble.

"Cranky," Vanessa spouted under her breath as she squeezed by the mammoth-sized demon.

Bobo scoffed. "I was promised coffee." He lifted his hand and motioned in air at all of the wonders of the foreboding hall.

She forced a mock smile. "You'll get it. You'll just have to practice patience."

"Ha. If I practice patience with you, I'll perish whilst holding my breath," he teased.

Per usual, Vanessa ended the argument with silence and pressed on toward the end of the hall where the Second Chosen office doors were. Despite the fact that she had been cleared of any faults and had a new ranking to prove her worth within the Coven, it didn't stop her heartbeat from hammering away at her chest like a herd of galloping unicorns as she approached the ominous double doors at the end of the hall. It was the dreaded doors that led to the High Priest Council. She delighted in them slipping from her view as she turned sharply down the next hall.

Her finger traced the air over the gold nameplates mounted outside each office door as she searched for Second Chosen David Reham's office. Success was met just a few moments later.

"A-ha!" she exclaimed quietly. With a triumphed grin, she confidently lifted her fist and knocked lightly over the door.

The knob jingled, turned, and the door slowly opened, revealing a somewhat small office inside. There was a bookshelf to one side, a couple of chairs fixed in front of a medium-sized desk, and a large, wooden, grandfather clock with bronze embellishments ticking rhythmically behind a man who hovered over a document. After a moment, David started to scribble away ferociously on the bit of parchment. Without lifting his head, he spoke, but the emotion seemed to be sapped from the words. "Come in." Lifelessly, he motioned to the chairs in front of his desk. His attention remained on what he was writing.

"Second Chosen Reham?" Vanessa questioned cautiously in a low tone as she stepped carefully through the threshold.

The writing stopped, and the man lifted his head. Upon seeing Vanessa, he plopped his quill into an inkwell and rose from his desk. Quickly, his demeanor changed, and he headed for her and Bobo with an inviting smile. "Spellweaver Peterson!" He ushered them further into the room and waved a quick will powder spell to close the door. "Come in. Come in. How can I help you?"

The young witch smiled as she asked, "Are there any missions for information retrieval?"

David threw his head back and laughed heartily. "My, my. They weren't joking when they said that you had a thirst for mission scrolls," he stated once the laughter subsided.

She could only nod sheepishly in return before the shyness was replaced with an impish sparkle in her eye. "So, are there any?"

"Sadly, there are not," Second Chosen David admitted.

"What a shame. We came, we tried, and we leave empty-handed," Bobo announced gaily as he turned and fully swung open the door. "We bid you good day, you amazing man with beautiful eyes!"

David blinked, taken aback by the compliment, but smiled awkwardly as he looked nervously at Vanessa who responded to the stunned man, saying, "He's happy that you don't have any missions."

"*Oh,*" the wizard mouthed.

"But he's right. You do have stunning eyes," she confirmed and then waved as she headed for the impatient ogre tapping his foot out in the hall.

David called out to them, "I'll crystal ball call you if anything comes up!"

"Thanks!" she shouted back, and the two headed back toward the main floor. Once they were a safe distance away from Second Chosen David's office, Vanessa turned and glowered at her pet.

"Careful, my dear. Your face may get stuck that way, and *I'll* be revered as the pretty one," the ogre stated with a smirk.

"You didn't have to rush us out of there," she hissed.

Bobo scoffed and fussed with his tie. "Of course I did. Leave you in that office long enough and you would have tried to convince him to let you take on a light labor mission scroll."

Vanessa perked up, "You think I could have?"

As soon as the witch started to turn to head back to the wizard's office, Bobo's hand was there to spin her around and pushed her further down the hall to stay in stride with him. "Not today," he barked.

She shoved his hand off her shoulder and remained silent the rest of the walk down to the lobby. Near the teleportation gates, Vanessa saw Leon lazing about as he leaned against the wall and casually waved at beings he knew as they passed.

Seeing the Summoner made Vanessa squeeze the tin of cookies again as she smiled to herself. She knew, even though she hadn't hid it very well, that Bobo had figured out the real reason she wanted to stop by the Coven. It was scrolled all over the ogre's face as he quietly chuckled beside her. She knew that he was holding back a mountain of teasing comments. She could feel it in her witchy bones.

"I didn't expect to see you back here so soon," Leon admitted, pushing off the wall as the Spellweaver and demon approached. His eyes became fixated on the rusty-red tin clutched in Vanessa's grasp. "Say, what is that? You've been pretty clingy with it."

SMOKE, LIES, AND GRIMOIRES

She looked down as if she had forgotten that they were there and became lost in a moment of thought. "They're ... uh, cookies," she said finally.

"Cookies? I could go for one right about now. I skipped breakfast this morning because I slept in past my Tinker Bell's Spirit alarm that I had cast, so I wasn't able to eat before leaving the house."

"Breakfast is the most important meal of the day, my good man. You shouldn't skip it," Bobo informed in almost a fatherly fashion.

Leon chuckled as he rubbed his belly. "Yeah. Not planning on making a habit out of it, buddy. Thankfully, I can take a break and grab lunch with you guys. But a cookie would tide me over until we get to the Grim Bean. There's a lot of cobblestone between here and the café," he verbally prodded the witch in an attempt to persuade her.

Gladly, almost too gladly, the witch opened the container and shoved it in Leon's direction. "Take as many as you like," she urged.

For a second, the Summoner reconsidered the offer. But they did look appealing resting in the tin, their chocolaty morsels taunting him as the florescent lighting overhead shined on the baked goods. Without a second thought, he reached in and grabbed a cookie and took a bite out of it.

At first, he smiled. But soon that smile soured on his face and he looked confused at the item in his hand as he turned it from side to side, inspecting it for flaws. The chewing slowed, and it appeared as though he had to muscle swallowing the first and only bite he had taken.

"Oh, dear," Bobo's hardly audible words were unheard by the others as Leon frowned hard.

"Uh, Vanessa?" Leon started.

"Yes?" she asked while looking at him with hope gleaming in her russet gaze.

He pointed, with the cookie hand, at the tin she held. "You need to get your money back."

"Why is that?" she asked, her beaming face contorting into confusion.

SMOKE, LIES, AND GRIMOIRES

He shook his head, and the frown deepened. "Those things are spoiled. I'm sure of it. You should get your money back. Where did you get them?"

The young witch looked crestfallen as each word left the Summoner's mouth. She took in a breath to speak, but whatever she was about to say was halted by the sound of another joining the conversation.

"Ah, Spellweaver Peterson, you're starting to be my new favorite witch to run into," Riker said with a sly grin. "And bringing me cookies? You shouldn't have. You know that the Coven will talk if you start bringing me little gifts like this," he joked.

She turned, and instantly Riker's hand reached in and plucked out a cookie from the tin.

"I wouldn't—" Leon tried to warn.

But it was too late.

Riker snapped the cookie in half with his mouth, chewed it without flinching, and swallowed. He made a face of approval, finished the rest of it, and snagged another two from the container. "I hope you don't mind?"

"You like them?" she asked perking up.

The smile that overtook Riker's lips was strange. It was both warm and, if a smile could be cunning, Riker pulled it off. "Indeed, I do, Peterson."

She grinned wildly in reply. Meanwhile, Bobo leaned over to Leon and tried to mask his words between clearing his throat and lightly coughing. "She made them," the gentleman-beast quietly informed the wizard before he pretended to finish turning away from everyone to cough.

Leon watched as Riker took another bite out of a second cookie, and the Summoner swallowed hard as he paled at the sight. "The man has an iron gut," he whispered.

"Good news. The High Priest Council wishes to speak with me later on this afternoon. I believe we shall see our mission scroll soon, if not within the next few days. Running into you saved me the crystal ball call to inform you."

Vanessa giggled happily. "That is the best thing I've heard all day!"

"I thought you might enjoy that bit of information," Riker said. "I'll leave you to the rest of your day." He turned and paused, his attention returning to the Spellweaver. "Oh, and Vanessa? Keep up the baking."

She beamed wildly then. She practically lit up the Coven lobby as Riker walked away. Leon did a triple take from Riker to Vanessa to the tin of cookies before he steeled his resolve and lurched forward. Desperately, he grasped a handful of cookies.

Just as Vanessa noticed, she gasped, "Hey!"

Leon slammed the handful into his mouth and chewed like it life depended on it. He coughed and Bobo reached out, but Leon held up his hand and finished chewing and swallowed while clutching his fist so tightly that his knuckles went white.

"You, sir, are a saint and a hero," Bobo whispered.

Vanessa had a toothy grin as she closed the container and leaned forward to give the Summoner a quick, chaste kiss on the cheek. "Don't spoil your appetite," she said with giddy laughter and bounded out the Coven doors.

Leon hiccupped and burped before slurring, "Too late," in a grumbling fashion.

Bobo chuckled and aided in turning the dazed Summoner toward the exit. "Come on. Let us wash that palate out with some better food and a tasty beverage."

"If I didn't have to clock back in, I'd wash it down with mead at Tasgall's," Leon admitted as they headed out to catch up with Vanessa.

 ## Chapter 10:

While Leon walked half hanging on Bobo's arm like a wounded soldier—Vanessa practically skipped all the way to the Grim Bean. Occasionally, she'd turn around, oblivious to the poor wizard's plight, and urge the two men to pick up the pace before bounding further ahead of them.

"She's a cruel serpent of a woman," Leon rasped.

"You knew this before you fell in love with her," Bobo reminded. "Suck it up, my good man."

"I'm sure she knows that she almost killed me. That's why she is so happy," the Summoner claimed in a whine.

"It was just cookies," Bobo hoarsely reminded.

The Summoner turned a sickly green and stifled a burp. "Don't remind me."

Scoffing, the ogre replied with, "Come now, you're making a fool of yourself."

Leon had hurt etched in every line of his face as he gawked up at the demon. "Did you eat any of them?" he asked almost angrily.

"Ha! I'm smarter than that," Bobo lied.

"You're as cruel as her," Leon groaned while limping along.

As they neared the café, Vanessa spun around and walked backward. "This is like a first date!" she exclaimed excitedly.

Whimpering, Leon shook his head. "I've been on dates. This is murder. She set me up for death, I'm sure of it. She'll be the end of me."

"I tried to warn you," Bobo mumbled and forced the man to stand a little straighter.

The glare burning its way through his demonic hide was ignored. Leon huffed, "I don't remember you trying to stop me at all."

There wasn't much of a reply, only the soft chuckles of an ogre as they crossed the street over to the Grim Bean.

Outside of the café stood Leslie. He had his head propped up in his hands, and his elbows rested on the outside windowsill of the shop. Every few seconds, a soft, content sigh escaped the imp who practically had his nose pressed up against the glass. It was a wonder that the window wasn't fogged over from top to bottom with all the heavy breathing the small demon was doing on it.

"What in the name of magic are you doing now, Leslie Templeton?" Vanessa asked. But instead of the imp turning to defend his good reputation (or so he'd claim), he simply remained glued to the glass and sighed again. "Are you okay?" The young witch was now concerned as the usual banter was skipped. Though she carefully approached, she expected that this was all a ploy to get her close enough to pick her pockets with his sticky fingers.

Leslie spoke, though his attention never wavered from whatever they had been fixed upon long before everyone had arrived. "Now dat," he started dreamily. "Dat's an imp."

She checked Leslie over, still suspecting foul play, before she clutched her coin purse a tad tighter and leaned in closer to the window. Using her free hand, she blocked the glare of the sun warming the glass as she attempted to see what had the imp so entranced.

Inside the café, Freeda smiled and laughed at a few gremlins as they all chatted away near one of the counters. Her long, violet hair was hastily flipped behind her shoulders as she turned to look over the shop. The black sundress she wore was littered in a large, sunflower print, and it complimented her green skin. The creamy white, knitted shawl was repositioned after she pushed a few stray locks out of the view of her hazel, almond-shaped eyes.

Slowly, Vanessa turned her attention back to the bewitched Leslie just in time for her to watch him sigh *again*. "Oh, goddess above. You're smitten!" she shrieked.

"Do ya have ta yell like dat?" Leslie whined while digging a finger into his ear.

"She really is a tumultuous creature by nature. You really shouldn't expect otherwise," Bobo stated in an exasperated tone.

The imp aggressively snapped out of his daze and turned on the three with pepper in his tone. "Hey, hey! Can yous guys see I'm havin' a moment 'ere? Move it along," he shot out at them and proceeded to shoo at them before going back to his previous position at the window.

Bobo shook his head. "We best be on our way. He's lost," he mumbled while throwing open the doors to the building. "Imps are obsessive creatures when they first fall in love. But who could blame him for falling for such a beautiful being?" the demon bellowed to gain Leslie's attention and then walked through the entrance.

Leslie whipped around with his eyes bulging. "Is he gonna say somethin' ta 'er? I mean, I'll fight him ... From out 'ere ... Wid words, ya know?"

Vanessa looked lost as Leon made a sound that said he doubted that the imp had a chance both in love and on the battlefield. "I don't know, little guy. That's a lot of demon strutting in there." The Summoner's voice was taunting in a grave tone. "Just look at him," Leon said while gesturing to the ogre inside the café.

The sound of the imp's face slapping against the glass was followed by the whine of his skin sliding over the smooth surface. His voice was muffled as he tried to talk to the wizard and remain focused on the ogre approaching Freeda. "*Eep!*" the small demon squeaked. His ears dropped. "He-he-he wouldn't dare," the imp stammered, unsure of his own proclamation.

Leon groaned, "Oh, I don't know." He leisurely looked into the Grim Bean and gasped.

"What?" Leslie cried out and pulled away to look to the Summoner before plastering his face back onto the window. "What? What'd I miss, huh?" The poor little guy's voice was filled with panic.

Leon leaned close to the demon's ear. "I think I just saw her eyes light up when she laughed. You know that ogre has a way with words."

"No ..." Leslie whispered.

"Oh, yeah. I'm pretty sure I saw it," Leon said.

Meanwhile, the scene of Bobo chatting with Freeda carried on. The images of them laughing and talking made the imp sink further and further down from his perch.

Again, Leon made a sound of surprise as he pointed and pretended to get closer to the glass. "Is she? No ... she couldn't be," he said, all while hardly trying to hide his sly smile.

"What! What now?" Leslie shrieked and bit at his nails.

"Oh ... it's nothing," Leon said with a sigh.

Without warning, the imp leaped up onto Leon's lap and grabbed him by his shirt and jerked him close to his gnarled, impish face. "Give it ta me straight!" he wailed.

"I just thought I saw her blush," Leon replied casually.

"She ... he ..." He sounded so despondent, and his shoulders slumped, his ears flopped back, and his eyes dropped to the sidewalk. Suddenly, the imp snapped out of it. Throwing himself off of Leon's lap, he squared his shoulders and marched with purpose to the front doors, kicked one side open, darted into the building, and yelled out, "Get away from my girl ya bag ah muscles!"

"*Leslie!*" Freeda gasped.

The imp rushed over to the flustered demoness. "I know he looks impressive, but don' judge a book by its cova. He gets ya hooked and strings ya along. I know a succubus dat's been charmed by him." Shimmying past the ogre, Leslie shot out, "Back up, big guy. She's spoken for!"

"Leslie, what are ya doing?" Freeda asked with concern for the fellow imp's sanity.

"He's tryin' ta woo ya!" Leslie informed in a hoarse tone.

Freeda looked from Leslie to Bobo, back to Leslie, and dropped her voice down to a level that only the two male demons could hear. "He was askin' 'bout the specials," she corrected.

"Da—da specials? *Oh.*" Leslie gulped and lost some of his bravado. "But, yous was blushin'," he whispered back to her.

The demoness seemed to blush harder to those words. "Well, I mean ... What girl wouldn't, huh? He said my eyes sparkled when I talked about the menu," she admitted.

Leslie searched Freeda's face. His features morphed into a softer version of himself. Both of his ears flopped back. His large, black eyes drank in every bit of the female before him. "Your eyes don' sparkle, Freeda." The words made the demoness frown hard. "Dey shine. You're like, tha brightest thing in *all* of Raen. Ya bring sunshine whereever ya go. And, I'm pretty sure, dat even when ya cry, ya manage ta make flowers sprout wherever ya tears fall. You are tha only light I need in my life."

"Oh! Oh, *Leslie*," Freeda cooed. "I never knew that you felt dis way!"

"I was too scared ta say somethin'. Not anymore. Freeda, I like you some kind of bad, ya know?" the imp admitted.

"Get over here," Freeda commanded as she took one of his ears in each hand, tugged the imp forward, and dipped the male imp in her arms. "Kiss me!" she cried and planted her lips over his.

Too shocked to do more than follow, Leslie looked surprised right up until her mouth met his. To which he stiffened and whirled one foot in the air as their lips remained locked.

The whole café erupted in a chorus of cheers, whistles, hollers, and a flurry of congratulations. Even Bobo added in a generous clap. The two imps separated and blushed at the onlookers. Freeda pressed her hands against her cheeks and bashfully turned away from everyone. "I'm so sorry, everybody," she stated as she turned redder than what one would expect from a being with green skin.

"No apologies needed, my dear," Bobo said with a nudge to the embarrassed imp.

Leon and Vanessa were standing inside at the entrance doors.

Bewildered, Vanessa looked to the wizard at her side. "How did you know?" she whispered to him.

Shaking his head with a chuckle, Leon replied with, "You didn't pay attention during demonology class, did you?"

Puffing out her cheeks, the young witch huffed. "I might have slept through that class."

Rolling his eyes, he informed her. "When imps choose a mate, it's for life. They can actually read a spouse in a matter of minutes. It seems these two had enough time to fall for each other."

"Oooh," the Spellweaver's voice echoed with her enlightenment.

After everything had settled down, Freeda gushed about renovations and additions. Which only led Vanessa and the others on a tour that took them outside to the newly made patio seating. There were still small details needing to be added and minor decorating to be done but, aside from the drying paint, the space was almost completed. Leslie and Freeda walked hand in hand as each detail was pointed out to the stunned group.

"It truly is amazing. This place has grown so much since it's been in your care," Vanessa spoke while her eyes trailed over the view, mentally trying to piece in all the new additions that would be introduced in the days to come. "I can't wait to see it finished."

Nodding, Bobo added, "I couldn't agree more. This is simply a marvelous idea. Truly, it shall be a seasonal hit."

Freeda winked. "I'm a businesswoman at heart." She giggled and motioned to a long bench lined with empty flower beds.

They all walked over and took a seat. Vanessa looked from one end to the other and paused while deep in thought. "Say, Leon, where is Lyx? I thought you went to go fetch her before you went on break."

"Oh yeah!" Leon stated while snapping his fingers. "She called me from her compact while I was looking for her. Though, I couldn't make out much of what she was saying she was chattering away so fast. Said something about clothes shopping for the perfect outfit and she'd see me at home later on tonight."

"Sounds like she had plans for the day," Vanessa said with a short burst of laughter.

Clearing his throat, Bobo awkwardly rose from his seat and noted the sun in the sky. "Speaking of plans, I have a prior engagement to attend to," he informed.

"You have no friends," Vanessa stated flatly.

"Correction, my glib-tongued girl, *you* have no friends." He sniffed and tugged at the lapels of his jacket. "It's my week to pick the literature for our book club," he stated proudly.

The Spellweaver looked bored and dryly added, "That doesn't sound like friends ..."

With a haughty laugh, Bobo snapped back, "Like you could tell the difference."

"Sounds like you have an entertaining night ahead of you," Leon cut in as he peered around two imps nuzzling noses and murmuring lovey-dovey nothings to each other.

The ogre smiled. "That I do. I shall see you all later on this eve."

With that, the gentleman-beast sauntered off, leaving the other four behind. "What about you?" Leon asked as he turned to Vanessa.

She blinked in reply, unsure of what he meant. "Hmmm? What do you mean?"

He shrugged. "Lyx is gone for the rest of the day, Bobo is off to his book club, and ... what about you? Do you have any plans for tonight?"

Opening her mouth, she went to reply, but she realized that she didn't have any plans. This was the extent of her plans. She let out a breath and raised her hands in the air. "I suppose I don't," she said with a laugh. Leon's stomach grumbled just then. "We were supposed to grab you lunch!" Vanessa exclaimed.

The Summoner chuckled and waved for the witch to calm down. "Don't worry about it. I'll snag something now, come on."

"You two have fun," Freeda said in a dreamy voice, her eyes lost in the black orbs of the imp cuddled up against her.

Leslie just nodded and swept his hand through the air as he silently shooed the two away.

As Vanessa and Leon rose from the bench, the Spellweaver's crystal ball jingled profusely from its bag hanging from her hip. "Oh, double-dip a candlestick," she cursed and shoved the tin of cookies at Leon, who immediately looked like he had been handed a ticker spell.

Quickly, the young witch dug in her satchel and pulled out the device. "Spellweaver Peterson!" she blurted out before she could see who had made the call.

"Just the witch I've been looking for," Second Chosen David said with a chuckle. "I happened to get my hands on a mission a little while ago that has your name scrolled all over it."

She couldn't hide the excitement. With a beaming smile, she pushed her face close to the glass of her crystal ball. "Really? What is it?"

He laughed and waved the scroll in front of his device. "Seems that the Coven wants to dig around Runerite for information that will give them leads to who's been throwing up unauthorized summoning portals."

"I'll take it," she shouted.

"I figured you would." There were threads of laughter woven into his voice as he waved at the orb. "It has a deadline for tonight, so you can—"

"No, no! I can come get it now and turn it in before this evening," she shot out.

This earned an eruption of laughter from the Second Chosen. "My, my. You are an eager one. Very well. I'll meet you in the lobby in …" He trailed off for her to give him a timeframe.

She thought, sort of, and quickly replied with, "I can be there in about twenty minutes."

David nodded. "I'll see you then, Spellweaver Peterson."

The orb winked out and dulled to its usual blacked-out state. As she put it back in the satchel, she looked up to Leon, who was frowning hard in her direction. "What?" she asked.

"Oh, nothing. I was only trying to ask you out for dinner tonight," he stated while he schooled his features to a more neutral expression.

She visibly cringed and bit at the side of her lip while attempting to think of a way to get out of the very deep grave she had just dug. "I—I just haven't been on a mission in a long time. I got excited," she started to defend herself.

Leon looked away with a shrug. "It's no big deal. Don't worry about it," he said in an even tone.

She lunged for his hand and tugged him back to her. He couldn't hide the surprise from his face as he was forced to stand toe to toe with her. Her bright, hazel eyes looked up into his, searching them for a long, quiet moment. "I'm sorry. I should have called you at some point over the past couple of days, and I should have taken a minute to talk to you first just now. I shouldn't have let my excitement cloud my judgment, and I shouldn't have so easily dismissed your feelings or input. This is all still ... new to me, Leon. I'm not used to having friends, and I'm even less used to future-gazing with someone."

The tightness in his shoulders released, and he gave a light smile with a sigh. "All right. You win, Vanessa. I can't completely fault you for how you've reacted recently. We are still trying to get used to this. Besides, I know how much working for the Coven means to you. I forgive you. But you need to give your own life some attention too. Not just the Coven."

She perked up. "I'll get better. Promise. And there is still a chance that we can have plans tonight. This job is easy. I can finish it before tonight and then—" She stopped as she saw his hand raised and a singular finger ticked from side to side.

"I know you. Things happen," Leon informed, and his blunt approach made her pout. "Sometimes without you even trying to. Let's not have everything slammed into one day, okay?"

Though it made her a little sad, she nodded. He was right, and it was better to plan a dinner together when there wasn't a chance that work was going to get in the way. This was the price she would have to pay for snatching up the mission scroll so quickly. Maybe work wasn't the only thing that could fill her time.

"You're right," she said softly.

"Ah, music to my ears, those words."

She slapped at his arm with a scowl marring her cute face. "I've got gold dust and I'm not afraid to use it," she warned.

Rubbing his hand over the side of the cheek that held the shadow of a bruise, he said, "And one hell of a right hook."

They both laughed and slowly drew into one another. Their arms wrapped around each other in a sweet embrace. Leon squeezed her a little harder and drew back enough to look down to her. "How about we plan something for tomorrow evening when you get off work today?"

"I'd like that."

"Well, my break is almost up. I'm going to grab a smoothie to tied me over until I get off work in a couple of hours."

"What's your next mission?"

"Eh, probably not a mission. It is most likely more summoning training. Mrs. Willow wants to see if I can hold my ground in a smaller summoning group."

"You haven't had any more issues during your sessions?"

He shook his head. "Not since we came back from the Black Forest," Leon admitted.

She opened her mouth to say something and decided to let it go. Smiling, Vanessa said, "I'm glad." A second later, she rose up onto her tiptoes and laid a soft kiss on his bottom lip.

 *Chapter 11:*

Back at Coven headquarters, Vanessa reminded Leon not to eat too many cookies, and urged him to keep the tin of treats. He had looked down to the container and blanched with an awkward smile. Since he had been holding on to them since he took them back at the Grim Bean, she figured he was too shy to ask for the rest of them.

After Leon ran off to his Summoner's practice, she stood in the lobby area searching for Second Chosen David alone. While waiting, a male pixie carrying several jars of ink zoomed near her head, and the Spellweaver managed to dodge it just before the flying being slammed into her face.

"'Scuse me!" the pixie yelled back to her while continuing on about its work. She waved the being off, gesturing that it wasn't a big deal, but she had a feeling that the creature didn't notice.

The soft jingle of magical bells sounded beside her, and a cloud of yellowish magic billowed and formed the body of a man before the electric blue eyes of Second Chosen David formed from the mist. "Ah, Vanessa." His voice sounded slightly distant and echoic like he was stuck between worlds. The Coven member finished materializing before brushing himself off. Slowly, the puffs of magic dissipated. "Sorry to keep you waiting," he said while patting away the remaining clouds.

"It's fine. I'm surprised you didn't use the stairs," she mentioned while giving a pointed look to the spiraling staircase in the distance.

He looked back and groaned with a shudder. "Those things will be the end of me. With all the times I go up and down them, I'm surprised I haven't wasted away by now."

"You do look like you've lost weight," she said.

He smirked and slapped at his tummy. "Dropped twenty-five pounds since the promotion!"

She gawked. "That much?"

He nodded while pressing his lips into a thin line. "Yeah. Even with my unhealthy snacking, I've still managed to lose a bit of weight. Those stairs. A blessing and a curse they are." He straightened himself up. "The missus doesn't complain, though." David reached under his cloak and retrieved the mission scroll. "I'll be handing this to you. Ask Second Chosen Winona for help if you have any questions.

The Spellweaver paled at the name and tried to not gulp out of sheer reflexes. "W-why? Where are you off to?" she almost squeaked out. Every nerve in her body was screaming at her. The last thing she wanted to do was speak to *that* woman. She scared Vanessa, and the Spellweaver couldn't exactly figure out why.

"She was the one that brought the scroll to me earlier. And I'm actually off for the day as of now. The missus and I have a date tonight. Managed to get reservations at that new popular restaurant in Adalith called The Chalice of Fire. The missus loves spicy food, and they apparently have the best in all of Raen, or so the buzz is saying."

Vanessa laughed. "I can see why you chose to use an expensive teleportation spell then." Though, inwardly, she wondered why so many people were talking about dates. Perhaps it was the spring season to blame or her newly acquired social skills that gave her a deeper connection with her co-workers. Whatever was to blame, she still found it hard not to smile.

Instantly, Second Chosen David's face lit up like a torch. But his eyes were fixed on something behind Vanessa. Slowly, the Spellweaver turned to see who he was looking at with such a loving gaze.

She didn't know what to expect when she turned around. But there, walking through the main entrance of the Coven, was a short, curvy, night-shaded female. Her chin was held up proudly, and her dark brown eyes had an ethereal glow to them which made them breathtakingly entrancing. Long braids of ebony bounced around her shoulders as she swiftly sauntered closer to Second Chosen David. It wasn't until the woman smiled that Vanessa noticed two incredibly sharp fangs that protruded down from the upper gums. She was a vampiress! Clearly, she was one that had a spelled artifact that enabled her day-walking abilities.

"My love!" David shouted. "You are early."

The female rushed over with a bit more pep in her step while calling out to him, "My light!"

As if Vanessa didn't exist, the two closed the distance, and David picked up the vampiress in a tight embrace and twirled her around as she giggled. Slowly, he set her down on her feet again and pressed his nose against his wife's. Feeling a bit awkward as the two nuzzled noses with ear-splitting smiles, Vanessa cleared her throat.

Breaking their loving gaze, David blushed, and his wife laughed. "I'm sorry. I get caught up when she walks into a room. Eleven years together and I still can't help but hold her and smile."

"Oh, you," his wife said with a playful pat on her husband's chest.

Motioning over to the Spellweaver, David looked to his wife and said, "Adaeze, this is one of the Coven's newest Spellweavers, Vanessa Peterson. She was just picking up a mission scroll as I was clocking out."

"Oh, you're Vanessa?" She clapped her hands together excitedly. "It is such an honor to meet you!" she yipped and lunged forward, snatching up Vanessa's hand in her icy grip, and she proceeded to shake her hand a little too enthusiastically. Vanessa felt her eyes jumbling about her skull as the strength of Adaeze jerked her about. She was only saved by David who reached out and calmed his wife with a gentle hand resting on her shoulders.

"Dear, your strength," he whispered.

Like she was burned by the young witch, his wife released her and exclaimed, "Oh! I'm so sorry!"

"It's all right," Vanessa assured, feeling slightly dizzy. "Adaeze, was it? That is a very pretty name, and I can see that Second Chosen Reham is smitten with both your inner and outer beauty."

The vampiress giggled and flushed. "I like you," she admitted joyfully.

"My love, we better hurry, or we'll be late," David reminded sweetly.

"Oh, yes. Dinner! It was nice meeting you, Vanessa. Take care. And keep being an amazing witch!" Adaeze chirped, hugged the unsuspecting Spellweaver, and then tugged her husband out the door.

The last thing she heard was David shouting back to her, "Remember, turn it in by nightfall!" before he was swept away and out the front doors by his demanding wife with a glowing smile.

Vanessa had stepped out of the bustling Coven to check out the finer details of her mission scroll. Out on the sidewalk, she pressed up against the stone fence lining the courtyard to avoid any passersby and unwound her scroll. Her eyes glazed over the ink scribbled therein. She had only read a few lines when she realized why Second Chosen David had thought she would be best for this particular mission. She was to dig around for information on who there could be linked to the summoning circles on the academy grounds, and maybe even a motive. After everything that had happened, she was closely tied to the events since the start. It made sense that she would be part of its end.

Rolling the scroll back up, she pursed her lips to the side in thought. Exactly how was she going to get information from any of those stuffed-shirts on the academy board? She sighed. Normally, she would just intimidate them with Bobo. Today, she had to rely on herself and herself only.

"Welp, this is going to be frustrating," she muttered. But she did this to herself. Accepting her fate and attempting to be more confident in her abilities, Vanessa pressed on for Runerite Academy.

Already tired from walking all afternoon and from the hours of baking she had done, her poor body wasn't up for another few miles of hiking. So, she opted to teleport using the Coven pads. That way she didn't have to purchase from a street vendor the teleportation ingredients for the academy, and she didn't have to hail a coach. She could get to Runerite quickly and save some coin while she was at it.

It was the best option, really. She hadn't exactly given herself a lot of rest time after her last mission, and her brain was still trying to digest all the information that she had found thrown into her lap within the last week. She wasn't fully human, lies from the elves, newly discovered spells, and magic had been dying in their world for hundreds of years because of blind hate. She couldn't understand some of it. Other parts were hard to accept after such a long time of not knowing anything about her family. So, she tried to learn something new or lose herself in work. But now? She just wanted to go home, crystal ball call her aunt, have a cup of tea with Bobo, and read her grimoire while she leaned against Leon on the couch. That thought made her smile.

Stupid spring.

Just as soon as she had gotten lost in thought, she found herself at the door leading into the front office. The halls had been relatively clear. Most sessions were done for the day, and the remaining night classes were already in session. She found herself thankful that she didn't have to weave her way through beings like she did at Coven headquarters.

Peering into the office through the glass on the door, she realized it looked nothing like it did the last time she saw it. There weren't supplies thrown about or papers littering the space. It was all clean and organized, right down to the last inkwell and quill sitting atop the counter space that faced a few large sofas pressed up against the wall.

Twisting the knob, she pushed the door open and stepped in. Inside, there were three beings taking care of the front office. The first was a golem, who sluggishly moved about the room as it fixed quills that were about to fall and organized workstations. Eventually, its large, clay hands slowly combed a filing cabinet drawer as it thumbed through for a document. It was large and beefy but lacked some of the finer details newer golems had. This one was smooth and bulky. The head even had slits for eyes hallowed out, but there was no mouth or nose. Its terracotta body was decorated in multiple rune belts. Most likely, the items were spells that bound it to the school grounds.

The second being that Vanessa took quick note of was the Hobgoblin positioned by the break room. A mug was in hand, and it was eagerly pouring a cup of coffee for itself. The being was hardly a head taller than Leslie and covered in deep, forest-green fur. It wore a discolored white shirt under a shabby pair of blue overalls and a pair of old sneakers with one of the soles so loose, Vanessa could see its mauled-up sock peeking back at her. Its hair was clean and well-groomed despite its tattered attire. As it turned, sipping happily at its coffee, she could see the yellow, cat-like eyes looking at her from over the rim of the mug. She gave a quick smile and short wave before diverting her attention to the third being in the room. The last thing you want to do is accidentally catch the attention of a hobgoblin. They tended to have between two and ten different personalities, and their bodies would morph to match each respective one. She didn't have the time to figure out how many personalities it had, and—furthermore—she didn't have the time to politely excuse herself multiple times if it did start talking to her.

Vanessa made way for the front desk where a white-haired female with lilac skin so pale she seemed to glow stood. But this being wasn't human either. She was a Muricidael. On the woman's back was a large, whirling, ridged, and spiral-shaped shell. Its royal purple color was only obstructed with creamy white stripes as it followed a beautifully dizzying design. Along the surface were countless spiny horns that flowered out like rocky blooms. Muricidaels were, for a lack of a better term, a human and snail hybrid. She remembered them from her social studies class during her academy years. They were predators. Typically, the beings were calm in nature and often very shy despite them being predators and lovers of meat. If frightened, their bodies would magically recoil into their shell where they would give off a series of clicking sounds as a warning to their attackers. If not heeded, or, if the beings felt threatened, they would then spit poisonous needles at the assailant which would paralyze them upon impact. Usually, it was a hunting method, and one not widely used as often as they had years ago, but it was definitely a great means of defense nowadays.

The Muricidael looked to Vanessa with soft, lavender eyes as her antennae gradually swayed back and forth atop her head. The Spellweaver instantly noticed that the woman looked incredibly youthful, almost younger than Vanessa. Her smile was as sweet as her voice as she sheepishly gained the Coven member's full attention. "Welcome to Runerite Academy, how can I help you?"

Smiling back, the young witch let her gaze drop to the nametag pinned to the front of the woman's white blouse. "Hi … Floretta. I'm Spellweaver Peterson, here on Coven business. I need a pass so that I can question a few people on the school grounds."

Floretta beamed with pink sweeping over the apples of her cheeks. "Sure thing. I just need to see your insignia and have you magically imprint our sign-in sheet!" she softly exclaimed.

"Okay," Vanessa stated while reaching for the clipboard on the counter. She picked up the thin, cheap wand clipped to the top and zapped the paper below. The spell popped and bits of brightly colored magic hopped around the surface before quieting down to a simple glow that morphed into her signature. Floretta took the clipboard, blew away the excess magic, inspected the signature, and nodded her head to Vanessa.

"Let me get that pass for you," she said quietly and reached into one of the desk cubbies but found nothing there. "Oh, pointless potions! We're all out again," she whined. Then she made a few clicking sounds as she turned to face the golem. "You forgot, didn't you?" she hissed. That soft voice was now scary. Vanessa already had one hand on her amulet around her neck, and the nearby hobgoblin had snuck to the front of the counter to avoid any trouble from the Muricidael.

"She's gonna blow!" the hobgoblin warned in a whisper-yell before morphing into a creature with longer, pastel-blue body hair, a slightly longer nose, and two sets of short horns. "This is going to be good. She's fun when she's angry." Again, its fur shifted color, becoming a bright yellow, and it slightly shrank in height by a foot. Its ears elongated and fell flat behind its skull. "D-d-don't say that. Sh-sh-she's scary," the hobgoblin quietly cried.

"Goddess, help me," Vanessa whispered and prepared herself to be ready to dive out of the path of any projectiles.

The clicking ebbed and Floretta, thankfully, took a calming breath. "I'll just print out some more," she announced in a despairing manner.

"Aw nuts." The hobgoblin pouted and then looked to the mug. Gasping, it realized how low it was as its fur changed back to the deep green Vanessa had first seen. "What the …? Banish a banshee, I just filled this thing," it griped and wandered off to refill it.

"Here we are!" the snail-woman exclaimed softly. Even though Floretta's voice was sweet, Vanessa had not expected to hear it, and, after such a nerve-wracking moment, it caused the poor witch to practically detach from her body and become a wandering ghost of the school.

With wide eyes, the Spellweaver turned her attention to the Muricidael. "Hmmm?" Her surprised gaze laid upon the pass, and she felt some of the tension melt away. "Oh, right. Thank you," she said, gathering up the hall pass. "You have a good day," she called back as she rushed for the door.

"Don't forget to come back and sign out!" Floretta reminded.

"I won't," Vanessa assured. Although, truth be told, if Floretta hadn't said anything she would have forgotten.

Stepping out into the hall, Vanessa quickly shut the door and let out a sigh of relief. Fishing around in her orb satchel, she pulled out her crystal ball. "Okay, Kristal ICE. Set a reminder to sign out in the main office."

The ball lit up, and a feminine voice responded. "Okay, when do you want that reminder to go off?"

Vanessa pondered a moment, quickly estimated, and replied with, "In one hour." She waited for the device to register it. That should be more than enough time to question some of the teachers and compile a list of people that were present that day and where they were in the building when the explosion happened.

Pocketing the crystal ball, she combed the halls and nodded to herself. It was a lot of ground to cover, but she figured she might as well get a start on it. The scroll had a list of the teachers that had crystal ball called when the event first took place. She would start there and work her way through.

 *Chapter 12:*

The first few beings questioned weren't much help. Not beyond what they had provided when the accident originally took place. The first few professors only restated everything that had been documented previously. The others remembered most of their statements, but their memories of what had transpired were either gummed up with students, lectures, the passing of time, or the chaos that had recently permeated through the city. She simply thanked them and moved on to the next teacher. Each time hoping that something would bring her closer to an answer that would aid in solving what was going on under the school's nose. How was demon summoning happening and none were the wiser to it until that day? The tunnels, the prisoners, the scroll-summoned guard ... there was too much happening for someone not to be suspicious before now. Who could cover something up that well? And not a soul had more information or the faintest clue as to what had been transpiring deep in the belly of Runerite. Things within the academy were clean.

Too clean.

As Vanessa walked through the hall, she heard the bell chime overhead. From her years attending the academy herself, she knew the drill. Move with the waves of students or plaster yourself against the wall to avoid being trampled over. She chose to lean on the closest wall. There, she waited for the sea of chattering students to all branch off into their respective classrooms before peeling herself from the safety of her hiding spot near a water fountain.

It was then that she noticed her next—and last—target for questioning. Little did she know that the being she was supposed to be borderline interrogating was a sirin. She marveled at the being as it swept through the hall in more elegance and style than some of the most proper noble farmers of Tolvade.

The sirin was tall. If Vanessa had not been so used to Bobo dwarfing everything surrounding him, she would have been intimidated by its height alone. It was seven feet tall—easy, and Vanessa's neck was already dreading how much she'd have to look up to it during the upcoming conversation. But the beautiful thing that Vanessa could not quite understand was that the very posture of the being made it appear taller. A regal air almost emitted from the creature as it swept through the hall. Feathers that reminded Vanessa of lily petals encased the being in a snowy mantle that dragged behind it like a cape. But this cape melted into the being's body. It crept up the neck and cradled the head, leaving only the beautifully angled features of its deep gray face free of feathers. The eyes were larg, with massive black pupils and surrounded by thin irises spun in a golden orange. The face was made up of large, over-exaggerated features that only added to her beauty instead of making it come across uncomfortably unnatural. Its feet reminded her of the owls that would try to make a home in the attic of the orphanage during the spring and fall seasons. The sirin's toes had hooked claws, and they were covered in rough skin masked by layers of small, puffy feathers. The hands were similar, though they were longer, slimmer, and the patterns that ringed around its fingers and wrists were beautifully woven like they were artfully sketched onto the being.

In one arm, the sirin carried music scores, a canvas, and a few stray art supplies. They were lovers of art, sirins. They lived and breathed the simple life of creation and beauty. Seldom did they seek anything outside of that. Power, fame, even gold held not a candle to the charms of the artistic world for these beings. They could lose themselves in it. And, if not careful, they could become so obsessed with the arts that they could lure others to produce beautifully designed creations. Not that the act itself was bad, but sirins have a tendency (when they get lost in their love for art) to make other beings forget about basic needs. The creators would get so lost in their craft that they perished from simply forgetting to drink, eat, and sleep. But such a case hadn't happened in many, many years. It did make people leery of the beasts. But as long as you were in certain spelled parts of the city, the chances of a sirin enchanting you were slim to none. And within any academy, your chances of being charmed were next to impossible.

Just as the being's free hand reached for the door, Vanessa jogged over while calling out to her, "Excuse me, are you Professor Nafdah?"

The being paused and slowly (much slower than the witch had expected the bird-woman to move) turned her head to set her gaze upon the Spellweaver. "*Who* might you be?"

"I'm Spellweaver Vanessa Peterson. I'm here on official Coven business. I was wondering if you had any further information that you could provide on the demon summoning portal incident? Do you have a moment to answer a couple of questions for me?"

The being seemed to ponder over an answer. Then, quietly, it combed the halls with a careful sweep of her large eyes before she nodded her head and spoke softly. "Please, step inside."

"Thank you," Vanessa chirped, excited that she might have some fresh insight to the past occurrence.

Inside the room, there was the traditional setup. A cauldron was in the far corner for potion brewing. A large chalkboard took up the majority of the space of the front-facing wall, and a desk was set up dead center with a podium nearby. Rows of seats ascended on the other side of the room with two narrow passages splitting up the collection of desks for easy access through the sea of furniture. A communal crystal ball was connected to the wall next to the door for both students and teachers to use, and tucked into the front corner was a skeleton with horns and pixie wings. A Changeling Child skeleton was often used in classrooms for anatomy references and even for art purposes because Changelings were the closest body structure to the majority of most magical beings in Aeristria.

The sirin took an extra moment as she checked the hall and then closed and locked the door. "Now, how can I help you, Spellweaver ... Peterson, was it?"

Vanessa turned around and mentally changed her tactics as she noticed that the sirin had seemed on edge since she mentioned the summoning portal investigation. To take some of the tension out of the air, she added a touch of warmth to her smile and let it reach her eyes. It was the kind of smile that you'd give an old friend after not seeing them for days on end. "Please, call me Vanessa, Professor Nafdah."

Standing taller, the sirin mirrored Vanessa's smile. "Vanessa," she greeted with a bow. "You may call me," she raised her head to lock eyes with the Spellweaver as she said her name, "Kasmira."

The moment that Vanessa heard the sirin's name, she felt like she had been slammed in the chest with a lightning spell. Her body jolted on high alert, and she had no control over her actions as she gasped, trying to draw in a breath to fill her lungs, only they reached their limit and she didn't want to breathe out. Her eyes widened, and her chest rose up, her back bowing as her heart tried to climb toward the heavens. Names were powerful things. Said the right way, with the right intention, with the appropriate gaze, mentally reach out (or with the proper potion or dust), and you can unlock a thousand emotions and a million enchantments. For a brief moment, the Spellweaver feared that she was being manipulated.

"Don't scream," the sirin ordered in a hissing whisper.

Oh, but she wanted to … Yet, Vanessa did as instructed, she didn't scream. Instead, she focused on steadying how she inhaled and exhaled. Her mind spun in a way that felt like she had taken some kind of awful potion or drank too much as Tasgall's. "Why shouldn't I?" she asked, and every ounce of distrust interlaced with her words as she narrowed her eyes at the creature.

Kasmira motioned with her taloned hands for the witch to calm down. "I was giving you permission to connect with me …" she informed.

The Spellweaver opened her mouth, but the words didn't come out. She could have asked any question she wanted, but she already knew the answer. The sirin was scared. She could feel it. Kasmira's heartbeat was a perfect melody of chaos inside of Vanessa's mind. The witch bent her brow and closed her mouth as she it surged through her. Distrust, worry, panic. It was like a finely brewed mead, and each flavor unfolded on Vanessa's tongue as she pressed with her mind deeper into the connection between them. Who was causing this unease? Why did she pick this way to communicate?

A soft jingle sounded through the room before the crystal ball near the door lit up. "Professor Nafdah, are you in your classroom?"

The being didn't make a single movement, but in Vanessa's mind, she could see a ghost of the sirin's form face her and lay a single digit over her lips. "Headmaster Fleeton," she called out to the orb, and slowly a face appeared on the glass. Kasmira's body hid the image that manifested on the orb as the sirin turned to face the device. "Is there a problem?"

The heartbeat that played a frantic tune was deafening as Vanessa tried to discern what was her and the sirin and what was in the waking world. She felt like she was floating between two realms, and her hand had a firm grip on a rope to each plane of existence. She was being painfully strained by it.

The conversation that carried on the orb was muffled, and many of the words were lost as Vanessa tried to navigate a clear understanding of what was happening in her mind. She normally had Bobo to magically ground her. He wasn't here now, though. She was traveling blind through uncharted waters. The room spun for a moment, and the witch swayed before she threw out her hand and landed, half-standing half-hunched over, on the desk next to her.

"Who's there with you? What's going on?" The concerned voice of the Headmaster held threads of heat to his words. Was he mad? Vanessa couldn't be sure.

One moment she heard the chirping sound of the crystal ball disconnecting abruptly from the call, the next there were plumes of red smoke slowly rising up out of the floor as the Headmaster materialized in the center of the room.

The connection between the sirin and Vanessa was getting blurred. Their heartbeats were now synchronized. Her chest felt tight, and the rhythm of her once steady beat was stumbling to match that of Kasmira. Vanessa was practically choking for air, and she pushed herself to stand straight up. But the presence of a strong demon in the room made the action difficult. Finding her footing, she tried to act like a light sheen of sweat wasn't building on her brow as she struggled to perform simple tasks.

"Ah," she managed to say without sounding winded. "Headmaster. Glad to see you here. I was on my way up to you," she lied. But each remark took everything in her to speak and not sound like she was barely holding on.

The hard, green-eyed glare that had once been fixed on Kasmira was now bearing down on Vanessa. She smiled at the Satyr as he turned to face her. His chestnut, shoulder length hair fell in lazy half-curls around his neck. It matched the beard lining his jaw, the coat of his cloven-hooved legs, and the thick eyebrows that were bent angrily. His long ears were lined in multiple gold hoops, and they twitched as he inspected Vanessa. He reached up and moved some of his hair resting between his large curved horns. His nostrils flared as he exhaled heatedly. Vanessa caught a glimpse of his tail, a small tuft of fur in the same deep brown as the hair that he was covered in. Around his hips was a pale blue and white striped sash that somewhat hid his plain leather loincloth. The fabric was fitted in place with a thick piece of lightly tanned leather adorned in flat, gold discs. There was no shirt, only flawless mocha skin surrounded by patches of clean, well-groomed hair. Like most Satyrs, the Headmaster didn't seem to like the idea of clothing. But he wore enough not to make anyone uncomfortable.

As Vanessa tried to get a grasp on her thoughts and put up metaphysical walls to slice through the fear snuffing out her clear thinking, she noticed that Mr. Fleeton was stepping closer to her. Her eyes immediately pinned themselves to his form as he strutted closer. It was done in a way that made the witch feel uncomfortable. He eyed her in a way that made her skin crawl and made her feel like she had to protect herself. Slowly, she straightened to her full height as her eyes searched his face for some telltale sign of what she could expect to happen next. The features she found were a perfect blend of animal and human. He was handsome, she couldn't deny that, but there was something about him that she didn't quite like. Something felt *off* about him.

"And exactly who are you?" he asked, motioning to her in such a blasé manner that she felt partially offended by the action.

Blinking, she tried to swallow through the thick heartbeat stuck in her throat. Mentally, she could hear the sirin speaking to her like she was flagging her down and yelling from yards away. *"Be careful,"* she heard Kasmira mentally say to her.

She knew when to take a hint. "I'm Spellweaver Peterson, here on Coven business."

His glare was deadpan before he stifled a quick laugh and drew in a leisurely breath that he exhaled just as slowly. "Well, seeing that Professor Nafdah will be starting class in a while, we can let her prepare for her next batch of students, and you can come with me to my office. I'm sure I can provide you with the information that you are looking for." His eyes felt like they were physically reaching out to her. His body alone demanded that she look at him and ignore everything else in a room. She felt drawn to him in a strange way.

Was he trying to charm her?

Banish a banshee!

Kasmira stepped forward. "Headmaster, I've already prepared the work for the next class. It's not a bother—"

Mr. Fleeton held up his hand. There was an expression passing over the Headmaster's features, and Vanessa couldn't figure out exactly what it was. "Professor, these students depend on your flawless teachings. How could I rest easy knowing that I didn't try to aid you properly? We wouldn't want your mind muddled with this Coven member's questions right before your next class." He turned his attention to Vanessa fully once more. "It's no trouble at all, Peterson. If you would just—"

Vanessa pulled away and glowered at the Satyr. "That's Spellweaver Peterson to you. I'm on duty, Headmaster. And I would appreciate it if you would respect that fact along with my ranking. As for following you for further questioning, I have no problem with obliging you." The Headmaster smiled triumphantly. *"After* I have finished my questioning of Professor Nafdah." When those words left her mouth, the smile that Headmaster Fleeton wore faded faster than it had appeared. "Now, if you don't mind, I would like to continue my investigation without further interruption," she stated and then walked over to the class door, opened it, and motioned with a sweep of her arm the path that the Satyr could take out of the room.

He straightened himself out and looked down at Vanessa. "Very well," he stated through practically gritted teeth. The click of his hooves as he left the room echoed through the empty space. When he was at the threshold, he paused and faced the Spellweaver saying, "I'll be in my office."

"Oh, I promise, Headmaster, I'll be there shortly," she said with a grin and then closed the door behind him. But the fiery glare that the Satyr shot in her direction remained with her even as she turned away and faced Kasmira. The anger had aided the young witch in regaining some of her senses and made it easier to separate her feelings from those of the Professor's. Stepping closer to the sirin, Vanessa got ready to speak, but the sound of Kasmira's voice inside her mind gave her pause.

"The crystal ball is a gateway, he can still hear us. I'm not safe to answer honestly out loud," the sirin explained telepathically.

Vanessa nodded while thinking a reply. *"That's why you linked us?"*

"Yes."

"Don't worry, I understand. I'll ask my questions. Speak out loud whatever you think would keep you safe, but answer me honestly through your mind." Quickly, she stated loudly, "Now, where was I? I'm sorry. I had to calm myself after that encounter. I don't like to be interrupted. Give me an extra moment to collect myself and proceed with the questioning."

"I understand. Take your time," Kasmira replied. *"I'll do the best that I can for you."*

Vanessa withdrew the mission scroll and pretended to scan the contents like she didn't have every question memorized. "Where were you the day that the explosion took place?"

"I was here, teaching my class," Kasmira answered without hesitation.

Vanessa waited a moment or two before she asked the next question. Almost all her questions were met with a quick verbal reply. She had started to wonder if the sirin had lost her nerve until she asked, "Did you know that there were demon summoning portals in the basement level of the academy?"

The sirin paused and then tilted her head in an unnatural angle, the action mirroring that of a curious bird. She was thinking long and hard about her reply. "No ... I ... Should I be concerned for the students?" she asked, blinking her large owl eyes at the Spellweaver. *"Yes. I knew. The Headmaster and Administrators all knew. They were the ones that had done it. They performed the magic!"*

"Wh—" she stopped and tried to erase the surprise from her face as she continued like the sirin hadn't dumped a ton of spell dust in her lap. "No. Your students should all be fine. There was a meeting with the High Priest Council and the academy's staff and its board. It has been deemed safe to continue schooling as long as the basement level entrance remains closed, locked, spelled, and the other talismans stay in place in the tunnel system found underground," she answered honestly. *"Does the board know?"*

"They are the ones that ordered members of the staff to do it."

Vanessa's eyes widened, and she looked at her scroll, pretending to read things that weren't there until she could regain composure. "I want to thank you for your help today in this matter, Kasmira," she said softly with a smile.

"It was an honor, Vanessa." The Professor then bowed to the Spellweaver.

The connection faded and then was gone. One moment it was there, the next it was quiet and calm. She could almost feel the spiritual essence of the teacher drawing out of her and slipping away. In a way, this made her sad. She didn't feel alone when she had been invaded like that, and she didn't mind the deep connection that they shared. But as soon as her head was free of the extra being, she found peace in that as well. It was like she had slowly been losing herself in the last few moments.

"I'll be on my way then. If you think you might have forgotten anything," Vanessa reached into her spell pouches and pulled out a small herb bag with a rune mark on the front, "just use this to establish a clean crystal ball connection with me," she whispered.

The sirin gracefully retrieved the bag and tucked it under her feathers. "Thank you," she whispered back.

 *Chapter 13:*

Vanessa dreaded meeting up with the Headmaster again. As she walked the halls on the way to his office, her pace became a touch slower. She took the extra moments to mentally prepare herself for whatever tricks or lies that the Satyr would more than likely throw her way. Just knowing that he had a hand in the whole demon summoning scheme made her hotter than a hellfire ember. The fact that they had staff members in on it made her fume, but they had those that were opposing the idea too scared to speak up to the Coven. To think what measures they had gone through to silence the weaker staff. It was both disgusting and dreadful. It made her wonder what was promised to them to keep their mouths shut? If the board was in on it, coin could very well be the cause of many staff members' silence. Gold could purchase just about anything and strip you of any justice while it was at it. Power could be another thing. Many sought after it, but if you had connections why would you step forward and lose what was often so hard to gain? And, finally, there was plain and simple threats. Their lives and safety could be at risk. That would be enough to keep many quiet too.

Her expression hardened. She wasn't afraid of anyone. Especially a Satyr on a very obvious power trip. Maybe he just needed someone to knock him down a peg or two. Vanessa knew of just the witch to put him in his place.

Coming around the corner, Vanessa avoided a large, bushy fern and a wall littered with flowering plants. The hall went from cold, gray stone to a miniature jungle faster than she could process the transition. A small stone path cut through the tiny trees and abundant greenery and led to the large, circular, wooden door of the Headmaster's office. Nearby, a nature spirit was kneeling as she sprinkled water and spoke to one of the plants. As she finished up her job, she stood and turned to Vanessa. "Here to see the Headmaster?" the spirit asked.

The young witch held her tongue and kept more honest comments to herself and answered with, "Yup. Hope to get this all over with before dinner."

"Good luck," the spirit said with a giggle and then frolicked further down the hall and toward the main courtyard.

"I'm going to need it," Vanessa whined to herself and made her way along the stone walkway.

The door stared back at her from the end of the path, and Vanessa grimaced at it. She had her fair share of investigations filled with all different sorts of beings, but Headmaster Fleeton was definitely in the top three of the most annoying.

This was the last person that she needed to question. And, from what she had gathered already, there was enough evidence to put together a request for an investigation of the board. All she had to do was question the Headmaster and leave. She took an extra second at the door to mentally prepare herself before she shook off her worries and knocked.

"Come in," Mr. Fleeton casually ordered.

By the goddess, why did his tone bother her so much? Why did his voice run over her skin like sandpaper? She drew in a breath and opened the door. "Headmaster," she stated, walking through the opening.

He was standing by his desk looking out the window with his hands clasped behind his back. "You're here sooner than I expected," he stated, his eyes still glued to the courtyard below.

She forced a smile. "There wasn't a lot of information to gather. Most of those questioned today didn't have much to give me that the Coven didn't already know."

"Oh?" he asked, turning his head slightly to the side. "Interesting."

"Interesting?" she asked, plucking a brow over one eye as she gave him a confused look.

He gave a soft, almost inaudible chuckle while he turned to face her fully. "Forgive me. I meant to say that I was hoping we'd be able to provide you with something more to aid with your investigation, Spellweaver Peterson."

Yeah, sure you did ... she thought to herself. But she only stared at him unbelieving.

He grinned, and it made Vanessa's stomach churn. The Satyr motioned to a chair in front of his desk. "Please."

The last thing that she wanted to do was get comfortable in his office. However, all the walking from the day had her feet screaming at her. Besides, most of her bumps and bruises were still healing from her last mission. Her whole body ached, and the thought of sitting for a few minutes while she wrapped up her questioning didn't seem like such a horrendous thought.

"Thank you," she quickly spat out and tried to actually sound thankful for his kind gesture. Though, she doubted his sincerity much like he probably doubted her own. She rested her staff against his desk. "It won't take long. I just have a few questions," she said, seating herself in the large, tall-back chair. Much to her dismay—and to her surprise—the Headmaster leaned against his desk, half sitting on it, in front of her.

"Take your time," he stated once he was comfortable. Resting his hands behind him, he looked down at her and let that grin grow to an uncomfortable width. "I insist." The way he dragged out the words made her skin crawl.

Attempting to look at anything else in the room, she made note of his office. A large tree grew in the corner behind the desk, and the trunk of it molded itself against the wall and crept up to the ceiling. The branches spread out like vines, and leaves covered the space overhead. But the most disturbing thing of all was the fruit that dangled from the boughs of the tree.

They were a sickly peach color with a touch of yellow spots that bled into the rest of the rough and bumpy peel. But set deep into the most unappealing skin of the fruit was a face. Each fruit's face was different and unique. Much like the beings of Raen. But fruit shouldn't have faces, nor should it move.

"Heeheee." One of the fruit faces giggled. Another next to it chuckled too. The branch they were on shook as they laughed relentlessly.

"Hmmm ... wait a moment. They can get out of hand once they start," the Headmaster advised.

Doing as instructed, Vanessa waited for the giggling fruit to stop. "Hahahaha!" The flower petals atop its head started to fall, and, once all the petals of the twittering fruit fell, it also plummeted from the tree. Its mouth became forever frozen with a wide cackle. The silence that came over the room was thick. It felt like she had just watched something die, and the cause of death was laughter. It was very unsettling.

"Should that be...?" Vanessa pointed to the disturbing fruit on the floor and moved as though she were going to pick it up.

"I wouldn't touch it if I were you," he warned.

His tone alone made her stop in mid-motion. "Oh, is it dangerous?"

"Quite," he said simply and lifted his wand hand and magically picked up the fruit and put it in a basket near the base of the tree. "The Jinmenshi fruit is both rare and dangerous. It can cause a being to go mad. Only certain kinds of spirits and creatures can withstand the maddening poison. Those beings typically turn it into a very sweet and potent wine."

She gawked at him and then the tree. He just casually had a Jinmenju tree in his office? Shifting in her seat, she tried to focus on something else in the room. "Sounds lovely," she lied, which earned a chuckle from Mr. Fleeton.

"I don't wish to keep you from your evening, Spellweaver Peterson. Please, ask your questions. I'm happy to provide you with information if it is within my power."

Again, Vanessa smiled, but the action held no heart or warmth. She had been face-to-face with far too many villains to not pick up on his untrustworthy vibe. "I'm glad to hear it." She pulled out a pad and turned to a page free of writing. "Let me start off with asking where you were the day the incident took place?"

He pondered a moment, though the action came across almost playful. There was no doubt in her mind that he was toying with her. "Why, I was here at the school. Naturally," he stated and smiled. She could feel it, an overbearing presence that wafted out of him. And that smile of his didn't settle with her quite right. It felt wrong. She couldn't explain why, but she didn't want to look at him, so she focused on writing down his answer.

The annoyance she had toward him seeped out as she asked, "Could you clarify where in the school, Mr. Fleeton?"

"Call me Sylas," he urged.

She suppressed the need to groan. It was rude not to give your first name when someone else gave you theirs. There was also the fact that she didn't want the Satyr to be even more on his guard than he might already be. If she was going to drag information out of him, she was going to need to come across like she didn't already suspect his involvement in the matter. Even if she already knew that he was.

Lifting her eyes, she slowly licked her lips and said, "Vanessa." Then, she dropped her eyes back down to her pen and paper.

It was around that moment that she felt something in the air, but she didn't say anything as Sylas was explaining where he was the day the event took place, finally. "I was here in my office with High Priest Dmitri, if I remember correctly."

"H-high Priest Dmitri?" she gasped.

The Satyr nodded.

She narrowed her eyes as she brought her gaze up to meet his. "Why were you seeing him?"

The Headmaster looked practically apathetic as he quickly replied with, "It was the end of the quarter. Naturally, he was here to see if there were any potential candidates for the Coven this year. He was taking the names of beings that they should ask about come the end of the school year."

"I see," she half mumbled. It was also a job that a Second Chosen could have completed. There was no need for Dmitri to come down to the academy himself or any High Priest for that matter. She didn't say that to Sylas though.

Again, she felt the brush of magic caress her body, and she shivered visibly but made the appropriate notes before she continued with her questioning. "Did Dmitri seem off during his visit?"

"Not that I was aware of."

"When did he leave?"

"Shortly before the explosion. He hardly made it off school campus when the event took place."

"And the witnesses, no one saw anything strange coming from the area where the blast came from?"

"Everyone that had been questioned had the same answer, mostly. They were all in class when it happened. We evacuated the grounds soon after."

"Mostly?"

The Headmaster shifted his weight and crossed his legs at the ankles while leaning further into his desk. One of his clawed fingers tapped on his forearm as the questioning continued. "There were a few students roaming the halls between classes. A few mentioned smoke, others had stated they heard loud howling, but there was nothing aside from those statements made."

Vanessa jotted it all down and paused to think. It felt warmer in the office suddenly. Her palms were sweaty, and another fruit giggled uncontrollably until its face froze in mid-laugh and dropped to the floor with a *thud* that made Vanessa cringe.

"Are you all right, Vanessa? You seem a bit jumpy and anxious," Sylas asked.

"I'm fine," she stated with pepper in her tone and threaded a stray strand of hair behind her ear. If being around him wasn't unnerving enough, the giggling fruit wasn't helping.

Sylas hummed, and she didn't like the sound. Tapping at the scroll, she stopped when she thought of her next question. "Has there been any strange communications between staff members?"

"What do you mean?"

"Has anyone seemed scared or like they felt threatened by other members of the staff?"

His tapping came to a sudden halt. He went perfectly still. She noticed it but was sure not to make any sudden movements to give away the fact that she had seen the action, or lack thereof, take place. She was mentally listing all the things that were adding up in very bad ways.

"I'm not sure what you mean?" This time, when Sylas spoke, there was an undeniable wave of power that washed over Vanessa. It made her feel lethargic and calm. Not exactly something you want to feel when in the middle of an investigation with a potential threat.

Her head lulled for a moment, and she rubbed at her eyes. "Mr. Fleeton ... are you ... are you trying to charm me?" she asked. This time, she locked eyes with him angrily.

"No, no. I wouldn't dream of doing such a thing. I was only worried about you. You seemed very anxious. I was merely attempting to ease some of the tension in the room."

She didn't believe him. And for good reason. She should have been scared at that moment. But she was just so calm and relaxed. The urge to curl up and take a nap had to be physically fought off with her pinching her thigh as she slid her hand under her cloak. She tried to hide the action. The last thing that she needed was Sylas knowing that he had her in the palm of his hands. Academies were one of the spelled places in Tolvade where a being is (usually) safe from being charmed, mentally manipulated, or spelled without consent. If the Headmaster could still get her this calm with that spell in effect, she was in trouble.

Unless ...

Her eyes widened at the thought, and her bewildered gaze burrowed deep into the Satyr's own. "You didn't," she whispered. It made so much sense now.

"Spellweaver Peterson ... I mean ... Vanessa. There is no need for you to be so guarded around me, hmm?" He knelt down slowly. A knot formed in her stomach as each of his hands ran along her thighs and rose up to grab the arms of the chair. The wood whined as she heard his inhuman grip squeeze. His face inched closer, and she felt the prickles of his magic invading her space. It rolled over her in suffocating waves. Vanessa gulped for air, but her head spun. "Sylas."

"Sh-shh-shhhh. Just let *go*. Trust me. Everything will be better if you just let go," he hissed in a seductively vile tone.

"Stop," she demanded. Vanessa tried to move her hand in a way that wouldn't gain attention. She just needed a proper grasp on her wand or powders, but the darn appendage practically flopped around like a fish out of water when she tried to move it.

She could see him. His outline fading in and out as her vision struggled to keep every detail of the world crisp and without flaw. His smile inched dreadfully closer as he came to her ear. Hot breath washed over her neck as he spoke, and she shivered with every word that he uttered. "You've had a long day, Vanessa. Just *relax*. I'm here to help you ..."

She had to pick her words carefully. If she said anything that would hint to her suspicion of him, there was no telling of what he would do. She had to play dumb and innocent. At least until she could fling a proper spell at his grinning mug.

"I'm fine, really. There's ..." her voice trailed off. What was she saying? She just wanted to rest for a moment. That would help her remember. Yes, just a short nap to help recharge herself. That is what she needed. Her eyes fluttered open, and he was inches from her face. He sniffed over the line of her body and shuddered.

"Back. Off." Suddenly, she felt a little more awake now.

The Headmaster's short tail was swishing back and forth behind him, and his eyes were glowing with power. He boldly remained where he was. Eyeing her over like she was a new toy.

"Rolling a member of the Coven with magic during an investigation is grounds to hold the being overnight for questioning. Do you really think you should pu-push the limits, Headmaster Fleeton?" Speaking alone felt more draining than it should have.

He laughed, the sound booming over her as she felt the pressure of his power being fully unleashed. She cried out and felt her body press into the wood of the chair. Her nails clawed at the arms of it as she forced herself to stay awake. Wood slipped under the bed of her nails. Anger, pain, and fear were keeping the sleep at bay, but she wasn't sure how long she could keep it up.

"Do you really think I'm that stupid?" he spat out.

Double-dip a candlestick!

"What are you—?"

"Cut the crap, Spellweaver. You've been onto me ever since you chatted with Professor Nafdah. What did she tell you?"

She wouldn't put Kasmira at risk. There was no telling what Sylas would do to her if Vanessa couldn't get the professor somewhere safe. "She didn't tell me anything ..." She grinned back to him. Victory glinted through the fog of her tired gaze. "But you just did," she said with a short spout of laughter.

The Headmaster snarled. "It won't matter. No one will believe a word you'll say if you're insane." He smirked as he walked over to the freshly fallen fruit from a moment ago and picked it up off the ground. "It is such a shame that I have to do this. You are such a talented witch. But I can't risk what you may know." He snapped his fingers and whispered something under his breath. If she wasn't so sluggish, she would have realized what he was doing. Why there were so many plants by his office. He was a Satyr. He could control plants growing! This whole office was one, giant trap!

Thorny vines swiftly snaked up her chair and bound her to it. The thorns scraped over her skin, and she tried to jump up from the seat. Only it caused more damage. Vines shot up all around her. One of the thorny extensions slapped her across the face, sending Vanessa flying back into the chair. They whirled around her legs and arms, and only the comfort of her clothing kept the press of the thorns from drawing blood. She jerked from side to side and then looked to the door. She had one thought that sung through her whole being. Like her voice could cast a spell, she screamed, "Help! Help! Someone *help!*" All the while she twisted about trying to free herself, and the more she struggled, the more the vines dug in. She could feel the tiny rivulets of warm blood running down her calves and arms.

"Oh, please. Like I didn't spell the thing before you came to my office. You gave me plenty of time to prepare. Perhaps things would have been different if you would have just come with me when I asked nicely."

Vanessa snapped her dagger-filled glare at him. "Traitorous snake! Do you have any idea of the crimes you are committing?" she seethed with rage and jostled about in the chair.

He laughed again. "If everything goes according to plan, I'll be a hero to all of Raen! And you? You'll go missing. Poor little orphan girl. No one will miss the witch with no friends and no family. Alone in life and alone in death."

The rage boiled over and she screamed as she writhed about the chair trying to scratch or kick him. She wiggled her hips and

SMOKE, LIES, AND GRIMOIRES

stretched her fingers in a desperate attempt to hurt him. Banish a
banshee. If she could just reach a spell pouch.

Sylas cackled as he watched her. Dark mirth swirling in his
power-hungry gaze. Sweeping his chestnut curls out of his face, he
knelt back down. "Did anyone ever tell you that you look cute when
you struggle?" His fingers quickly opened one of the satchels at her
hip, and he whispered to the crystal ball in his hand, "Do not disturb,
hold all the calls, I don't wish to be bothered with twinkling crystal
balls." The orb winked out to a pitch-black, and he slipped it back into
her pouch with a light chuckle.

"I'll get out of this and make you regret every horrible deed
that you ever committed."

He sniggered. "Yeah, whatever you say, little Spellweaver."
His claws sunk deep into the fruit and the juices ran down his fingers
and hand. The poisonous juice coated his digits. "Look on the bright
side; they say that this fruit is the sweetest and most delicious fruit
you'll ever eat. I mean, sure you'll go stir-crazy, but, hey, at least it'll
taste good." He started to bring his coated claw to her mouth, and she
spit at his face.

"Why you little," he snarled and slapped her so hard that it
sent the chair flying. She screamed, and the furniture hit the floor with
her bound to it.

Think. Think. Think, Vanessa! She mentally tried to calm
herself. She couldn't reach her spell pouches. She couldn't reach her
wand. Hex it all, her staff was propped by the desk. And, double-dip
a candlestick, he turned off her crystal ball!

There wasn't a lot that she could do.

The muffled sound of the Headmaster's hooves clicking over
the carpeted floor and reverberating over her skin had peeled her
vision from her bindings to the approaching threat. Her mind reeled.
A spell. Something. Anything!

She looked at him in horror and felt nothing but fear grip her
as the realization that she could potentially lose her mind to the
poison of the fruit, all the lies and innocent lives that would be buried
with her silence raced through her mind. It spelled her veins to feel a
touch of frost. It made panic swell inside her. Mentally, she scoured
her being for a drop of power. Reaching deep within, trying to find

111

any amount of magic that she had felt in recent months. She watched another drop of juice fall from the Satyr's claws and she thought, *Stay back!* At the same time, her mouth opened, and she screamed, "Force. Push!" Immediately, she felt the familiar rush of warmth that her hidden power usually held.

That one command shot out of her. She could feel it all over her. Like the words manifested and were being ripped out of her being. The sensation of the spell rippled over her body and then it blasted out of her like a shockwave. The room held a low hum as the magic propelled across the space between them and slammed into Sylas, sending him flying backward and crashing into the front of his desk. The furniture scraped over the floor in a half-howl that mingled with the Headmaster's painful wail right before he slumped to the floor.

A moment later and he was heaving himself upright. He wiped the side of his mouth and inspected his hand. Instantly, he noticed the blood smeared over the back of it. He snarled and shot his hand out in her direction. *"Fen mortum!"* he bellowed.

Before she could blink, the roots of the Jinmenju tree were crashing through the floorboards of his office and stretching out like wooden rivers rushing out of control and heading straight for her. She closed her eyes and turned her head to avoid the onslaught of debris that exploded in her direction. The roots uplifted and slammed into her chair, sending her reeling across the room again. She yelled as she felt the bindings bite deeper into her skin as she was tossed about. She plastered herself against the back of the chair to avoid her face smashing into the floor, but it mattered little as the chair tumbled about. She felt her head hit something, but it all happened so fast she wasn't sure what. Her forehead had a white-hot heat spread over the inflicted area right as the chair connected with a bookcase on the far side of the room. She came to a sudden stop, and she sputtered with a coughing fit as her head swam, and she felt her stomach threaten to heave. She drew in slow breathes and tried to regain focus.

"I'm going to …" he said and started to stand. *"Ugh …* enjoy feeding this to you, you little brat," he threatened. He was getting up a lot faster than she had hoped.

She opened her mouth, but, instead of air being sucked in, she felt like she had been metaphysically punched in her gut. Another wave of the charming spell took her over. It was all she could do just to focus on the simple act of breathing. "You ... removed ... the barriers ... aro-around the school," she wheezed between strained gulps for air.

His grin was sinister. "You're definitely smarter than I had anticipated. Unfortunately for you, it is going to cost you ..."

The power bore down on her from every angle. Her eyes rolled, and her head lulled until it fell to the side on the ground where she could only gasp for fractions of breaths. Still, she fought it. Her eyes were lazily drooping before shooting wide as she could get them.

He laughed again. Power was rolled up in that dark chuckle, and it washed over her. Caressing every muscle and commanding her body to just relax and stop struggling. "What a shame," he stated and knelt next to her. Gingerly, a clean talon moved a bit of hair from her face and then he snatched her jaw in his grasp.

Tears welled in her eyes.

She couldn't focus on the words. She was too tired to draw power. It took everything in her to just fight to stay awake. "No, p-please," she whimpered as she watched the fruit come closer.

One moment she was there, seconds away from defeat, and the next there was a thunderous crash, and the office door was thrown off its hinges. The object hurled across the room and crashed through the window on the other side. Screams from the courtyard below were heard as cascading glass hit the ground seconds before the loud 'thwack' of the door made contact with the concrete.

"RAAAWR!" There was a bestial vigor in the tremendous roar that shook the windows still standing in the room. Items on the racks rattled. Books on the shelves shook. A second after the bellow rumbled through the room, a green flame wrapped around the Satyr.

The Headmaster pulled back and slapped at the lapping flames growing all over his body while screaming. Bobo barreled through the opening, and with a sweep of his hand pulled off the hellfire before his free hand balled into a fist and slammed into Sylas's jaw. The Satyr flew like he had no weight to him at all and fell in a heap by the filing cabinets behind his desk. The metal objects teetered and collapsed, toppling over him.

"Vanessa!" Lyx rushed in and quickly came to the witch's side.

Bobo stormed over to the heap of office furniture and threw one of the metal cabinets to the side where it bent upon connecting with the wall and fell to the floor. He stared down to the spot where red plumes of sparkling clouds were dissipating.

"He escaped," he snarled in a heated tone.

"Bobo?" Vanessa managed to squeeze out.

The ogre turned on heel, and all the aggression that coated every fiber of his being died when his blue eyes rested on his master.

"My dear," he breathed.

Anything in his path was moved like he was brushing away jungle leaves. He shoved the desk, and snapping sounds erupted from it as it hit the wall. He tossed a chair to the side and pushed a lamp out of the way. All of them bent or broke as he ran to her. And not a single thing on all of Raen could stop the tears that welled up and flowed down Vanessa's face in thankful droves.

 *Chapter 14:*

The two cut Vanessa free of her bindings, and the witch attempted to slowly explain what had happened. But she didn't give the pets long enough to say much of anything before she quickly asked, "How did you find me? How did you know I was in trouble? Where is Leon?"

That earned many awkward glances between the demon and demoness before Bobo cleared his throat. "I can't really explain it that well myself, Vanessa. But I felt you call to me. Or, rather, call out for help. I just happened to pick up on it."

She looked confused. "How?" was the only thing she could think to ask.

The ogre tapped the side of his head. "I heard you up here."

"By the goddess ... Bobo, did we?" Vanessa started to ask.

He nodded and replied. "I believe so. We seem to have synced up recently. As a result, I think I could hear you telepathically."

"That—That's amazing!" Lyx burst out happily. "To think that the two of you are actually close enough to share that kind of bond!" She stated with a massive smile. It swiftly fell, and she stared off into the distance. "If a certain someone and I had a close connection like that, I wouldn't have had to suffer so much when you all were lost in the Black Forest."

Vanessa couldn't help but laugh, and Bobo joined in with a light chuckle. Attempting to stand up, the young witch hissed in pain.

"Careful, my dear. Seems you have quite the bump on your head."

"Ugh, you don't have to remind me. I can feel it," she groaned, holding her head.

Lyx reached up to keep Vanessa steady. Concern was scrolled all over her face as she told the young witch, "You really need to get that looked at."

For once, the Spellweaver didn't fight the suggestion. "I'll need to make a report at the Coven. I can get checked out and mended while there." Besides, magically healing beyond a basic patch-up or muscle relief spell, healing wasn't Vanessa's forte. You had to be trained to be a healer to do more than simple quick fixes. "It's definitely on my list of things to do."

"Why does it sound like you are going to be doing more than filing a report to the Coven?" Bobo asked with a less than pleased expression.

She half-laughed and paused as she held her head, regretting the happy outburst. "Because we are going to finish the investigations after we've questioned those double-crossing snakes rotting away in the oubliette."

The sound of distant thunder rolled outside as if on cue. Lyx slowly brought her fingers to her lips. "What are you saying, Vanessa?" the demoness questioned, confused.

Vanessa faced her. "I'm saying that Headmaster Fleeton knew about the summoning portals. Many beings here at the academy knew. And, if my hunch is right, Dmitri is connected to it. He might have the missing pieces to our puzzle."

"Well, well," Bobo stated, rising to his feet and brushing off his slacks. "It would seem that the magic has hit the fan."

"Oh, it has," Vanessa confirmed. "I don't know where Fleeton went, but I'm sure I need to quickly go to the Coven and question Dmitri before I can make a proper report."

Lyx swiftly rose up and pointed a clawed finger in the young witch's direction, "Don't you dare forget to go to the Coven infirmary!"

The Spellweaver nodded. "Promise," she said with a reassuring smile. And no one really doubted her. She poked at her lump and hissed in pain. "I don't think my body will let me avoid it this time," she admitted. All the while, her fingers traced the edges of the bump as she felt how far out the bruising went. It was a wound that could not go unattended for long. Pleased with the witch's reply,

Lyx went to inspect the damage out in the courtyard through the broken office window.

"Very well, then. I suppose we should be off to seek danger and all that," Bobo stated, motioning to the gaping hole in the wall where the door used to be.

Vanessa puckered her lips and scowled. "I don't like danger," she defended.

If the ogre's expression wasn't a dead giveaway to his disbelief in his master's words, his sarcastic comeback was. "Of course not. Why, an innocent thing like you with a squeaky clean nose and an unwavering moral compass? I'd dread the day you sought danger."

She raised her chin as she went to pass the gentleman-beast. "My nose may not be the cleanest in Aeristria, but my moral compass always points north."

"That, my warrior with a wand, not a soul— living or dead— could deny," Bobo expressed with pride and helped the young witch walk through the opening.

"Wait for me!" Lyx yelled as she ran to catch up to them.

Vanessa couldn't concentrate well enough to use a teleportation spell. Even if it was an easy-breezy one like using the Coven insignia to jump back to the arrival pads in the headquarter's halls. Walking wasn't exactly a witch's best friend at the present moment either. The storm was building up and would be blanketing Tolvade in heaps of rain within the hour. The deep gray clouds rolling through the sky from the north filled the air with the scent of promised rain. The rush of winds and rolling thunder in the distance gave them enough warning to not try to head back on foot. So, after a bit of fussing, and Lyx answering a crystal ball call from Leon, they hailed a carriage and took it back to HQ. Though, with the swaying of the carriage, Vanessa had to steady her breathing and focus on the passing scenery through the small windows or she was going to lose it. As her stomach did sickening flips, she started to wish that they had walked instead.

When they exited the carriage, Leon was there. "What in the name of magic happened, and why are you always in the middle of trouble?" the Summoner asked, his voice a little loud as he tried to speak over the rising winds.

"It likes her. They are on a first-name basis, she and trouble," Bobo muttered stepping out of the buggy. He turned and aided Lyx down the steps while perfectly ignoring the heated glare from his master.

"Come on, we need to get you healed up," Leon urged.

"No." Vanessa strained to push out the single word as she loved the stillness of the ground beneath her feet. Her head swayed involuntarily for a moment.

"Are you crazy?" he asked in a hoarse tone.

"I'm in the middle of an investigation," she snapped back.

"Wonderful, I'll put that on your tombstone. Want anything else chiseled in while we are at it?" The fire in his words was matched with the burn of his unrelenting gaze.

She bent her brow and opened her mouth, only to hear Lyx add in with finality, "That's it! I'm tired of putting your health at risk, young lady."

Everyone blinked at those words, and the succubus's hooves clicked angrily over the sidewalk as she came to stand in front of Vanessa. Her hair was no longer black, but a bright, fiery orange, and her amber eyes were glowing as she spoke. "You can side-step disaster with some other demoness, but not me. Not today." Her finger pointed aggressively to the building. "You are going to march your cute butt through those doors and go straight to the doctor's office."

The Spellweaver looked like a child who had been told they wouldn't get sweets for a month. "But I'm —"

Lyx would have none of the witch's excuses. She cut her off faster than she could have dipped a finger into a pouch of gold dust. "You're injured! And the more you put yourself at risk, the more you are going to put your investigation at risk and everyone who cares about you too. Heal first, work later!"

It was final. It was final because Lyx was right. Vanessa knew when to throw in the towel. "You're right. I just ... I got wrapped up in everything and wanted to do my best to give the Coven answers."

The demoness lost the pepper in her tone, and her hair changed from the bright orange to purple and finally back to the deep, silky black. Her features softened, and she said, "You can do your best only when you are feeling your best, Vanessa."

"She is right, you know," Leon whispered to Vanessa.

"Neglecting your needs is poor form, my dear. Self-care should always take priority. Or you'll always put others before you and forget yourself entirely," Bobo added.

"All right. All right. Sheesh. You guys win. I already said that I was sorry," Vanessa griped.

Lyx pouted playfully. "You're not mad at me, are you, darling?"

Vanessa sighed and then gently shook her head. "No. You were just worried about me. I can't blame you. After everything we've been through, I should know better by now. I don't have to get swept up in the excitement and forget about my health. You win, Lyx. I'll go see the doctor first. Then I will continue my questioning before making my report."

"Thank you," the succubus said with her tail swaying behind her happily.

Inside, the four of them all traveled toward the hall that would take them to the medical wing. While they walked, Vanessa asked Leon, "Have you heard anything from Raven?"

Lyx answered for her master. "She actually crystal ball called him a while ago. She had tried to contact you but couldn't magically connect."

"Yeah, Sylas turned off my crystal ball," she seethed as the memory seeped back into her mind. "Oh! That reminds me." She instantly reached for the object as they walked and laid it in both of her palms.

"You really shouldn't activate that while walking," Leon warned in a sing-song tone.

She made a sound and continued with the task. The orb lit up to its usual dark gray, and she slipped it back into her pocket. "I'll call her when I get home tonight."

A call to her aunt would be a nice addition to a cup of hot cocoa, curling up with a blanket, and reading her grimoire while listening to the storm. The plan sounded like a dream to her. However, first things first.

"Leon," Vanessa said as they approached the door that would lead to the infirmary. "What time is it?"

"Why?" he asked.

"I'm worried that I might not have time to question Dmitri. The Coven dungeon is off-limits when the sun goes down," she whispered back.

"And for good reason. Blood mages are more powerful at night," Bobo reminded.

"Blood mages. Dmitri. What exactly are you up to, Vanessa?" Lyx chimed in.

"I'm trying to get answers," the Spellweaver quickly replied.

Leon hummed as he noted the hour and shook his head slightly. "I'm afraid you won't have the time you were hoping for."

She sighed. "Drat. I'll have to ask for an extension then. I am supposed to turn this mission scrolls report in by this evening."

"Yeah. Seems like luck isn't on your side with this," Leon replied.

"Don't worry, darling. They're stuck in a dungeon. Not like they are going anywhere anytime soon," Lyx stated while gently rubbing Vanessa's back.

Vanessa smiled and gave the succubus a half-hug before reaching for the door. She looked everyone over as she said, "I just know that I'm on to something with th—"

But her words were cut short by a small, red head poking out of the door and yelling, "Do you have an appointment?!"

Out of pure reflexes, the young witch screamed, all the others jolted in surprise, both from the tiny demon's sudden presence and the Spellweaver's yip. Before she could stop the action, her leg drew back and extended, kicking the red imp far into the room. She slammed the door shut, and the realization sunk it. "Oh. Oh, no!" Just as quickly as she had closed the door, she opened it and rushed inside crying out, "I'm so sorry! Are you okay?"

Savannah Snow was speaking with a pixie at the far end of the room. The winged-being floated closer to gather a medical chart and prescription for a patient and fluttered off to give it to the herbal staff. Meanwhile, Savannah turned around and plucked a quill from the air and signed her name on a floating clipboard before tossing the willed feather pen back into the air.

"Fortitude, what did I tell you about jumping in front of beings? You need to be more careful," she reminded her pet before turning her attention to Vanessa and the others.

The smile that overtook the doctor's lips was a cross between sweet and curious. "My, my. If it isn't Hu ... *Spellweaver* Peterson. Aren't you late for your checkup?"

Three sets of eyes turned and bore a hole right through Vanessa, who shrank in on herself with a cringe. Bobo grunted and shook his head at her, Lyx puckered her lips to the side, threw her hands on her hips, and tapped her hoof on the floor while glaring at the young witch, and Leon didn't look surprised, but his expression was far from thrilled.

The Summoner's voice matched the look on his face as he said, "Really? Really, Vanessa?"

"A lot of things happened, okay?" she snapped back in a hoarse tone.

Savannah giggled and—thankfully—lifted all the harsh stares fixed on the Spellweaver. "Don't worry about it. I wouldn't have been able to see you. We've had an influx of injured members, and I've been moonlighting at a local healing office to help the citizens of Tolvade. The numbers have dwindled down in recent days, which has been nice."

"Now I have two things to feel better about," Vanessa admitted.

The doctor motioned for Vanessa to come closer and then gestured toward an empty medical cot. As she passed by the rows of beds, she noticed two red imps marching with a stretcher as they headed for the one lying motionless on the ground.

"*Hup, hup, hup,*" they barked in sync with their footsteps. Placing the stretcher on the floor, they rolled the limp imp on it, hoisted it up, and marched off toward the back.

"Sorry," Vanessa whispered as she walked by.

Savannah smiled sweetly. "He'll be fine."

"Perhaps it will serve as a lesson," Bobo tried to turn the negative situation into a positive one.

The doctor's smile faded as she added in a deadpan voice, "That's the sixth time this week."

"Oh." The gentlemen-beast widened his eyes and looked off to the side.

"Now, let's get you looked over shall we?" Savannah said sweetly.

Vanessa sat on the edge of the cot. Doctor Snow dipped her fingers into a dust pouch and summoned a light spell and made the orb small as she inspected the young witch's ears, nose, and eyes. She sprinkled the remains of the spell off to the side. "Looks like you got a pretty nasty bump there," she noted out loud as she continued to look the Spellweaver over. "Any other aches I should be aware of before I start healing?"

Vanessa lifted a hand and pulled up the hem of her skirt. Leon looked away as his face glowed red, Bobo shielded his eyes saying, "Give a gentleman warning, won't you?" and Lyx giggled at their reactions.

"Hmmm. I see." Savannah murmured.

"There are more along my arms and wrists. Nothing too deep," Vanessa added.

"I'll make the appropriate adjustments to the spell to help heal those." From behind the doctor, the clipboard and quill floated over, and she spoke to it quietly. "Multiple minor lacerations to the legs and arms, bruising to the forehead and cheeks, and a large welt near the crown. Possible traces of magic fatigue will be treated alongside the visible wounds." She stopped and turned away from the paper and pen, facing Vanessa. "Are there any odd or even beneficial happenings that have taken place in your physical or metaphysical forms?"

There was a silence in the room. Sure, there were a lot of things Vanessa could say at that moment, and most (if not all) of them were positive. However, she wasn't sure who she could trust with certain aspects of information. She was half Dark Elf, and one with a considerable amount of magic. At least, she suspected that much. And her birth and existence had been a secret for so long. Even Ell hadn't brought it up. So why should she say anything about it now? Until she was sure of who she could trust with the information, she played it safe and answered with, "I've been learning how to control my magic. It is a slow process, but I'm managing."

Savannah looked the witch over while deep in thought. Nodding, she continued as though she were happy with the reply. "Good." She grabbed a small note from out of the air after it tore off of a small pad, and she called out, "Temperance!"

From one of the medical cupboards, a red imp exploded out yelling, "I retuuurn!" and landed on the floor with an ungraceful *thud*. Sitting up and giggling, the female red imp wiggled about and jumped to her feet. "Coooomiiiing!" the being bellowed gleefully.

Slamming into the side of Doctor Snow's leg, the creature looked up to her master with its large, black, doe eyes. Blinking innocently up at her, the imp asked, "Whatchu need?"

Savannah handed the imp the note, "Get this filled for me and bring it back. I'm going to perform a healing spell."

The imp stood tall and at attention, even saluted the doctor before swiping the paper. "You got it, boss!"

As Temperance waddled off for the herbal room with her arms flailing over her head excitedly, Doctor Snow called after the creature, "And tell Prudence to bring me a fresh pouch of gold dust!"

The only reply that was received was insane giggles from the other room. "*Ehehehehee!*"

Turning back, the doctor smiled. "Now, let's get you healed up and forms signed so you can get back to work."

"What are the herbs for?" Lyx asked.

"Hopefully, to knock her out," Bobo mumbled to himself.

Leon attempted to stifle a laugh and failed, which earned a heated look from Vanessa. But Savannah ignored the exchange and answered the demoness. "It's a mild blend of herbs that help with the pain that is going to hit her as the night goes on. It will also help to bring down the swelling around the head injury. Even though magical healing does a lot visually, the body still feels the remaining effects for a few days. As always, medicine and rest can help anything a spell can't mend."

"You won't hear me complaining," Vanessa stated, happy that she would have something to take the edge off the pain later on that night.

"It would be a first for you, I'm sure," Bobo was quick to put in his two coins' worth with a grin that made Vanessa roll her eyes.

Savannah went to work. She started to focus on the head injury first. She then moved on to the other scrapes, bumps, and bruises. The soft minty glow of her magic pulsed as she focused on her task. When finished, Prudence came rushing in with a bag of gold dust in one hand and the filled herbal prescription in the other. "

"Special delivery!" Prudence yelled as she ran over to the doctor.

"Thank you," Doctor Snow said, finishing up her healing spell and dipping down to retrieve the items. "Where is Temperance?" she asked.

But the doctor's question was answered when the sound of a ceramic jar smashed on the floor behind the desk. Large cotton balls rolled over the floors as Temperance swayed atop the desk while she held her neck with bulging eyes. She landed face down on the floor with a groan stifled by cotton balls.

Two other red imps jumped off the writing area onto the choking imp's back, and a handful of cotton balls erupted out of the imp's mouth. Gasping for air, the imp looked to Savannah and smiled while the other two looked at the mess shaking their heads.

Savannah looked off into the distance, almost like she was imagining being somewhere peaceful, and drew in a long, slow breath. Turning away from the imps, she resumed speaking to Vanessa. "Take this tea once in the morning and once at night before bed. If you have any concerns, crystal ball call me."

With that, the doctor turned around pointing to the mess. "How many times do I have to tell you? These are *not* cotton candy!"

Lyx visibly shuddered. "I never want to see cotton candy again," the demoness whispered.

The image of parading imps being yelled at by their master was quickly snuffed out by a pixie flying over at a breakneck speed. "Sign here, please," the flying being asked sweetly.

Chapter 15:

They had exited the medical area and headed for the main lobby as quick as they could. None of the group was faster than Vanessa. She was practically sprinting down the hall toward the vestibule.

"Could you slow down?" Leon asked as he jogged to keep up with the fast-paced witch.

"I *have* to get to the oubliette before they put a hold on beings going to and from there," she reminded.

"You could come back tomorrow after asking for an extension, what's the rush?" Bobo asked.

Her countenance twisted as she tried to figure out the answer herself. "I'm not sure, to be honest. I just have this feeling of urgency."

"All right then, Vanessa. Let us carry on with haste," the ogre announced with finality.

Lyx gave Bobo a look and said, "You always tell her to stay out of trouble and complain but here you are encouraging her behavior."

Leon thumbed to his pet. "What she said."

Bobo nodded, understanding of their thoughts. "Yes. I cannot deny that. I shan't deny it either. However, I will follow that little witch to the underbelly of Hell and back if she has a hunch."

There was only one way in and out of the Coven dungeon, and that was on the second floor across from the Great Orb room. A room on the other end of the hall. A small room. A dark room. A room that none in the Coven openly spoke of. It was a place better forgotten and given no attention to. That room led to the Coven dungeons, or what was better known as the oubliette.

As to why no one talked about the room, there were many reasons. For one, it was revered as a cursed place. The oubliette itself was a place that held the worst of the worst, the traitors of Aeristria, though they were few. Another reason was because it was never intended for the use that it had today. But possibly the main reason why no one spoke of the place was because of how it came to be revered as cursed.

Back when the Coven was rebuilt in the heart of Tolvade, there was a talented wizard who had recently joined the ranks, Archimedes. He was ambitious, smart, and a wiz with spells. He had collected artifacts through the years, though only a handful. Archimedes proposed to the Coven Council that he would donate the artifacts if they'd fund a project he wanted to start. A dungeon that could strip demons of their powers. When the High Priest Council of that time inquired his reasoning for wanting to build such a place, he reminded them that feral demons could still be a threat to the citizens. The Council agreed and made the proper arrangements for the funding of the project.

A few years later, the dungeon that Archimedes had been building was no closer to being completed, according to the High Priest Council. And, after many meetings over the funding of the project, it was seen as a money pit with no payoff. Many in the Coven ranks had even staked claims to the fact that a feral demon sighting had not happened in so long, and that there was no need for such a place.

Oh, if they only knew then what they know now …

Archimedes was denied further financial assistance for the project. Though, he didn't fault or blame the High Priest Council. In fact, he even let them keep the artifacts that he had promised to them. Four of them, to be exact. The fifth, and final, artifact could only remain in their keeping if they agreed to let him continue on with the project. They agreed, though they never gave him further funding. The wizard used his own coin for years to follow until he vanished without a trace some years later. It was later announced that he died during one of his expeditions out into the wilderness, searching for lost artifacts he claimed were still scattered about Aeristria. His death left behind his unfinished work and no known family. The project

SMOKE, LIES, AND GRIMOIRES

then turned into what was known today as the oubliette. A pocket dimension nestled within the Coven. It wasn't strong enough to strip demons, but it could slowly siphon out the magic of any other wielder captured within it. A curse, in a sense. The High Priest Council wouldn't kill the caster, outright. They would keep the being in the dungeons for three to four months, draining them of power slowly. Right before they had nothing left magically, they would be removed from the prison, a probation trial would be held, and, if released back into society under tight watch, they would barely be able to make a crystal ball call and hardly able to function without feeling weak and tired all the time. They would live being borderline magicless for the rest of their lives.

It was the cruelest thing you could do to a being that had magic integrated so deeply into their lives. More often than not, it was considered too cruel for most magic-based criminals of Aeristria, especially since it could kill the being if left in there too long. There were exceptions to this, of course. Traitors were one of the top exceptions.

One by one, the four of them climbed the stairs to the second floor. The portion of walk space between the Great Orb room and the entrance to the oubliette was coated in shadows. The light seemed to burn less brightly here. It was as if the magic-eating spell consumed the illumination as well. The door was guarded by a Coven member, and his eyes narrowed suspiciously at the oncoming group.

"Name and rank!" He shouted long before they arrived at the door.

None could blame him. This was where they held the highest regarded enemies of Tolvade. One slip up and you'd have a mess on your hands. One Vanessa wasn't willing to be associated with. She stopped not a second after the guard asked, and she was still a few feet away from both the guard and door when she replied, "Spellweaver Peterson and her pet Botobolbilian."

Leon stiffened up and called out, "Summoner Zvěrokruh and his pet Lyx."

The guard nodded. "Let me see your insignia," he said while holding out a crystal ball in his hand.

Both the witch and wizard made their emblems more visible and waited for confirmation from the guard to continue. A moment passed, the orb was pocketed, and the guard poured a few drops of a potion over the knob. The moment the liquid connected with the metal, the door slowly creaked open.

The floors were made entirely out of jadeite. The walls were smooth, wavy quarts that still held slight signs of how they had been hastily chiseled by hand, and dead center of the room was a double-sided mirror that hummed with power. It was taller and wider than Bobo and stood on large metal bird feet. All of the metal was a dingy brown color and brushed in bronze. Along the sides, swirls of the creature's tail feathers rose up to hug the edges of the mirror. Near the top sides two great, fiery wings rose up to the ceiling. On the very top, the head of a phoenix was pointed up and its beak open wide as if crying out an empowering song for the broken to rise from the ashes with it. The glass itself shifted like it was a pond softly rippling in the spring breeze. The image therein changed from that of the room and reflecting all those present to the scene of another room. It was a darker room with jewels sticking out of black-as-coal cave walls. Each gem twinkled under the nearby lamplight.

As they watched two guards look back at them through the glass, Vanessa turned to Bobo, Lyx, and Leon. "Stay here. I want to talk to him without crowding the oubliette."

Leon looked a little disappointed but nodded, silently agreeing. She smiled to them all, took a deep breath, and stepped through the spelled glass. Cold embraced her and sunk down past what a fire could bring comfort to. Even though she had expected it, she shivered out of reflex. Within seconds, her hearing was swallowed up in the ripples of deep purple that surrounded her and made up the spell. The outside world from either side of the mirror became lost and distorted as she pushed through the wall. All around her, the cool sensation made her feel like she was swimming in a pool hidden in a deep and shadowed forest but she never got wet. Her clothes and skin remained dry while she pushed through to the other side.

There was a brief moment of a blank, black void before she felt herself slip into the pocket dimension. She practically stumbled out of the mirror and swiftly caught herself before things got too bad.

Both of the guards standing watch eyed her over as if asking silently, *"Are you okay?"* She grinned awkwardly at them, and both guards resumed their post as usual.

The dungeon air felt like it had been soaked in the waters of Banshee Bog and then hung up to dry in a damp, sunless cellar. Smelled like it too. Vanessa crinkled her nose as she eyed over the objects lining the circular dungeon room. Fifteen long, rectangular mirrors were hung all around the black, jewel-encrusted walls. Most of them were empty, but three of them were filled. One was a criminal Vanessa had never heard of. It wasn't a secret that she hardly paid attention to the tabloids and news. She was more concerned with flinging spells and practicing magic rather than who had been the top captured criminals of Aeristria. So, the name of the culprit mattered little to her as long as they were captured and dealt with appropriately. The other two were filled with Isolde and Dmitri. Each of them harbored in their own private mirror prison.

"Fifteen minutes before the gateway is closed down for the night. This is for your safety," the female guard informed, bringing Vanessa out of her daze.

"I understand," she replied while dashing for the mirror where she saw Dmitri, huddled in a corner, with his back facing the glass.

Reaching out, she let her fingers roll over the edge of the mirror's metal flourish design. Her magic connected with the mirror, creating an open connection. Next, she traced the glass with one of her fingers, scrolling a rune upon it. The mirror rippled. It was protocol for those wishing to speak to prisoners. You had to leave a magical imprint. She had done the rune spell to amplify his voice. Mirrors were not known for having the best reception, even if they were transmitting between dimensions. The picture would be clear, but the voice could come through as distant or echoic.

"Dmitri," Vanessa called to him.

He didn't turn to face her. Only a cold, "Go away," was muttered in the witch's direction.

She sighed. Five seconds into the conversation and she was already emotionally drained. Hardening her expression and squaring her shoulders as if she were heading to the frontline of a battlefield, she drew in a breath and held a commanding tone. "I'm not leaving until you give me answers."

Slowly, he turned. His eyes widened when he saw her, and then they narrowed angrily. "Haven't you done enough damage?'

She didn't show if the comment bothered her or not. She remained unmoved by his words. "What about you? Are you done causing harm to Aeristria and the Coven?"

He stood then. Every portion of the action was teeming with rage. "Harm? Harm? You know nothing of what I was trying to do. I was doing what I needed to for the greater good. And because you couldn't follow orders, I was branded a traitor and locked in here!" he snarled and spread his arms wide, showing off his personal prison.

"I know that you were working with Headmaster Fleeton," she quickly shot back.

That caught him off guard. Enough that he teetered and took a step back to balance himself. "What do you know?" he whispered.

"I know that the academy's barriers were taken down. I know that the staff knew about the summoning circle. I know enough to link you and him … but I need your help to fill in the gaps."

"Why would I bother?"

"You said magic was dying!" she shouted. The guards shifted and looked nervously at her.

Dmitri stood a little prouder. "And? What of it? Why do you care now?"

"What if I told you that I believe you, that I believe that magic is dying? What if I said that I knew you were doing what was right? Even if I don't agree with your methods … I think there was real concern that drove you."

There was a silent pause as he drew in a thoughtful breath. "So what if you do?"

Vanessa braced herself on either side of the mirror and got close enough to the glass that her nose almost touched it. "What if I told you I saw the elves, I found one of the hidden temples, and the Coven is already in possession of two of the four magical tablets needed to restore magic on Raen?"

Dmitri raced across his cell and mirrored her pose. "You found them? Then, there is still hope that the magic can be restored!"

Slowly, the Spellweaver slipped away, feeling uncomfortable that close to his image. Dmitri remained as he was. "Yes," she replied simply. "But I need your help in trying to restore things to normal. And those in power at the academy are more concerned with themselves than returning magic to the land. Something isn't right. I need your help. I know that there is something good in you. You cared enough to go this far. Help me and repair your image. Help me save Aeristria."

He looked off to the side as he considered it.

"Tell her nothing!" the sharp command of Isolde rang through her mirror next to his on the wall.

He heard her and took a step back from the mirror. Vanessa was losing the little ground she had made. "Don't. I just need to know who. Help me. Help the beings of Aeristria. Don't let these beings go unpunished while you suffer the price for all of their crimes."

"Heh. Crimes? We were doing you all a favor," Isolde snapped.

"Silence!" Vanessa ordered. She turned her attention back to Dmitri. "Please," she begged. "Help me."

He brought his thumb to his mouth and pressed down while looking at the floor. He was battling with himself. And, when she felt her heart sink and assumed she was on the losing end, he stepped closer and said, "Sylas is ... he's part of a group that is tied to the board."

"Who?"

"Don't tell her anything!" Isolde hissed.

"Two minutes!" one of the guards warned.

"I'm not sure. Whenever I went there, we didn't talk about it much. What I do know is that they had been searching for a hell gate so that they could open it."

The Spellweaver pinched her brow as she processed the information. This had been planned for months, possibly longer. How had they managed to keep it all hidden for so long? Who all was involved? "Why did they need the hell gate? Why were they summoning demons?"

"Because they needed them for a ritual." He stopped and seemed conflicted. His gaze looked at her in a peculiar way. Guilt was scrolled over his features. "I-I've said too much." His eyes shifted about.

"One minute!" the other guard yelled.

Vanessa pressed her lips together and then huffed quietly. If she just had a little more time. "Dmitri, think about any information that you believe could help me. I'll be back tomorrow. I might even be able to tell the Council what you've done and ask them to cut you a deal." She didn't know if it would do much. He was a traitor, after all.

Dmitri looked to the mirror with hope in his eyes and nodded. Nothing more was said between them. There was only the guard yelling, "Last call," as Vanessa rushed for the main mirror. She stopped by the exit, took one look behind her, and smiled as she announced, "I'll be back tomorrow." Then, she slipped back to the other room where Bobo, Leon, and Lyx were waiting for her.

 *Chapter 16:*

As soon as she stepped through the mirror portal, she shivered and rubbed her arms, though it did little to chase away the chill. She would have to wait for the spell's residue to wear off before she wouldn't feel cold anymore.

The three of them stared at Vanessa expectantly.

She frowned and sighed while shaking her head. "There wasn't enough time to find out everything I hoped to."

"Don't worry about it, my dear. I'm sure you warmed him up to spilling magic beans for you tomorrow," Bobo said, trying to make Vanessa feel better.

"Did you happen to find out anything useful?" Leon asked.

Lyx looked to Vanessa hoping that there was some good news.

The Spellweaver nodded and bounced her head from side to side as she said, "Sort of. Mainly, I found out that there is a group pulling the strings behind the event back at the academy. I'm just not sure how deep it goes. Isolde didn't want him to talk. I'm hoping that she doesn't diminish the little headway I've made and convince Dmitri to seal his lips back up."

"We can find out tomorrow. Let's go get you that extension so we can all go home and rest, darling," Lyx urged sweetly.

"Yeah," Vanessa said with a sigh. She felt like she was holding a handful of potions with no labels. Sure, they could be helpful ... if she knew what they were. All of these tidbits and leads were no different. She had theories and ideas, but without hard evidence, it was a waste of time, breath, and energy. Feeling drained, she expelled a lungful and looked at Lyx and Leon. "Would you guys like to stay over at my place tonight?"

Lyx looked like she had all of her dreams come true while Leon looked to Vanessa with a sly smile. "I don't know. Are you going to wake up angry about me being there?"

She blushed while the others giggled softly. "N-no," she mumbled.

"We'd love to," he admitted.

"Darling, would we!" Lyx shouted with a beaming smile.

They all headed down to the main desk area where Vanessa filed the proper paperwork for a mission scroll extension. Because it was only for an information retrieval mission, she didn't have to wait long or go into a verbal meeting with a Summoner to get approval. With all of her work said and done, it was time to call it a day at the Coven. It was a day of unexpected work. Work that had made her feel better about her recent collection of days off. But it was draining nonetheless, and going home to rest was at the top of her list.

Outside, the storm had already begun, and it didn't look like it was going to relent anytime soon. Deciding that trudging through rain and intimidating bolts of lightning was one of the few dangers Vanessa wasn't willing to endure, they decided to use the Coven teleportation pads to get home. They landed in front of the building, took the lift, and sluggishly piled through the apartment door.

"Ugh, I didn't think I'd be happy to see home so soon, but I'm so mentally exhausted," Vanessa admitted as she immediately plopped back into the soft cushions of her couch with a groan.

Everyone but Leon mirrored the young witch. The wizard had shuffled off to the kitchen and was rummaging through the fridge.

"Leon," Lyx gasped. "Have some manners," she demanded.

He pulled his head out of the fridge far enough to let her see the perplexed look on his face. "I lived here once," he reminded.

"And now you don't," the succubus heatedly reminded in turn.

"Pffft. Once you live somewhere, you never go back to being a guest," he warned and dove back to searching through the icebox.

"Ugh," Lyx growled. "If I wasn't tethered to you ..."

"Pay it no mind," Bobo stated with a lazy wave of his hand. "It has been a long and arduous da—week. Let the man find himself some sustenance."

Fluffing her hair, Lyx pouted and shimmied back into the cushions. "If you say so, I suppose it's all right then."

Rolling until she fell flat along the couch, Vanessa then turned her vision to the kitchen and yelled, "You're not going to find anything."

"You don't have to tell me twice. Why is your kitchen so bare?" Leon griped.

She sighed audibly. "Well, I haven't been able to go to the market. With all of the many adventures and almost meeting death, I simply haven't had the time."

"What? What?" Bobo fluttered his lashes at his master's words. "You just went to the market a few days ago. You didn't want to get more than the baking goods and said you'd go back for the rest later."

Vanessa waved at the thought like it was a swarm of annoying pixies. "I don't know what you're talking about."

He made a few sounds and flattened out his tie, "You, my dear, are a horrible liar."

She turned her narrowed eyes in his direction and then something clicked. She rose up and pointed at him. "Why did you come with Lyx when you saved me?"

His eyes practically popped out of his head. That was not what he had expected to come out of the witch's mouth. "I-I-I see that we are not going to get not a scrap of food here, and suggest that we order out," the ogre stuttered as he tried to change the subject.

Leon came in and jumped on the couch behind Vanessa and twisted his orb from side to side in one hand. "All ready took care of it, big guy. Pizza will be here in thirty," he announced and tossed the crystal ball to his free hand before pocketing it in his side pouch. "So, what's going on?"

Lyx was doing anything in her power to not look at everyone sitting in the living room while the poor ogre looked like he was suffocating from choosing to hold his breath.

"Did I, uh, miss something?" Leon whispered to Vanessa.

"Oh, we are all about to find out. Spill the magic beans, Botobolbilian! Why was Lyx with you when you came to save me at the academy?" Vanessa pressed with a serious tone.

The flustered gentleman-beast kept opening and closing his mouth as his hands seemed to move in a way that he was about to speak and forgot what he was about to say. A rush of hot air escaped the demon as he shook his head and looked to the ceiling. "Goddess, help me," he whispered. A moment went by, and he straightened up and faced Leon and Vanessa. "The truth is ... I ...was on a date."

"We bumped into each other!" Lyx shouted a fraction of a second later.

"What?" Leon and Vanessa gasped together in awe.

Lyx's tail flicked behind her as she looked at Bobo. Her eyes were a mix of emotions.

The ogre stood swiftly, straightened out his attire, and took the succubus's hand in his. He pulled her gently to her feet. Patting the top of her hand, he soothed her as he said, "It's all right, my dear," in a low tone before facing both the witch and wizard once more. "We were on a date."

Both the Spellweaver's and Summoner's jaw unhinged. The room fell quiet. Everyone had been stunned into silence. All except for Lyx. Her hair was a pale pink, and her eyes were transfixed on the ogre standing beside her. Slowly, her clawed hand closed over the one holding hers. She smiled and breathed, "Booboo."

He puffed out his chest a bit more. "I'm not ashamed. However, I wasn't quite ready to speak about my personal affairs. Not when so many have their own opinions tied so close to the matter. I wanted to give it some time before I ..." He motioned to the room. "Well, before I did this," he admitted.

Lyx was practically purring as she clung to the ogre's arm, and her tail gradually wrapped around the demon's side. "It was a lunch date, and I went to a book club meeting with him," the succubus said.

"So you didn't lie," Vanessa expressed, amazed.

Bobo scoffed. "I am a gentleman, Vanessa. I may be vague and omit a detail or two, but I promise I will never lie."

A rush of strong wind from outside slapped large pellets of rain against the window, and it sounded like tiny pebbles were hitting the glass. Thunder rumbled, and a sheet of lightning lit up the dark clouds before a bolt of blue and orange light ripped the scene of the town's rooftops in two.

Vanessa turned her attention back to the two demons in the middle of the living room. "I … I don't know what to say," she admitted.

Bobo gave a quick smirk as he replied with, "A gift from the goddess herself."

"Ha, ha," the young witch snapped back and felt the familiar aches and pains returning. Her hand reached around and rubbed the small of her back. "I don't have the energy to think much more." She paused and pointed to Bobo in a wordless warning, and the ogre lifted his hands in defense and looked innocent. She continued on saying, "I just want dinner, a hot drink, and to cozy up on the couch and read my grimoire."

"Don't forget your medicine," Lyx reminded.

Leon guided Vanessa into a more comfortable position on the couch. "I'll get your grimoire and medical tea, you just rest easy, okay?"

She smiled up at him and spoke softly, "Thank you."

The Summoner nodded to her with a grin and then jutted his chin at Bobo, "Hey, big guy. Can you get the door if the pizza comes?" He pointed to a bag on the coffee table. "If they do, there's the coin, and be sure to tip them good."

"Consider it done," the ogre replied.

"As for you, what'll it be for that hot drink?" Leon asked Vanessa in a lower tone. One that was just for her.

She smiled and melted into the couch a bit. "Hot chocolate," she replied dreamily. "But put extra water in the kettle for Bobo, please?"

"You got it," he replied. Dipping down, Leon planted a quick kiss to her forehead and then went to the kitchen.

"Oh, Leon! The grimoire is on my nightstand," the Spellweaver called out to him.

"Gotcha!" he yelled back.

During the quiet reprieve, it was easy to tell that Lyx and Bobo were trying to have a quiet and private conversation. And, though she was dying for the details, Vanessa thought it best to fish out her orb and make a quick call to Raven to keep her from 'accidentally' hearing what the two were discussing.

As she drew out the item, she couldn't help but smile. Once her life and apartment had only consisted of her and Bobo. Now, it was so busy and full of life. She bumped into beings who recognized her, she fell easily into casual conversations with others almost daily, she and Leon were happily working on building their relationship, and she had family that she could reach out and crystal ball call whenever she wanted. She felt full. She felt like she was in some sort of dream that she would never want to wake from. The bliss and joy that came with all of these additions were enough to make her burst at the seams. Everything felt so wonderfully normal. Like this was the way you were supposed to live your life.

There was no chasing the grin off of her face as she glided her fingers over the device and closed her eyes. Mentally, she thought of Raven and her starlight hair and eyes colored like the night sky. Hardly a second passed after she had reached out with her magic and the orb was filled with the smiling face of Raven.

"Little shadow!" the Dark Elf sang happily. Her cheeks were slightly red, and her smile looked a bit sloppy. This was not the refined woman she had been so used to.

"Where are you?" Vanessa asked, curiously.

But not a second went by before Ell was jerking the orb hand in her direction. "She wouldn't stop worrying about you. I told her what Leon said when we called, but she wasn't going to be happy until she—" Ell paused to hiccup, giggled, and then resumed speaking. "... Uh, what was I saying?"

"I was worried!" Raven barked and slammed her free hand onto the bartop.

"You're at Tasgall's, aren't you?" Vanessa roared with laughter and shook her head. "I don't think that is the best way to deal with your worries, Raven."

"See? She doesn't respect me at all. Doesn't even call me auntie," Raven whined to Ell.

"Auntie," Vanessa called to the Dark Elf in a song-like voice.

The female elf dramatically turned the orb to face the witch entirely. "Awww. That's more I like it, little shadow!" she said with a massive, toothy grin.

"What did she say?" Ell half-whined.

"Tomorrow, I shall teach you hand-to-hand combat," Raven announced sitting straight up.

Vanessa laughed. "I think you'll be too busy nursing your hangover."

"Nonsense," Raven growled. "I've excellent alcohol tolerance."

"I have to go to the Coven tomorrow. Maybe we can meet up later on?" the witch asked with a hopeful glimmer in her eyes.

Raven nodded once at the orb. "Yes."

"I'll let you get back to catching up with Ell," Vanessa said with a smile.

Just then, Ell's voice carried through the crystal ball call. "Whoa, whoa!"

THUD!

The cackles of Raven were all Vanessa could hear and then the image swirled as the elf turned the orb in the direction of the giggling blonde that was flat on her back with a barstool laying over her chest.

"Yeah. Let me take care of this mess," Raven said still laughing while thumbing to the happy receptionist on the floor.

The call winked out, and the glass resumed its pictureless state. She hugged the orb to her chest and didn't try to hide the curl of her lips. She didn't say anything. She didn't think about anything. She was just there, relishing the happiness that swelled through her. The young witch was met with a blanket snuffing out the light as Leon covered her from head to toe in a soft throw.

Just as she peered out from under the covers, there was a knock at the door. "Pizza's here," the Summoner announced, and he snatched up his coin purse on the way. The Spellweaver noted the grimoire resting on the coffee table as Leon rushed to answer the door.

They all ate while trading small stories from the past few days. Bobo's mainly consisted of teaching Vanessa how to bake while Leon's were filled with how Summoning training was a breeze lately. Lyx tossed in tales of her new adventures, all of them in the book world. She was new to reading and, after some effort on Bobo's part, had found that she was quite fond of tales of romance and adventure.

Soon after eating, Vanessa was nursing her second cup of hot chocolate and reading her grimoire while resting her back against Leon's side. The Summoner cradled the witch while he scrolled through news reports on his orb. Bobo was propped up reading his newest find while Lyx rested her head in the ogre's lap as she read her novel, though she looked like she was battling the urge to fall asleep as she did. A cozy hush had fallen over the apartment. One that didn't need to be filled with idle chatter. It was the kind of quiet that came when you were in good company and happily existing in your day.

Vanessa flipped another page in her book as she tried to mentally digest half of what she had been reading in her family's notes scrolled within the massive tome. Through countless pages, she had come across so many suggestions and tips and tricks, spells and runes, incantations and potions, and various ways to create the same spells she already knew of but using alternate reagents or how to perform them without the aid of any outside sources. The next page she flipped to had her mother's name scrolled over the top. In the writing, it explained how magic was all connected to the goddess, Saellah. Vanessa's eyes widened as she read eagerly.

All magic is connected to the goddess we were all created by. The tears she shed for how empty Raen was made the elves, and she birthed the celestials from her womb. Later on, the elves paired up with humans. We are all sons and daughters of Saellah. We all have magic flowing within us. Learn to control what you have, and your power will be even greater when reagents are applied.

Vanessa stared at the text. "That name," she whispered.

"Hmmm?" Leon hummed as he came disconnected from his orb and looked over to Vanessa. "What name?"

She pointed to the grimoire's page. "That name," she stated a hair louder. "That is the same name that I heard whispered to me countless times. She looked up to Leon to explain more, but his face held concern and the faint hints of judgment. She puffed out her cheeks and yelled out, "I'm *not* crazy."

"You do a poor job of proving that bold statement, my dear," Bobo muttered while flipping a page in his book.

Exasperated, she pointed to Bobo, "Tell him about the voices. Tell him about the ones that whispered to me in the hall under the academy. The voices we heard near the summoning circle when the candles all lit up."

The ogre gave a knowing nod as he remembered. "Ah, yes." He sighed and gave Leon a serious look, "I'm afraid she's right. We indeed heard them. Why are we bringing this up?" As the gentleman-beast spoke, he gingerly removed the book gripped in the slumbering succubus's hand, marked the page for the demoness, and placed it upon the coffee table.

"The name that we heard back then, Saellah, the voice called me a daughter of Saellah," she reminded excitedly.

Leon and Bobo both nodded and waited for the witch to continue explaining her findings.

"Saellah is the name of the goddess!" she informed, her index finger poking at the open grimoire in her lap.

Leon shifted and leered over Vanessa's shoulder as he read the page. "The goddess? Like ... *the* goddess, goddess?"

Vanessa nodded. "The lore written in here matches with what we've always been taught. Her name is Saellah, and ... guys, not just elves can do magic without amplifiers."

Bobo bounced his hands in the air as if he was channeling spirits. "Wait a moment. My word, that makes a lot of sense."

"It does?" Leon asked, his face twisted in confusion. "How?" The Summoner sounded as though he doubted it to be true.

"Think about it, my dear man. Demons, both feral and tethered, can all use some form of magic without amplifiers or reagents."

"Yeah, hellfire is a type of magic too, Leon," Vanessa added.

Bobo continued after the excited outburst. "There isn't a being I can think of that cannot use magic without a single amplifier needing to be applied. Except for ..." he trailed off and motioned to Leon.

"Except for humans," the wizard finished the thought for him.

Everyone nodded.

After a long moment, Leon asked, "Why is that?"

Vanessa was the first one to speak up. "Yeah, why?" But her tone insinuated that she didn't believe what they had been taught all her life. She scanned the room and said, "I think that humans can. But they were never taught how to. The Light Elves saw to that, and they tried to destroy the Dark Elves before they could teach them. Then they scattered the tablets which ate up yearly magic. Less people have been born with magic. Powerful spellcasters have been dwindling in numbers each year. Guys, Dmitri was right! Magic is fading, and the first signs were exhibited in humans, but we didn't know any better. We fixed the broken flow of magic with stronger reagents."

"Gold dust and will powder," Leon whispered.

"Yes. Exactly. What could be stronger than the ashen remains of pixies? It was only a temporary fix, though."

Leon pulled the grimoire closer to himself. "Does it teach you how to use magic without amplifiers?"

The succubus stirred and yawned with a short stretch. "It's a grimoire, Leon, not a cookbook. Yes, it will teach her," Lyx stated with a tired snicker.

"Ha, ha," he shot back at her.

"I say, Vanessa, this is quite a find. Do you plan on telling the Coven?" Bobo inquired as Leon and Lyx stuck out tongues at each other.

She looked off to the side and muttered, "Eventually."

"Eventually?" Leon was quick to end his back and forth child-like spat with Lyx to question the young witch.

"Yes. Eventually," she repeated a bit louder.

"They need to be told right away," he argued.

"And they will be, after I tell someone that I think needs to know first, and after I look into more details." Her tone alone told everyone in the room that she had made up her mind.

"Who are you planning to tell that is more important than the Coven?" Lyx asked while rubbing one of her eyes.

Vanessa felt it resonated deep in her bones. "Kasmira, Professor Kasmira Nafda. I feel like telling her is the right thing." She raised her gaze from the book and looked to everyone in the room. "I want beings to be able to be taught how to do this. We've gone so long with missing information and with magic not being the way that it should be in this land. I want to take a step in the right direction. I want the beings of Aeristria to benefit from this. Our world is changing in good ways. I want this information to be my contribution to that."

Leon sighed and drew Vanessa back into his side, wrapped his arms around her chest, and hugged her. "Then I support you. If you feel that strongly about it, then do it."

"I told you, Vanessa. Your heart is never in the wrong place. And I couldn't agree with you more on your choice of action," Bobo said proudly.

Vanessa smiled. "Thank you."

"No need to be so thankful, darling. That's what friends do. We support you when you feel strongly about something. Now," she stretched and yawned again, "let's get some shut-eye, m'kay? This momma needs her beauty sleep." She turned and winked to Bobo.

The ogre immediately became flustered and looked away. "I-I agree. We all are in need a good night's rest."

"Right. In the morning, I'll head over to the academy and tell Professor Nafda about what I found. Then I'll go to the Coven and report it to them before I try to talk to Dmitri again."

They all went into their respective rooms for the night. Leon stayed on the couch, Bobo went to his private quarters, and Lyx bunked in the room with Vanessa. Behind closed doors, the witch couldn't help but crack open her book again and read while asking the succubus about the juicy details of the demoness' blossoming romance with the proud and proper Botobolbilian.

"I wouldn't start ringing wedding bells just yet, Vanessa," Lyx said with a giggle. "He wants to take things slow, and I'm respecting that. But he is such a devoted ogre. He doesn't go in with half-baked attempts and sweet nothings." She smiled and played with the seams of the comforter. "He is attentive and caring. It is such a nice change in pace." The sound of her voice mirrored the content look in her eyes. Leaning back into the pillows, she sighed out loud with a grand smile. "Tonight was … it just felt like a leap in the direction that my heart has been craving."

Vanessa smiled and snuggled into the covers. "I know. I guess I'm just excited for you," the witch admitted.

Lyx curled up into the Spellweaver's side and nodded. "I'm excited too. But he and I are just at the start. Today was the first time we went out. It was just a book club meeting and lunch but it was so nice. He had it all planned out. I've even picked up a new hobby. Who knew?" she giggled again and yawned as Vanessa played with the succubus' hair.

"I'm happy for you two, and I hope for the best," the young witch whispered.

Lyx nodded again and was so tired she only hummed out a reply. "Mhmmm." Soon after, the demoness was fast asleep again.

Closing her book, Vanessa looked at the object and then the nightstand that was just a hair out of reach. *Double-dip a candlestick.* She really didn't' want to wake up Lyx just to put the book away and blow out a candle. The idea hit her then. What if she tried to use magic to do it? Just to practice. Putting a book away and blowing out a candle should be a cakewalk.

Right?

She hoped it would be, at least. Last thing that she needed to do was upset a succubus with a bullwhip in reach. Gauging the distance and then making sure not to trouble Lyx, Vanessa thought about her power. Just like she did back in the Headmaster's office, she imagined the power behind a door that was left slightly ajar. She reached in mentally, trying to grasp just a smidgen of that power. All the while her mind thought of a basic levitating spell, but she eliminated all the words and dust powders needed. She only latched onto the feeling that she was familiar with when she would levitate something.

Her hand hovered over the book. It was just a simple spell. *Simple.* The more that she thought the word, the less stressed she felt about performing the magic. She closed her eyes for a moment. Inside she felt her usual power swirl, but she ignored it, probing the deeper parts of her spirit. Pushing past the usual cool river of magic, she searched for the golden light full of warmth and power. She could see it. A door at the end of a long-forgotten hall, the seams of it alight with a yellow glow, and the strangest urge to just open the door wide as it could go hummed through her body. She walked her inner halls and reached out to that hidden room.

"Levitate," she said softly. Mentally she thought, "*Then blow out the candle.*"

It all happened at once. She opened her eyes and saw the book hovering and then a gust of wind swept through the room. Her hair fluttered in the burst of air, the candle flame went out and then the candlestick toppled over on the nightstand, her concentration wavered and the book fell flat on Lyx's face.

The succubus sat straight up and gave a short cry of surprise. Her eyes blinked rapidly as she surveyed the room and then saw the book on the bed where her head had once been and Vanessa cringing as she stared at the demoness.

"Sorry," the witch said softly as her hand reached out to inspect the rather large red mark on part of the succubus's face.

Rubbing her cheek, Lyx asked, "What happened?'

"I ... uh, was practicing magic before bed."

The demoness sucked at her teeth and said, "You know better than to practice while tired."

The Spellweaver bit her lower lip and nodded quickly. "I'm done for the night. I'm sorry, Lyx. I didn't mean to hurt you."

She sighed and shook her head. "It's fine. Let's just go to sleep before you try another spell."

 *Chapter 17:*

The next morning Vanessa rolled over in her bed and sniffed. The scent of sweet, warm, fluffy pancakes swirled around the room. "Mmmm," she groaned dreamily. With her eyes still closed, she reached out and patted Lyx to wake her up. "I think Bobo's cooking," she mumbled half into her pillow. But there were no horns, tangled mass of hair, or wings under her hand, just the puffy mounds of pillows and a bunched up blanket.

She peeled one eye open to inspect the other side of her bed. It was empty. Sitting up, she yawned and rubbed her eyes. "Where'd she go?" she wondered out loud.

Slowly, she climbed out of bed, got dressed, and headed out toward the kitchen. As she rounded the corner, she saw Bobo and Lyx cooking together. Lyx was finishing up the last of the pancakes. A plate mounted high with golden brown delights stared back at the Spellweaver, reminding her of how hungry she was. Bobo tended to the eggs that sizzled in the pan next to the succubus.

"Would you be a dear and wake up Leon?" Lyx asked after taking notice of Vanessa standing behind them.

"He's been slumbering like a cursed princess. Nothing is waking that man," Bobo added.

She stretched and nodded. "Yeah. I suppose I could."

"I was not sleeping like a princess," Leon grumbled from behind Vanessa.

"Ah!" the young witch yelled out in surprise, turned around, and slapped the Summoner across the shoulder. "Warn somebody, would you? Always sneaking up on people."

He blinked, clearly still half asleep, and pet the top of her head. "Mhmmm ... that's nice ..."

She bent her brow in anger. "Are you even listening to me?"

"Where's the coffee?" Leon asked.

"I'd take that as a no, my dear. He's practically sleepwalking," Bobo added.

Turning off her side of the stovetop, Lyx wiped her hands on the bottom half of her apron and sighed. "I'll get it for you. Honestly, you're such a grumpy baby early in the morning."

Bobo plopped a set of dishes and utensils in Vanessa's unexpecting hands and pointed to the table. "Be helpful and set the table, would you?" He paused and eyed her over. "You do know how to do that, right?"

Vanessa scoffed and breezed through the crowded kitchen as she headed for the dining room table. As she walked, she did her best to hide how anxious she was to get back to the Coven and continue to question Dmitri. The only thing she hoped for was that Isolde hadn't convinced him to stay silent. Whatever secrets they were hiding, Isolde was spell-bent on keeping. Even if he was a traitorous snake, he was still Vanessa's best shot at getting clear answers. Something in her nagged her to hurry. Something in her warned that this twisted web of deceit could end them all if she didn't get the answers she needed, and soon.

She turned around and Bobo was there. He let one, giant digit from his hand extend and press against Vanessa's mouth not a second after she drew in breath to speak.

"Before you suggest that we hurry, there is plenty of time for you to rush off to the Coven after we all eat," the ogre informed.

Just then, there was a knock at the door.

"Who on Raen could that be?" Vanessa questioned with a perplexed look twisting her features.

"I hope you don't mind," Lyx began as she rushed for the door, tail flicking erratically behind her. "I know how work has a tendency of getting out of hand, and she called us earlier this morning." She opened the door and any further information or questions dissipated at the sight of Raven quickly stepping in through the threshold.

"A lot better than I imagined it would be," Raven stated, eyeing over the apartment with a quick sweep of her black-as-night eyes. "Clean like your father and organized like your mother," she said to herself and nodded in approval.

"It's clean and organized thanks to me," Bobo mumbled to himself.

"Raven!" Vanessa shouted with glee.

The Dark Elf turned sharply and ticked her finger from side to side. "What did I say ...?"

For a moment, Vanessa was lost until she remembered their conversation from the night before. She flushed a bit and said, "Auntie Raven."

The white-haired female shook with joy and flew open her arms. "Come to auntie, little shadow!"

Happy to oblige the Dark Elf, Vanessa ran into the woman's embrace with a bright smile and squeezed her hard. "I didn't expect to see you until much later today," she said, her words muffled as her mouth was pressed into the folds of the female's crimson cloak.

"I didn't expect to either, little shadow. However, I received a message from Rakka recently and need to go to the borders of the Black Forest to check on a few things. I fear I won't be back for a few days, and I wanted to see you again before I left. Plus, Lyx informed me that you were skipping out on taking a rest from work and had to finish up a mission scroll later on today."

Vanessa visibly cringed. "Oh. Yeah." She looked off to the side and avoided the stern, concerned look from her aunt. "Do you plan on training me in hand-to-hand combat when you get back?" she reminded, attempting to change the subject.

Thankfully, Raven let her.

"Of course, I am. Who else could I confidently leave you with and trust them to teach you?" she asked.

"I could—" Leon started.

"No," Raven replied before he could say more.

Leon's mouth unhinged before slamming shut with a disgruntled look settling in on his visage. Lyx choked back laughter while Bobo came into the room with a hot pan in hand.

"Come now. Fuss later, everyone. Let's not let breakfast get cold," the ogre gently ordered.

"And I got you coffee," Lyx coaxed to her master as she put his mug down at the table.

The Summoner needed no further spurring and headed for the drink and plopped down in the chair it had been placed in front of. Bobo and Lyx fussed with the ritual of getting everyone's plates ready while Vanessa and Raven sat down next to each other.

"I heard about your fight with Sylas," Raven said, finally.

Vanessa stared at the food piled on her plate as she tried to think of something to say. But she kept drawing up blanks. Her mind propelled her back to yesterday in the Headmaster's office. She could feel his hands sliding up her legs. She could remember the way he looked at her. She visibly shivered and swallowed hard. "Yeah. I was careless. I should have kept my staff on me, or prepared a spell to counter possible charming magic. I just ... I never thought."

Raven's hand reached over and rested on hers atop the table. "It's not your fault. You learned from it. It was a painful lesson, and one that you were lucky enough to live through." She squeezed the Spellweaver's hand with a light smile. "Anything else worth talking about?"

"Well, everything else is classified to Coven members," Vanessa admitted.

Leon choked on a bit of his eggs. "She's following rules," he wheezed.

Bobo calmly handed the man a cloth napkin and used his own to dramatically dab below his eye. "They grow up so fast."

"Be nice, you two," Lyx hissed with a heated look to the teasing duo.

Shaking her head, Raven laughed and waved off the rest of the group while Vanessa thought about stabbing Leon with her fork. However, she didn't want her breakfast tainted with the taste of blood and huffed as she aggressively stabbed at the meal on her plate. "Oh!" she cried out, remembering that the hag stone had fallen out of the grimoire a few nights ago.

All eyes rested on the young witch as she shoveled forkfuls of eggs and meat into her mouth before jumping up from her seat and jogging to her room. After rummaging about her nightstand, she ran back with the hag stone. Rushing to her seat, she placed the object on the table and said, "That fell out of the family tree page in my grimoire."

Hag stones were incredibly hard to come by, and, unless you went into specific magical training, its purposes were not widely taught in local academies. Vanessa was hoping that Raven would be able to explain it in depth without her needing to make a trip to their local library to dig up information. By the expression the Dark Elf wore, the Spellweaver was left to assume that she knew something about the item.

Raven reached out and let her fingers gently caress the edge of the stone. A smile that was wrapped up in faded memories that were far from Vanessa's dining room claimed the woman's mind. Her lips faintly curved as she was lost in thought. *"Simma vall l'ae,"* she whispered. "It has been so long since I've laid eyes upon it." She curled her digits around the item and drew it closer to her as she lovingly inspected it.

"Auntie?" Vanessa gently pressed.

As if she had a spell broken, Raven snapped out of it and looked around to everyone intently watching her. *"Evantis."* Placing the stone back onto the table, she sighed and leaned back in her chair. "That stone is old. Very old. Your grandmother found it when she was younger than you. Gave it to your mother long before she left the city. At the time I last saw it, your mother was preparing the grimoire for you." She stopped and shook her head. Pain settled into the fine lines of the elf's face as she recalled memories that Vanessa would never understand. "Sometimes, I wish she would have kept it on her," she admitted quietly. After a long moment of silence, Raven drew in a deep breath and let it out quickly before she tapped a finger over the surface of the stone. "They are nature's blessing to us," she stated. "Able to ward off curses, see into the spirit realm, and can even aid in healing many ailments, a hag stone is about as precious to an owner as your amulets are to a Coven member, little shadow. Keep it close. Keep it safe."

Scooping the hag stone up into her hands, Vanessa cradled it and placed it in one of her spelled pouches until she could get a proper necklace to put it on. "I will," she assured.

The tension had grown in the room, and Lyx broke it with, "Who wants another cup of coffee?" Several hands rose in the air, and the succubus looked to the pot with a slight pout. "I'm going to need to make a lot more," she admitted with a laugh.

Everyone joined in the joyous sound and the rest of breakfast was full of chats about Vanessa's youth from Raven's perspective while others told the Dark Elf various adventures that the young witch had in the city.

Raven threw her head back and laughed while saying, "You got your love of trouble from your father!"

Even though her face was bright red, Vanessa couldn't help but giggle along with everyone else.

 *Chapter 18:*

With their bellies full and minds lighter, they all stood outside Vanessa's apartment complex exchanging hugs. "Remember, I'll only be gone a few days. When I come back, expect to get a workout," Raven warned.

Laughing, Vanessa nodded. "I look forward to it. Crystal ball call if you need anything. Oh, and do you want something from my apartment?" Without waiting for a reply, the Spellweaver snagged her teleportation pouch and shoved it at Raven. "I promise, I'll replace my pouch and pick up more reagents on my way to the Coven. But I want you to take this. My home is your home."

Raven didn't grab the bag. She dove in and gave the young witch another big hug. "Thank you," she said softly, and then drew back before taking the bag. "You stay out of trouble."

"You ask too much of her," Bobo muttered.

Raven smirked and winked at the ogre and Leon. "I know she has good company to help her with the task."

"Somebody has to keep her in line," Leon announced with a toothy grin.

"Don't worry, we'll keep her in one piece until you get back," Lyx assured.

"I'm counting on it. Be blessed, little shadow. I shall see you all again soon." With that, Raven waved them all goodbye and headed into the Vemeese district on her way to the Black Forest.

"I say, I rather like her," Bobo admitted.

Lyx was watching the Dark Elf fade from sight as she agreed. "Mhmmm. Makes everything feel more like home."

Home.

Vanessa beamed at the thought. "Maybe I should look into getting a bigger apartment. Or, I don't know … buying a house," she stated out loud. Her eyes were transfixed on watching Raven's red cape sway in the wind as she dissipated from sight. Too focused on their target, she missed countless looks from various people present. One was from Leon who shoved a hand in his pouch and stared at the contents with a long-lost look in his eyes. Another was from Bobo, who knew that his master was contemplating on having her aunt live with them. And the last was from Lyx, who eyed the Spellweaver over with an understanding glinting in her amber hues.

"I demand larger quarters with a private bathroom," Bobo claimed with a grin.

Vanessa tore her gaze from her aunt's distant image with a giggle. "You've got it!"

Coven headquarters was swamped more than usual that morning. The congested halls and main rooms gave Vanessa an uneasy feeling in the pit of her stomach. She frowned hard and furrowed her brow as she scanned the multiple groupings of Coven members huddled together while speaking in hushed tones to each other.

"I've a bad feeling," she admitted finally.

"That makes two of us," Bobo muttered at her side.

Leon paused a step behind the two and pulled out his crystal ball. The ringing had almost gone unnoticed due to the drone chatter that blanketed the lobby. "Hello?"

On the other end of the orb was Mrs. Willow, and her stern glare penetrated through the glass at Leon. "Come straight to the summoning grounds and bypass the urge to gossip, Zvěrokruh."

"Ma'am?" he blinked at the orb feeling lost.

Flipping her long, silver braid over her shoulder, she sniffed and looked down at a sundial on her wrist. "Sixty seconds," she stated and then the image winked out.

"Well, looks like we have to part ways here," Lyx said.

"Banish a banshee," Leon hissed, pocketing the orb. "I've gotta run. Literally." He rushed forward and pecked Vanessa on the lips and quickly turned to head off for the summoning grounds. "Let me know how it goes," he called out to her as he and Lyx rushed off down the hall.

The young witch stood in the middle of the lobby as she tried to hide the rising heat that was eating at her cheeks. Leon had just kissed her in front of countless Coven members. Instantly, she assumed all whispers were targeting her and the moment that transpired between her and Leon. She felt like her heartbeat was trying to carry her away to lands far off and unexplored.

"My, my. Aren't you a scandalous witch?" Bobo teased.

It only caused the color in her face to brighten even further. "You're a wicked pet, you know that, right?" she whispered heatedly.

"Oh, I've been coming to terms with it slowly, my dear," he admitted with a smirk.

She shook her head. "Oh, hex it all. Come on," she hissed. "I want to talk to Dmitri and file my report."

"Lead the way."

Silently, they shimmied through the crowds and headed up the spiral staircase to the second floor. Once on the second floor, they went to the end of the hall only to be halted halfway there.

"No one is permitted beyond this point until further notice," the guard warned.

Plucking at the edge of her phoenix seal, Vanessa started to say, "I'm Spellweaver—"

Quickly, the guard cut her short. "It's not a matter of ranking, ma'am. We had a security breach. One missing, one dead, and four injured."

Vanessa's mouth unhinged, and she felt the color drain from her face. "But ... I ..." Her words escaped her for a moment before her expression hardened. "Who?"

"I'm sorry, I'm not at liberty to say," the guard replied stiffly.

"I'm on a mission to discover who could have been responsible for the demon summoning under the academy. Dimitri was my closest shot to getting any answers. I demand to know who was killed," she shot out with authority.

"My, my. She does have a backbone," Bobo muttered under his breath.

The guard looked like he was torn on how to respond. "I-I-I ..." he stammered with zero grace.

"Who?" she barked.

"Dmitri, ma'am. The coroner said that he was sliced with a piece of the broken mirror and bled dry," he sputtered out quickly.

Vanessa's eyes narrowed. "Did Isolde escape?"

The guard nodded reluctantly.

"Double-dip a candlestick!" she screamed.

It all made sense now. Why the Coven was such a mess. Why there were so many members chattering away. Why Mrs. Willow took the measure of reminding her pupils that summoning training was to continue despite the new wave of drama. The unthinkable had happened. All of the sudden, the impenetrable Coven didn't feel so impenetrable anymore. And that sparked a whole new wave of fear and doubt in the young witch.

Bobo waved the guard away and guided Vanessa over toward the top of the stairs. Once there, the young witch spoke in a hushed, peppery tone. "I knew it. I knew something was going to happen. Everything in me was pushing to get the answers out of him. If I could have gotten there sooner," she snapped.

"If you would have gotten there sooner it wouldn't have changed a thing," Bobo stated.

The glare Vanessa shot him was full of venom and daggers. "I could have found out a hex of a lot more than I did," she retorted.

"From what you told me about how he was acting and how Isolde had shaken him, I doubt it."

She puffed out her cheeks, held her breath, and let it out loudly. "Ugh ... You're right ... I just—" She sighed hard and closed her eyes. "I was *so* close."

"That is why Isolde killed him, because you *were* close. But now that she has flown the coop, so to speak, that leaves a much larger, glaring issue."

Rubbing her temples, the Spellweaver dared to ask, "And what would that be?"

"Who is helping Isolde? There had to be some powerful magic behind her getting out," Bobo informed.

Hope ignited in her once more, and she beamed as she shot out, "The Great Orb would have picked up on the location of the spellcaster and where it was focused."

"The focus point was here at the Coven when they helped Isolde escaped."

"And the other is where we will find the culprit behind the breakout!"

"I suggest you file your report and ask for access to the recent black magic spells that have pinged on the Great Orb."

"Right."

Both of them rushed back down to the main lobby to file the report and then headed straight over to the Great Orb room. To say the place was packed was an understatement. Witches and wizards were darting about while countless others collected ping locations and sent them to the appropriate dispatch receptionist.

"Bless. My. Spell," Vanessa gasped.

Bobo was wide-eyed as he looked about, but he managed to say, "What in the name of magic is going on here?"

"A pure meltdown, that's what." The voice came from beside them. Turning to inspect the owner of it, they saw a tall—really tall—woman with auburn hair and deep, coffee-brown eyes. Her short hair tickled the sides of her chin as her eyes scanned over the room with purpose.

"Is that so, miss …" Bobo trailed off for the woman to finish the thought.

She waved lazily at them as if shooing away something in the air. "Miss nothing. The name is Colleen."

"Are you the overseer, Colleen?" Vanessa asked, slightly hopeful.

"I am the head overseer, yes," she affirmed.

Bobo motioned to the room. "What is going on?"

"Well, for starters, the Great Orb blacking out almost a week ago caused a lot of issues. Took us a bit to get it up and running again. After the Blood Moon Festival, and word of the Great Orb shutting down, black magic spells seem to be popping off left and right in Tolvade." She paused and turned to face the two at her side. "And that isn't even including the feral demons that are lighting up the orb like an altar on a ritual night."

Everyone slowly turned their attention back to the orb. Vanessa watched countless balls of light carrying missions bob down to each respective room. The low hum of magic radiating off the Great Orb was accompanied by hundreds of hushed murmurs as crystal ball calls were placed and mission orders given.

"Is there a chance that you could locate a spell that went off sometime last night?" Vanessa asked, but hope in her was already sinking.

Colleen sighed. "If you're referring to the spell that would have been linked to Isolde's breakout from the oubliette, our hands are bound. Seems that whoever she is linked to is not only powerful but has deflectors in place. Powerful ones at that. Meaning that the chances of tracing the spell to the caster is—"

"Slim to none," Vanessa finished for the overseer.

"Right," Colleen agreed.

Bobo looked to his master with concern. The Spellweaver simply gave him a look, lightly shook her head, and motioned with a pointed look to the exit. "Thank you for your help, Colleen," the witch said trying not to sound too disheartened.

The overseer gave a nod and then turned her attention back to her job, leaving Bobo and Vanessa to see themselves out.

 *Chapter 19:*

Back down in the main lobby, Vanessa leaned against the wall next to the communal crystal balls. She had been resting there for some time, lost in her thoughts before she spoke up. "This whole thing just gets more complex," Vanessa grumbled to herself. "I feel like every time I have it a little figured out, we are back at square one with a new piece to the puzzle."

"Indeed," Bobo said while flipping a page in his book.

"Can you help me figure this out rather than reading?" she snapped in a half-whine.

"What if my reading was my way of helping you figure it out?"

Vanessa gave the ogre a deadpan stare.

The gentleman-beast smiled, bookmarked his place, and put the tome away. "I was merely passing the time while you collected your thoughts."

"But I can't," she admitted.

"You did the best you could, Vanessa. It isn't like another lead is going to land in your lap, so … do what you do best."

"And what is that?" she asked, pouting.

"Meddle, my dear. Meddle and stir up trouble like you've never done before."

Vanessa laughed then. Leaning onto Bobo, she sighed again and nuzzled up against the ogre's side. Slowly, he put a massive arm around her shoulder. "You'll figure it out. You always do."

"Thanks, Bobo. Sorry for being so grumpy today."

He gave a light squeeze to her. "We all have our moments. Some more than others." He stopped to give her a pointed look. The Spellweaver punched him lightly in the side and giggled. "But you were frustrated just like anyone else would have been over the situation."

She nodded and sighed.

Across the lobby, near the entrance, there was a ruckus on the rise, and Vanessa could hear it all the way over on her side of the room. "What in the name of magic is going on now?" she muttered.

"I would say that it's none of our business, but, knowing you, it won't remain that way," Bobo sighed.

"Your fault."

"I beg your pardon?"

She gave a toothy grin and said, "You told me to meddle and stir up trouble."

He groaned. "I have made a grave mistake. May the goddess forgive me."

The young witch giggled and practically skipped off in the direction of the commotion. The ogre watched and gave a corner smile as he mumbled under his breath, "And all on Raen was as it should be."

As they neared, they could make out more of what was going on. A cloaked being that was about a head shorter than Vanessa stood near the entrance and swatted away the hands of a male Coven member that tried to guide him out the way he had come in. It was brief, but Vanessa saw a fluffy tail swish under the hem of the mantle belonging to the loud, distraught being.

Only one creature in Aeristria had a tail like that. It had to be an azbanonite. They were sentient beings that were bipedal and held similar traits of various animals across Raen. Traditionally, the beings preferred to live along the borders of Tolvade because they very much enjoyed nature and having easy access to wide-open spaces with less technology and buildings. Vanessa couldn't be sure which clan this particular one came from until she got a closer look.

"I will not be swept out the front doors like yesterday's trash. I demand to speak with someone a higher rank than …" the being paused and a black, clawed paw reached out, the tip of the dagger-sharp nail plucking at the edge of the Coven member's bronze emblem. "*Hunter* status," the being hissed as he said the ranking.

"We can just as easily help you," another female Hunter explained.

"I said I need someone of higher status!" the being yelped out and held its head. "It's no use, I'm going to die," he whispered. The hopeless phrase was followed by a series of short, high-pitched chitters.

"What about Spellweaver status, is that high enough for you?" Vanessa asked from behind them.

The creature spun on heel, and glowing yellow eyes revered her from under his hooded cloak. It was quite clear what clan this azbanonite hailed from. The Sleekit clan. It was evident by the reddish fur covering its body, the snowy underbelly, and the black-socked feet and hands. A skinny, canine snout protruded from under the fabric and was tipped with a wet, coal-colored nose. Fangs, sharp and tiny, were present in the azbanonite's maw, and they were glistening in the lighting as the being picked at something between his teeth. The tail was now more visible. Fiery fur tipped with a dollop of white and wrapped possessively around the being's lower half, it was almost as long as the creature was tall. Puffy, loose, khaki-colored pants covered up the creature's legs and waist but his feet remained bare. Along his hip was a bright cobalt sash that held in place an assortment of weapon's belts. An open, unstrung, hunter green vest covered (somewhat) the being's upper body. An assortment of jeweled beaded necklaces hung around the being's neck, and they sparkled like enchantments and clattered about as he leaned forward.

The Sleekit sniffed about as if trying to decipher her sent before it spoke again. After a moment, the azbanonite straightened up and looked down his short, pointed muzzle at her. "Depends, are you a Spellweaver?"

Confidently, she pointed to her silver insignia. She then eyed each of the members trying to help and gave a silent nod and pointed with her chin to another portion of Coven.

"Thanks, Vanessa," the male said in passing.

The female member pat her on the shoulder and explained, "We'll let the higher-ups know that you're handling a walk-in."

"Thanks guys," she said with a smile and waited for them to be out of earshot before she turned her attention back to the azbanonite.

But it was Bobo that that broke her view of him as he outstretched his arm protectively and took a step in front on her. She was about to ask what was wrong, however, she noticed his nostrils flaring and his ocean-blue eyes were locked onto the Sleekit in a suspicious manner. "Explain yourself or meet your end here," Bobo warned through gritted teeth.

The azbanonite took a step back, shifted his eyes to the other inhabitants of the building and spoke in a hoarse tone. "You got me. Red-handed, okay? But mind if we move the conversation to somewhere a bit more private, huh, boss?"

Vanessa looked around the room, and already a few passersby had taken slight interest on what was happening between them. Gently, she reached out and placed a hand on the ogre's arm and whispered, "He's right. Let's not do this out in the open."

Relenting his gaze long enough to survey their surroundings, he loosened up after a second and pointed to one of the corridors branching off of the main lobby. "The interrogation hall," the demon ordered.

"Fair enough, big guy," the Sleekit muttered.

"Bobo?" Vanessa pressed.

"Not now." His eyes scanned over the room aggressively. "Not here," he said just loud enough for only her to hear.

She trusted him and gave a quick nod before starting to take a step to lead the way. However, Bobo's arm shot out again and, sweeping elegantly behind him, he put her at the rear of the grouping. There were no words. There didn't need to be. Whoever this cloaked figure was, he couldn't be trusted. So much so that Bobo lost his charm for a moment. He had hunched forward and the clasp on his battleax holster was already unsnapped. He was ready to strike and all he had done was looked at and smelled the creature. What did Bobo know that she didn't? Regardless of who this being was, there was no way Bobo was about to let him get close enough to Vanessa to cause harm. In the ogre's mind, the safest place in all of Raen was behind him.

They marched with purpose toward the interrogation hall and quickly found a vacant room. Bobo swung the door open and stepped off to the side. "You first, lad," he practically growled to the Sleekit.

"Testy," the azbanonite stated with a quick sniff. "Think your iron's low, you sound a little grumpy."

There was a low, guttural growl that emitted from the demon as he towered over the much smaller being. Instantly, the creature's fur puffed out, and he raised his hands palm up to show he didn't want the trouble (or pain) that Bobo was sure to inflict if he felt the need to.

"Was only a joke. I'll have to mark you down as the serious type." With that said, the azbanonite slunk into the room like a zipping snake disappearing into tall grass. Only the chitters of the nervous being echoed back out into the hall.

Vanessa tugged on Bobo's jacket and gave him questioning eyes. He responded with, "Keep your distance and have your spell pouches loose. I don't trust this mongrel past the hair on his face."

"All right. You've got it," she replied, and then the two of them entered the private room and shut the door.

 *Chapter 20:*

The walls inside the room were washed in pale, cool, gray paint that bordered along blue, and the floors were the same marble floorings that extended throughout the Coven's ground level floor. In the middle of the room were a few outdated metal chairs and a plain, tall, rectangle table. Just standing inside the room made Vanessa feel like she was the one about to be interrogated. She tried to hide the shiver as the cooler air and lifeless atmosphere rushed over her.

Once the door had shut, the being had lowered his hood. Under the intense lighting and without the shadowed depths of the cowl tucking away the being's features, she could now see that the eyes were not the yellow she had originally seen, but a deep, warm golden shade.

"Talk," Bobo ordered.

"How about we ask his name first?" Vanessa asked.

The being chuckled. "Ah, goddess help me. You two are the worst at this. The classic good Coven member versus bad Coven member? Ah, I didn't think ya'll still had this in the playbooks anymore!"

Both of them stared down the cackling being with flames lapping at their irises until the Sleekit's laughter ebbed. "Oops. Guessed that wrong," he quietly declared before clearing his throat and gulping audibly.

"Very well then, I agree with the lady. I do not wish to lower myself to referring you to as simply your clan's name. So, what is it?" Bobo urged.

"Malachi."

"And what are you doing here?" Bobo steamrolled on to the next question.

Malachi sighed and ran his claws through his hair and scratched at his chin. "Look, big guy—"

"Botobolbilian," the ogre corrected.

"Ookaay, Botobol—man, did your parents hate you or somethin'? I mean, that is one heck of a mouthful. How about I call you Bo—"

"You will call him Botobolbilian and knock off the idle chatter, or you'll find my wand where you would least like it," Vanessa snapped.

"Whoa. Full of fire and brimstone, are you?" Malachi said with a grin that was almost sinister. Almost. However, the twinkle of mischief in his eyes was far greater than any glimmer of evil residing in his smile.

Vanessa pushed Bobo off to the side and leaned on the table. Her voice dropped to a pitch that gave a cold, uncaring air around the Spellweaver. A threatening promise clung to her eyes as her words wrapped around Malachi, holding the being captive as each syllable made alarm bells sing inside the being's mind. "I'm about to find out exactly what you are made up of."

The Sleekit's eyes grew wide, and he blinked, trying to hide that the action had ever taken place. Recomposed, Malachi sank back lounging in his chair. "You're a lot colder than I had anticipated, Vanessa," he said with a smirk.

"I've been through a lot, lately," she snapped back.

Like the words were an incantation, her mind flipped through images. Each one was a memory that broke her heart and remade her from the inside out.

A hellhound lunging hungrily at her, held a breadth away. There was barely an inch between life, death, her, and its jaws.

Countless magically-mangled ogres reaching out for help.

Bobo on his knees. His words, "You summoned me!" echoing loudly inside her brain.

Spells flinging as she crawled across the floor to Bobo's motionless body.

Leon's face looming over her cold-as-stone morphing features as she felt herself slipping away to the Gargoyleism.

Seeing swirling shadows and darkness all around her as the spectrals tried to claim her body for their own.

Giant wolves surrounding them, the hope of any escape seeming like a dying flame.

A knife.

Eyes consumed with pain.

Blood covered hands.

A single word whispered, and it carried away the innocence that she had kept for so long.

"One."

Sylas running his hands up her thighs right before being bound to a chair by thorny vines.

The panic. The fear. It soaked the memories like a single moment hadn't passed since they had taken place. She managed to not flinch or give any indication of the struggles that she battled under the surface as she leveled with the being and refused to relent her hold of his gaze. It must have been there. Somewhere on the surface, no matter how much she tried to deny the emotions, there were slivers of them swimming in the brightness of her hazel hues.

Malachi looked off to the side and sighed as if he had been defeated. "I haven't helped in that department," he murmured.

"What did you say?" she asked as she narrowed her eyes to mere slits at the being.

Another sigh. Nervously, he scratched at the snowy patch on his chest. "I know I've contributed to some of your recent struggles," he admitted.

"What do you mean?" There was venom lacing her words, and Bobo put a hand on her to ensure the young witch wouldn't dive across the table and strangle the answer out of the Sleekit.

Too many secrets. Too many lies. The web she was caught in the middle of was wrapping her up and suffocating her. Her heartbeat thumped against her chest like a feral demon hammering away at an open hell gate.

"You were the being that was spying on us the night we were at the Flustered Dragon. Why?" Bobo broke the ice with the first question that shed some light on the subject. It opened up the Spellweaver's eyes to why he was so reluctant to let her follow behind the azbanonite earlier.

"You?" Though it was a question, there was too much heat in the singular word for it to come across as such. Instead, it came out angry and dripping with the desire to magically bind him and throw him into the oubliette!

The azbanonite picked up on this and closed his eyes, reserving himself to a verbal backlash that was justly earned. However, Vanessa bit her tongue. An act seldom performed by the young witch. Instead, she waited for the being to finish.

Malachi peered out of one golden eye and scanned the room. Gauging the reactions and expressions, he let go of a breath he had knowingly held. "And my head is still intact. Full of surprises, you two."

"I can fix that for you if you are disappointed," Bobo stated in a flat tone.

The Sleekit cleared his throat and tapped his claws wildly on the table. "We're getting off topic."

"Mhmm," Vanessa hummed in agreement.

"Look, you two don't know what you are in the middle of," Malachi whispered and scanned the room, sniffing at the air.

"I know a lot more than you think I do," Vanessa corrected.

The twitchy azbanonite shifted in his seat and asked, "Are there any scrying mirrors? This conversation should be ... well, let's just say the less that know the better your chances of living are."

Bobo shook his head *no*.

Instantly, tension in the being's shoulders melted, and he sighed again. "By the goddess," he whispered to himself as he patted his chest over his heart. He noted the two beings staring him down as they waited for information. Straightening up in the seat, Malachi licked at his snout and nodded a bit. "Right. Information." As he rubbed his sweaty paws on the fabric of his pants, he started to explain everything to them. "This thing is deep. It is so deep that after a bit of digging, I knew I was in trouble. Big time." He licked at his snout again and flicked one of his furry ears.

"Yeah. Two High Priest Council members betrayed us, and I recently found out that the Headmaster of Runerite was in on it too," Vanessa added.

Malachi laughed and stood up from the chair. Walking around the table, he sniffed about her and gave a series of short yips. "You think that he is the big bad to all this?"

She went from looking confident to confused. "What do you know that I don't?"

"Depends on how far down the rabbit hole you want to go there, princess."

"All the way."

He drew in a long breath and looked about the room. "The Council members were pawns," he explained.

Bobo looked bewildered. "They are highly respected members of Aeristria. How are they—"

Malachi showed no fear as he raced over and stood toe to toe with the ogre. His hoarse voice clipped out the words like they were the lines to a trusted battle spell. "They have been orchestrating this for years. Years!" His golden eyes flicked between the two. "The blood mages, the recent feral demon summonings, the pinpointed hell gates that have slowly been reopened all across Aeristria, and even the betrayal of the blue cloaks. It's all connected so deeply and intricately that it's hard to see where one stops and the other begins. It has all been meticulously planned from the start. They had nothing but time to figure it all out. They had time to manipulate every being they got their hands on. They had nothing but time to find answers to slowly arising questions. And time was sucking out the magic from your beloved Coven that Tolvade depends on so much."

"What are you saying?" Vanessa asked.

"I'm saying that the Coven isn't safe anymore, princess. There aren't a lot of places that are, I'm afraid. If you want me to sing, I want you to protect me."

"Protect you? From what?" Bobo inquired.

"The people that hired me to follow you that night," Malachi informed.

"Who are they?" Vanessa pressed.

"Your word and a safer place to talk than here. I have said what I intended to. Either you believe me and give me your binding promise, or let me leave. Though, I doubt I'll live much longer without your aid."

The time stretched on as Vanessa thought about it. She was either walking right into a trap or she was just given another lead to her previous mission. Either way, only time would tell.

"You have a deal," she said finally.

"Vanessa, you can't be serious!" Bobo cried out.

"I don't have a choice, Bobo," she said while searching her spell pouches for the needed materials to perform a binding promise spell. She didn't really like that she was about to be bound by two magical promises that could bring harm or death to her, but she needed answers. All of Raen was depending on them.

The azbanonite let his jaw unhinge as he furrowed his brow. "She gets to call you—"

"If you even attempt to say the nickname she has so cruelly placed upon me, make peace with it being your last spoken word for I will gladly have your tongue as payment for it ... *sir*," the demon warned.

The Sleekit threw his hands up in the air and turned to walk back around the desk. There suddenly was a strong desire to have both distance and furniture between him and the towering ogre all of the sudden.

With the being now distanced from them, Bobo turned his attention back to his master as she laid out various ingredients on the table. He shook his head as he took into account that they were, indeed, all needed for a promise binding spell. Specifically, a Bound by My Word spell.

"Are you really going through with this?" he asked in a hoarse whisper that was full of displeasure.

"Yes. He is my only lead right now!" she snapped back in the same tone.

"I'm saying, do you want to put your faith in a being like that? You don't know if he'll stab you in the back, swipe your coin purse, or finish the job he started the night we met him in the Flustered Dragon," Bobo shot back in a hissing whisper.

"Well, I guess we are going to find out because I'm not letting him walk out of here without some answers."

"You're a daft fool and a lover of risks," he blurted out.

"Oh, and, Bobo, I thought you said another lead wouldn't fall into my lap?"

"Logic cannot predict dumb luck, my dear."

"Maybe that dumb luck is going to save my ... what was it? Suicidal hide?"

"It wouldn't be the first time it did, my dear."

"And I have you for all the others."

He couldn't help it. The gentleman-beast cracked a smile and shook his head. "Get on with it, then. There is no persuading you once you've made up your mind."

Malachi motioned between the two with a mock look of concern scrolled over his furry face. "You two done?"

"Get over here before I change my mind," Vanessa groaned.

Without needing further instruction, the azbanonite rounded the table and stood toe to toe with the Spellweaver. She grabbed a small needle and pricked the tip of her finger. She did the same to Malachi's paw who, surprisingly, made no fuss over the ritual or the needle. He didn't seem to mind the sharp object. In fact, with each ingredient that was added, he seemed to lose tension and became slightly more relaxed. Pressing a drop of blood each into a travel-sized mortar and pestle, Vanessa began to blend together a few pungent leaves and a couple flower petals. But it was the thorns and snake scales that scraped over the stone that made Bobo grimace with worry.

After mixing, the young witch poured the contents into her hand and then held it out, palm up, for Malachi to take a hold of. There wasn't a second of hesitation from the being. As soon as she presented her hand, the Sleekit slapped his black, rubbery paw over her appendage and locked his eyes with her own.

There was a moment of silence as they searched each other. Vanessa sucked in a slow breath and sprinkled gold dust over their hold of one another, the incantation following soon after.

"Weights are now tied to the words that we've spoken, light as feathers they'll be to the souls they are bound, though they'll be heavy as stone if ever broken, and will drag the being to the realm underground, I claim that my words are just and true, and now I ask it to be bound to me and you."

They both felt it. Even her pet felt a portion of it, for the spell was as deep as the elven oath and the being was tethered to her soul. In some ways, they were two separate beings, her and Bobo. In others, they were tied by the soul and shared each other's pain and joy. It was a silent reminder, at that moment, as the magic took its hold, that not all spells were blessings and not all magic made life easier.

Tightness in her chest revisited. Though, this time, it felt like something was constricting her heart. The two magically binding promises squeezed her rapidly beating heart. Every *thump, da-thump, da-thump* were twisted in old magic and new magic imbued with the promise of it becoming more than a spell. Promising to turn into a curse should she fail. She winced in pain and held her chest. It felt like it was on fire and thorns from the elven magic threatened to poke a hole clean through the panicked muscle.

"Aah!" she tried not to yell, but it came regardless of how hard she tried to hold it back. The burning sensation grew in intensity as it slowly spread out through her body. It traveled through her veins like lava and seared a path over the twisting vines of the other spell. It blanketed the thorny magic until you couldn't tell where one ended and the other began.

Malachi looked bewildered. Not just because of Vanessa, but because Bobo had dropped to one knee clutching his chest as well. Was it all in her head? Was sound dissipating from this realm? Was … was her heartbeat slowing down?

Thud-dump

Thud-dump

… Thud—dump

The world started to turn hazy. A deep void threatening to envelop her vision seeped into the corners of her view. She blinked and tried to suck in a lungful of air. The ringing in her ears was almost deafening, making it hard to hear anything else aside from it. Malachi was speaking, but she couldn't make out the words. She could feel him trying to let go of her hand, but she clamped down on it with a vengeance.

She could make out the tail-end of his frantic blathering. "... this up you're going to get yourself killed!"

"I'm ... stronger ... than ... that," she proclaimed torpidly. There was a pulse of magic from deep within, and she felt the darkness ebb. Her vision brightened, and she could see the finer details that had been blurred before.

She reached for that power. The way she had grown used to calling to it. She searched for the door, the one that was down at the end of the metaphysical hall and glowing at the seams with glittering, gold light. Mentally, she envisioned reaching out for the door handle and swung it open.

"Let it be so!" she yelled out, her voice cracking at the end. But it didn't matter how warbled her voice sounded. The spell was completed. Quickly, she let go of Malachi's hand. Throwing herself back against the wall, Vanessa rested there with her eyes closed as she tried to even out her breathing.

The tightness in her chest swiftly died off, but the pain remained a moment after like a haunting reminder that it was there. That it was waiting. The soreness around her heart sung a quiet song of warning, reminding her that if she failed the Allatari and elven people or Malachi, the debt that was to be paid for it would be collected.

A promise was a promise, after all.

Chapter 21:

Even though a few minutes had passed already, the magic was still coating the air of the interrogation room. Thick as honey, it clung around them, making the small room almost insufferable. They would have left if it wasn't for the fact that you weren't exactly allowed to magically bind yourself to a suspect, especially while you were on duty. And most definitely not while in an interrogation room if the suspect had not been given the chance to seek council from a lawyer first. Being Resources and the Council would be all over this like nobody's business.

Vanessa tried to ignore the stack of taboos she had just performed under the Coven roof without batting an eyelash. One of the reasons she did it was obvious. She wanted information, the Sleekit had it. There had to be an exchange of some sort. But the other, the one she didn't want to openly admit, was that he claimed his life was in danger. Stupid as it might be, she believed him. And she had joined the Coven to serve and protect the beings of Tolvade. *No!* The beings of Aeristria. She wasn't going to let Malachi walk out of there and be at risk.

However, there was the glaring issue of him being a criminal. Most would turn their backs on him. And, where she could understand most beings that would do that, she also couldn't turn away someone in need. Everyone deserved a second chance, right?

Before her mind could throw at her a million possibilities and scenarios that would rip that theory to shreds, she shook it free from her mind and took in another deep breath. The slowly fading magic that strangled the room made the simple act of breathing a touch more difficult. However, with every passing moment, it became easier to draw in a lungful without feeling like she had a slumbering dragon on top of her chest.

"How are you holding up, Bobo?" she asked breathily.

The ogre grunted at first before saying, "Next time, have your magic ready. You don't go into a spell like that and not have your magic fully open."

"I'm still getting used to *that* magic," she whined with her head tilted back, resting against the wall behind her, and with her eyes closed.

"You're the queen of excuses," he muttered back with a grin.

"You both are insane!" Malachi finally found the perfect moment to shriek out what had been bouncing around in his mind since he felt her magic connect with him. "Two. Not one, but two promise spells?"

"So you could feel it?" she said, eyes still closed.

"Ha. Feel it. She's asking if I felt it. Girl, that spell on you was so strong it jumped out and smacked me right upside my snout! Who, in all of Raen, did you make an oath with that was that strong?"

"The Allatari," she muttered.

"The Ala-who?" Malachi asked, jerking back with a dumbfounded expression.

She sighed and opened her eyes before rising up off the floor. "The leader of the elves. Though, don't tell my aunt that I described him that way. I'll never hear the end of it. But I'm too tired to try and remember and explain it without messing it up," she admitted.

"Well, I'll be a gorgons uncle," the Sleekit announced and plopped his rump down on the interrogation table. "You just keep those surprises comin', don't ya?"

Bobo was on his feet and patting at his chest. "I'm not the young ogre I used to be, Vanessa. Warn a demon next time, won't you?"

She came to his side and lightly hugged him. "I'm sorry, Bobo. I rushed in and didn't prepare my magic properly."

"It's been a long time since you messed up a spell like that. Try to remember that emotions don't just get you killed. They can get everyone around you harmed as well. Try to keep them under control and take a moment to think before you act."

"You got it, big guy," she said as she pulled away.

Turning her attention back to Malachi, she ran a hand over her raven locks as she tried to smooth out any flyaways produced from the recent spell. "You," she stated with a pointed look in the azbanonite's direction. "I held up my end of the bargain, it's time for you to fulfill yours."

"Not one to waste time, I see. I like that." He hopped down from the table and sniffed before pulling up his hood. "Lead the way, princess," he half-teased with a grin, his golden eyes glowing in the shadowy depths of his cowl.

Vanessa didn't know if she should be cautious or mesmerized by the dazzling gaze. She turned away and quietly said, "Stop calling me princess and follow me," as she opened the door to leave.

"Any funny business and you'll find one less head on your shoulders," Bobo muttered to the Sleekit as he came to stand behind the creature.

The azbanonite froze for a moment, his fur standing on end as the fear visibly took hold of him. His eyes, large as moons, quickly shrunk back to their normal size, and the being rolled his shoulders as if unaffected by the threat. "Trust me, buddy, I am the least of your worries."

"We shall see about that," the ogre stated gruffly and poked at Malachi's back with the head of his ax.

A stifled yip was caught in the azbanonite's throat. And, with a disgruntled look behind him, Malachi huffed and headed out the room behind the Spellweaver.

Vanessa had given the hall a quick sweep before she'd rushed out into the corridor. She wanted to ensure that no random Coven members would try to slip in and try to use the interrogation room immediately after they left. Though the more powerful remains of the spell had all dissipated, there was still a tinge of magic floating about the room. She didn't want it to be blatantly obvious that she had performed the spell. Last thing she needed was to be questioned by her peers on her way out. Thankfully for them, the halls were blissfully clear, and walking back to the main lobby was a breeze. The room would be cleared up in a minute or so, and Bobo made sure to close the door behind them as they left so none of the remaining traces of magic would seep out into the hall.

Back in the main lobby, Vanessa shifted her view from one side of the building to the next and motioned for Malachi to keep up. "We are going to head out of here for the day and go straight to my place." Her words were hushed and hurried. After informing him of their plans, she homed in on the archway that marked their exit and quickened her pace.

"Ah, Spellweaver Peterson!" Riker called out.

"Oh goddess," Vanessa squeaked.

She stopped dead in her tracks, and Malachi bumped into her backside, followed by Bobo slamming into the Sleekit soon after. A series of grunts escaped the group, while poor Vanessa was sent flailing toward the ground.

The witch watched as the immaculate floor got closer and screwed her eyes shut, bracing for the pain that was sure to follow. All the while, she attempted to prepare her pride for the embarrassment the fall would bring. But she never connected with the hard surface. Instead, she felt solid arms around her. She blinked and looked at the tiles below. A shiny boot taunted her with the gleam of overhead lighting bouncing off of its glossy, black surface.

Riker cleared his throat. Vanessa looked up to see his perplexed look. She forced a smile and scrambled out of his embrace. "S-sorry," she frantically stuttered.

The man seemed unfazed as he deposited his crystal ball into a satchel at his hip and dusted off his open, night-shaded coat-cloak. Two, shining silver clasps were on either shoulder of the garment, and the mantle flowed down his back and arms like a still, black waterfall. A coal-gray suit with rich, burgundy trimming and hems were decorated in leather straps that held various weapons, dust pouches, and a small collection of vials. A few of his medals were hidden under a panel of his cloak, and a few of the tassels from them danced from side to side as the man shifted his weight and stared down the Spellweaver in front of him.

His lips slightly corked at the corners, but quickly died away as he noted the addition to her company. "Did I catch you at a bad time?"

"No." She tried to sound confident as she made her claim, but the singular word came out a little too shaky for her taste. She swallowed hard and repeated the word with a touch more coolness, "No." And the young witch tilted her chin up proudly like she wasn't guilty of committing crimes behind Coven walls. She suddenly felt sweat beading on her brow.

Was it hot in here?

His grin slid over his lips, and it made her blood run cold. With just a look, Riker could make it seem like he had already figured out every secret you've ever buried and picked apart every lie you've ever told.

"Leaving for the day?" As he asked, his brow lifted over one, cold, silver eye. His voice was void of emotion, and his gaze held an overbearing weight to them.

Already, Vanessa felt like she was in a steaming cauldron. Her heartbeat rose to an unsteady rhythm while her face maintained the façade of complete calm. Or, at least, she hoped that it did. "I've finished my most recent scroll," she admitted.

Riker laughed. The sound jerked her nerves into high alert. "Hahaha! You were always quite the worker. You were supposed to be relaxing," he reminded.

"I fear she doesn't have that word in her vocabulary," Bobo informed.

"I was actually heading on my way out, so—" she stated while pivoting slightly to face the exit. Her eyes alone told Bobo that they were a hair away from big trouble.

"Not so fast, Vanessa." The hardened veteran's voice lacked warmth and spelled Vanessa's heart with an icy touch.

This was it. She was going to be locked away for sure. She felt her spirit sink as she reserved herself to the fate of living out her days in Zaraltrac prison. Blood drained from her face. Her skin was clammy. Her heartbeat tripped up. "Hmmm?" she hummed, trying not to come across as guilty as she felt in that moment. Turning to face him again, she waited for it. She waited for her impending doom to rain down upon her.

A scroll lifted. "Do you have a few minutes? I was actually about to crystal ball call you when I saw you and your pet across the lobby," he admitted. "I'd like to go over the details of our upcoming mission scroll that we've been assigned to."

"Oh," she said, perking up to the news. The best news. The greatest news in all of Raen! "Oh, sure. I don't mind at all." She gave a passing look behind her.

"Is there a problem?" Riker asked, eyeing over the hooded and cloaked figure behind her and Bobo.

"No. Not at all. Bobo can easily escort this being to his destination and meet up with us later," she advised.

Riker nodded. "Very well, then. Mind if we discuss it over lunch?"

"Huh? Oh, I don't mind," she said with a smile. She was a little hungry. Practicing magic always used a lot of her energy. "Let me tie things up with Bobo, and I'll meet you outside."

With a quick nod, the man was marching out of the building and leaving Vanessa to practically melt on the floor as the tension held in every limb of her body died off.

"Is that guy a golem? Man. Gave me the shivers, that one," Malachi grumbled and then trembled slightly.

"You've no idea," Vanessa whispered.

"What are we going to do?" Bobo whispered to her.

She gave a quick glance to the area around them and spoke loud enough for Bobo to hear. "I don't see the big problem. Just take him back to the apartment and come meet back up with me."

Bobo scoffed. "I'm not leaving this riff-raff alone in our humble abode."

"Why not?" she asked.

"Yeah, why not?" Malachi chimed in. His face was suddenly huddled with their own.

Bobo glowered at the being before he turned his attention back to his master. "We may not have much in our home, Vanessa. But I will not be naive and leave a sticky-fingered thief alone there and expect nothing to be swiped in our absence."

The azbanonite's mouth unhinged in mock surprise, and he laid a hand over his heart like he had just heard the most scandalous news in all of Tolvade. "I thought you were the type of ogre that didn't judge."

"Shut it, you," Bobo grumbled.

"I really don't feel comfortable splitting up when I'm stuck with Riker," she heatedly replied.

The gentleman-beast seemed to understand the poor witch's plight and took a moment to think it over. "Hmmm. Yes. However, we cannot trust the Sleekit on his own."

Malachi swished his tail back and forth as he crossed his arms over his chest. "Hairless wretches," he whispered angrily.

"Call Leon on the way over there," she exclaimed as the idea hit her. "He can watch over Malachi while you and I talk to Riker."

The ogre rested his chin under his thumb and the crook of his finger. "Yes. That does seem like a wise choice. It is approaching the hour he'd be taking a break from practicing. Very well, then. I shall escort Malachi and meet up with you ... uh ... I do say, my dear, where are you two going again?"

"The—" She stopped and blinked absentmindedly. "Double-dip a candlestick, I forgot to ask him."

"Ah, I see I've chosen the brightest of the Coven to protect me. My fears are demolished by the wit and intelligence that you two ooze," Malachi snapped teasingly.

Vanessa peered around the looming figure of Bobo to snap back, "He oozes charm and handkerchiefs, thank you very much!" And stormed off through the exit.

The Sleekit blinked confused and then eyed over the ogre inquisitively. "So, uh ... is it a medical condition or ...?"

"Ugh. Why is fate so cruel to me?" Bobo whined and grabbed the azbanonite by the shoulder and forcefully guided him toward the front of the building.

Riker was already outside and eyeing over the streets looking for someone to correct or a practitioner to magically bind for going against code or standard procedure. Did he ever really clock out?

"Riker!" Vanessa called to him and waved him over to the bushes that lined the front of the Coven underneath one of the large, stone sorcerer statues.

With one more suspecting glance to the cobblestone roads, the Summoner rolled his shoulders and waltzed over to Vanessa and the others. "Are we all heading out then?"

"Not yet," she half-laughed. "I forgot to ask where we were going. Tasgall's? The Grim Bean?"

The wizard shook his head slowly. "Merlin's," he informed.

She didn't expect that. Merlin's wasn't expensive, but it definitely felt too formal for two Coven members discussing the details of a mission scroll. "M-Merlin's?" she croaked.

He merely nodded in response.

Turning to face Bobo, she saw nothing at her side and whirled around until she saw his mammoth form, occasionally prodding Malachi in the back with his weapon, in the distance. That ogre moved too fast for something that large!

"Bobo!" she called out to him, a few beings paused to watch the scene unfold.

The demon only waved over his head and yelled back, "I'll meet you at Merlin's, my dear!"

Slowly, she turned and looked to Riker who shot her a warm smile, but held her with eyes that were as cold as winter. Nervously, she gave a quick grin and a short burst of laughter. "Looks like it's just me and you for a while," she said.

She could almost hear Leon in her mind, warning her to keep her yapper shut or she'd be shackled and thrown into an interrogation room before sundown. Riker was not a man to be fooled or played with. He was the best of the best. And, rumors had it that the Summoner had turned down the chance to be a Second Chosen three times. It was often a complaint of a new High Priest. When it came to choosing a trusted being to take the seat when they passed down the position of a blue cloak, Riker wouldn't give the offer a week, a day, or even a second thought before he proudly turned them down and walked away. And she was going to go have lunch with him. Then be stuck with him for however long this mission was going to be.

Leon was right. She was doomed.

Holding back the urge to gulp, she shifted uncomfortably under the wizard's slate-colored eyes.

"I reserved a private area for us, and I've asked them to have a table prepared with a privacy spell," Riker informed and then swept his arm out to the walkway hugging the main road. "Let's hail a carriage, shall we?"

 *Chapter 22:*

The ride was long and awkward. To pass the time, Vanessa repeatedly rubbed her sweaty palms over her robes, and, occasionally, her eyes would wander over to the stoic being sharing the coach with her. He sat across from her with his eyes glued to the world beyond the glass of his window. More than once, he'd glance her way and catch her staring, and she'd grin anxiously before pointing her vision out her side's window and in the direction of the buildings that they passed by. Well, Vanessa was not staring at Riker so much as his many medals that were peeking out from behind his cloak. No one really ever saw them. It was something the man didn't necessarily flaunt. Not like the wizard needed to. His war stories alone were something to marvel at. The Summoner was pushing thirty and had more accomplishments, plaques, medals, and history in the Coven than some of the High Priests.

Why wear them at all if you're not going to let people see them? she thought to herself.

"It's required that Coven members display their medals on their uniform when on duty, protocol says nothing about them needing to be fully visible," Riker announced while looking out his window.

His voice startled her just as much as his words had. Banish a banshee! Could he mind read? She must have looked as panicked as she felt. Slowly, Riker turned to face her and she visibly paled.

"You were trying to look at my medals, right?" he asked in a bland tone.

"I … I mean … yes?" she replied a bit confused. How did he know?

"It wasn't difficult to tell where your eyes were homed in at. Besides, I highly doubt you were swooning over me from afar as I'm twice your age."

She didn't know why, but she felt incredibly embarrassed at that moment, and her whole body began to lightly perspire as warmth licked over her skin. "Oh," she quietly whispered.

"You can't be in the game as long as me and not notice a thing or two about the way beings act. The way someone talks, looks, or moves can betray everything about them. Not many have learned the art of masking their emotions, and those that do? I suggest you fear them or keep your distance from them, for they can fool you faster than anyone else."

"Is this something you picked up from the Coven?"

"It's something I picked up after learning that you can only rely on yourself. Everything else provided to you is either by luck or chance."

Her mind wandered as she let his words sink in. There was an unmistakable hurt beneath his stone-cold visage. It made her curious as to what had made Riker become the way that he was. Spell-bent on law, order, and upholding the truth so much so that he seemed to have morphed into this cold and distant man. A being focused on his work and nothing more.

The carriage stopped just outside the restaurant. The braying of the horses indicated their restlessness and desire to keep moving despite having reached their destination. Vanessa watched Riker exit first, and, once he had reached the pavement below, turned to offer a hand to help her down.

She stood from her seat and thanked him as she exited and waited by the main doors of the establishment while the wizard paid the coach. The unease that she had at the start of this adventure was no longer present. Her curiosity was far stronger than her fear. A commonplace reaction she often displayed in stressful situations. Perhaps that was her blessing, though Bobo would claim otherwise.

Vanessa couldn't help but notice the Summoner's watchful gaze shifting from street corner to street corner. Ready to pounce on the opportunity to shackle any being misusing their magic, improperly wielding a wand, or breaking the law in some way. It made her frown. How was she supposed to feel at ease at all when around him? She sighed heavily, and the wizard took notice.

"Is there something the matter, Vanessa?" he inquired.

She blinked, not sure how to respond. Finally, she started to shake her head *no* but stopped in mid-motion. "Actually, yes. There is."

Oh, goddess help her. She was either about to make the biggest mistake of her life or make the last mistake of her life. She wasn't quite sure just yet, but it surely wasn't going to end well. That was for certain.

The Summoner actually looked surprised at her admitting that there was a problem. Patiently and quietly, he waited for the reason. Hoping her heartbeat wouldn't trip up her words, Vanessa found her inner courage and propped her hands upon her hips as she boldly probed, "Do you ever clock out?"

This time it was Riker's turn to blink, confused. "Daily, Spellweaver Peterson. No one can stay clocked in. It's against Coven policy." He seemed perplexed as to why she even thought that he never was off duty.

She shook her head and knit her brow in frustration. "No. No." She pointed a digit in his face. "You are always looking for your next suspect. You're always on the lookout for the next criminal. Don't you ever just ... I don't know, unwind?"

His face turned deadpan.

She threw her hands up in the air. "I'm stuck with a stiff-neck!"

Something flashed in Riker's eyes. It was quick. Like a bolt of lightning during a midnight storm, waking the slumbering world for a fraction of a second and then returning to the quiet darkness. "I can unwind," he proclaimed.

She turned to eye him over, suspicious of his claim. "Oh? Can you now?"

His chin tilted up, and he looked down his nose at the young witch. "Yes," he stated earnestly, a slight, wintery bite lacing his reply.

She smirked. "Ha! I bet you can't for thirty minutes!"

"Ha," he mocked her laughter. "I'll do it for forty minutes!"

She stepped back, amazed at his counter. "Oh. Okay, big Cerberus joining the game, here." She nodded, approving. She reached out with her hand and asked, "Mind putting your dust where your mouth is?"

A long moment passed, and she feared that he had lost his resolve. Slowly, her hand started to fall away, but Riker grabbed it and threw a handful of dust over their clasped hands. "Let it be!" the Summoner shouted the short spell as the dust twinkled around them.

It was a short incantation used between friends to show good faith. If the bet was lost, the loser would feel a slight pain in their hand. Nothing serious, but it was a reminder that your word is just as important as a spell pouch. For a moment, Vanessa gazed between Riker and their clasped hands with a look of dumbstruck surprise. Riker. The notorious Riker just made a bet with her!

Feeling rather victorious, the young witch wasted no time in rolling up the Summoner's sleeve to note the time. Pointing to his wristwatch, she announced gleefully, "Don't start the timer until we are sitting down."

"Fair enough," he stated, though he looked like the extra time tacked on would do him in. Again, a look flashed in his eyes, and the man smiled warmly. "Is this how you manage to always find yourself in trouble?"

She couldn't help but laugh at that. "Probably," she admitted delightedly.

With that over, they entered the building, and Riker informed the lady at the front that he had previously made reservations. Meanwhile, Vanessa gawked at the interior of the building. She had only been in once before, but it was always such a stunning sight to behold. Ornately carved metal lanterns swayed overhead. The intricate shapes and spaces from the carving gave birth to rays of warm light splashing against the walls and floors. It was only broken up by various atriums that were littered across the entirety of the building. The lush foliage inside with wide, flat leaves were all nestled into white, smooth rocks and rich, black soil underneath. From the second story, a mini waterfall flowed down into a large pool of water near the center of the room.

After a moment of checking her book, the hostess nodded and grabbed two menus. "Follow me, please," she instructed.

Wordlessly, the two followed. Passing by a set of double doors on their way into a private area off of the main dining area, they noticed a few spread out tables. Only one of the various tables was occupied. An older gentleman with white hair and worn robes in hues of washed-out grays and blues adorned him as he dined.

"Your spell has already been prepared," she informed and motioned to the table before laying down the menus. "What can I get you two to drink?"

"Water," Riker announced lifelessly.

The hostess looked to Vanessa expectantly, and she replied with, "I'll need a moment to look over your teas." She had a picky ogre, after all.

Riker seemed to be keeping a keen eye on her. As he sat down, he said, "I didn't know that you liked tea."

She gave a short bout of laughter. "I used to not like it. It's something I've started to grow to enjoy thanks to Botobolbilian."

"Hmmm. I see. And will he be joining us soon?"

"I hope so," she mumbled under her breath but said to Riker, "Should be along shortly."

As soon as her butt hit the comforts of the cushioned seat, Riker tapped a button on the side of the wristwatch. Gradually, his gaze lifted to hers, and he flashed a devilish smile. "Is discussing the mission scroll going to be too wound up for you?"

She thought it over with a playful gleam in her eye. "Let me think about that." Tapping her chin with the tip of her index finger, she toyed with the thought before saying, "I suppose that is the reason we are here. I'll allow it."

"Heh, you're a tough one," he said and reached for a large, hard, leather container at his side. Uncapping the end of it, he slid out the parchment held within and plopped it on the table. A scroll never looked so daunting.

A small dagger was removed from one of the various leather straps dangling across the wizard's chest, and he unsheathed the blade to break open the seal. A tinge of tangerine magic popped around where the seal had been broken. The sign of a high-class mission scroll. The paper was unfurled, and Riker's eyes glossed over as he read the ink scribbled therein.

Moments stretched by while the Summoner read the mission. Unable to hold back, Vanessa reminded Riker that she wanted to know what the mission details were. "Well, what does it say?"

He gave a hum of displeasure. "Seems that there are more than the two tablets that you and Spellweaver Bauer brought back to the Coven," he began.

She nodded. She knew that there were more, she just didn't know their locations. "Does it say where the others are, or how many?"

"Two more," he informed quickly and tapped a point on the scroll. "Says that the report Spellweaver Bauer and Summoner MacBain turned in matches with the two unidentified magic pings that went off on the Great Orb right before it blew out during the Blood Moon Festival. A few scholars were monitoring some strange waves of magic that were pulsing on it right before four locations with the same magical imprint went off. One was in Herbon. The other was on the banks of the Gentle Titan River in the Vemeese district."

She was practically lying on the table she was so enamored with what he was saying. All worries about being stuck on a mission with the Coven's warm-blooded golem were obliterated. "And the other two?"

"One was marked as being somewhere in the Red Tipped Mountains," he explained. "But the other one was marked as being both in the Jungle and somewhere in Tolvade."

As if the notion had pushed her back into her seat, she flopped back with a perplexed look scrunching up her features. "But there are only four tablets," she reminded. "How can there be four tablets but five pings made on the Great Orb?"

"I'm not sure. Neither is the High Priest Council. That's what you and I are to investigate. We are to look into why traces were marked both in the Jeweled Canopy and in Tolvade, locate the final tablet, and bring it back to headquarters immediately." He leveled his gaze with the young witch. "I cannot express how important these tablets are, Vanessa."

"You don't need to," she said while playing with her fork. "I already know why they are important."

He blinked.

Rolling her eyes, Vanessa scooted into an upright position and explained, "I spoke with an elemental when I found the first tablet. It … well, there were a lot of things said in a short amount of time …" she grumbled.

Interest piqued, Riker raised a brow over one eye. "Like?"

She cut her eyes to him and suddenly got an idea. "Nope. You're being too serious," she said with a sigh.

Ever so slightly—almost unnoticed—his mouth unhinged, and she had to lift up the menu to hide her ear-splitting grin. Looking overly interested in the tea options, she sniffed and read through the descriptions. All the while, she ignored the stare from Riker that practically burned a hole through the menu.

"What do you want in exchange for you telling me?" His expression had returned to normal, and he appeared unphased by her holding back the information.

Her grin widened. "My, my, Summoner Alastair, I didn't know that you were the impatient sort."

"I'm a great deal of things, Spellweaver Peterson."

She rolled her lips into her mouth and thought a moment. This was her chance to crack open the ice lord. But she had to be careful. Asking Riker a question was like asking the jinn to grant a wish. You had to be careful and meticulous with your words. One sentence could open a floodgate or lock the doors forever. Her vision became fixed onto the wizard before her. She took everything in from the scar on his head to the gleam of his half-hidden medals on his chest. Finally, she had it. The question everyone wanted to know but no one dared to ask. The question that had birthed countless theories and tales amongst their peers …

"Why did you join the Coven?" she asked.

His face twisted. The amount of emotions that crashed to the surface were swiftly managed faster than a vampire schooling their features. He sat straight and proud in his chair. "Forget it," he mumbled.

"I knew it. Stiff-neck through and through." She huffed and crossed her arms over her chest and glared off to the double doors across the room. A short time passed, and she took a chance to steal a peek at the stoic man. She noted that he seemed cold, calculating, and staring at her with an intensity that made her feel like he was reading her soul like an open book. Her pouty demeanor faltered, and she squirmed under his unrelenting gaze. "I didn't mean to—"

"You remind me of her," Riker said in a tone that held the breath of winter and the vision of a freshly dug grave. It shot through the air like an arrow of ice and pierced her heart.

She couldn't stop herself from asking, "Who?"

He was looking at her, but it was clear Riker wasn't seeing Vanessa at that moment. No, what he saw was a ghost of someone he used to know. "Silver," he whispered. "You remind me of Silver." There was a longing in his voice, and it took his eyes captive, and, suddenly, the Summoner became a million miles away from her as he remembered a time long ago.

Vanessa was afraid to speak. He appeared content. It was as if his past was both a blessing and a curse. A place he visited and strayed away from. But the curiosity pulled the words out of her despite not wanting to disturb the wizard.

"Who is Silver?"

His trance broken, Riker blinked rapidly and refocused on the young witch. Drawing in a calming breath, he breathed out the reply, "She was my very first friend."

There was a pause then, as the waitress came with the drinks. "The hostess said you wanted to pick a tea?" she reminded sweetly.

"Oh, right," Vanessa grimaced and pointed to a random tea on the menu.

With a slight bend, the woman read the item off the list and nodded. "I'll go prepare that now. And have you thought about your orders?"

"Just bring out two specials, please," Riker instructed like the previous moment had never transpired.

"Thank you," Vanessa expressed sheepishly as the waitress walked away. Immediately, her attention was pointed back to the orange-haired male. "Where is she now?"

The idea that this being had such an impact on Riker was far more interesting than anything else. She didn't even mind that her food had been ordered for her.

"She's dead." The comment was made so simply. While Vanessa struggled with trying to not look like she had just been slapped across the face, Riker sipped at his water.

"I'm … I'm so sorry," she uttered disheartened and looked about the table, lost in saddened thought.

A slow, deep breath was inhaled and released by the wizard. "I was seven when I first met her." The witch perked up as she curiously eyed Riker over. He crossed his arms and leaned on the table. "I grew up in the Borlimane district. My dad … he had a real nasty gambling habit. He was horrible at it to boot, drove him to drink. What coin the gambling didn't steal away, the bottle did." He sighed then. "Should have gone to Tasgall's. Would at least have a decent brew to go along with the sad story." Regardless, he sipped the water and resumed speaking before Vanessa could convince herself to tell him he didn't have to. "One night, he bet the unthinkable."

"Your home?" she quietly guessed.

Slowly, Riker shook his head. "Me. He bet me." Vanessa's eyes grew owlishly large, and her jaw dropped. "Naturally, he lost. The following day, the man he lost to came to collect his debt. Dad was drinking with some buddies to escape the monumental mess he had made. My mother was inside weeping while I was outside playing with a few other children. I had no idea that anything was wrong. While playing with the neighborhood kids, a fight broke out nearby, and the chaos seeped out into the street we were playing on in front of my home. My mom rushed out to grab me." Again, he shook his head. "She shielded me from an arcane blast from a blood mage. I could feel her body growing heavy as she continued to cling to me in order to keep me safe. Between the man that came to collect me and the efforts of the Coven rushing in, the blood mages dispersed while others were incarcerated. And I got a lifetime of nightmares from watching everyone, my mother included, die." Another sip of water, the glass was now half gone. "Barnaby Jargen was the man my father lost a bet to. He ran a local gang primarily filled with children from off the streets. Taught them to pickpocket, haggle, and run gambling carts throughout Tolvade. I expected the worst when I left with him that day. I had never thought I would know happiness again after everything I had been through and everything I witnessed. Until I met

Silver." He laughed then. A foreign sound coming out of the Summoner. "She was a spry little Sleekit halfling. Caused nothing but trouble, could hardly pickpocket, and was horrible at managing the gambling carts." He laughed louder then. "She gave me a new name, Riker." His smile faded at the edges, and he twisted his glass on the table from side to side. "We had a rule growing up together for those five years. Don't go out on the streets alone, and when the moon rises, you lock the door and stay inside." His eyes glassed over. "She didn't come back one night … I searched everywhere for her … I found out later that she had tried to pick a pocket late at night, and it happened to belong to a blood mage." Riker's free hand balled into a fist. A long moment passed in silence. "Barnaby was the illegitimate son of noble. In those years growing up with him, Silver, and the others, I learned a lot of things I would never have hoped to learn while living in a hovel in the middle of Borlimane. After begging him to send me to school, Barnaby used the gang's savings to put me through Perriline Institute of Sorcery. Studied for three years before I was picked up by the Coven." He leveled his gaze that blazed with fire and stirred with embers. "So, the shorter version of your question, Vanessa, is I joined the Coven for good old fashion revenge. And you? I felt drawn to you because you are so much like her. A piece of me misses that sly Sleekit girl laughing at me and causing trouble every day."

Bobbing her mouth open and closed like a fish on dry land, Vanessa struggled to find something to say. But she couldn't find a single thing that would matter at that moment. She slunk down in her chair and looked heartbroken for the wizard. "I see. You didn't have to tell me all of that," she managed to say finally.

"I think I wanted to tell someone my story. You were the first one to really ask. Besides, you told me to unwind," he reminded.

"That was a bit too loose," Vanessa griped as she reached for her glass of water.

"I trust my story will not be hung to dry for all of Tolvade."

She shook her head rapidly in reply. She wouldn't dare!

"Now, you were saying about the tablets and speaking with elementals?"

 *Chapter 23:*

As quickly and efficiently as she could, Vanessa explained everything she, Leon, Bobo, and Raven had discovered when the Undine, Meladrious, spoke to them back at the forest temple. Afterward, she went on to tell him about the mission scroll she picked up and how Dmitri had been tied to the Headmaster and the summonings that went on under Runerite Academy. She only paused in telling the story when they were served their food.

The Summoner sat back in his chair, rubbing his chin in deep thought. "This is interesting, to say the least."

Vanessa pushed away her half-eaten plate of food as she said, "I know that the tablets are important, but if we waste too much time on searching for them, we won't be able to hold off on the spell before the sun will change its position during the Spring Equinox. The tablets are a key point to the spell ..." she let her words trail off.

Riker nodded, "Perhaps, if it comes down to it, we could only use a few of the tablets for the ritual and use all four next year after we've found them all?"

"Well, that sounds harebrained if you ask me." The old wizard that had been seated behind them was now pulling out an extra chair at their table and nestling into it with a groan of comfort. "Hmm," he hummed as he patted down his worn-out robes. "Where'd I put that confounded ... ah, here it is!" he exclaimed as he withdrew a long-stemmed pipe from the many folds of cool-toned fabric. The twisting wood of the stem had been dyed in varying blues, and the base was an all white carving of a twisting sea serpent cradling the bowl. Again, the wizard seemed to have lost something as he reached into pockets and slipped into the depths of his attire in his search. Pulling out a small, cloth pouch, he grinned victoriously and stabbed the back with the tip of his pipe. "There you are, ya little rascal." Ignoring the fact that he was sitting with two strangers during their private conversation and invading the spelled space, the old being began to pull out a dried, sage green substance peppered with bits of deep brown leaves and stuffed it into his pipe.

"Are you lost, old man?" Riker practically growled. Any warmth that the man might have obtained in the short time that he and Vanessa had been conversing evaporated. He was even reaching for his wand.

Quickly, the young witch tried to dispel the anger forming. "You made a bet with me," she reminded in sing-song form. Then she turned to the older gentleman. "I'm sorry, sir, but we've paid for a privacy spell—"

"I know," the old wizard stated plainly as he tried to make a small flame appear on the tip of his finger. It sparked once, twice, and then ignited. He hovered the flame over the bowl.

"Then why are you still here?" Riker snarled.

The old man paused and lifted his gaze up to the seething Summoner. "Your conversation sounded interesting," he admitted before resuming lighting his pipe.

"You heard us?" Vanessa breathed unbelieving.

Again, he paused and now looked to Vanessa. "Yeees," he confirmed and poised the flame once more.

"How? You shouldn't be able to!" Riker snapped. "We've been swindled," he roared and rose from the table, ready to pick a fight."

"Calm down," Vanessa gasped, rising to her feet.

Sighing over still not being able to light his pipe, the wizard thumbed to the Spellweaver. "You should listen to her."

"We paid for a privacy spell," he informed, explaining the cause of his rage.

"Well, I mean, you have one. There is no doubt that the spell has been cast," the wizard said.

"I'm getting a manager," Riker hissed while narrowing his eyes into mere slits.

"Sit down, it's not a big deal. We can figure this out calmly," Vanessa urged.

The old wizard slammed his palm down on the table, and the contents atop it rattled with the force. "I'm going to light this pipe, and you are going to sit down and listen to me."

"Hex this. I'm cuffing him." Riker sounded like he had made up his mind and not a single being on Raen was going to stop him.

It all happened at once and so quickly that none of them could react. Faster than one would suspect a man his age could move, the wizard had pulled a thin, gnarled, white wand from his robes and zapped Riker with a spell. "Sit." The command was simple and effective. Though the Summoner tried to fight it, the spell forced him clumsily back to his seat, and he steadied himself by vice gripping the table.

Clearly, the privacy spell was in effect, otherwise, the whole restaurant would have had their attention on them, and, surely, servers would have gathered to see what the commotion was over and to see if they could help. Instead, the doorway was free of beings, and everyone was paying more attention to their plates rather than the drama playing out.

"Do you have any idea of the mistake you just made?" Riker's voice was hauntingly low and each word was wrapped up in warning.

Unaffected by the dagger glare of the Summoner and the awestruck eyes of the Spellweaver, the wizard smiled at the brief moment of silence and lit his pipe. Deep mauve smoke curled with copper sparks around the top of the bowl before dissipating into the air overhead. The old man held his breath for a moment with a satisfied grin. A light cough and then he exhaled. "First of all, young man, you don't scare me." He took another puff and eased back in his chair. "Secondly, I cast the bloody spell you're fussing about," he informed.

"You?" Riker couldn't even hide the confusion in his voice.

As the wizard went for a second puff of his pipe, he paused and drew in a long-winded breath. "That's what I said," he answered snarkily and brought the pipe to his lips.

"How?" Vanessa's question stopped the wizard in mid-motion.

He smirked at the young witch. "What? It's not like it's hard."

Riker, again, reached for his wand at his hip. Catching the action, Vanessa called out to him, contesting the action. "Hold on, Riker. It may sound strange but let's hear him out."

"That is exactly how trouble starts and people die, Vanessa!" Riker barked, swiftly pulling out his wand.

"Trouble? Oh, no, no, no!" coughed the wizard with dusty purple smoke rolling out of his nostrils. "Not in *my* establishment."

"*Your* establishment?" Vanessa parroted.

The cold, focused glower of the Summoner rested on the old wizard. Wordlessly, he waited for the wizard to explain himself.

"Yup. My establishment," he reconfirmed.

"You're Merlin?!" she squawked.

The wizard sighed heavily, again. "Hex it all. I'm starting to remember why I don't talk to Coven members. Nothing but questions and wand flinging."

"Fine, you're Merlin, and you personally prepared the spell for us. I fail to see how that invites you to join our company. Is there a reason you're at our table?" There was no warmth to Riker as he spoke those words.

Merlin perked up and snapped his fingers as the reason for him joining them revisited him. "Oh, yeah. I almost forgot." Though, the way he had said it implied on its own that he had very much indeed forgotten up until then. "You two were talking about something ... what was it?"

"The tablets," Vanessa reminded.

"Vanessa!" Riker boomed, amazed at the young witch for giving up such important information.

"What?" she whined angrily.

"Tablets!" Merlin burst out excitedly.

"Can you put the wand down and listen to him? Please?" Vanessa pleaded with large, hopeful eyes.

Physically fighting the urge to yell, Riker turned a red that matched his hair and slammed his wand back in its holster before shaking a finger at the girl. "I better not regret this," he snarled.

"Me too," she mumbled under her breath and pulled her chair closer to Riker's, just in case he got the urge to reach for his wand again, and sat down.

Purple smoke swirled around the old wizard's head as he puffed away at his pipe, waiting for the two to get situated once more. After a very long, quiet moment, Merlin said, "It has been forever since I last heard another being speaking about the tablets." He smiled fondly. "True treasures of Tolvade, they are. Surely, it is one of the greatest artifacts that I've found to date."

"Wait. Wait." Riker pinched his brow in a crude mixture of confusion and annoyance. "Wait a spell-flinging minute here. You have found one of the tablets?"

The old man drew in another breath of smoke with his eyes closed, and slowly released it, the act making him look like a slumbering, fire-breathing dragon. "That's right. I have it in my possession to be exact."

She couldn't mask the amazement from her face. "You have it?"

"You guys sure like your questions, you know? If you'd just slow your casting for a dust-making minute, you'd have all your questions answered without sounding like a couple of surprised parrots." Laughing at his own joke, he pointed to the two of them. "Could you imagine yourselves with beaks like a couple of Harpies?" He giggled to himself. "Heeheeehee. Just ... hahahaha ... imagine your feathered faces. Bwahahaha!"

Meanwhile, Riker looked like he was about to explode on the spot, and Vanessa reached out timidly to touch the side of this arm. She didn't say anything. She only waited for those cold, slate hues to land on her. Her expression alone was asking him to unwind, to calm down ... to trust her judgment. The Summoner searched her gaze for a moment before he sighed, and—with the exhale–all the tension was washed out of him.

Wiping away a tear from his laughing fit, Merlin recomposed himself and continued on with his story. "It was years ago, now. I had stupidly ventured too far from my camp. I had gone out with several other artifact hunters and scholars to the edge of the Jeweled Canopy. We were trying to monitor the magical barrier that surrounded the jungle and why none of it seeped out to affect the rest of Aeristria, or if there was the possibility of it doing that in the years to come. There were also several clues hinting at possible artifacts along the area. One evening, I had a cyan spider monkey steal some of my equipment and run off with it. It was late and hard to see. I chased after the cheeky bugger nonetheless." A soft sigh escaped him. "I had stumbled past the barrier while not paying attention. I continued chasing that blasted monkey without realizing it. After chasing it for almost an hour, I victoriously snatched back my things and pulled out my compass to head back to camp ... but it didn't work."

"You were lost in the Jeweled Canopy?" Vanessa breathed.

Merlin nodded. "For over a week."

"I don't believe him," Riker grumbled.

"Let the man finish," Vanessa whispered.

"I managed to stroll upon a broken-down temple while I was there. It was guarded by all sorts of strange beings and creatures. I could sense a great deal of magic pouring out of the ruins and went in. That's where I found the tablet."

"You didn't," Vanessa gasped in disbelief.

"I assure you, I did. Because there were two things I was certain of at that moment. One was that the tablet inside those ruins was powerful enough to level the whole continent if placed in the wrong hands, and two, if I didn't take it and use some of its power I was going to die in that jungle."

"Is that how you got back to your camp?" Riker asked.

The old wizard groaned and tapped his pipe into an empty plate on the table. "It was. Though, a good forty years had passed. Most of my colleagues had died. The construction on the oubliette was never completed. Many of the High Priests had already been succeeded by their Second Chosens. And I? Well, heh, they thought I was dead."

"You're Archimedes!" Vanessa shouted.

The wizard gave a smile that was all teeth. "That's me."

Riker floundered for a reaction and could only come up with confusion. "You were in the Jeweled Canopy for over a week and ..."

"And forty years had passed," Merlin finished for him.

"Why didn't you come back to the Coven?" the Summoner asked.

"Why would I?" He watched the surprise register over their faces before he continued. "Look. I was a laughing stock at the Coven. I was fearful of the chance that someone out there was going to use one of the natural Hell gates to summon feral demons. I was trying to find a way to fix it ... but I could never perfect it. I could never get it to work on a demon. And the Coven? Well, regardless of them knowing that fact, they weren't concerned with feral demons when one hadn't been sighted for such a long time."

"But the tablet!" Vanessa cried out vehemently. "You could have given it to the Coven. They could have—"

"Young lady, what do you think they would have done? Hmmm? I'm not one that's fond of questions. Coming out of the Jeweled Canopy alive and without a pocket portal ... I'd have been answering questions for the rest of my life. As for the tablet, I didn't trust who was in power during that time. Why would I hand over a powerful artifact to someone I didn't trust?"

"Good point," Vanessa mumbled.

"Besides, I had a feeling that I was either going to go get all the tablets myself or someone would present me with an opportunity to hand it over without the Coven knowing I played a hand in it."

"Whoa. Whoa. So you knew what this thing was and how important it was to magic in the country as a whole, and you just ... did nothing?" Riker was a cross between amazed and fuming, and Vanessa didn't know how to calm him down.

"If no one else did anything, I was going to do it, eventually," he murmured and looked for his tobacco pouch again.

"You put countless lives at risk," Riker's voice dropped an octave.

"Correction, keeping the tablet saved lives. Could you imagine what those two double-crossing blue cloaks would have done to Tolvade if they got their hands on that thing? They would have leveled the city to the ground by the end of the day. Mark me, they were out for blood and the tablet would have been like giving them a knife. I'm not that sort of wizard."

"But keeping the tablet didn't really help, either," Vanessa added with a hard frown.

"Again, you are wrong. I knew that there were more tablets. But I wasn't the wizard for the job. For various reasons. Look, have either of you been scared? Worried that one wrong move from you would put the whole world in danger? Thankfully, I was lucky enough to get a message from the Celestial while she was in isolation before she took her elixir. She told me that the goddess had a message for me. I was to wait. That a girl seeking the tablet would come to me, and I was to trust her. As each year passed, my doubts grew. I can't really deny it. I prepared myself to head out and find the tablets myself because doubt is an ugly thing, and it started to silence my belief in what the Celestial had said."

"The goddess," Vanessa breathed.

"The goddess had a message ... for you?" Riker asked unbelievingly.

Merlin shrugged. "Apparently."

"Why hadn't you left yet?" Vanessa asked.

"Oddly enough, I was heading on my way out of the city when I was blasted onto my backside by a spell's shock wave. Not too long after that, I saw isolated lightning over the Vemeese district. The power from both of the tablets was palpable. That's when I knew, my destiny was never to gather the artifacts. I put my faith in what the Celestial told me, and waited for when you would come to me."

"The Celestial ... sent you a message *personally*?" Riker repeated. He still sounded like he didn't trust what Merlin was saying.

The old wizard plucked a bushy, white brow over one eye. "I'd tell you to ask the being yourself, but she doesn't remember after taking the elixir."

"Convenient," Riker muttered.

"I'll say," Merlin said with a chuckle.

Vanessa leaned over the table a bit as she asked, "Do you still have the tablet?"

With a small amount of dust, a short, whispered spell, and a wave of his hand, the stone tablet appeared on the table, and Vanessa shot up to her feet. "By the goddess, it's just like the other one." She tilted her head as she examined it. "Though the writing on it isn't the same."

"Each one has a different portion of the ritual and various spells locked away within it. I would hope it wouldn't have the same writing," Merlin announced.

Riker reached for the item, and the wizard slapped his hands with the butt-end of his pipe. "Not so fast. I want to ensure I'm not going to be pestered. I want the last of my life lived out in peace and without worry."

Narrowing his eyes at Merlin, Riker hesitantly asked, "What do you want?"

"A promise. An unbreakable one," Merlin demanded.

Vanessa threw her hands up in the air. "Not it!"

Riker shot her a look.

"You can point those daggers elsewhere. I've already got too many promises to keep. I don't want to add to that growing list," she defended.

"Fine! I'll do it," he said while reaching for his dust pouches.

While the two wizards fussed over what specific spell to use, Vanessa looked out through the room's double doors to the slowly filling main dining area. Carefully, she scanned the room, fearful that they might be watched. Too many strange things had transpired recently for her to feel comfortable in the middle of a crowded restaurant while they performed spells, talked about tablets, and had an insanely powerful item just resting on a table like it was a basket of breadsticks.

"Can you two stop your fussing and hurry up? I don't feel comfortable with that thing just hanging out in the open like that." Her words caught both wizards off guard.

Merlin declared, "I like her. She's spunky."

"Spunky is one way you could describe her ..." Riker said with a look. But despite his cold eyes, Vanessa saw something twinkle in them. His smile, half-hidden, was full of warmth too.

"Just get the spell over with so we can get the hex out of here with that tablet," she reminded hotly.

"All right. All right. I didn't know that you were the type to get bossy when you're anxious," Riker teased.

Looking back out into the hall, she saw Bobo at the front. "Bobo's here."

"Who?" Merlin asked.

"My partner. You two finish up here, I'm going to go get him. I don't want the hostess coming over here right now."

"Good idea," Riker agreed.

Bounding across the private dining area, Vanessa made her way toward Bobo and intercepted him flawlessly from the hostess. Kindly dismissing her, the young witch pulled Bobo over to their table while the demon griped about Leon taking forever to get to the apartment to Sleekit-sit while he rushed over to meet up with her. In the middle of his fussing, he furrowed his brow at the old wizard finishing up the promise spell with Riker.

"I say, Vanessa. What have you managed to get into while I was gone this time?"

"I'll explain in the safety of the privacy spell," she assured.

"Oh, dear," the ogre mumbled.

After explaining everything to her pet, Bobo sat at the table with his arms crossed over his chest. His empty plate was pushed into the middle of the table with the rest of the dirty lunch-ware. Pointing to the tablet resting in front of the wizard, Bobo said, "How are we going to deal with that?"

"We're going to take it to the Coven, of course!" Riker boldly stated.

"I don't think that is a good idea," Vanessa admitted and flinched, ready for the Summoner's outburst.

As if expecting the answer, Bobo made a face and nodded. "Honestly, I do hate to admit it, but she's right."

Riker looked between them like he was given the most outlandish news of his life. "You two can't be serious! That," he pointed to the stone, "is one-fourth of a ritual that we've been performing wrong for countless years, and you want to wait on turning it in?"

"Well, yes." She let out an exasperated breath. "Think about it, Riker. If we walk into the Coven now, hours after a high-ranked mission was assigned and turn in a tablet, what do you think is going to happen?" She paused and watched the wizard think it over. Merlin just bobbed his head as his eyes darted to each new speaker, puffing away happily on his pipe. "After so much betrayal and as the secrets keep pouring in, do you think, for a second, that they are going to trust us?"

Quietly, Riker stared out the windows on the far side of the room. His arms were stacked on his chest as he took one deep breath after another. Clearly, the Summoner was attempting to calm down. Turning to face Vanessa again, he looked between her and Bobo and said, "What do you think we should do, then?"

Ignoring the very evident displeasure in his voice, the Spellweaver pressed on. "One day. That's all I'm asking for. Give me one day to come up with a plan."

"A ... plan?" Again, he held back his anger as he parroted the reply.

"Yes. You are magically bound to a promise, and I won't let you get hurt." Those words jerked an emotion out of Riker, and the man quickly covered up any traces of it as the young witch continued on. "We can't afford the Coven distrusting those that are working so hard to protect it and the values it was built upon." She sighed heavily. "So, yes, I'm asking for one day to think of a way to handle all of this."

Riker loomed over the table, displaying one digit held high in the air as he replied darkly, "One day." There was a finality to that short answer. His eyes said everything his terrible tone of voice didn't.

Vanessa gulped and nodded. "One day," she whispered with a lack of confidence.

"There is still one glaring issue, my dear," Bobo informed dreadfully.

Riker was the first to look upset over one more problem presenting itself. Vanessa didn't look any less irritated. Merlin ... continued to puff away, drowning himself in a sea of mauve-colored smoke.

The gentleman-beast pointed a clawed finger at the stone slab on the table. "How are we going to hide that?"

All eyes turned to the tablet.

With a faint coughing fit, Merlin interjected with, "Take my bottomless bag." Gripping the pipe with his lips, he pulled out the bottomless bag, reached forward, and stuffed the tablet into the bag. Vanessa's eyes grew wide as he tossed it to her.

"I'll bring it back as soon as we turn in the tablet," she assured.

"Eh, keep it," he expressed lazily with a single wave in her direction. "I've got a million of them."

"It's a-a-a Morgan Le Fay bag!" she yelled, noting the gold stitched embroidery of the initials on the deep crimson, velvet bag.

"Yup," he replied flatly.

She stuttered for a moment. "I—I couldn't keep it."

"I insist," he mumbled while eyeing the bowl and jabbing at the contents with the tip of a butter knife.

"I couldn't possibly ..." she breathed.

Leaning over toward his master, Bobo whispered through a forced smile, "If you won't, I will. That is a Morgan Le Fay bag, my dear. I suggest you stop pushing a gift away and accept it with the hidden grace I know you possess."

"Uh ... thank ... you?" Vanessa answered unsure of how to accept such a monumental gift.

Bobo patted her on the head. "That'll do, my dear. That'll do."

She cut him a dirty look, and the ogre grinned.

 *Chapter 24:*

Standing outside the building after paying the bill, Vanessa was trying to convince Riker that everything was going to be okay.

"Nothing bad is going to happen, I promise. Just go home for now, and I'll think of something by tomorrow." She felt like she had said that same phrase so many times already, and all they had done was go from the table to the register and out the front doors.

Riker still looked as unbelieving as he had when she first presented him with the idea. Even though this was (theoretically) the best option, it didn't make the man feel any better. And it was scrolled all over his face. His slate eyes drifted over to Bobo right before he asked, "Is this a common occurrence with her?"

"I'm surprised you're even asking after witnessing it firsthand. But yes, it is I'm afraid," the ogre replied with a shake of his head.

"I don't know how you do it," Riker sighed as he rested his crossed arms over his chest.

"Neither do I," Bobo chortled.

The Summoner couldn't help but smile himself, but it was short-lived. He cut his gaze at Vanessa and shook a finger at her. "Mark me, Spellweaver Peterson—"

She huffed, "I thought we'd grown past titles."

He tried not to crack a grin at her comment. The corners twitched, and his harsh tone didn't match the fondness in his eyes. "You better not make me come to regret what happened here today, or I'll happily file a long report to the High Priest Council about you," he warned.

She threw her hands up in the air. "That is the last thing I want." Patting at her new bag attached to her spell belt, she smirked and said, "Let me and this thing get home. I've got a lot to think about tonight."

"All right. Good luck, Vanessa." Riker turned his attention to the ogre at her side and pointed from his eyes to Vanessa. "Keep an eye on her," he commanded.

"Round the clock, sir. You have my word," Bobo replied with his chest puffed out.

With that, they parted ways and headed for home.

As they were approaching her apartment complex, her crystal ball jingled from the bag around her waist. Who would be calling her now? Pausing in her stride, she fussed with the tassels, opened the bag, withdrew her crystal ball, and answered it.

Instantly, the device came to life, and Leon's face was inches from the glass. "Vanessa," he whispered. "Are you expecting company?"

She shook her head in reply.

In the background, Vanessa could see Malachi hunched over next to Leon. Further back, she saw Lyx's tail jittering about aggressively as her amber eyes remained glued to the front door. A hiss tickled the succubus' throat. He too looked to it, and then immediately turned back to the young witch and shook his head. "I've got a bad feel—"

KABOOM!

A thick haze rushed into the room, and debris flew across the surface of the orb seconds before the connection winked out. If there had been a shred of doubt that trouble was bubbling at her doorstep, that notion was snuffed out as she saw puffs of black smoke rolling out from her apartment windows a few floors up.

"Banish a banshee!" she hollered and rushed inside.

Already, beings were shoving their way through the lobby and running to make an escape from the apartment building. The flat workers included.

"The stairs," Bobo announced, leading the way.

Pushing past the new wave of bodies that were pouring out of the stairwell, Vanessa tried to not get trampled over as she fought to go in the opposite direction of the masses. It was like trying to swim upstream. The current of beings tried to carry her back as she struggled to push forward. Frantically fleeing for the front doors for their lives, a collection of frightened souls swept Vanessa up, and she cried out in frustration.

"Bobo!" she screamed over the chaotic melody of mixed voices and hysterical wails.

Whipping around, Bobo could see Vanessa practically fighting off those that were trying to escape in their blind panic. To his horror, he watched as she was slammed into and hit the floor. Mustering up his inner ogre, the gentleman-beast lost all of his composure and roared a terrible roar. The walls shook, and every being immediately went to cover their ears with meek whimpers. He combed with ease past the less crazed crowd and helped Vanessa to her feet and then hoisted her up to his shoulder as he said, "We need to hurry."

She nodded, agreeing, and reluctantly clung to his neck while saying, "I can walk."

"I promised that I would keep an eye on you. I do not take my word lightly. So, considering that I cannot account for those around us presently, close to me you shall stay," he explained while taking the steps in leaps and bounds.

"You're right," she whispered.

"Of course I am, now get a spell ready. I don't think our visitors are the well-mannered sort."

There was no denying his assessment. As Bobo focused on climbing up to their apartment floor and trying not to hurt (or get hurt) by anyone running for the exit, Vanessa quickly dove her hand from spell pouch to spell pouch. She grabbed dusts, runes, charcoal, parchment, and pieced together a spell. Every now and again, she'd inhale sharply as she'd almost mess up her writing, but she didn't say anything to the demon as he continued on.

As they neared the landing for her floor, the crowd thinned out. However, there wasn't comfort in seeing the dwindling numbers because the few trailing beings skittering by clung to wounds and limped down the stairwell. The master and pet shared a look before he put her down.

Vanessa's eyes were glued to a faun with blood running down his arm as he wobbly made his way down. His clumsy hoof-falls echoed in the small space. Again, the duo traded glances.

Shaking her head, the young witch whispered, "This isn't good."

The ogre hummed in agreement. "Indeed. They seem to lack a caring for harming the innocent."

Biting her lip, she clutched her spell bag and took in a deep breath. Suddenly, there was a rumble, and it shook the floors and walls. The two braced themselves on the railing and hunkered down close to the floor.

"What on Raen was that?" she asked hoarsely.

Bobo only shook his head in reply.

Her chest tightened. The thorns of her magical promise were slowly waking and moving around her heart. *Not good!* There was no time, they had to move now. Leon, Malachi, and Lyx needed her. She couldn't just hide away in a stairwell.

Inching for the half-opened door, Vanessa poked her head out. Instantly, her eyes widened, and her jaw went slack. The heat of the spells was wafting through the halls, and she could see flashes of wand shots. But that was not what surprised her. She expected those. It was the bodies that she didn't expect. She darted her eyes from motionless being to motionless being on the floor. Her stomach knotted. Her eyes watered from the smoke lingering in the air, but mostly from feeling pain while the numbers mounted in her mind. Each frozen body was a life she couldn't save. Vanessa went so still, one would think she had been turned to stone. Her eyes were assaulted with smoke and her vision blurred, but she recognized one of the bodies that lay still in the middle of the floor was her neighbor, Mrs. Garrett.

Casualties.

It was the first lesson that they give new members when they joined the Coven. That there was bound to be casualties and that you couldn't save everyone. No matter how much Vanessa wanted to disbelieve it, she knew it—deep down in her heart—to be an unwavering truth that split her soul in two. But she had managed to escape it for so long. Much like she had dodged the second lesson that they taught at the Coven: *You will kill a being at some point in time. It's unavoidable.* She had always been warned that these inevitable truths would come to pass in her line of work. Hex it all, she expected them. But she was blessed by the goddess to have never encountered them.

Until recently.

The overhead fluorescent lights that were usually a bright, white light were now dingy with smog, and the yellow glow hardly illuminated the wide hall. Even the bursts of spell casting from across the hall couldn't penetrate far down the corridor. She frowned hard and was about to pull her head back to tell Bobo that she could see the commotion from around their apartment when she heard a cough.

Her nerves sung through her body as she jolted, unexpecting of the sound. Quickly, hope flared through her and replaced the dimming light from within. Turning, she saw a pixy with one wing, its leg clearly broken. The being was desperately holding hands with a kobold in a wheelchair. She looked around and saw that there were others, unable to walk or move due to injury or disability. The flat was out of commission, and they were stuck here, unable to make the trek down the stairs. The smoke was building and surely the fires that had been started would soon spread.

A shout from down the hall tore her vision from the huddled mass of beings, and she could scarcely make out Leon's form as he slammed into a wall. A bulk of black-cloaked beings emerged from the apartment, and the crack of Lyx's whip snapped through the air. Purple energy crackled around the weapon as she cleared the crowd encircling her master. Malachi threw a few daggers at a select choice of poised wand hands, but they were outnumbered.

Again, Vanessa's chest tightened and she hit the floor. But just as she caught her breath, a blindly flung spell came ripping down the hall. She looked at the beings as they cried out and hugged each other and hid their faces from the danger that was fast-approaching. Without thinking, Vanessa rushed into the hall to block them all from the blast.

No spell ready.

No weapon in hand.

No plan.

Just her body as a shield.

Time felt like it slowed down for a moment. She could see the flash of the speeding magic heading right for her. There was no time to grab a wand or search for the proper powders. She felt the lack of weapon on her and cursed her recent absence of preparedness, despite knowing better. There wasn't anything she could do but throw her hands up toward the wand bolt. Everything that she felt, the want to protect those scared beings and the desire to get to her friends, it all raged inside her. She yelled like she had never yelled before, *"NO!"*

It flooded her. Power. Unbridled and coursing through her at a speed she could not control. A pulse of blue light emitted from her palms. She turned her head to the side out of instinct, but the blast never came, the pain never washed over her … the spell never connected. Looking through one eye, she slowly peered in front of her. The bolt was suspended in mid-air, stopped mere inches from her body. It jostled about as if fighting with her power, and she felt a bit more confident. Then heat poured out from a spell pouch, and the magic burst into nothing but raining sparks.

"Vanessa, are you all right?" Bobo asked, grabbing her and spinning her around to face him.

She nodded dumbly.

"What was that?" he asked breathily.

"I think it was my magic and some of the tablet's." She reached for the spell pouch and clasped it tightly as she added, "And I think the wand bolt was obliterated by my hag stone."

Just then, they heard one of the dark-cloaked figures yell, "Kill the Sleekit, reinforcements are coming!"

And the words were like a spell cast all on their own. Clutching her chest, Vanessa clamped her mouth shut as she felt a wave of pain envelope her heart. Thorny vines slithered and snaked through her chest before they tightened around the muscle. The dagger-like tips of the barbs teased the soft tissue underneath. Threatening to pierce it clean through and bleed her dry.

"Ah!" she cried, unable to hold back. She had to save them. All of them. But she didn't know where to start. She felt so torn as to what to do and time was running out to make a choice.

Bobo was there, grounding her, and bringing the young witch out of her haze of agony. His massive hands felt warm against her cheeks as he forced her to look into his ocean blue gaze. Giving a light shake to wake her from her daze, Bobo grabbed her attention before speaking. "Go to them!" he urged in a hoarse yell. "I'll attend to these beings and bring them to safety." She didn't move. She didn't nod. She just searched the sea of his eyes like she had a thousand times before. Only, this time, she found thoughts and feelings and things she had let go unspoken within his orbs. Her hand rose up, gently laid over his, and a single tear blazed a path down her cheek. "Are you well enough to stand?" he asked, and waited for her to come to her senses and nod to him, and then he turned her toward the commotion. "Go, then."

"Thank you," she said before rushing into the fray.

It was hard to make out, but she could vaguely see Leon on the ground fighting back with all his might, Malachi dodging grabby hands and side-stepping disaster from a pointed wand, and Lyx wildly trying to keep enough distance between those that were trying to attack her master, the Sleekit, and herself with each wild snap of her whip. Between the billowing clouds filling up the halls and the stinging tears that it produced, the young witch had to strain her vision to make out any details beyond that.

As she trotted quietly through the hall, she tripped over a bit of debris and sucked in air to refrain from crying out or yelling a curse. She had to use the edge of her cape to hinder the smoke from stinging her lungs, though the garment almost did nothing to stop it from doing so. Each breath left her wanting to wheeze and cough. Every inhale was tinged with bitter, ashen flavors. Her nose burned with the scents of melting wires, singed plastic, burning fibers, and blazing wood. The swirling clouds of smoke were thick enough that the images down the hall were now mere black blobs when spells weren't being flung. She could still hear the commotion of them all yelling as they battled.

"Force push!" Leon yelled.

The backblast from the spell cut through the smoke. *Double-dip a candlestick!* Quickly, she grabbed a nightingale feather wrapped in enchanted twine and dusted it with cobalt powder. Faster than the flick of a wand, she whispered, "Conceal me from their vision, hide me from their eyes, my body will be hidden, so I may have the element of surprise." The feather shimmered and melted, growing as it did. Swiftly, the spell encased her, just as the last of it wrapped around her, one of the cloaked members standing in front of Leon turned to face the hall. Weapon held out suspiciously as their eyes combed the narrow passage.

Even at this distance, Vanessa could see the being home in on Bobo helping the others. His twisted smile overtook him. The look was far too sinister to be considered kind. "Oh, no you don't," he whispered.

Noticing what was about to happen, Vanessa readied herself to stop any spell he was about to fling. But his words had gained the attention of his brethren, and they turned to see what he was eyeing up. It was only for a split second, but that was all Leon needed. His hands were quick as lightning as they dipped into a pouch and withdrew two items. Runes were tossed into the air and he chucked the gold dust at the carved stones as he roared, "Ignite!"

A blazing fire and a trail of embers exploded in front of the cloaked beings. They yelled and shielded their faces from the oncoming onslaught of heat and growing flames. Nearby, a cloaked woman was far away enough from the spell that she could find her footing and point her wand. Her mouth opened to call out an incantation, but Lyx snapped her whip at the female assailant.

A scream ripped through the hall as the wand was dropped. Blood splattered the ground. Shaky hands held the side of her face, and the woman wailed, revealing that Lyx had sliced the female's face from the corner of her lips to the side of her cheek. A dagger flew across the room and landed, dead center, of the shrieking woman's chest.

Lyx followed the line of sight and saw Malachi stab two members simultaneously with two more blades. One of the men was close enough and had the strength left to lift his hand and point his wand at the Sleekit's arm. "Slash!" the dying cloaked being croaked out the battle spell before falling lifelessly to the ground. A slice ripped through the azbanonite's clothing and skin. Malachi yipped in pain and drew his arm close to his body. Vanessa drew in her lips and bit down hard to stop herself from crying out in pain. She could feel her skin rip open and hot blood trickle down her arm. Her chest tightened, and she hit the ground again. She was forced to watch everything unfold as the thorns squeezed around her heart, and her vision swam in and out of focus. The cloaked members swarmed them again. The furry being growled and bore his teeth at them as they encircled.

From the safety of her spell, Vanessa could do two things. One, she could get close enough to do damage with her properly prepared spell, as soon as she could stand on her feet again. And two, she could also tell that these beings ... they *weren't* blood mages. Which was a good thing, because—if they had been—Vanessa and the others would all be dead. But they did have the mannerisms and magic of blood mages. They lacked regard for human life. They attacked anything that moved. They had a love for violence and fought until death to carry out their task. That made Vanessa wonder, where they recruits of blood mages? Or were they something else entirely?

The sound of Lyx struggling as one of the beings grabbed her from behind tore Vanessa's vision from the injured beast to the thrashing demoness. "Get your filthy hands off of me!" The succubus bellowed before slamming the back of her skull into the nose of the brave being trying to keep a hold on her. Breaking free of his grasp, Lyx took to the air overhead and quickly closed the short distance between her and the Sleekit, aiding in battling off those enclosing around the injured creature. Nails elongated and she hissed at the cloaked beings in warning.

Finding the strength to rise up off the ground, Vanessa fought past the pain and willed her feet to press on, one in front of the other, toward their destination. All the while, she tried to steady her breathing through the smoky air. Her lungs felt like they harbored fires. The pungent air stung with every inhale through gritted teeth. She could taste ash and heat. It saturated her mouth and nose as she struggled for a decent lungful of clean air. All the while, she kept pressing on. Nothing was going to stop her. Nothing.

Almost close enough.

She needed to be dead center or there wouldn't be enough of them caught. Sneaking into the crowded space, Vanessa did her best not to break concentration and not touch anyone, for they were the only things that would break the spell keeping her hidden.

She was doing so well, until Leon kicked one of the beings off of him, sending them tumbling backward and slamming into Vanessa. Two things happened at once. Vanessa gave a shrill cry, and then the concealment broke. She stood dead-center of the chaos fully exposed. Three of the cloaked beings spun around and pointed their weapons at the Spellweaver, ready to blast her into the next life.

Vanessa yelled, "Amulets!" before yanking off her necklace and tossing it to Lyx who caught it.

Was Vanessa fully exposed and going to be hit? Most likely, but this was her best shot. It was this or breaking her promise, and, to be honest, there was a better chance of survival in the middle of the battle than there was with her breaking her promise.

"Vanessa, no!" Leon cried but growled, infuriated, as a few of the cloaked beings rushed at him to intercept him.

One of the beings rushed at her with a dagger and wand, screaming a spell she couldn't make out. When the tip was inches from her face, it stopped. Flicking her eyes down, she saw a small hand protruding from the being's chest. Gargles escaped the assailant before they fell with a sick *thud* to the floor below. With a bloodied arm, the one-winged pixie paled, panted, and gave a shaky smile while stepping back from the lifeless body.

She wanted to thank them, she wanted to tell Leon it was all going to be okay, but couldn't waste her breath. There wasn't any time. Her gaze spoke in volumes. Grabbing the Pixie with haste, Vanessa tossed her to a very upset Leon, who caught the one winged-being and immediately activated his amulet.

Thankfully, she had prepared the spell beforehand. Raising the dust-covered scroll over her head, she feared the worst but said the incantation nonetheless. "My rival surrounds, on every inch and all around, make not a sound, and level it ... TO THE GROUND!"

Light brighter than the sun shot out from her hand, the floor quaked, the walls trembled, the ceiling crumbled, and it all started to come undone, brick by brick, around them. The few beings that tried to escape the spell quickly fell through the growing hole surrounding them and disappeared into the yawning abyss. Their shrieks and cries gave no comfort to those left behind and unable to do more than watch in horror.

Vanessa screwed her eyes shut as she poured out her power into the spell. The floor beneath her opened up, bits of concrete fell away underfoot as she stood her ground.

"Not on my watch!" Bobo bellowed before diving across the hall and slamming into the young witch. His arms encased her, and they slid across the carpeted floor. As they rolled to a stop, the ogre's hug protected the Spellweaver as the remainder of the spell went off.

Through slits of space between the demon's embrace, she could see Lyx carrying Malachi toward her and Bobo and could see the pixie and Leon jumping from one stable bit of flooring to the next as they were in hot pursuit. But the cloaked beings, they all fell several floors down, and then the ceiling rained down over them.

 *Chapter 25:*

"I told you they were trying to kill me!" Malachi snapped irately. His snout was poised over his wound and sniffing all around the inflicted area. After thoroughly inspecting his injury, his tongue rolled over the opened flesh. Lyx tried to stop him and look at it, but the Sleekit repeatedly, and wordlessly, pulled away from her touch while possessively clutching the arm.

"Well, excuse me! I didn't think that the assaults would take place within the hour!" Vanessa yelled back.

Malachi scoffed. "She didn't think it would happen within the hour. And you call yourself a Spellweaver! Why do you think I didn't want to leave until I knew I'd be protected?" he shouted in return.

It was a valid point, even if her pride didn't want to agree at the moment. "Are you alive?'

"Barely," he mumbled.

She pointed to the gaping hole in the middle of the apartment building. "I doubt they are. Want to join them?"

He looked over his shoulder at the impressive remodeling they had just performed on the building and then looked back to Vanessa. "Nooo," he answered, finally.

"Then stop your complaining," she said as she came to her feet. "Are you all right, Bobo?" she asked in a far sweeter voice than she had used with the Sleekit.

"I'm not a brittle being, my dear. It will take more than a tumble to harm me," the ogre replied with a faint grin. A frightful coughing fit started, then.

"Booboo!" Lyx cried and slammed into the demon with a vice grip hug.

Completely caught off guard, the gentlemen-beast floundered and tapped at the succubus whispering, "There is company, woman. Restrain yourself." Clearly not listening, the demoness only hugged the ogre tighter. With a sigh, Bobo hugged her back and said, "It's all right. You're all right, my dear. Come on now. Let us get out of this smoke-infested pile of rubble and somewhere safer. And preferably," he paused to cough. "… With far cleaner air."

"Where exactly are we gonna go to now, hmmm?" Malachi queried.

"Where a fire isn't trying to burn down the building is a nice start," Vanessa informed with a tight smile.

"To my place, but if you're going to have more sass than her," Leon stated while thumbing to Vanessa, "then I'm going to toss you into Zaraltrac and be done with you."

Malachi rolled his eyes. Without warning, the azbanonite sneezed a few times before lapping at his snout. "The sooner we go, the better. The smoke is so thick here that I can't think straight."

"I think that problem started before the smoke," Vanessa grumbled.

Bobo snickered.

Checking the exit behind them, Leon made sure that the stairwell was clear of debris and fires before waving everyone over. "All's clear. Let's get the hex outta here."

"Gladly," Bobo announced, coming to his full height and pulling up the distraught succubus with him.

They all headed down but were met halfway by a team of cleansers. There was a chain of beings where buckets of water were passed by non-magic users while spellcasters summoned rains and flooded the floors with the provided water. All the while, Vanessa and the others were looked over by the medical teams that had shown up on-site while they uncomfortably explained what had happened.

Why was it uncomfortable? Because none other than Riker had shown up to the scene. And the whole time he was silent, Vanessa felt pings of panic race through her core. Was it too late to go on that vacation the Coven had been pushing her to take?

"Peterson … Why?" he asked simply. But the young witch never gave a response. "I just left you. I. JUST. Left. You," his second reiteration was far louder, and angrier, than the first.

"You really shouldn't be surprised," Bobo mumbled.

Riker cut the ogre a look, and the gentlemen-beast whistled a tune while stepping away from the group to assess the damage to the building. Cold, slate eyes resumed their chilling hold on the Spellweaver. "How do you manage to get into these situations all the time?"

"I'd tell you it was luck, but that would be a lie," she tried to joke.

Leon added, "Right? It's more like a curse."

Riker flashed his gaze over to the Summoner. "A curse, indeed." He straightened up as he took in a deep breath of air and released it slowly. Vanessa could see the man visibly calming himself through breathing exercises. "Where's the tablet?"

"Safe," Vanessa quickly informed.

The war veteran's eyes narrowed into slits at her. "Safe and you do not go hand in hand."

Leon sputtered with laughter and looked away from the heated stare Vanessa was tossing his way. She sighed then and said, "Riker, I know I'm trouble on two legs—"

"Wait, wait. Where's Bobo? He needs to hear her admit this," Leon stated while whirling around looking for the giant demon. However, the gentleman-beast was nowhere in sight.

Pressing on like she had never been interrupted, Vanessa finished with, "BUT! I keep the important things safe."

"My faith in that statement is wavering, Peterson ..." Riker announced in a drone tone.

"Goddess above, aid me ... I promise I've got this! Trust me." Her begging eyes pleaded silently with him as she folded her hands in prayer.

As the Summoner thought it over, Bobo called out to Vanessa from the front of the apartment complex. A few cleansers were all around him, and he was waving a book in one hand and clutching a cappuccino machine under his arm. "Vanessa! Vanessa! I had them recover your grimoire!" he exclaimed excitedly.

Riker darted his vision from the ogre back to the young witch, who already had the tablet removed from the magic satchel and was holding it out in the Summoner's direction. He raised a brow inquisitively at the Spellweaver. "And here I was questioning the depth of your sensibility." Snatching the stone from her, he put it in an empty bag at his side. It seems as though he already determined her unfit to watch over the artifact before making the trip to her apartment. Which only made her frown harder. He saw her expression and sighed while darting his eyes from place to place. "I ... *hem* ... It would be better for me to have it in my possession. If the Coven was to find out about this, I—naturally—would be far more capable of explaining the reasons why we hadn't turned it in yet."

Her pout turned from real to playful as she jutted out her lip even further. "You don't trust me," she whined under her breath.

"No, Vanessa. I don't trust the trouble you tend to find yourself in," he corrected.

Slumping back against the medical carriage, she groaned out, "Fiiine. You're right."

"Go ho—" Riker stopped and examined the half-burnt building in front of them.

"They're coming to my place," Leon informed. "The cleansers said that they'd have everything cleaned up in three days. Until then, they have a home with me."

"Good. Before any more mishaps and misfortune can find you, I urge you all to be on your way," Riker said with finality.

And none of them argued with him.

After filing a short report and submitting an insurance claim at the Coven, they all headed over to Leon's place. Which Vanessa had no idea was located in the Adalith district. Despite knowing who he was and what family he hailed from, the Spellweaver couldn't keep her jaw from unhinging as she gawked at the monumentally large home that stared back at her.

Malachi whistled at the two-story home with double, curved staircases leading up to the second-floor balcony. The deep brown of the siding was complimented with the stark white trim and latticework that hugged the white-painted beams and facing of the home. Rich brown tinged with red tiles coated the entire top of the sharply angled roof. On one side of the home was a beautiful, tall turret. The earthy tones cut with white beams made it look like the largest gingerbread house Vanessa had ever seen.

"Impressive," the Sleekit remarked. "I'd try to steal from it," he quickly added his admission.

Leon only laughed instead of threatening the being.

"This is your house?" she screeched.

"Yes?" Leon replied.

"Exactly how rich are you?" The young witch turned to look at Leon with large, bulbous eyes.

"Well, I mean ... I'm not rich. My parents are," he informed.

"This really is your parent's house?" Surprisingly enough, she had a calmer demeanor as she asked the question.

He nodded.

She shook her head. "Nope. I'm not living with your parents for three days." Turning on heel, she started for the front gate. Only, Bobo slid into her way to stop her.

"Hold on, Vanessa, my dear. You're such a charming creature. This really is the best option. A young, unmarried witch sleeping in a man's one-bedroom abode would be frowned upon. Surely you cannot be afraid of meeting his parents to the point that you'd have us sleeping on the streets, correct?" The ogre dripped with confidence, but Vanessa knew all too well the angle he was coming from.

"You just want to sleep in a place that mirrors your posh spirit," she mumbled heatedly.

The ogre got a tad bit flush in the cheeks and rolled his lips in trying to hide his growing grin. After a quiet moment of him collecting himself, he added, "Oh, come on, Vanessa! How often do we get to stay in something this amazing? I'm sure the flagstones we're standing on could pay a few months of our rent alone."

She leaned in close and whispered, "You're a money-hungry ogre."

He scoffed, shifted his weight, and repositioned his cappuccino machine under one arm. "No, I'm an ogre who appreciates quality. And that," he pointed to the mansion behind her, "is the finest quality home I've ever seen. Now, turn your cute butt around and get in that house."

Jutting a finger up into her pet's face, Vanessa drew in a breath to retort. But before she could counter the gentleman-beast, Vanessa was twirled and pulled over to Leon who then guided her a few steps back from the others.

The Summoner's eyes became fixed with hers, and his mouth looked like he was trying not to frown and failing. "What's wrong with staying at my place for a few days? There is more than enough room—"

"It's not about space, Leon," she half-whined.

"Tell me what the problem is so we can fix it together. Walking away isn't going to make anything that you're feeling right now, in this moment, disappear."

She huffed and looked away.

"Vanessa?" he pleaded.

She sighed heavily. "Leon, I've always known you've come from a pretty well-known family. I was reminded enough during my years at the academy and when I first joined the Coven. Everyone always whispered about you. They always talked about how if they could just rub elbows with you that they'd be set for life. Me? I never cared about that. So much so that I forgot about it." She looked back to the beautiful home. "But this is a reminder of how different we are."

His grip on her tightened, slightly. "Are you … breaking up with me?"

She pulled back and slapped him over the shoulder, hard. "What?! No!" she shrieked. "I'm just saying that I'm worried that … you know … me being—"

It was his turn to interrupt her. "An orphan is going to make my parents look down on you and question my taste in women?"

She nodded and looked down.

Drawing her back into his arms, he smiled and gave her a strong hug. "I'm sorry that the world you've had to live in was cold, lonely, and cast in shades of black and white. But the world isn't so stark all the time, Vanessa. There is a rainbow of choices and actions out there that you've not been privy to, but I have been. I'm sorry for that."

"That world I've always known exists no matter how much we don't want to acknowledge it," she whispered into his chest and squeezed him.

He pulled back enough so they could look in each other's eyes once more. "Let me share my world with yours, then. That's the only way to defeat it."

She smiled. And it rivaled the sun. Jumping up and wrapping her arms around his neck, she spoke only loud enough for him to hear. "Thank you for loving me." She dropped down, flat on her feet again, and said, "I love you, Leon."

He chuckled and kissed her gently. "I love you, too," he breathed against her lips.

Bobo shielded his eyes. "And my nightmare of your public displays of affection continues."

"Oh hush!" Lyx snapped with a smile. "I think it's adorable!"

"You'd be the only one," Malachi interjected.

Bobo thumbed to the Sleekit with a look of silent agreement.

 *Chapter 26:*

Standing at a front door had never been so nerve-wracking. Vanessa was wringing her wrists until the skin bled white while Leon rang the doorbell. It made her heartbeat scramble to a tempo that threatened to choke the life out of her.

"A-are you sure they'll like me?" she whispered to Leon.

He leaned over to her and whispered back, "I don't think you understand what is about to happen."

She felt like she swallowed her heart when he said that. A knot grew in her stomach, and everything told her to forget it all and run for the front gates. But the door opened and it was too late.

"Young master!" the butler's elated voice echoed through the large foyer.

As if summoned, a woman with straight, glittering blonde hair came bustling through from the other room. "My little Leo! Mommy missed you!" she said in a sweet, high-pitched voice. Dashing in high heels across the pristine marble flooring, the woman threw her arms around Leon's neck and forced the Summoner to bed down to her shorter height.

As he gasped for air, he reminded the woman holding him in a near headlock saying, "Mother, I visit here often and was just here a few days ago." He managed to pull free of her suffocating embrace.

"Doesn't matter," his mother expressed. "Working for the Coven is dangerous, and there are far too many ferals out there right now. What would happen if my baby boy got hurt or —" she gasped and covered her mouth while shaking her head. Holding back a wail, she threw her arms back around her son and hugged him tightly.

Leon chuckled. "What are you going to do when I start staying at my own place more?"

The woman practically screamed as she pulled back to inspect her son's face. "Aah! Leon! Why would you say such a thing?" Her lip quivered. "You don't want to stay with mommy?"

Before he could reply, a taller man with brown hair and a mustache of matching color announced his presence by saying, "Look at the young man, Patricia. He's hardly a boy anymore."

The mother cut the man a harsh look that could smelt rock. "Don't you come in here just to dash my hopes and dreams, Robert!" her sweet voice was peppery as she shot out the command.

"My dear, Patricia. The light of my life. The sun in my sky," Robert started.

The flames died out in her eyes like her husband had thrown a bucket of ice-cold water over them. "Yes?" she asked, honey coating her words.

"Someone must be the voice of reason in the family," he informed while giving her a dashing smile.

Vanessa now knew where Leon got his looks from. His mother, but that smile? She could see it in his father as plain as day.

The father flicked his brown eyes to the succubus. "Hello, dear." Lyx waved back with a smile before hugging Leon's mother. The father looked to the Sleekit and nodded to the being. Who gave a quiet nod back. Then Robert looked to his side and scaled up the length of Bobo's body. Stopping at the head, he stared at the demon while remaining quite still.

"Well. You most certainly didn't skip your vegetables. Look, Leon. I told you, eating your peas would have given you a physique like this fine being. You missed out because your mother coddles you!" Robert proclaimed.

"I'm allergic to peas, dad!" Leon shouted.

Vanessa couldn't help it. She laughed. The action brought far more attention to her than she would have expected. She had been hiding behind Leon, struggling with her fear and trying to calm her nerves.

Patricia's head popped out from Leon's side. The woman blinked her baby blue eyes as the young witch. A smile formed. Though, Vanessa wasn't sure if it was forced or not. "Leon … Who's this?" she asked through her teeth and all while blinking wildly.

"This is my partner," he announced.

"Ah. Works at the Coven, eh? I wonder, what is your status there?" Robert piped in.

"Spellweaver," Vanessa replied proudly, albeit on the meeker side.

Robert lit up. "Spellweaver? Why, you look so young. A breadth away from twenty, I'm sure! And you're a Spellweaver? Tell me, what is your name, young lady?"

Leon cleared his throat. "Mom. Dad. This is Vanessa Peterson."

The father blanched and bumbled about his speech for a moment. Vanessa shrunk in on herself. Any minute, the speech would start. The orphan troublemaker couldn't be seen with their son. Would it be better that she quietly see herself out now, before she was thrown out in the trash heaps for the Skrittish to collect?

"Leon, how could you?!" Robert finally roared.

"Honestly," Patricia balked. Her hands reached for Leon's and held them in her own. "How could you do this to us?" she whispered. Her hurt expression turned up to the Summoner, her blue eyes searching his own for answers she would never find in their depths. The mother's eyes teared up. Again, she asked, "How could you?"

The father motioned to the world outside their front door. "If we would have known!" He stopped and tried to get his anger under control. Shaking his head, Robert scowled at his son. "I don't even know you."

Vanessa's heart shattered. Her throat tightened like a spectral was wringing her neck. Her eyes blazed with heat as she fought back the urge to cry. There was no loss of dignity if she just turned and walked out now. But what hurt the most was that she had trusted Leon. He said it would all be okay.

And she believed him.

Robert hid his face with the palm of his hand, shaking his head over and over while the room fell deathly silent. The tension was so thick you could reach out and grab hold of it. Slowly, the father's gaze rose to rest on his son. Anger filled in his laugh lines. He shook his head again. Finally, he turned to Vanessa. "Let me start by apologizing to you. You … didn't deserve any of this. But … because of a *poor* choice on our son's part," he stopped and let his lips thin out into a straight line, and he audibly exhaled through his nostrils, "all of this could have been avoided," he whispered.

It hurt. It hurt so much.

"Leon," the mother chided softly.

"If you would have told us that we were having such an esteemed guest, all of this could have been avoided! We could have had petals lining the path, and a party could have been arranged. Patricia. Patricia, tell him what I was just saying earlier!"

The mother nodded. "It's true. He was talking about wanting to have a party. A ball, in fact," she informed.

"A ball, Leon! I could have had a grand ball prepared for the occasion. And food!" he cried out and laid a hand over his heart as he stumbled back. A maid caught him, helped him stand upright, and resumed her dusting like nothing ever happened.

"You know your father loves party food best," Patricia whispered to Leon.

"All my unplanned plans ruined! And now she's going to look down on us!" The mother only nodded in agreement. "Get out! Get out all of you. We'll have to do this all over and do it right from the start." He waved the butler over, "Jasper, see them out. I have a ball to plan!"

As they were being shoved out by the butler—who had far more strength than one would have expected—Lyx snapped to her master, "Hex it all, say something!"

Leon grabbed a hold of the doorframe and yelled back to his parents, "Her apartment was damaged, and she has nowhere to go!"

Robert slapped at the butler's hands. "What are you doing? Didn't you hear my son? She has nowhere to go. How heartless are you?"

"Forgive me, my lord," Jasper said with a bow and stepped back from the chaos.

"Why didn't you say something sooner?" Robert asked.

"Not like you gave him the chance," Bobo mumbled to Vanessa.

"Well, I was trying to tell you something *else* first!" Leon barked, exasperated.

Patricia scooted up next to her husband and said, "There's no need to yell, Leo."

Although the Summoner looked like he was about to at that moment, he managed to cool off quickly and took a few deep, calming breaths. "Vanessa isn't just my partner." He grabbed Vanessa's hand. The parents' vision followed the action. He pulled her in close. His mother and father watched with large eyes of amazement. Holding the Spellweaver close to him, he announced, "Vanessa and I are future-gazing together."

"F-f-f-future-gazing!" Robert floundered.

"Oh. My. Goddess!" Patricia screamed. "My little Leo has a girlfriend! He's brought home his very first girl! Aaaah!" She shoved her son out of the way and drew Vanessa in for a hug.

While the mother squeezed the very breath out of the young witch, Robert leaned in close and asked, "Is he blackmailing you?"

"I'm right here!" Leon yelled.

Ignoring his boy, Robert continued, "Whatever dirt he has on you, I can get rid of it. Come now, tell me." Immediately, Leon's father held up his hand. "On second thought, don't tell me. The less that I know the better. Just give me a list of names, and I promise all your problems will go away by the end of the week."

"Are you serious?" growled Leon.

Lyx was too busy trying to mask her laughter to add anything to the commotion. Trying, and failing. She giggled into her hand and held her stomach as she stifled her cackles as best as possible. Malachi was busy touching a vase, and a maid slapped his hands when he reached to pick it up.

Bobo, however, seemed just fine with letting everything carry on the way that it had been like he had expected the whole ordeal from the start.

"I'm not blackmailing her, dad," Leon half-whined.

Robert scoffed and turned to face his son. "Well, why else would she be future-gazing with you?"

"Oh hex," Lyx gasped between quiet cackles and quickly tightened the hand covering her mouth, a grin peeking out from behind her perfectly manicured nails.

He motioned to his son. "You still haven't reached Summoner status."

"I'm training. All I have to do is go through the ceremony, but the Coven already considers me a Summoner," Leon said in a flat tone.

"Certainly she isn't attracted to your sense of style. Your taste in fashion is atrocious, my boy." His father steamrolled on, ticking off the reasons why Vanessa wouldn't be interested in him.

Bobo perked up and added, "That's true!"

Leon looked to the ogre and the gentleman-beast stared in the opposite direction. Robert's hand rose and gently lay on the back of the demon. The two beings exchanged a look and a quiet nod before they resumed looking at the Summoner.

Another voice joined the mix. It was soft like the mother's but held a child-like lilt to it. "Dad must be at it again."

Entering the room was a shorter female with deep brown hair like her father. She had the same blue eyes as her mother, and she had a cute, button nose placed between two dimpled cheeks. Her long, pink, flowing gown glided just above the floor as she waltzed in with grace and poise that rivaled a queen.

"Sara," Leon said the name like he was greeting his own, personal savior. "Help your brother out, would you?"

She laughed into the back of her hand. The sound was pure, proper mirth. "Brother, you know that I have to stand by father in all decisions that he makes."

"Ah. The child that has the most sense in this family, come." Robert rolled his hand, churning the air as though it would cause a current that'd bring his daughter to him swifter.

She obediently came to his side and gave him a hug. "Are we going to have a party? I heard you say something about a ball," Sara inquired.

Robert frowned. "No. Someone didn't give me a proper warning. Sadly, there shall be no party."

"How can someone plan a building blowing up?" Leon seethed.

"Please, don't tempt her. She'll find a way," Bobo warned.

Lyx lightly slapped the ogre's shoulder. "Be nice. She doesn't always get into trouble."

Malachi snorted with laughter. "Word on the street says otherwise."

Sara pouted at her father, but Vanessa could tell it was all for show. "Oh. What a shame. You always throw the best parties." She sighed. "If only we had the coin to urge the caterers to come up with a simple but wondrous meal for the occasion, and, if we were to plan now, we could try to throw it in a few ... no. No. It was silly of me to think you would do that," she said to herself.

"Well, let's not be rash dear. Daddy is a capable man, you know," Robert stated, perking up to his daughter's ideas.

Patricia clapped her hands together excitedly. "Robert, we could send out invitation messages using flitter on our new crystal balls!"

Robert waved a finger at his wife. "You're as smart as you are beautiful. Come, my love, we have a grand event to plan!" Swooping in to hook his wife around the waist, Leon's father started out of the room. Pausing in mid-stride, the man turned his gaze to Vanessa. "My dear, it was a pleasure to meet you. I do hope you'll like the ball we're planning for you. Stay as long as you like."

With that, the two parents practically danced and giggled out of the room. All the way out, mummers of ideas were passed between the two of them until they faded from sight.

"Clever as always, Sara," Leon chuckled.

She grinned and flicked her hair over her shoulder. "One must be in this house."

They both laughed and hugged before he straightened up and turned around to motion to Vanessa and Bobo. "This is—"

"Vanessa Peterson," she finished for him. The smile on her face was large and radiating warmth. "Oh, bless the moon and stars. I never thought I would get to meet you in person," she gleefully announced, rushing over and shaking the young witch's hand. "You've no idea what an honor this is. To meet someone of your caliber is equal to meeting one of the legendary members of the Coven. You're up and coming and soon to stand with the greats. I heard that you can perform magic without reagents!" she gabbed excitedly.

Bobo coughed at her side, and her beaming smile brightened all the more. "And you are—without a doubt—the *great* Botobolbilian, the loyal, true, and strong partner of our young and upcoming witch here. I heard you battled a pack of hellhounds all on your own while Vanessa prepared a spell. How heroic!"

The ogre was about to say some rather honest things to put the girl straight about his master, but she did have a point. He was pretty heroic. He straightened up his tie and flattened out his soot-smudged suit and bowed to her. "Greetings, my dear."

Sara curtseyed.

Leon faced the butler, "Jasper, please gather Matilda and see that the rooms in the west wing are in order. My friends will be staying with me on my side of the mansion for a few days."

"Of course, sir. Right away," Jasper replied before heading out of the room and up the main staircase.

Placing a gentle hand on Vanessa's shoulder, Lyx turned the young witch slightly to face her. "You can bunk with me in my room!" she whispered happily. "I've got more than enough space, darling. You're going to love it."

Her mind was still a whirlwind of emotions and thoughts. She could only nod in reply with a faint, genuine smile.

"I have to get back to my lessons," Sara admitted with a real pout this time. "Leon, would you join me in the music room later?"

He nodded. "I can. Let me get them taken care of first."

"Okay. Goodbye, everyone!" Sara waved happily before rushing off toward another one of the various rooms in the large home.

Lyx was already tugging Bobo to follow her down one of the main halls. Eyeing over the Sleekit, the Summoner pointed to Bobo, and Malachi held up his hands while following the pair ahead. "I know, I know. I'm following him," the azbanonite grumbled.

While the others walked ahead, Leon and Vanessa fell behind the group and took a more leisurely pace. "I told you," he whispered.

"Hmmm?" she immediately realized what he meant and smiled, bumping him with her hip as they walked. Her lips curled and she laughed. "I can't lie, I was a little worried."

Putting an arm around her, Leon drew her closer to him and said, "I would never put you in a position that I know would hurt you mentally, physically, or emotionally."

"I trusted you," she admitted. "Just, when they were saying—"

"I know." He squeezed her side, and she mimicked him.

After letting out a heavy sigh, Vanessa felt better. "I like your family," she said.

"You can have them," he joked.

And they laughed while following behind the others. Again, Leon's hand dipped into a small pouch by his hip, and he got a peculiar look in his eyes.

 *Chapter 27:*

"You get your own room, big guy," Leon informed the gentleman-beast when they had reached their destination. A few of the maids were still rushing about the halls and darting in and out of rooms with fresh linen, feather dusters, mops and buckets, brooms, and various trays. Newly filled oil lamps were being brought into the bedrooms while Vanessa, Leon, Bobo, Lyx, and Malachi waited out in the corridor.

Bobo curled his lips into his mouth and gave a short, stifled, cry of joy. Wiping away a tear that wasn't there, the demon approached Leon and embraced him. "I shall never forget this."

"Okay," Leon gasped, tapping at the ogre's arms. "Let the Summoner breath."

"Yes, sorry." The demon released him and cleared his throat.

Malachi's ears were twitching, his tail was swishing wildly to and fro, and his eyes were large with wonder. "What about me?"

Leon's smile faded a bit. "You're staying in my room."

The Sleekit's bottom jaw went slack. "What?"

"You think I'm going to let you have your own room?" Leon asked, truly astonished.

Crossing his arms over his chest, the azbanonite grumbled, "This is clearly a judgment based off of creature profiling."

"You said you would try to steal from my home," Leon reminded.

Malachi looked hurt. "I would never—" He stopped when he saw multiple sets of unbelieving eyes resting on him. "Okay, fine! But why can't I bunk with him?" he asked, thumbing over to Bobo.

The Summoner visibly cringed and quickly masked the expression. Even if he didn't trust the Sleekit completely, he still didn't want to subject him to the horror that he, himself, had lived through. "Trust me. I'm doing you a favor."

During dinner that evening, Leon convinced his father that it would be best to wait to hold a party to greet Vanessa. He used the excuse that she didn't have the funds for the proper attire and threw in mission scrolls as an extra bonus. Luckily, between the Summoner's justifications and Sara's cunning speech, they managed to sway Robert to hold off until after the ritual of the Wild Hunt. That way, he wouldn't be competing with the grand yearly event.

Every year, the Coven performed the Wild Hunt ritual, even though they had been doing it wrong practically from the start. During this ritual, the High Priest Council would focus on performing the spell and keeping a barrier up around all of Tolvade while the entirety of the city would attend a ball that would be held shortly after the Wild Hunt was summoned. This spell had two functions, or, since they've found the tablets, three. One, it called forth the Wild Hunt to judge the souls of the departed so that they could be at rest before being escorted on into the next realm. Two, it gave those that were grieving a chance to say goodbye, and a massive ball was held so that both living and spirit could attend. Though, there were fewer spirits showing up each year. The reasoning for that still eluded the Coven and inhabitants of Aeristria. And the third and final purpose of the ritual was to give back all the magic that had been accumulated throughout the year or (in this case) all the magic that had been stored within the ritual tablets for a couple hundred years.

After explaining that the extra time meant that the party could be even larger and more magnificent made the father more than happy to put off the plans for a bit longer. He did offer to aid in purchasing Vanessa's new clothes for the occasion, though. She accepted his kindness. Primarily because he wouldn't take no for an answer and was putting the coin purse in her hand despite her constant, polite rejections.

Once dinner was done, they said goodnight and piled into Lyx's room to hear out Malachi. The Sleekit was far from happy about the extra ears joining the conversation but didn't fight them on it too much considering the situation. Lyx and Leon aiding in keeping him from becoming a corpse helped a bit too. He waited while they all poured into the large room and closed the door.

"Lock it," he demanded. "I don't need a larger audience."

Agreeing, Leon locked it before coming to sit down next to Vanessa on the couch at the end of the massive, purple, canopy bed.

"To catch everyone up, I was the being that snuck into the storage room the night you all went to the Flustered Dragon," Malachi reminded.

Whipping her tail back and forth with a look that could curse, Lyx asked, "Why?" in the most non-threatening tone she could muster.

Bobo patted the top of the demoness's arm to calm her, though his look portrayed his lack of trust that he still had toward the Sleekit. "Continue," the ogre urged the being.

Malachi paced like he was cutting a path into the elaborate rug in the center of the room. "I was hired by the Elternian," he started.

Already, everyone was lost.

"The who?" Leon asked.

"Was it to get the treasure box Vice gave to me?" Vanessa questioned.

"What do they want?" Bobo inquired.

The Sleekit growled, and his ear flicked as if trying to discard all of the mounting questions. "Hush. Hush. Hush. You bunch of hairless wretches," he hissed. He sneezed and lapped at the sides of his muzzle.

Lyx spoke up then. "Let Malachi speak. He'll get to answering all of our questions without us prompting him, I'm sure."

Malachi pointed to the succubus with a grin. "Yes, thank you."

The smile that formed over the demoness' lips was sinister and made a shiver run up the Sleekit's spine. "If he doesn't then I'll handle disposing of him myself."

The azbanonite gulped audibly.

"Please," Bobo said with a grin that was more threatening than friendly, "… continue."

Malachi's nose twitched, and he nodded slowly. "Yes ... well." He took a moment to pause and regain his lost courage. "The Elternian is a more recent group of magic users that have come together in the last few years. But their influence is great, their power immeasurable, and the original group wanted — at all costs — to find a way to put magic back into the land." He scratched at the patch of fur on his chest. "Dmitri was tied to that group."

"And Isolde," Vanessa reminded.

Malachi shook his head. "No, she was part of something darker. But one thing at a time. Let's focus on the Elternian for now." The room fell silent again, and the Sleekit continued. "They didn't want the treasure box. They wanted me to kidnap you and your partner, Bobo."

"What! Why?" Vanessa didn't mean to interrupt him again. It just naturally slips out after someone states that they wanted to kidnap you.

Malachi sniffed and paused in his incessant circle walking. "They had been trying to summon ogres from the underworld. They were trying to get a powerful creature that would also have enough devotion, magic, and sense to be part of a ritual to put the fading magic back into the land."

"They — they were the ones summoning all of those — " Vanessa stopped and looked away. She had laid them to rest, but that didn't stop the memory from haunting her. She hadn't, until now, ever counted them as kills. She had released them. She had sent them into a dream state that they would never wake from. Unlike Denmarius, whom she had run through with a shadow blade. She shut her eyes, and her head spun for a moment. Had she ever tried to come to terms with these actions? Were a few weeks enough time to come to terms with such things?

She took a slow breath in and released it gradually. Opening her eyes, she noticed all eyes on her. Attempting to avert everyone's attention, the Spellweaver spoke to Malachi. "So, they summoned all those ogres ... why didn't they go ahead with the spell? Why need me?"

"They lacked intelligence and a proper tether." This time, it was Bobo that spoke up. His eyes were fixed on the Sleekit.

Malachi rose to his full height and nodded very slowly. "Yes," he admitted.

It took a moment, but Vanessa gasped as she caught on and stood to her feet. "They wouldn't!"

"I'm proof that they would, Vanessa," Malachi shot back.

"What exactly are you getting at?" Leon asked carefully, his body looking as though he were fighting back the urge to grab his wand.

Running a hand through the fur on his head, the Sleekit sighed and said, "All those summons were failures without proper tethering. They didn't time the intelligence spells right. Some had been hit twice and suffered more than the others." He took no joy in explaining it all to them. "But you, Bobo," Malachi pointed a clawed finger to the ogre. "You were a perfect specimen and already tethered to a powerful witch."

Vanessa's eyes narrowed. Not at Malachi, but at the notion that she had come to realize what she meant to this Elternian group. "An expendable witch with no family to speak of."

"Alakazam! She's got it!" Malachi yipped.

Lyx let the tips of her talons rest on side of her face as she thought out loud, "You were there to snag the two of them for this sacrificial ritual to put magic back into the land but why did you know how to use black magic? How are you not— you know? "

"Driven insane?" Malachi finished for her. "That's where Isolde comes in. She was part of the original group before it started to become corrupt. There was a disagreement amongst the members, and a divide in goals came into play. Once they realized that the tablets were the source of magic being withheld and that the balance could be restored—"

"They wanted to tie up all the loose ends and silence anyone that could out them for their crimes against the Coven and against all of Tolvade," Leon guessed.

The azbanonite nodded. "Exactly."

"Which is why you fled to the Coven seeking someone powerful enough to stand against any assassination attempts made by the Elternaian," the Summoner finished.

Again, Malachi nodded.

"Then, what of the other group that Isolde was a part of? Why did you perform black magic?" Vanessa asked.

"Well, to explain that," Malachi started and began pacing again. "The other group, the Night Order, had already delved into practicing black magic to achieve many goals that the group had laid out. Summoning, attempting tethers without proper reagents, curses, and the like. With each spell, they noticed that their magic was more powerful when they practiced black magic. Isolde was one of the first to figure out the reason for that. She had been assigned by the Coven to investigate why the blood mages had recently been growing in number and in power. She was a double-agent, though. She gave information to the blood mages about Dark Market raids, watch schedules, and anything else that would benefit their nasty deeds and kept any information that would tip the Coven off from reaching the High Priest Council."

"What was causing the growth in power," Bobo asked, trying to keep the Sleekit on topic.

Snapping out of his angry daze, he resumed explaining. "Restless spirits. Less and less show up each year to the spring ball. Haven't you ever wondered why? They aren't being judged. They aren't passing over. They are stuck and slowly they turn into something dark. That is where black magic gets its power from. It draws it from the angry spirits of the dead. Slowly, over time, those restless souls try to take over a body. If they can't pass over into the next life, they try to take over a living host."

"But you show no signs of long-term use," Vanessa said.

"Because I'm not dumb enough to use it all the time. Besides, Sleekits naturally have a higher tolerance to black magic," Malachi informed.

Bobo added, "You used it that night at the Flustered Dragon."

The Sleekit half-laughed. "I'll admit, I panicked. I had hoped that the spell going off would cause you all to stay behind and cleanse the area, but you didn't."

"So you summoned those gargoyles?" Leon asked.

Malachi shook his head. "I knew that they were sealed there. I was just using what was available to me to my advantage. So, I broke the seal just in case."

"You almost got us killed!" Vanessa shrieked.

"I wasn't trying to get you killed. I figured if there was a slight chance that you would follow, that maybe you'd split up. The old divide and conquer trick. But you all rode on the waves of my magic."

"Most of us did, anyway," Lyx huffed.

"Those spells you slung—" Vanessa started.

"Would have knocked you out at best," Malachi interrupted heatedly.

Leon shook his head. "But you realized you were outmatched and ran."

"I did. I managed to give you all the slip and tried to recollect myself for another attempt when you got the attention of those blasted gargoyles. Do you know how hard it is to seal those things?"

"Did you follow us into the woods?" Vanessa asked.

"Ha! Unlike someone in this room, I don't have a death wish," the azbanonite replied smugly.

The room fell silent again. Vanessa was too focused on what Malachi had said to try and banter with him further. It would be a waste of breath trying to explain herself to someone that didn't know her personally. Out of everything that he had said, she realized a very dangerous truth. The number of restless spirits were growing and quite rapidly in the past few months as well. "Something bad is going to happen soon." Her voice was low and full of dread.

Malachi sighed softly. "I'm afraid so. Though, I don't know what or when. Both sides were starting to realize that the other group didn't align with the other. The divide had happened long before that. There is no telling how long they've been planning everything. But the real trouble was brewing with the groups when my contract to kidnap you expired and I had to run for my life. Otherwise, I'd give you every bit of dirt on those—" He bit his tongue. "Doesn't matter. If we can shut them down, my hide can live in peace until the natural end of my days."

Vanessa held her head. She had this to deal with and still had to come up with a plan for Riker. "I don't know what to do," she whispered.

"It's a lot to take in," Bobo expressed. "Why don't you and I come up with a plan for Riker?"

It was like the ogre knew. Goddess bless that behemoth demon! "Please. This is too much catastrophe for me to take in."

"I find that hard to believe," Bobo said with a grand smile.

Vanessa shook her head and laughed even though she had tried to fight the urge to. "Blast it all with hellfire, Bobo," she giggled.

"Come over here, darling," Lyx begged while tugging at Vanessa to the head of the bed. "Let's try to figure all this out like we'd try to figure out eating a dragon."

"Oh? And how would we do that?" Vanessa asked with a tired expression.

Lyx laughed then. "One bite at a time, of course." The demoness winked then and patted on the soft pillows propped up on the bed.

Across the room, Leon had taken Malachi over toward the windows to talk a bit more. Even though she was curious, Vanessa's head hurt too much already. The last thing that she wanted to do was add to the growing pangs of pain. She'd much rather take Lyx's advice and tackle the whole situation one problem at a time.

First problem: how was she going to explain to the Coven how she and Riker had gotten the tablet within hours of getting the mission scroll and not tell them it was Merlin? And Merlin was actually Archimedes who was presumed to have died years before. If they did find out, Riker would suffer for not holding up his promise to Merlin.

Her head hurt just thinking about the things she did know. Trying to tackle this, even in parts and pieces, was going to be one hex of a task.

Taking her time, she explained everything to Lyx and even filled Bobo in on a few things he had missed before his arrival at the restaurant. It was a lot to take in considering everything that had happened over the past ... well, for a while now. Afterward, Lyx frowned, and Bobo pondered while Vanessa looked equally as stumped as the other two.

"I fear to say that I cannot come up with a good plan, my dear," Bobo admitted.

Sighing, Lyx added. "Yeah. I don't have a clue on how to help you there."

Nodding, Vanessa shrugged, accepting her fate rather well. "I don't think I'm going to have the answer come to me as soon as I thought."

"What are you going to do about Riker?" Lyx asked.

Vanessa bit her lip and then grinned awkwardly. "Ignore him?"

Bobo stared at his master with a bored expression. "Do you honestly believe that is the best course of action?"

"Nooo. But it can buy me some time? I can't avoid him forever, but I can dodge his crystal ball calls until tomorrow at least. My brain feels like it's filled with pixy dust. I just can't seem to think straight, and I need to find a way to keep Malachi safe." As she spoke the last line, she held a hand over her heart. Not just his life was riding on the promise she made with him.

"All right, then, Vanessa. You don't have to play me a sad song on an enchanted fiddle," Bobo huffed. "No sense in pulling a half-baked idea out of your head."

"Don't beat yourself up. With some proper rest, I'm sure you'll come up with something," Lyx assured.

Vanessa hoped that they were right.

Lyx opted to break the doom and gloom mood that was saturating the room. "Things have been too serious, darling. Do you know what we all need?"

"Hmmm?" Vanessa hummed.

"A good show on the magic mirror and some late night snacks!" The succubus was all sorts of giddy over the idea.

Leon snapped his fingers and turned away from whatever he was discussing with Malachi. "It's spring. I'm sure that the professional Runeball games have begun. Given the hour, I'm sure it's about to kick off."

"Banish a banshee. I had forgotten that it was Runeball season," Vanessa gasped.

The Summoner could only laugh. "That's what happens when you get obsessed with mission scrolls."

Bobo had quickly grabbed his spectacles from his side pouch and rushed over to the large magic mirror on the wall. "Confounded all. How does one finagle with this enchanted contraption? We'll miss the first serve." His large hand ran over the edge of the mirror, and a call opened up.

The reflection faded, and the image of Leon's mother formed. She was sporting a pale pink silk nighty and a lacey magenta robe with matching fluffy feathers lining the hems. Patricia was paused in mid-action of brushing her hair with her comb still in hand, and she blinked at the image of Bobo staring back at her. "Oh … Uhmm … heh …" She waved to the mirror and pointed to the other side. "If you're trying to watch something, the image-spelled side is over there."

Clearing his throat, the gentleman-beast gave a half-bow and nodded. "Thank you, my dear." And he quickly cut the connection. He gave Leon a look. "Could have warned an ogre that you had your mother dearest on speed call," he mumbled, and rand a finger over the other side.

The Summoner laughed boisterously. "And miss out on stuff like that?" he expressed, thumbing at the mirror. "I think not."

Lyx tugged at Vanessa's sleeve and whispered excitedly, "Come on. Let the men fuss with the hanging glass while you and I go to the kitchen to see what's brewing in the cauldron!"

Before the Spellweaver knew it, they were out the bedroom door and flying through the maze of corridors. Trying to memorize how they wound up in the kitchen was dizzying for Vanessa. Despite her own two feet making the trip, she was lost the whole way and had not the slightest clue on how to make it back to Lyx's room without the succubus holding her hand. Thankfully, that wouldn't be a concern for her.

Inside the cooking area, slow, lapping flames ate away at hunks of logs in the fireplace on the far side of the room. A blend of new age electronics blended into old fashioned. Lyx pointed to the pot pulled away from the fire. "That's where Beatrix makes the kettle corn," the demoness whispered dreamily.

A large, plump, older woman—with her back facing the two girls—sliced away at a pear and delicately plated it with an arrangement of other freshly cut fruits. "Lyx, is that you? Don't you go putting your hands in nothing that I've been preparing. You know how master Zvĕrokruh likes his Runeball snacks," the cook warned.

The succubus skipped over to the cook. "What about the young master?" Lyx asked, sporting a rather impressive pout.

The cook, Beatrix, slowly turned and pointed with her knife to the succubus' lip. "Don't point that at me."

Lyx sneered and pushed the tip of the knife away, "Don't point yours, and I won't point mine."

"Hmf. You won't get your way with me, missy."

"Oh, come on, Beatrix. Can't Leon and I have some snacks?" Lyx whined.

"No," the cook replied flatly.

Lyx lay on the counter dramatically and whimpered. "Pleeaase!"

Beatrix scoffed. "Look at you begging for scraps like a Cerberus pup. I'm not giving in to you. You said you were on a diet to lose a few pounds."

Lyx practically fell onto the floor and turned an unflattering deep purple. Whispering heatedly, the demoness placed a clawed digit in front of her lips. "Beatrix. Shhhh." With a pointed look in Vanessa's direction, the demoness hinted to there being more than just cook and succubus in the kitchen.

Vanessa watched quietly and awkwardly waited for the cook to lay down her knife and turn around. Her brunette hair had strips of silver peeking out of her bun-styled hairdo. Her eyes were a warm chocolaty color, though they were large and quite round. The young witch smiled when their eyes met as she felt the urge to freeze in place rise up. The cook wasn't human. She was part bugbear. Hair the shade of tea leaves covered the woman's arms. Her nose was bulbous and bumps covered her face. But somehow, the smile that Beatrix gave was soft, warm, and inviting. Like she would hug your fear right out of you and send you on your way with a freshly baked cookie and a cup of milk. Any fear that Vanessa had was thwarted by the image of that smile. That, and coupled with Bobo reminding her that bugbears were beings just like everyone else, Vanessa released a breath she hadn't realized she was holding.

Calmly, the witch said, "Hi," and waved with a grin.

Beatrix turned to Lyx with flames lapping in her eyes. Her hoarse voice teemed with anger as she snapped, "You didn't say that the snacks were for guests!"

Lyx blinked. "I thought it was obvious, darling."

"If Robert finds out about this, he'll have my month's salary, and I'll carve off those pretty horns of yours! Shoo with you, now. I'll prepare it and have one of the maids run a cart up to the room."

Giving the cook a quick hug, the demoness jumped back and grabbed Vanessa's hand. "Come on, we'll miss the first quarter if we don't hurry back."

They rushed out of the room as Beatrix's voice called after them. "Don't fuss with me later about your diet, Lyx!"

Vanessa couldn't help but laugh as they ran through the halls back to the succubus' room.

The rest of the night was spent with them yelling at the magic mirror, laughing, and devouring snacks. By half-time, everyone had piled up onto Lyx's bed. The quiet slowly took over the group as the banter and giggles ebbed. By the time the game was over, Vanessa was fast asleep.

 *Chapter 28:*

The next morning, Vanessa was woken up with bright, happy sunshine assaulting her vision as the massive plumb curtains were ripped open. Groaning, the young witch pulled the comforter over her head and murmured, "Five more minutes." Feminine laughter roused the Spellweaver from her attempted slumber, and she peered out from under the covers.

Sara stood near the windows. Her laughter ebbed, and she hummed happily to herself as she smoothed out the front of her teal dress. The gold trimming and midnight blue sequins glittered in the morning sun. "Good morning, sleepyheads," she said with a smile.

Yawning, Lyx mumbled, "Good morning."

"Leon is in the dining room. The family would like to discuss the financial implications of what transpired at your apartment complex and request your presence during our morning meal."

The succubus rose out of bed whispering, "Robert can't keep his coin satchel out of anything."

Sara giggled. "You know father. He has a soft heart and the coin to aid where he cannot. Let him dote upon my sister-in-law."

Vanessa, who was just getting out of bed, fell to the floor with a loud *thud*. Could she ever get out of bed gracefully? Sheepishly, the witch looked to everyone present. "I … Leon …We … I mean … we're not—"

As Sara approached the Spellweaver, she tried not to laugh. Her smile was wide and cute, and the look in her eyes matched the teasing of her words. "Do you always tumble out of bed?"

"I could fall up the stairs most days," Vanessa admitted shamefully.

Still laughing, Sara helped the poor girl up to her feet. She leaned in and whispered, "I used to be really clumsy too. Mother and father hired two etiquette tutors, and, some days, all that they taught me still isn't enough to save me from my two left feet."

They both giggled.

"Leon and I, we aren't—" Vanessa started again.

Sara placed a finger in front of her lips and softly tapped it there before saying, "You aren't there … *yet*. You two aren't future-gazing to breakup. You're together because you think you can build a life together. Stay positive, and let everything else fall where it may. But never forget, Vanessa, you are in control. Now, let's get you dressed."

If anyone would have told Vanessa that she was going to be dressed in one of the finest robes she had ever laid her eyes on today, she wouldn't have believed them. Yet, there she was, decked out in a long, flowing robe that dragged the ground behind her as she walked. Being that it was one of Sara's, the colors were far more vibrant than what the witch was accustomed to. It was white with a shimmery teal centerpiece with a dark, flourishing embellishment. It was corset styled with a thin, black, silk rope drawn in as tight as her frame would allow it to go. Gold trimmed the edges and cuffs of the large belled sleeves. She didn't know if she felt pretty or pretty ridiculous. But it was this robe or one of the robes in a varying shade of pink. At least her feet were a touch too large to fit into the heels that Sara was determined to shove Vanessa's tootsies into. Thankfully, she was wearing her boots. She would have been just fine in her outfit from the day before, but Sara insisted on having it washed because it smelled like a day old campfire. When Lyx didn't fight back against the statement, the Spellweaver relented her usual clothing and borrowed one of Sara's.

She tried to ignore how out of place she felt in the robe that she was borrowing as she walked into the main dining room. As she mindfully kept track of her feet placement under the tighter robes, she found everyone chatting away at a table that looked more like a runeball field. On one end of it sat Patricia, Leon, Sara, Bobo, and

Malachi with Robert at the head of the table. Noticing that she and Lyx had entered the room, Leon gawked at the Spellweaver, shook his head, quickly stood, and motioned for Vanessa to join them. Bobo and Robert both rose when they realized the young witch was now entering.

"Good morning," Robert stated proudly to the both of them.

Everyone gave their own greeting, and Vanessa smiled as she replied softly, "Morning."

Lyx sashayed into the room with her tail ticking behind her, "Good morning lovely family."

The gentleman-beast that he was, Bobo pulled out a chair next to him for Lyx, and Leon followed suit with the chair at his side for Vanessa. Battling her rising heartbeat and trying to breathe slowly to fight back the heat that was washing over her face, the young witch quickly crossed the room and sat down in her chair. Once all women were seated, the men took their own again.

"Wh-where was I, Patricia?" Robert asked.

"The chandeliers, my love," she reminded.

"Right! We'll buy new ones!" he announced.

Sara almost dropped her fork, "New ones? We just bought new ones three months ago."

"We'll donate them to a local orphanage," Robert informed.

"Because that's what orphans need, chandeliers, not families," Leon mumbled into his cup.

"What was that?" Robert asked with a brow corking over one eye.

"I think the kids would love it," Vanessa interjected. She was being honest. She was also saving Leon from a potential argument. But if she was in the orphanage and a chandelier was installed, she and the other kids would, without a doubt, pretend to be royalty. "I think it would lift their spirits," she reaffirmed.

Robert slammed his hand down on the table and then pointed to Vanessa. "Consider it done! Jasper!"

The butler, standing behind Mr. Zvěrokruh, came rushing to the master's side. "Yes, M'lord?"

"Order that all the chandeliers are to be taken down and split them amongst the orphanages in Tolvade, and purchase new ones to replace them," Robert demanded.

Patricia spoke up, "Oh, with lots of raw crystals and silver!"

"Patricia, my love!" Robert yelled out and quickly took his wife's hands into his own.

"Yes, my love?" she replied dreamily as she inched closer to him.

"You're a genius, did you know that?" he whispered, gradually closing the distance between them.

"We should donate to them as well," she passionately told her husband.

"Mmm, yes. Donate," Robert replied.

They got lost in each other's eyes and were almost about to kiss when Bobo coughed lightly into his fist, bringing them out of their loving gaze. Slipping back into their seats, they went on to take a few bites of their meal while calming down.

Patting at his mouth with his napkin, Robert grunted, pleased with his ideas. Smiling, he looked at Vanessa again. "So, tell me young lady, what is the price you're looking at for the damages to your home?"

"Oh, uhm, well, because it was a Coven-based incident, the Coven is actually covering anything that the insurance company isn't. So, it doesn't look like I'll have much of a bill," she answered honestly.

"Oh." Robert looked crestfallen over the good news. He stared at his plate and pushed a bit of sausage about with his fork with a heavy sigh.

Leon leaned over and whispered into Vanessa's ear, "He likes helping people with money."

She fought the urge to shiver and whispered back, "I'm not sure I feel comfortable with accepting a gift like that."

Snapping back into his spot, Leon loudly stated, "Vanessa says that she didn't really like the furniture that got damaged. And the bathrooms are too small. She also told me that poor Bobo has to sleep in a room that hardly fits the giant ogre."

Lifting a single digit, Bobo announced, "Dare I say, this is the utmost truth."

"Bobo!" Vanessa snapped.

Slamming his fist down on the table, the ogre snapped back, "You got a grimoire, a lost aunt, all the dangerous fun you could ever hope for, and a Morgan Le Fay bag. Let me have nice things, woman!"

Boisterous laughter cut through their bickering. Robert held a hand over his stomach as he rolled in newfound joy. "By Jove, I think we have it, Patricia."

"Are you thinking what I'm thinking, my love?" Patricia asked with hope twinkling in her baby blues.

Simultaneously, they both cried out, "Pocket portal constructor!"

"We can reform the whole thing!" Robert exclaimed.

Excitedly, Patricia added, "New everything! Singed or broken, we fix it up and donate it and give her whole apartment a whole new look!"

"We can have them contacted today," Robert said.

Across the table, Sara shook her head as she watched her parents go on and on about the endless possibilities of upgrading the entire interior of Vanessa's apartment. "By the goddess, we've lost them," Sara mumbled as she swirled her juice in her crystal goblet.

Ignoring his parents and Vanessa's heated glare, Leon pointed to a dish on the table. "Could you pass the eggs?"

After breakfast, Leon whisked Vanessa away on a tour of the gardens. His family owned a great deal of peacock griffins and had them roaming around the large maze in the backyard. Their enchanted bracelets kept them contained to specific areas so they wouldn't eat or peck away at Patricia's prized roses and herb gardens, and so they wouldn't fly right off the estate. Their gentle coos accompanied the two as Leon walked the young witch down the stone-lined path and through the grapevines that mingled with morning glories on an open, arched gate.

"I'm sorry about this morning," Leon said.

Vanessa turned away from him as if she was angry, but she couldn't control her urge to smile. "Seemed to me like you were pretty fine with what you said."

Rubbing the back of his neck, Leon sighed. "I was trying to make my dad happy. But I also felt like it was my fault that your apartment got blown up."

Turning to scoff at him, Vanessa shook her head. "I was the one that took on Malachi, and I'm the one that had him sent to my apartment. How is that your fault?"

"Because I could have left with Malachi and avoided everything that happened," he admitted.

Crossing her arms over her chest, she shot back with, "If they thought that Malachi was in my home, they were going to break down the door and turn the place upside down regardless of whether or not you stayed."

Again, Leon sighed. "I suppose you're right."

"I am," she stated proudly.

Drawing her close, he dropped his tone down to something more intimate. "You're not mad at me? You'll let my dad go crazy on the redecorating?"

"Not too crazy, but, yes, Leon. And I'm not mad. Even if I wanted to be, Bobo has let it be known that he will not be denied this once in a lifetime opportunity."

Just as they started to laugh, Vanessa's crystal ball jingled.

"Oh, double-dip a candlestick. I can't catch a break," she groaned and pulled out the device.

Connecting her magic with the glass, the image quickly morphed into Riker. There were bags under his eyes and ... did she see the shadow of stubble on his chin? He looked like he hadn't slept all night. "Riker?"

"Have we gone and skipped formalities now, Spellweaver Peterson?"

"I mean..." She bit her lower lip as she tried to search for an appropriate answer. She couldn't think of one. "You just look like you've spent the night at Tasgall's." As she said it, she visibly cringed and was completely prepared to chuck the crystal ball into the hedge maze a few feet away if the Summoner chose to yell.

Ignoring the comment, Riker pressed on with the conversation. "Did you come up with a plan?"

"Now who's being rude?" she mumbled to herself. "Not... exactly."

"Are you—" He flared with anger and slammed his jaw shut as he visibly calmed himself with slow, deep breaths. "Peterson, tell me that there were concentration issues with your crystal ball, and I did not just hear what I thought I heard."

She didn't have the energy to lie to him. "No."

"You told me that you could come up with a plan!"

"Calm down. What's one more day?"

"No, Vanessa. We turn this tablet in today. For my sanity."

"Just one more day."

"No more lies and stalling."

"It's just a white lie," she countered.

"It's still breaking the law," he reminded.

"Riker!" she started.

"I've never broken the law!" he yelled finally.

Vanessa sat there with her mouth agape. "Never?" she inquired.

"Not since I've joined the Coven, and, trust me, you don't want me on the other side of the law."

"Fair enough." She caved finally. "When do you want to meet up to—"

"Now," he barked, without waiting for her to finish.

"What?!"

"I expect to see you on the teleportation pads at Coven headquarters in the next five minutes," he warned. And, with that, the connection winked out.

Vanessa stomped her foot on the ground. "Hex it all with hellfire!"

"Riker put his foot down?" Leon asked.

She nodded in reply.

"Leave Bobo here with me. Let him enjoy a day where he doesn't have to look at HQ. I'll keep the big guy happy while keeping a watch on Malachi for you. I highly doubt anyone is going to try and roll up on my family's property and start slinging spells."

Looking up to him, she asked, "Are you sure?"

"I'm sure," he replied before lightly kissing her on the forehead. "Now, you better use a transportation spell or Riker is going to have your head mounted on his wall."

She grumbled, "If he doesn't, the Coven will. I still haven't come up with a good excuse."

"You'll do fine. I know it. I dealt with you for years. I can confidently say that you are the best with coming up with a lie on the spot."

She laughed. "Oh yeah?"

Leon shrugged, "Well, I mean, most of the time, anyway. Just don't count that time you told me you weren't in the tunnels under the academy."

 *Chapter 29:*

Riker hadn't really given her a choice, and she wasn't too keen on finding out what he would do if she didn't show up at the drop of a pointed hat. Leon had grabbed her cloak and satchel for her, and she used the emblem to teleport to HQ. She had forgotten about her glamorous attire and, as she stepped further into the building, she realized she was getting a lot of stares. A quick glance down at her apparel reminded her that she practically looked like royalty. She would have preferred her campfire scented robes right about now.

"Banish a banshee," she whispered to herself.

She darted through the center of the Coven and tried to avoid all the unwanted looks her getup was garnering. When she was just past Ell's usual desk, Vanessa noticed Riker propped up against the end of the communal crystal balls. He looked far more haggard than he had appeared in the image of his earlier call. As soon as the Summoner spotted Vanessa, she froze a few feet away.

"Get over here," he demanded in a heated whisper.

She really didn't want to.

Gradually, she made her way over to him at a snail's pace. "What happened to you?" she asked what had been plaguing her mind since the call.

"I didn't sleep well last night," he answered back. "Are you ready?"

She gave him a look. "It's not like you gave me the option not to be."

His silvery gaze pointed at her, and she smiled and lifted one of her dust pouches and swayed it from side to side like a white flag.

Putting away his dagger-like gaze, Riker snatched at the bag at his side and displayed the tablet to the teasing witch. "I'm ready to be rid of this. Prepare whatever you want and I'll go along with it, but

I will not go down in flames, Peterson. We have an audience with the Council."

"What! Right now?" She gawked.

"Why do you think I told you to hurry here?"

She looked around the lobby and stepped in closer. "I don't exactly have anything prepared."

"Think on the way," he demanded.

Taking her hand, Riker pulled her toward the dreaded spiraling staircase. This was not the way she had planned her day to go. She didn't waste her breath on asking for more time. Chewing frantically on her lip, Vanessa let her mind race for something, anything, that would keep all of their promises kept and give a believable story to the Council so they wouldn't put Vanessa and Riker under surveillance or land them in Zaraltrac prison.

Stairs ascended.

Halls navigated.

Double doors knocked on.

And, before she knew it, the large barriers to the High Priest Council were opened. Goddess help her. She still hadn't thought up of a single thing. And now? She had all thirteen members of the blue cloak staring her down.

Was it hot in here?

"Spellweaver Peterson, Summoner Alastair, why have you sought counsel with us? We were informed that it was urgent and couldn't be discussed openly." The Celestial's light poked out of the cloak as she adjusted herself on her seat.

"Yes, High one, it is in regards to the tablet mission," Riker began.

Mia spoke up next. "I fear we've given all the information that we can, Summoner Alastair. The scholars did the best they could with what little information had been preserved from the Great Orb before it blacked out. The only details that we are aware of have been listed in the scroll."

Riker nodded as thinned his lips out into a straight line. "Yes, High Priest Mia. My only concern is … well … it isn't a concern. It's more of a—" he failed to complete his thought.

Torro was the next to speak. "If it's money, worry not. Simply file a request for funds, and we'll approve it within the hour. We are aware that Spellweaver Peterson recently had a catastrophe strike her home. We are prepared fully to fund the trip."

Shifting his weight, Riker again nodded. "Yes, High Priest McTaggart, however, it is not a funding issue. We've actually obtained it already. The tablet, that is," he informed.

"We understand that this trip will be—" Ronan started and abruptly stopped. "I think I might have heard that wrong, Summoner Alastair. Did you say that you already *have* the tablet in your possession?"

Was it too late to run?

"Yes, High Priest Vestal. We have it," Riker affirmed to Ronan.

"H-how?" Mia gasped, completely astonished.

"We had just discussed the mission scroll details," Riker started and then turned to Vanessa. "Vanessa departed before me and I was to catch up with her on the outskirts of the Jeweled Canopy."

All eyes turned to Vanessa.

"Is this true, Spellweaver Peterson?" Mia asked.

If internal screaming had a look, Vanessa was wearing it. Slowly, she nodded, unsure of her voice. This must be what sitting in a bubbling cauldron felt like.

Ronan gave her a concerned look. "Speak, child," he urged kindly.

Here goes nothing.

"Yes, it's true. I had gone to an area agreed upon to wait for Summoner Alastair to arrive. Before the attack on my apartment, we had mapped out a wide range of places to search according to the information we had been given. I had noticed some strange activity near the tree line and, not being able to let it be, I went to investigate."

Curiously, Ronan asked, "What did you find?"

"Blood mages, sir," Vanessa answered confidently. After a moment of letting the information soak in, she pressed on. "About twenty of them," she explained. "I can't be quite sure. It was getting late. But I could hear them talking about a magical item that would give them enough power to attack the Coven," she shrieked.

A few of the High Priests gasped and began to whisper. To her side, Riker had slowly turned to face her and was giving her a look. She ignored it. He told her to make it up. Continuing on, Vanessa shook her head. "They had it," she whispered. "The tablet was in their hands ... I ..." She balled her hands into fists. "I couldn't let them have it. Imagine the damage they would have caused!"

"How did you defeat them?" Mia asked.

"It wasn't easy," the Spellweaver admitted. Like she had become a hardened war veteran, she looked at the Council with a battle-hardened soldier's expression and said, "They spotted me. I managed to dodge the first attack and deflect the second. But it was getting dark. I knew I wouldn't last long. It was around the time that they had surrounded me that Riker showed up." She patted the man on the shoulder. "I would have died if he hadn't been there." Though, when she looked into his slate-colored eyes, they sent a chill through her. The shiver she experienced was witnessed by all of the Council. "Most of them escaped."

"We shall take care of the bodies—" Torro started to say.

Panic rose in her. She held up a hand and cried out, "No!"

Everyone stared down at the young witch.

"Why not, child?" the Celestial inquired.

She paused and looked off to the side, but it was all for show. Frantically, she came up with an excuse. "Strange creatures from the rainforest emerged. Riker and I managed to escape while the beasts feasted on ... on..." She hid her face in Riker's chest.

Pretending to console the poor Spellweaver, Riker hugged her and whispered in her ear, "What on Raen are you doing? They'll never believe this fairy tale!"

Torro slammed his fist down on the arm of his chair.

This was it. This was the moment that their lies would be exposed, and they would be shackled for their crimes.

"I knew those blood mages would try something like this!" Torro fumed. "Dirty, underhanded dogs. They've probably been searching since the Great Orb blacked out."

Seething with equal rage, Ronan added, "Spineless wretches. They're always plotting something!"

"It's a good thing you two were there to stop them," Mia chimed in. "After the incident with Spellweaver Bauer and Summoner MacBain, I'm not at all surprised that they got their greedy hands on it." She shook her head and sighed loudly. "Where is the tablet now?"

Speechless, Riker remained motionless and stared in awe at the Council members while Vanessa acted like she was regaining her composure and wiping away unshed tears. Sniffling, she turned to face them and untied the bag from Riker's spell belt. Reaching in, she retrieved the stone and headed toward the seated Council members to present it to the Celestial.

As the being reached for it, Vanessa thought that she saw a grand smile on her lips, but it was hard to be sure with the light that pierced through the being's cloak.

"You've done us a great service and suffered greatly these past months, Spellweaver Peterson. Due to the upcoming importance of the Wild Hunt ritual, we think it would be best if you take a two-week vacation. Paid, of course," Torro announced.

All of the Council nodded, and she instantly went from feeling victorious to defeated. Riker, on the other hand, couldn't stop smiling. And that smile only widened as Mia announced, "No mission scrolls for two weeks. You are hereby on vacation starting this moment!"

Ronan chuckled. "Enjoy your time off. You've earned it."

The Council room was buzzing with congratulations and victorious blathering over the newly obtained tablet. But Vanessa felt like she had been cursed by all thirteen High Priests and stood in a state of shock.

"A well-deserved ending, don't you think?" Riker whispered to her as he clapped her on the back. "Yes. A fitting end, I think."

Goddess help her.

Vanessa practically stormed out of the Council room after the meeting had been closed. "It's not fair!" she exclaimed once the doors had shut.

"I think it's rather fitting," Riker disagreed with a wild grin.

She stopped and spun on heel and pointed a finger in his face. "You're the one that told me to—" She stopped, looked around, and hissed quietly, "… *lie*." She huffed and resumed her scolding tone. "I only did what you told me to do!"

He slowly moved her finger from his face with a dead look in his eyes. "I asked you to find a way to keep us out of scrutiny. I never asked you to fabricate the legend of a tale you just whipped up in that room. "

She stifled a scream and turned to continue stomping through the halls all while Riker chuckled and shook his head at her. "Just like her." He laughed a bit more. "Scared of the devil one minute and yelling at him the next." His laughter grew.

"This is all your fault!" Vanessa yelled back at the cackling Summoner.

 *Chapter 30:*

It goes without saying that Bobo was thrilled about the news. While Vanessa mourned the loss of doing any kind of mission scrolls for the next two weeks, she sat out in the garden moping as she tossed bits of bread to the peacock griffins.

Leon came out to her side and nudged the crouching witch with the side of his boot. "You going to just sit there and pout all afternoon?"

She gave him big ol' Cerberus puppy eyes and a large pouty lip as she looked up to him.

He rolled his eyes. "So dramatic! It's a vacation, Vanessa. Not the end of the world."

"Could be the start of it. You never know," she muttered.

"Banish a banshee, you stop it." He sat down next to her and drew her into his side. "When was the last time you had a vacation?"

"I ... don't remember," she admitted softly.

"Don't you think you need to stop distracting yourself with work and do some things that make you happy?"

"Working for the Coven does make me happy," she whined.

"There is more to life than Coven mission scrolls. Come on, Vanessa. Spill the magic beans. Tell me your dreams, your goals, your aspirations, your wants! Tell me things that you've always wanted to do but never had time because you were *working*."

She looked at him, sighed, and tossed more bread to the colorful creatures pecking around them. Long moments passed in silence. Leon didn't pressure her. He waited while she thought it out. Even if she was silently throwing a fit, he would wait for her to finish and answer him. It was nice, despite the circumstances that had brought them to that moment, sitting next to him and feeding peacock griffins in the early afternoon was a blissful kind of moment.

Finally, after some thought, she spoke to him. "I've always wanted to go to the Festival of Farms," she admitted.

The Festival of Farms was a year-round carnival that was held on the outskirts of Tolvade's farming land. Mr. Brigget, the founder of the festival, ran a bed and breakfast in the heart of the bustling festivities. The theme circled around the harvests of each season. Though many of the Adalith area detested the noisy carnival and the owner, everyone else loved Mr. Brigget, his festival, and the bed and breakfast that he ran. He also gave yearly donations, fed the poor, and was overall a kind, warm soul.

Leon blinked at Vanessa. "Have you never been?"

She shook her head. "I tried to sneak out once or twice when I lived at the orphanage. I never made it far before Agatha found me and yanked me back by my ear."

The Summoner laughed.

As if she could feel the old caretaker tugging on her ear, Vanessa cuffed it with her hand and thought about all the times she swore she'd go there. But she never did.

"Why didn't you go when you left the orphanage?"

She sighed. "I got caught up in studies. A new door had opened for me. I ran and never looked back. Too worried that one slip up would land me homeless and penniless in the streets, I did what I could to stay in the academy. I studied through all hours of the night, often making me too tired to pay attention in class."

"I see."

"Reading made tests and quizzes a cinch, but it mattered little when it came to actually practicing. Because I slept through those, I missed out on important key points on how to focus."

"That explains a lot." Directly after saying that, Leon had to dodge a slap to the back of the head. Stabbing her in the side with his index finger, he chuckled when she squeaked like a mouse and glared at him. "Well, put the daggers away. I don't think they'll let you onto the festival grounds with a nasty look like that."

"We're going?"

"Yup," he stated standing up and dusting off his pants.

"Now?"

He nodded.

She looked down at her dress and turned redder than a cooked apple. "Let me change first!" she yelled before she stood, turned, and rushed into the manor.

A few hours later, Vanessa, Leon, Bobo, Lyx, and Malachi were all standing outside the festival grounds. The smell of buttery popcorn mingled with the sweet scents of caramel covered apples. To one side, a baker shouted out an order and passed out funnel cakes, and another vendor with smoked sausages called for the next person in line. A cotton candy booth yelled out, "Buy one get one for the next hour!"

Lyx paled to the pitch. "No, thank you."

Vanessa's stomach growled, and everyone turned to look at her. "What?" she snapped. "I haven't had lunch yet."

Lyx waved away any negative thoughts. "These places hit you with food at the door. Naturally, you'll be hungry after you pay the entrance fee."

"I'm not complaining unless I'm told that I cannot have anything," Bobo said to no one in particular.

"I thought you were on a diet," Vanessa teased.

"Diets have no place on the carnival grounds, my dear. I shan't be merry at these festivities if I cannot partake in the delightful food that they have to offer."

Malachi added, "So, what you're saying is, you want one of everything, and you'll complain about it tomorrow?"

Bobo straightened his tie and tugged at jacket. "Precisely," he announced with confidence and swaggered over to the ticket vendor at the main gate.

They all laughed and headed into the carnival. Bobo and Lyx went from vendor to vendor collecting various food items while Leon, Vanessa, and Malachi headed further into the carnival grounds with their sausage dogs. Music played far in the distance, a puppet show brought forth boisterous laughter from the crowd seated in front of it, and there was a great cheer from inside a nearby tent. Through the smallest sliver of an opening, Vanessa could see someone flipping through the air and then being caught right before they hit the ground. Her heart stumbled over its rhythm as she caught the glimpse of the ongoing show within.

Leon grabbed Vanessa's hand and pulled her closer as the crowd became thicker. "Where do you want to start?"

She felt overwhelmed for a moment. There were so many options. Glancing from tent to tent, vendor to vendor, and game to game, she mulled over her options. "How about a game first? I've always wanted to win one of those large, stuffed unicorns!"

"Typical," Malachi muttered.

Vanessa rolled her eyes. "Like a sticky-fingered Sleekit is unique."

Malachi gradually turned his head toward the witch and laid a hand over the side of his face with mock surprise. "Vanessa!" he gasped. "You cut me deep. I ... I thought we had something special."

"Ha!" Leon shouted. "You two are quite the pair."

"Don't curse me," Vanessa whined.

"Don't you mean bless, not curse?" Malachi asked, and— when they both looked at him—the Sleekit waggled his eyebrows.

Leon grimaced. "Please don't do that."

Malachi chuckled at the Summoner's displeasure.

"Over here!" Vanessa cried out right before she yanked Leon toward the game booth she wanted to try out. In a rush, Leon snagged the laughing Sleekit by his cloak and dragged him along.

"No-*gah*!" the azbanonite shrieked right before the sound gurgled from the fabric straining across his neck.

Rubbing his throat next to the booth, Malachi grumbled a few choice words under his breath while Vanessa eagerly pointed to the prize she desired. As described, it was an obnoxiously large, stuffed unicorn.

The vendor handed Leon a wand that was tethered to the booth. "You get three shots. Try to knock down the bottles," the vendor explained. "Good luck."

"Luck. Psssh. This is going to be a cinch." Leon took his stance, aimed, and fired away.

Half a coin satchel later and Leon was glowering at the grinning man behind the booth's counter.

"Would you like to give it another go, sir?" The vendor asked. "You were sooo close." The grin he wore said otherwise.

"Move over. It takes a con artist to beat a con artist," Malachi snapped, annoyed. "The girl wants to see more than this booth and your failures."

"Hey!" Leon griped.

"Ya hairless wretch," Malachi whispered under his breath.

Slamming the necessary coin down on the counter, Malachi snatched up the wand and took aim.

Zip!

Zap!

Crash!

In two shots, Malachi had toppled the pyramid of brightly colored bottles and won the prize. He yanked the unicorn from the vendor with a glower. "Things rigged. You outta be ashamed of yourself!" He then turned and tossed the reward to Vanessa. "Here," he stated flatly. "You're welcome." He shoved his paws into his pockets and pointed his chin at a ride further in. "There's a haunted magic carpet ride further ahead you should try."

"I would have gotten it in one more go. I was just warming up," Leon tried to convince everyone, even the vendor merchant.

Nodding, Vanessa rubbed his arm and said, "Of course you were. It's okay."

Malachi pursed his leathery lips to one side and snorted. "Yeah, okay, hero. Whatever you say," he muttered. "Come on, already. Wasted enough coin and time here. Let's get a move on already."

With that, they all trudged toward the ride that Malachi had mentioned. The next hour was spent with them joining the long lines to be seated on one of the various rides. Lyx and Bobo had caught up with them, though, the gentleman-beast turned green at the sight of any moving cart. He opted to sit on a nearby bench and let his stomach settle.

"Carry on without me," Bobo cried out as he plopped down onto the selected rest area.

"Poor thing. Let momma help," Lyx announced as she skipped over to the bench to dab the ogre's forehead with a clean handkerchief.

Vanessa, on the other hand, had determined that the next and last ride would be the fairy wheel. Which was a giant wheel consisting of carts that would loop around in a giant circle and would pause at the top to give the grandest view of the whole festival and most of Tolvade. The magic that propelled the suspended-in-air device in an endless circle was a large swarm of fairies. Their magical light and dust trails illuminated the fairy wheel area as they slowly spun the ride around. Nothing excited the young witch more than to know that she was about to behold a view her years had not gifted her with yet. Her eagerness was bubbling over.

"Rest, Bobo. And you two, hurry up, slowpokes," she exclaimed as she rushed to join the growing line. The sunlight was fading on the horizon and the fireworks were sure to start as soon as the sun went down. If she timed it right, they would be on the ride when they went off. She giggled as she imagined sitting next to Leon on the ride as the twilight sky lit up with bursts of brightly colored explosions.

It would be perfect.

"She gets excited and you just get swept up in it, don't you?" Malachi asked Leon as they struggled, while smiling, to keep up.

Leon chuckled and nodded. "But you have to admit, with her around there is never a dull moment."

Inch by inch, the line shrank along with the dissipating rays of fading light. Stars started to appear overhead when Vanessa, Malachi, and Leon were going to be the next batch of customers to be seated. In the distance, she could see the cannons being loaded and lined up. It was just like she had hoped it would be.

The gate was opened and everyone was taken in small groups to be seated. When it was Vanessa, Malachi, and Leon's turn, she was hit hard from behind, and she almost fell face first in the straw-covered ground. To make matters worse? She could feel that whoever had bumped into her had spilled their drink on her as well. While she accepted the fact that she was going to need to wash her outfit, again, she listened to another group of rowdy beings bicker with the employee at the entrance gate. She even heard glass breaking.

"Whoa there, missy. I'm sorry about that," the man said helping Vanessa to her feet and bringing her attention to the individual that had caused her to break away from the others.

She dusted off the front of her robes and stole a look further into the ride area. She saw Malachi and Leon being seated and she felt panicked. "It's fine," she lied. It wasn't fine. She wanted to sit next to Leon on the fairy wheel! If she hurried, she could still make it.

Before she could walk away completely, the man had grabbed her by her sleeve and pulled her back. He then began to beat bits of straw off of her. "Let me help you get you dried off at least," he insisted.

If she didn't get over there she was going to miss the ride. "No, really, it's okay."

The gate closed with a deafening *clack* behind her.

Vanessa jumped in place from the sudden sound and spun around. "No!" she whined. But there was nothing on Raen that would convince a carnival employee to ignore the rules that they held in place. She sighed and turned around to give some choice words to the man that had cost her a very special moment. However, when she turned around, the man was gone. She stood up on her tippy toes and searched the crowd. But he was nowhere to be found.

"Weird," she whispered to herself.

Just then, the ride started up. All she could do was watch from below with a hard frown fixed on her face. Golden glittering tails of dust fell to the ground as groups of fairies fluttered their wings and started to gradually spin the ride. Pings of jealousy rose up in her as she watched the fairy wheel turn, bringing the cart holding Malachi and Leon higher and higher.

Suddenly, one of the fairies fell from the sky in a dizzy circle. Caught by a few of her peers, the fairy was laid down on the ground beneath the wheel. "Must have magically exhausted herself," Vanessa whispered. But that thought was swayed when two more fluttered speedily toward the ground. "They really are pushing these poor beings, aren't they?" she quietly asked no one in particular.

As soon as the thought left her mouth, a handful more fell from the sky. Vanessa looked up, and as her gaze drifted up to the night sky and, to her horror, a multitude of the fairies controlling the wheel dipped and then fell. "Oh, goddess, no ..." But she knew that something was wrong as incalculable pain shot through her heart. Thorns sprung up around the muscle and squeezed. Her vision blurred, and she gasped as her knees connected with the ground. The fairies had all been put under a sleep spell!

The wheel creaked and with fading fairy magic there was nothing keeping it in the air which caused the device to teeter on its side. The crowed all collectively gasped at the spectacle. "Hex it all!" she grit out through the pain and jumped over the fence. She ran like blood mages were flinging spells. She ran like devils were hot on her trail. She ran like lives depended on it ... because they did.

Her hands dove in and out of the spell pouches on her belt. She had a rune and a handful of dust, but she knew it wouldn't be enough. Levitating something this large would normally need a whole team. But she didn't have time to call for backup or prepare a proper spell for something on the scale of this magnitude. She had to try to tap into her well of magic. She had to control the flow better. She had to. There wasn't a second option.

Beings surrounding outside the ride paused to snap pictures with their crystal balls and compact mirrors while others ran further into the festival screaming. Chaos was erupting all around her. Beings that had been around the fairy wheel scrambled past her in their attempt to find a safer place. The crowd quickly thinned out as she pressed on.

Racing across the straw-covered ground, Vanessa yelled out the incantation, "From the ground below, separate, as if it is without weight, and linger there, levitate!" Quickly, she threw the dust and rune skyward. The object started to fall back down but was suddenly halted in its descent. The rune glowed a dim blue before the illumination grew and a burst of power pulsed out of the engraved rock. As the fairy wheel lost more fairies, the ride started to fall. Screams erupted from the fairy wheel as the beings realized the doom that was about to befall them all. The spell rushed out, stretching and growing, until it had the whole ride under its command. Vanessa, with her feet firmly planted on the ground, held out her hands and tried to keep the whole thing steady. The magic inside her wanted to pour out of her in one, drowning wave, but she held it back. Willing her magic to obey her command and come out in a trickle.

Sweat was already forming on her brow. She wasn't sure she'd be able to keep this up. From the top of the ride, she heard Leon call out to her over the panicked shouts of the other passengers.

"Vanessa! Vanessa! Just keep hold of it as long as you can. I'm working on a spell to help and Malachi is crystal ball calling the Coven to report the incident."

"I don't think I can hold on until backup arrives, Leon!"

"I know! I'm here, though. So don't give up. I just need time."

"Hurry!"

They didn't talk anymore after that. She needed to focus on the spell and to keep the flow of magic just right. If she went all super powerful now, it would amplify the levitation spell to levels Aeristria had never seen before and—most likely—send the ride and all the passengers straight up to the goddess herself. Staring up at where Leon and Malachi were seated, she could see them fussing over the spell. She really hoped that he would hurry up. It was getting really difficult to keep this—

"You're a needle in a voodoo doll, you are." The voice that was in her ear was deep, husky, and dripping with anger.

Before she could counter with a witty comeback or elbow the being in the gut, she felt cold steel sink into her side. "You won't be much of a problem when your six feet under, little witch."

She-she had been stabbed?

Looking down, bewildered, Vanessa tried to not lose focus on the spell, but her vision swam when she saw the knife sticking out of her side and the blood running out of her body like a tiny river. The thick, metallic scent filled her nostrils, and any remaining hope that she had just been holding onto dissipated. It didn't feel the way she thought a stab would. It hurt more. The initial stab stung, but the longer the knife remained in her side, the more the pain grew. It grew until she couldn't hold back the scream anymore. Her cry pierced through the frantic wails of the ride passengers. As she screamed,

Vanessa hit her knees. Her hands remained outstretched, holding the levitation spell as best she could. The ward around the fairy wheel wavered for a moment, the whole thing creaked and tipped, and the swarm of screams that followed drowned out her wailing cry of pain. A dull, throbbing ache rose up and coursed through her. Gritting her teeth, she commanded her body to stay awake. To keep pushing the spell but her mind drew a blank when the knife was yanked out of her. She gasped for air and, again, the spell she was casting wavered. Shouting, yelling, and the frantic shouts of countless beings begging to be saved all erupted from the levitating ride. Swarms of beings mirrored them as they darted through the festival. It felt so had to breathe. She was barely holding on.

"You're with ... them, aren't you?" Vanessa wheezed out.

"Heh. The answer won't matter where you're going," he said with a sneer.

"Vanessa! No!" Leon howled.

The blade rose. It glistened in starlight and early evening moon glow. And it plummeted down toward her without remorse.

A second passed, and Vanessa was sure this was how she would meet her end. Until she saw an ax, wielded at a speed she could not follow, slam into the side of the assailant's head. The blade sunk deep into his skull. His attack lost momentum and then his arms fell to his side limply. Bobo, in all his rage and fury, flew across the field and roared at the man, "You dare to harm her? Your bones will know of HELL!" Green flames were surrounding his hands as he rushed over and grabbed hold of the being with his mighty grip. In an instant, the whole body of the attacker was engulfed in the eerie fire. But not a sound escaped. The assailant was already dead.

Bobo shoved the lifeless body to the ground, whipped around, and rushed over to her. "Vanessa—"

Her shaky hand covered his mouth. "If I stop, they die," she explained breathily and then gave a pointed look to the ride.

"I fell asleep ... I thought you were safe. I thought..." He looked like his world was being torn asunder.

"Ground me," Vanessa ordered, hoarsely.

"You're wounded."

"Ground me," she ordered again, her voice strained and raspy.

His brow furrowed and told her very well how much he disapproved, but his large hand reached out and cupped her wound, then put pressure on it. She didn't know if it felt good or worse. But she managed only to grunt in discomfort. Wiping her forehead free of the growing perspiration, Vanessa resumed the spell.

"Leon, I don't think I need to tell you how dire the situation is down here," Bobo yelled out to the Summoner, but there wasn't a reply.

"Leon?" Vanessa croaked, but the sound didn't carry.

It was Malachi that answered. "Everyone, DUCK!"

Rising up out of the cart was Leon. His arms were outstretched to either side of his glowing form, and he hovered over the fairy wheel as he recited the incantation. "For by the magic that I have, by the word that I speak, make my request known to both ground and sky, for with this spell ..."

"No. Leon," Vanessa gasped. "You can't!" she screamed and felt fear bubble to the surface. There was no grounding agent. He didn't have another caster. A spell like that could ... it could ... "Please, stop!" she cried. The strain that yelling put on her body forced her to cough and hold her side even tighter. Fresh, warm blood trickled through her and Bobo's fingers.

As for her plea, it didn't stop the spell from being spoken. Leon finished it without a moment's hesitation, "... I'm willing to *die*!"

A screech filled the sky. "I invoke the power of my tether!" Lyx's powerful wings propelled her toward her master, and she slammed into him and they spun in place as she tried to bring herself to a stop. Suddenly, her wings outstretched to either side and they hovered there, powered by Leon's magic and her grounding him with her life's essence.

"It won't kill them," Bobo whispered, but he sounded both relieved and unsure.

"No." Vanessa didn't sound a hundred percent sure either. Not when words and incantations held so much power. He was willing to die to perform the spell. A spell that was not exactly okayed by the Coven as it was more gray magic than anything. He was using a powerful spell on his own. He wouldn't die from it (thanks to Lyx), but he would feel like he was dying for the next couple of days. None of this made the witch or the ogre feel at ease that their future-gazing partner was toying with a spell that could take their life if the magic saw it fit to do so.

Vanessa looked around and realized that if she wanted Leon to use less magic to complete his spell, she was going to have to help him beyond levitating the fairy wheel. He was trying to take over so she wouldn't become magically fatigued, and from the throbbing heat that penetrated her wound in strangely soothing waves, he was trying to patch her up as well.

"Bobo," she practically whispered, her dry throat doing her speech no favors.

"Yes?"

She jutted her chin in the direction of the sleeping fairies. "I'm going to wake them up. Ground me just a little longer."

"Honestly, I'm glad you thought of it. Waking up the fairies and letting them do the work means you can stop and we can focus on getting you healed up."

Not trusting her fading voice, she nodded in reply. She needed to let Leon know what she was going to do. Letting go of the levitation spell could break his concentration if he wasn't prepared. "Leo—"

Before she could finish, Bobo laid a hand on her shoulder and smiled warmly at her. Taking over, he yelled out, "Leon, she's going to let go. Don't overdo it! Keep her steady until the fairies are awoken!"

Vanessa didn't wait for an answer. She slowly released her hold of the spell so she could focus on an easier task of waking the fairies. But when she looked over to the scattered winged-beings lying in heaps, resting, she doubted that it would be easier. That was a lot of fairies, and the spell cast over them was strong enough to put them in not only a deep sleep, but it was also a focused spell and wouldn't put anyone on the ride to sleep. How cruel did they have to be to put so many beings in danger and leave them awake to witness their demise? She pushed those thoughts to the back of her mind. Right now she needed to focus on waking them up, not the twisted mind of the culprits responsible for all this destruction.

She took in a deep calming breath and closed her eyes. Already, she could feel Bobo's hands on her back, the energy coursing through her. It felt like the warmth of a campfire on a cold autumn night was washing over her back and shoulders. It thrummed through her and made her teeth hum with the power. She lifted her hands skyward and called out, as if beseeching the goddess, "Your children are all asleep, forced by a foe, wake them up—I implore, let them dream no more."

From overhead, shimmering filled the sky. It looked like falling glitter, and it swirled and floated until it rained over the pile of fairies. Vanessa felt the power being pulled out of her. It was a large spell. It was a lot of bodies to wake up. The size of them didn't matter. She felt tired and Bobo's energy changed from warm to hot. He could feel her weakening.

"Stubborn girl. You said you wanted to do this while injured," he whispered.

She grunted and said, "It was that or both Leon and I risk being magically fatigued or worse with levitating the wheel until backup arrived. This way, the fairies can take over, and he and I don't have to worry about doing another spell to get everyone off the ride or focus on the difficult task of turning that massive thing."

Bobo chuckled softly. "I wasn't telling you to stop. I want you to hurry the hex up."

She looked behind her and smirked. "I'm trying," she said, and she could hear how tired she was by the sound of her voice.

Turning back around, she poured everything into the last of the spell. She noticed a flitter of wings, and then another and another. The first one that sat up slowly held its head and looked lost as it scanned the festival grounds.

"Hurry. Help the others, and get the wheel!" Bobo yelled.

Vanessa started to fall to the side, and the ogre was there to catch her and lift her close to him. She winced in pain, and his brow bent in worry as his ocean blue eyes trailed down to the wound that Vanessa was covering as best she could. He removed her hand from the inflicted area and he saw the fabric was visibly soaked in blood.

The crimson color spread, and fresh pools rose up to the surface. Leon had managed to heal a good portion of the inner damage, but the initial stab wound was still open and bleeding. His massive hand instantly cupped the injury, and he put pressure on the gash. Bobo hissed to himself having realized just how serious it still was.

"I'd slap you if you weren't hurt," Bobo grumbled, threads of worry soaking the statement he had used to try and lighten the mood.

"Lucky me," she replied in a strained whisper.

She felt so tired. Her eyelids drooped, and she willed her body to remain awake. The night air felt colder than it should. Sweat covered her body and made the chill even more unbearable. She shivered and stifled a groan of pain.

Bobo looked back at her and hurt swam in the pools of his eyes. Taking in a deep, slow breath, he hid his concern and searched the festival. "The backup from the Coven should be teleporting in, just hold on. We'll have a healer look you over."

"It's okay," Vanessa said quietly. Her bloody hand lay over the ogre's, and she smiled up to him. "Scorch it with your hellfire."

The ogre flinched. If she hadn't been resting her hand on his, he would have pulled away.

"We have to stop the bleeding now, Bobo." Her voice was so sweet. Too sweet for the burden she had just passed onto her partner, her friend.

"No," he answered. His voice was steady, sure, and held subtle hints of anger woven into the single word.

She drew in a breath, and the stress pulled at the torn flesh. She was so much more aware of how her body moved and how reliant she was on those muscles in particular. She made a small sound and snuffed it out as quickly as she could while her hold on his hand tightened. Any anger that had grown in him had instantly drained away.

"Vanessa—?"

She stopped him by lazily patting his hand. Her eyes slowly opened, and she forced a smile. Shaking her head, she said, "I'm fine. I just ... I moved wrong." All over her side, she could feel the fresh, warm blood cooling in the evening air. Her hand pressed down on the ogre's. She felt dizzy, and she could feel the shock lifting, giving way to new waves of pain that were crashing over her in unrelenting succession. "It's okay," she whispered through the pain. She pushed his hand down a little harder.

"It'll scar," he reminded softly.

She nodded. She knew it. Scorching it would always end any chance of the flesh looking smooth and unblemished. But she knew when she chose to be a Coven member that her body would take the hit. The scar wouldn't be something that would mangle her fair looks. It would be a reminder that she survived. That she visited the gates of Hell and walked away saying, "not today." It wasn't a blemish. It was a blessing. A permanent mark etched into her flesh that would forever remind her that when she could have died, instead of waiting for help that she was unsure would ever come, she chose to save herself. That would always mean more to her than perfectly smooth skin.

"I trust you, Botobolbilian," she said, and let her hand fall away from his own. "You once told me that I was powerful enough to do a spell that I had no faith in performing. Now, it's my turn to tell you that you're strong enough."

Bobo's bottom lip quivered, and the saddest sound escaped him. "Forgive me," he uttered breathily. She saw the trail of a blazing tear stream down his cheek as he touched his forehead to hers. Growling as he summoned the hellfire, the ogre masked his pain with the sound of fury, but Vanessa could still hear it, and it broke her heart. His tears hit her face. The flames began to manifest.

It hurt.

Goddess, it *hurt*.

As her mouth opened, the sounds that escaped were like raspy screams. Bobo's hold on her tightened, and she kicked her feet as she cried out in unfathomable pain. Together, the two of them let out howls of torment. They were hardly heard as the fireworks went off in the distance. It was a song of pain lost in exploding lights.

The scent of scorched flesh ebbed from her senses slowly. She could taste it in the air, and as she looked down at the blackened skin, she knew that the control Bobo had used to contain the fire and ensure it wouldn't do more than scorch the wound was as difficult as her controlling her inner power. The proud, gentleman-beast was turned away from the young witch as he blew his nose into his handkerchief.

"Are you all right?" Vanessa asked, sitting up as best she could.

The ogre laughed then, a soft sorrowful laugh. "I should be asking you that," he replied in a shaky voice.

"It's not my first time being scorched," she tried to joke.

Reaching out, she gently placed a hand on his back. "I'm all right," he whispered. "Thank you."

Blinking, she asked, "For letting you scorch me?"

He chuckled then, the happier laughter suiting him far better than the anguish that was settling into every crease and line of his face. "For believing in me, my dear."

"I never doubted you," she said with a grand smile.

"And I've never doubted you," he admitted, patting her thigh.

Wind hit them then, as Lyx flew over carrying a passed out Leon in her arms. "Let's not do that again anytime soon, okay? I don't think I can handle it," the succubus stated with a frown.

"How are you fairing?" Bobo asked.

Lyx gave a gentle nod, "I'm tired but I'm a lot tougher than I look. This lug, on the other hand, exhausted himself."

"Is he fatigued?" Vanessa asked concerned.

Shaking her head, Lyx said, "No. But it was the first time that he put out that level of magic in a long time. He's lucky I was there to ground him and to carry his heavy—"

"I'm not that heavy," the Summoner groaned while sitting up.

"Leon!" Vanessa cried out.

Turning, he noticed that they were on solid ground and that the Spellweaver was far paler than usual. "Vanessa," he shouted and shot out of the demoness's arms.

"Hey!" Lyx whined. She folded her now empty arms over her chest as she muttered, "Could at least say thank you."

She was ignored as he crashed into Vanessa. The hiss of pain escaping the young witch made him pull back and inspect the inflicted area. "You still had to scorch it?" he asked. He looked sad.

"It didn't hurt that bad," she lied.

The look Leon gave her said it all.

"The fairies are starting to get the riders off the wheel," Lyx informed Bobo.

"You all are a lot of insane casters, did you know that?" Malachi loudly snapped out as he clambered out of the wheel seating and stormed over to the group. "I thought you were going to be a goner," he said to Vanessa. "Good to see you know how to cheat death," he added with a wink.

"Yeah, I try not to encounter him often," she said with a smirk.

"Ha! You flirt with him daily, my dear," Bobo teased.

"Good to see you got your sense of humor back," Vanessa said while poking the ogre's side.

"What on Raen happened?" Lyx asked.

They all stopped to remember the events that had led up until that moment. A rather difficult task with the festival grounds still teeming with cries, screams, and shouts. It was Vanessa that had started to pick apart what she had seen and heard and put one and two together before anyone else.

"When we were being guided to the ride, I had someone bump into me. It was the same man that stabbed me," she started.

"Whoa, whoa. Wait a dust-making minute here. You were stabbed?!" she shouted in a panic.

"I'm fine," Vanessa attempted to assure her.

"No. Get a healer here now. How deep is the wound? Where did he stab you? Are you still bleeding?"

Bobo's voice cut through her chaotic questions. "I scorched it." He did his best to stand up and look proud. He tried to look like admitting it didn't hurt him.

Lyx and Malichi stared at him speechless and then at Vanessa with wide eyes of disbelief. She didn't say anything about it. In fact, she wasn't going to do anything to make Bobo feel worse about it. She, instead, pressed on with her previous train of thought like she hadn't been interrupted.

"When that man bumped into me, there was a group of other beings shouting and fighting with the employee, and then I heard glass breaking."

"It was a distraction," Leon growled.

"Yeah," she replied. "They set off a powerful spell that targeted only the fairies and then bolted before the mayhem hit."

"Except for the one that got to you," Malachi reminded.

"He probably stayed behind to see the job was done," Vanessa informed.

"They were targeting me," the Sleekit muttered.

"It seems to be the case," Bobo said with a sigh.

"What do we do now?" Lyx asked.

Vanessa tried to stand up and felt a ping of pain. Leon was there in a flash and whispered, "Don't overdo it. Just sit and wait for backup to arrive. There will be healers with them."

She nodded to him, agreeing. Then she went on to answer the demoness. "The best thing to do is put Malachi on house arrest and leave him with you, Leon."

"What?" Leon asked.

Thumbing to the Summoner, the azbanonite mumbled, "I'm with this guy. What?"

"They haven't made an attempt since we were there. Leon's home is fortified, spelled with protection wards that far exceed my own, and have multiple spellcasters living in the home that can further protect him. I'm just one witch. The best option is to leave him at your place until I can sort this all out."

"I agree with her," Lyx said suddenly. "They are cowards and with him on lockdown, I can sleep better at night knowing that you all won't be caught up in the assassination attempts."

"And you don't care for me?" Malachi asked drop-jawed.

"If I didn't you wouldn't walk back onto the property, sweetie," she informed. Her fanged grin sealed the deal.

Malachi shivered. "Fair enough." He then took a few steps over to Bobo and whispered to the ogre, "Get your girl. She's creepin' me out."

"I hold no intentions of bridling the woman's spirit. I rather like it," Bobo replied.

Finding it best to shrink back from both demons, the Sleekit went to hide behind the injured witch. There was shouting from behind him, and when the azbanonite turned to look, he saw Riker and a collection of Summoners rushing over to them.

At the wizard's side, there was a tall, white-haired female with glowing red eyes and skin the shade of alabaster stone. She wore boots that went up to her thigh and were decorated in golden wolf-headed buckles. Her whole outfit was leather with gold trimming and embellishments save for the creamy white tunic she wore under her corset.

As they approached, Riker assessed enough of the situation to know that Vanessa had been hurt. He pointed to the young witch and belted out his order. "Healers, assist Spellweaver Peterson. The rest of you aid the fairies with getting people off the ride, and for the sake of the goddess, get a calming spell put over the area."

"Yes sir!" two healers shouted before scrambling over to Vanessa's side while the others dispersed toward the fairy wheel.

The healer's leather suitcase of herbs and potions was dropped next to her, and one opened the bag while the other swept their healing spell over her. As they fussed over what to use and rebuilding what they could, Riker loomed over them and let his silver gaze trail over the wound that held black, charred edges. His eyes flicked over to the ogre who looked away with a frown.

"I see," the Summoner muttered. Turning to Leon, Riker asked, "What happened?"

Leon was quick to answer with, "Seemed to be the cause of some dark witches and mages. They compromised the fairy wheel and then stabbed Spellweaver Peterson while she was trying to keep the ride levitating."

"And what were you doing?" Riker questioned.

Leon looked like he a bit embarrassed. "I was on the ride, sir," he admitted.

"And you?" he asked Bobo with a pointed look.

The ogre shifted under the cold gaze and muttered, "I was resting on a bench after having partaken in too much carnival food, I'm afraid."

The vampiress at Riker's side spoke up. "Demon, you look as though you regret your actions like you should have been guarding her, why?"

"Leave it," Riker stated flatly.

The vampiress glared at her master. "You can't be serious? They're obviously hid—"

"I said to drop it, Aurora," he reminded in a cold voice.

Her lips pressed down into a thin line while her glowing crimson orbs burned into the Summoner. After a short pause, she said, "As you wish."

"As for the five of you. I don't want to know. Do you hear me? Collect yourselves and go home, and I don't want to see you battling blood mages or saving carnival goers or attempting to pacify drunkards at Tasgall's. If I see you get into the slightest bit of trouble, or if it manages to miraculously find you, I'll be asking a lot of questions, and—I promise you—that is the last thing that you want. Do I make myself clearer than a crystal ball?"

Vanessa gulped. She was sure the others did too. They all wordlessly nodded to the icy Summoner.

"Good," Riker snapped, and he started to walk away when he noticed the body a few feet away. "And, Bobo?"

Snapping to attention, the ogre responded with a military-like reply. "Yes, sir?"

The Summoner pointed with his chin and then let a digit reiterate where he was directing the demon to look. "You forgot your ax."

Following the Summoner's line of vision, the gentleman-beast noted his weapon sticking out of a finely charred corpse. Turning back to Riker, the ogre replied with, "Yes. I'll be grabbing that in a moment."

"Right," the wizard said. Drawing in a deep, calming breath, he looked the group over again and slowly exhaled through his nostrils. "Remember my warning, Vanessa. I want you healing at home. No mission scrolls. No trouble. Got it?"

She gave a thumbs up as she tried to not fuss over being poked and prodded and fed the most horrendous herbal potions that could be brewed. "Loud and clear, Riker. I've reached my quota for trouble."

"Have you?" hissed Bobo in a whisper.

"I sure as hex hope so," she said with a half-smile.

Chapter 31:

Even though Vanessa fussed over the cost of using another teleportation spell, they decided that it was the best option to get back home in one piece. There was too much of a risk limping home and being ambushed along the way, and doing a double teleportation to the Coven and then to Leon's home would do nothing for her aching body. Instead, they opted to drop on Leon's doorstep and rush to get the young witch up to Lyx's room before his parents could see that she had been injured. She didn't want to be a burden.

After she was settled into the room, Leon broke the news to his parents and asked for a healer to be arranged to see her in the morning. Patricia gave Leon some soothing tea to bring up to Vanessa to help with the pain through the night. She was rather amazing with herbs and potions and sold them in their local shop. It was a good thing too because Vanessa would have tossed and turned in pain the whole night otherwise. The Coven healers hadn't given her a proper prescription, and all the local apothecaries were closed by the time they got back.

The next few days were spent in bed in (what Bobo described as) uneventful bliss. Rune ball and various other Raen-wide shows and complaining about not being able to move around much combined with eating heaps of snacks filled the Spellweaver's recovery time.

"I'm getting fat. I can feel it," Vanessa glumly griped.

"You've not gained a single pound," Leon assured.

She groaned and placed a fluffy pillow over her face. "I need to get out of this house!"

Bobo flipped a page in his book as he sat on the sofa at the end of the bed. "No way on Raen that is happening, my dear. Better snuggle up in those covers and get used to this until you're completely healed."

She sat up and threw the pillow at the ogre who dodged it with ease. Unaffected, and not even peering up from his most recent read, Bobo flipped another page and said, "Still not leaving this house."

She sat back into the mountain of pillows and crossed her arms over her chest. "I can move without being in pain now," she reminded.

Leon chuckled. "Yeah, but the last healer that came to see you said that you still need to take it easy."

"And with your habits, stuck in bed is the best way to ensure it," Malachi added.

She tossed eye-daggers at the Sleekit who grinned back at her.

Lyx spoke next, saying, "They aren't wrong, darling."

Letting out a sigh, Vanessa slapped her hands on the bed on either side of her thighs. "I know."

"Quick, make note of this. She's admitting a fault," Bobo shouted, ripping off his spectacles and pointing at Leon with them.

"There is a de-summoning spell now. Don't make me use it," Vanessa threatened.

Snorting, the ogre repositioned himself on the sofa and muttered, "Don't threaten me with such a delightful notion." He then settled back into the couch to continue reading.

Lyx clapped her hands together excitedly. "I've got an idea!"

"Anything. Please!" the young witch whined.

"You could go to your apartment to oversee some of the alterations and additions. I'm sure that Mr. and Mrs. Zvěrokruh would adore you being there to give suggestions," she explained.

Vanessa sunk even further into the bed and pulled the covers over her head. "I don't think I can handle that."

Bobo scoffed, "Nonsense. You'll do fine. It'll even get you out of the house."

"I mean that energy. I'm not sure I can handle it," she admitted quietly.

Leon burst into laughter and held his side. "I'm their son and can hardly handle them. Don't worry about it, Vanessa."

She emerged from under the blankets a little bit. "It would be nice to get out of the house," she affirmed.

Lyx nodded.

"That means I can come, right?" Malachi asked, hopefully.

"No," Vanessa and Leon answered in unison.

"You're staying put right here. Where it's safe," Leon stated in a way that gave little room to argue.

Crossing his arms over his chest, Malachi huffed and walked over to gaze out of the bedroom window.

Bobo put his glasses and book away as he stood from the couch. "I'll even go with you," he assured.

Vanessa gave him a look.

"What?" the ogre snapped.

She tried not to smile. "Oh, nothing. I'm sure it has nothing to do with the fact that you could list a million additions you'd want applied to the apartment."

"And I would get to watch you squirm in company that makes you uneasy," he added.

Her look was far from happy. "Mhmmm," she hummed.

"D'all right!" the ogre shouted as he rushed over to her bedside. "You caught me, fair and square. I have dreamed for a moment like this, Vanessa. We could have magnificent crown molding, a tray ceiling, and the lighting ..." He swooned and had a far-off dreamy gaze. Snapping back to reality at the sound of Lyx giggling, he resumed fussing with Vanessa. "You know you don't care for interior decorating."

"You're right, I don't."

"Then, I implore you to search your better judgment and let me do this," he begged.

"Fine. Fine. I was only teasing. Go full ham. Just no suggestions on my room," she warned.

"I can make no promises." Gleefully, the ogre pulled out a notepad and a piece of chalk from his pouch. Scribbling madly, he made way for a more quiet area as Leon came over to sit on the bed next to Vanessa.

"How about you and I get some alone time in before you head out to the apartment with Bobo? No mission scrolls, no Coven business. Just you, me, and some unadventurous free time." The Summoner had a gleam in his eyes.

"I'd like that," she whispered with a smile.

"And I, regretfully, will decline on her behalf," Bobo butted in.

"What—?" Leon groaned.

The ogre gave the Summoner a pointed look. "Need I remind you the last time you two attempted a date it ended in disaster?"

She and Leon looked at each other and then off to the side, each of them cringed at having been reminded in front of everyone.

"It was just going to be a walk in town," Leon attempted to justify the innocence of the outing.

Bobo grunted with a bland expression. "This girl could get in trouble when picking out a pair of shoes. Do you really have that much confidence in calamity not befalling you two that you'll risk Riker's warning?"

Now, that earned a look from both the witch and wizard.

"The guy's got a point, ya know? Why not hold off on your lovey-dovey stuff until you've let the dust settle on everything, and my possible death isn't looming over us all and potentially ruining the moment?" Malachi asked.

Lyx grimaced and bit the side of her lip as she faced all the beings in the room. "I hate to be that girl, you know. But Bobo's got a point, and so does Malachi."

Looking slightly apologetic, Bobo added in a soft tone, "It's honestly for the best, my dear."

The young witch flailed in the bed for a moment and then abruptly stopped and let out a burst of air. "Okay. Okay. It's on hold. But I still want to get out of this house. Let me get up, get dressed, and grab some food so I can head on over to the apartment," Vanessa said with a sigh.

"Well, you heard the girl! Get out so she can get dressed. This isn't the Flustered Dragon. *Shoo. Shoo,*" Lyx ordered as she shoved Malachi out of the room.

"I know how to walk, you know?" the Sleekit reminded the succubus.

Bobo pocketed his book and approached his master. He gave a comforting smile and patted her hand under his massive paw. "I'll help set something up when everything is … well, less hectic," he assured in a low tone.

"Thank you," she whispered with a soft curve of her lips. Even though she didn't want to admit it, they were all right, and Bobo had done the right thing by stopping the date before it could start.

"We'll have a date night inside. My place is big enough. We'll find somewhere to run away to. For now, focus on getting the apartment designed," Leon suggested from the doorway and then left behind Lyx and Malachi.

"This is more boring than staying at Leon's," Vanessa grumbled to Bobo quietly.

He leaned in closer to her as he whispered back, "That's because you are just standing there like a steaming lump of imp poo."

After pulling away, she gave him a cold stare. The ogre chuckled and held up a few paint swatches. "Here, help me choose the color for the living room."

She eyed over the swatches and gave him a perplexed look. "They're all white."

He balked at his master. "I beg your pardon? Your eyes must still be recovering too because—clearly—this one is dragon eggshell," he stated, holding up one swatch, "… and this one is warm alabaster." As he said so, he held up the second colored paper. Then holding up the third, he said, "And this beauty is winter priestess."

Vanessa looked unamused. "White," she reiterated.

"Hopeless," the gentleman-beast said with a sneer.

She sighed. "This one," she shot out and pointed to the warm alabaster tone.

He stared at the swatch. "Really?" he questioned while holding the swatch up toward the living room wall. "I'm not sure. The pink undertones might be too much."

"If you were going to pick the opposite color from what I chose, why would you even bother asking me?" she half-whined.

He waved her away like she was an annoying swarm of pixies. "I'm still thinking," he defended. The young witch sighed heavily again, and the ogre looked at her from the corner of his eyes. Putting down the swatches, he let a slow-growing smile take over his lips. "Did you say something about needing a bigger apartment?" She turned to face him with questioning eyes. "He tapped his pointer finger against his chin and stared at the ceiling. "I believe a guest room would be a nice addition, and a room for Raven wouldn't be too much trouble to add in ..." When he turned to ask for the young witch's thoughts, she was no longer there. Instead, she was standing next to Mr. Zvěrokruh and the portal constructor.

For the next few days, the routine was the same. Vanessa ate breakfast with everyone at the mansion and then headed over to the apartment to aid in overseeing the additions. Despite her belief that she wouldn't enjoy the remodeling process, she found it really exciting to help form the interior layout with the pocket portal constructor. She even was able to make a couple of extra rooms. One for guests and one for Raven. She tried to remember Raven's home as she explained her design plan for the room to the constructor. She felt nervous and giddy as she thought about her aunt showing up and seeing a room designed especially for her awaiting. As the days flew by and the construction rapidly came into completion, Vanessa felt overwhelmed with giddy joy that when her aunt would return, she would not only see a new, roomy apartment but also find her own room to settle into. Vanessa walked around the finished room after all the furniture had been added. Every piece of artwork, every throw blanket, and every notch in the rugged dressers brought a smile to her face.

"She's going to love it," Bobo stated from the doorway.

Spinning around, the young witch grinned wildly. "You think so?"

"I know so," he affirmed.

She ran to him and hugged him tightly. After a long moment, she pulled back with a perplexed look on her face. "I think I lost track of time because of all the excitement, life-threatening events, and construction work," she admitted softly. As she spoke the next thought, her arms tightened around his waist. "Shouldn't—shouldn't she be back by now?"

The ogre looked confused and then worried. "Let me think a moment." But it was clear that he already knew the answer once the Spellweaver had reminded him. "Perhaps she popped by Ell's place?"

"Maybe," she whispered. "But, why hasn't she tried to crystal ball call me?"

Before Bobo could answer, Mr. Zvěrokruh entered the room. "I just signed the papers. It's all paid for, and the movers have brought everything in and arranged it to this magnificent beast's specifications. You can move back in tonight!" he bellowed happily.

"That's great!" But even as she said it, she didn't feel it. Because now that she hadn't heard from Raven by the time she had promised, her head was swimming with new worries and fears.

What could have happened to her aunt? Why had she not called or teleported in? Did she forget? Did whatever she need to handle take more time than anticipated? Was she spending time with Raka? Or had one of the wolves...

She forced a smile.

Bobo noticed the look on her face and rubbed her back. "I'll tell Leon to escort Malachi over, and I'll gather your things from his place and join him in bringing the Sleekit here."

"What am I going to do?" she asked.

He leaned down closer to her and said, "Try to call Raven."

Vanessa looked to him with a smirk and mischievous glint in her eyes. "Who's going to protect me?" she teased.

"Do you know who you are and the trouble you get into? No one can protect you."

They both laughed, and Bobo hugged her again. Softly, he said to her, "Vanessa, I think you've proven what you've doubted about yourself all along."

"What's that?"

"That no matter what, you can handle whatever this life throws at you."

She squeezed him with a faint curl of her lips. "Thank you."

 *Chapter 32:*

The whole time Leon, Lyx, Bobo, and Malachi all gathered up their things and headed back to the newly renovated apartment, Vanessa tried to contact Raven. But a connection was never established. It could have been that she was still in the Black Forest and the magic there muddled the connection. Which left Vanessa with only two probable outcomes: either Raven was with Raka and still handling the situation she spoke about before leaving, or she had been attacked by one of the wolves.

To keep her mind from wandering off to the worst outcome, she placed wards around the home and re-established new welcoming spells. As she walked from room to room, she found it very hard to admire what had been done. She kept thinking back to Raven.

Feeling like she was going mad, Vanessa thought it would be best to try and contact Ell. Maybe the receptionist had spoken with Raven recently and could bring her some peace of mind. Pulling out her crystal ball again, she thought of the blonde and waited. Within seconds, the orb lit up with Ell's face.

"Vanessa, are you all right? I just looked over a report from Riker. I wanted to call earlier, but work's been crazy!"

It was oddly comforting to hear the receptionist's voice. She was instantly smiling at the image displayed in the orb. "It's not a big deal. I've been pretty busy myself."

"Are you healing well?" she asked.

Vanessa nodded. "I'm back to my old self," she informed.

"Don't let Bobo hear you say that," Ell added with a giggle.

The Spellweaver joined her and then her mood slowly shifted. "Say, Ell, have you heard from Raven recently?"

Blinking at the orb, the receptionist replied with, "A few days ago. She said she needed me to look into something for her and that she'd call back later."

"What did she have you look into?"

"Mmmm ... I wrote it down." She was not visible for a moment while she rummaged about and then returned holding the paper. "She wanted to know if blood mages were ever known to work with darker beings and cursed creatures."

"Huh. What did you wind up telling her?"

Ell shook her head. "Nothing. She never called back."

Vanessa's heart sank. "Oh."

"Has she contacted you?"

It was Vanessa's turn to shake her head. "No. I haven't heard from her since she left my home about a week ago."

"I'll see if I can pull some strings and get a missing being report put in."

"Thanks, Ell."

"You take care, Vanessa. I'll keep you updated."

"You take care too, Ell."

With that, the picture winked out, and Vanessa was left alone with the three worst things a being could be stuck with: worry, silence, and her mind.

After going through countless scenarios that all ended in a horrific battle where Raven was hurt or left for dead, Bobo, Leon, Lyx, and Malachi arrived at the house.

"Sorry for the delay my dear. I picked up a few things when we came through the market. A first meal cooked with good company in the home will be a nice way to commemorate the occasion," Bobo announced as he started putting away groceries with Leon.

"I could have been ambushed while you all were gazing at meats and apples," Malachi griped and then turned to look the apartment over. "Not bad!"

Leon rolled his eyes. "I put a cloaking spell over you. You were fine."

It was Lyx that came over and drew Vanessa into an unexpected hug. The Spellweaver got lost in that hug. It was the kind of hug where you forget all the bad things in life. The worries melt away and you just exist in the embrace. The succubus smelled like spice and brown sugar, and it made the young witch relax all the more. She nuzzled into the demoness and drew in a deep breath.

"Bobo told us on the way over." Vanessa pulled back to look into Lyx's amber hues as she spoke. "We'll figure it out, okay?"

The young witch couldn't doubt someone that looked that sure and sounded that confident. She nodded without a word and hugged Lyx again, and the demoness didn't stop her. She squeezed her back and silently gave her all the comfort that she could.

"Where am I sleeping?' Malachi asked.

Leon and Bobo yelled from the kitchen, "The couch!"

"You—!" Malachi shot out.

"I just had everything put in order in my new room. I shan't have you rummaging about it," Bobo expressed.

Leon gave a quick, short laugh. "I've had my fair share of nights on the lumpy couch she had in here before. At least you're getting a new, plushier one."

"Bullies, the both of you!" Malachi swore.

Vanessa couldn't help it, she laughed as she and Lyx remained hugging. Meanwhile, the Sleekit snuck over to Raven's room and opened the door. "What about this room?"

"No," Vanessa said without giving a reason.

"You don't have a heart. You have a lump of coal resting in your chest," he muttered.

Lyx grinned madly. "We could contact Riker for you and see if he'd like to let you bunk with him?"

Malachi ran across the room, jumped over the back of the couch, and landed on the sofa. Drawing in a throw pillow to himself, he started snuggling into the soft cushions of the furniture. "You know, this thing is pretty comfortable."

"Careful, Malachi. That coffee table is glass. If you had landed wrong you would've made a mess," Lyx warned.

"Bah. I'm more graceful than a cat. Even if I landed on it by accident, there wouldn't be a scratch on it," he insisted.

"Somehow, I doubt that," Vanessa grumbled.

Bobo called from the kitchen, "This is not Leon's mansion. Stop your squabbling and come earn your keep." He thusly pointed Malachi to the sack of potatoes next to the sink. "Clean and peel these potatoes."

The Sleekit groaned in protest but started to get up off the couch. "Fiiine."

Slowly pulling away from Lyx, Vanessa asked the ogre, "What's for dinner?"

He poked his head out from the new, and much larger, kitchen to tell her with a grand smile, "Shepard's pie!"

Suddenly, from behind them, there came a massive crash as the glass coffee table shattered into a million pieces. Everyone shouted or screamed in surprise. The air felt electrified as the remnants of the teleportation spell ebbed gradually. Pins and needles raced over Vanessa's skin as she took in the view. A red-cloaked being sat in a sea of broken shards. White hair spilled out from underneath the hooded cape. Black, starry eyes rested on Vanessa.

"Raven!" the witch exclaimed and dashed over to the Dark Elf.

The female didn't respond. It looked like it took all of her energy just to remain sitting upright. Everyone rushed out of the kitchen, and Lyx was already behind Raven, lifting her up to her feet and wobbling as she took the elf over to the couch.

"I'm fine," Raven grumbled out in a tired voice.

"Gentlemen, we are needed," Bobo informed those in the kitchen.

Vanessa eyed over her aunt, searching frantically for any cuts. She found a sea of bruises and wounds that were both new and old. Her lips were cracked and bleeding, and her bright starry eyes had lost some of their luster.

"I'll get the vacuum," Bobo whispered. He rose and looked at the mess with a sigh.

Nudging at Malachi, Leon motioned back toward the kitchen. "She looks like a mess," he whispered. "Let's get some hot water and fresh linen to clean her up."

"Raven … what … what on Raen happened to you?" Vanessa asked with sad eyes taking in every cut, bruise, and swollen patch of skin that covered every visible inch of flesh on her aunt. She feared that beneath the Dark Elf's clothing, it didn't look much better.

Lyx ran, flapped her wings to gain speed, and grabbed a glass of water from the kitchen. Quickly, she returned and aided the battered female in drinking. "Slowly," she advised. "I don't think she's had water in days," Lyx informed Vanessa.

"I can check my grimoire for an herbal remedy," the young witch said frantically. She jumped up to her feet, but it was the scratchy voice of her aunt that halted any further movement.

"Call ... Coven," she panted while trying to gain her bearings. She drew the water back to her mouth and chugged until the glass was empty. While the succubus went to retrieve more, Raven motioned for Vanessa to come closer. When the witch was in range, Raven's arm shot out like a snake, she dug her fingers into the Spellweaver's garments and tugged her close. Caked blood covered the swollen and cracked lips of the Dark Elf. Two words trickled out in a raspy whisper. "They're coming."

Raven then collapsed on the couch.

 *Chapter 33:*

Vanessa dove forward and checked Raven's breathing. "She's alive," she whispered to herself. Jumping up, she told Lyx, "Watch her. I'm getting my grimoire for a healing spell."

The succubus nodded as the young witch darted out of the room. Bobo had already grabbed the vacuum and was cleaning up the shattered glass. The Spellweaver bumped into Leon on his way out of the main bathroom in the hallway with an armload of towels and washcloths. "Whoa," he cried out.

But she didn't stop. "Sorry," she barked back as she crashed through her bedroom door and scrambled to the bedside table. She opened it and felt her clawing heartbeat strangle her senses right out of her. "This will take too long," she muttered to herself. And then it hit her. She tapped into her power and said, "Show me the spell that will best aid my aunt," as her hand hovered over the book. Instantly, the book flipped through the pages as commanded. It didn't stop until it landed on a faded page splattered with brown, dried blood. "A Prayer for Mending," she read aloud to herself. Her eyes scanned over the spell and she repeated it over in her mind until she had it. Rushing out of the room, she slid into the kitchen and searched the spice rack. Clinks and clattering chaotically sounded through the room. Bobo looked at everyone and sighed as he powered off the device.

"I'm going to have to reorganize that," he expressed with a look of displeasure.

"Where's the mortar and pestle?" Vanessa angrily inquired while still rummaging through the cabinets.

"Next to the stove," Bobo informed while laying a sheet down on the couch and lifting Raven and placing her atop it with a pillow under her head.

Lyx had removed the Dark Elf's cape and boots and rushed into the laundry room with them. Leon loomed over the female as he did the only healing spell he knew how to perform. A minty orb of light surrounded them as he washed the spell over the white-haired woman.

"Why'd she pass out?" Malachi asked, leaning on the back of the couch.

Lyx came back just in time to answer. "I'm really hoping it's only because of lack of food and water in addition to using a long-distance teleportation spell, and not because there is internal damage."

"Shouldn't we contact a medic to be sure?" Malachi practically screeched.

"Watch out," Vanessa said in a hurry as she came to Raven's side. Lifting her aunt's head up, she fed her the concoction she had made in the kitchen. It was apparent by the passed out Dark Elf's features that even out cold the taste was still bad enough to wrinkle a nose.

Closer than the others, Malachi pulled back from the couch and held his sensitive snout. "By the goddess, what did you brew in less than five minutes? Are you *trying* to kill her?"

Vanessa was too concerned for her aunt to reply. While her watchful gaze was glued to the Dark Elf, Leon was behind them on a crystal ball call. His body was turned so the sprawled out Raven could be visible to the Coven member he had contacted.

Soft groaning came from Raven, and her bruised hand went to hold her head. "A Prayer for Mending," she said while smacking, the taste still coating her tongue. "Water," she croaked and was immediately met with a glass as Lyx handed it to her. A little more herself, the Dark Elf sat up and looked over the room confused.

Vanessa followed her trailing eyes, and she realized why her aunt seemed so lost. "We renovated the place with a portal constructer."

"Would explain why I landed on the table instead of the couch," Raven stated. After being informed of the renovations and thanks to the potion Vanessa had made, the Dark Elf could feel the fog that had consumed her mind gradually lift. Leon's voice had gained her attention, and she narrowed her eyes as she homed in on the crystal ball in his hands. "Leon, I need to speak with them!" she hollered.

The sound caused the Summoner to jolt in place and turned to face her. "What?"

"Give me the crystal ball!" she demanded.

He didn't ask why. There was a look in her eyes that was drenched in panic and unmistakable fear. He handed her the orb and Raven winced with a hiss of pain when she reached to grab it hastily.

"Careful," Vanessa whispered.

Patting the girl's arm wordlessly, Raven lifted the crystal ball to her face and addressed the Coven member therein. "What is your rank?"

"I-I'm a Summoner," the male started to explain.

"Patch the call through to a higher rank," the order lacked emotion and was more expectant than anything.

"Ma'am … I don't have the authorization to do that."

"All of Raen is at risk, and the information that I have is so highly classified that your insignia would be on the line if I uttered a word to you. Put. Me. Through to a higher rank," she heatedly demanded.

"Y-y-yes. Right away." The image blurred and there was silence while they waited.

Vanessa asked what everyone else wanted to at that moment. "What's going on?"

The Dark Elf shook her head but didn't say anything. The orb's clarity was returning and a new face lit up the surface. It was Second Chosen Winona.

"You've managed to scare a Summoner into skipping protocol. For what, may I ask?'

"Blood mages are colluding with feral demons and cursed creatures. They've been collecting in the Black Forest and causing trouble along its borders for the past two weeks. They are getting ready to launch an attack."

Winona's eyes grew wide and then she schooled her features just as quickly. "This is a rather unexpected bit of information. What do you think they are up to?"

"I had been captured by them. They tortured me for information on the tablets and were trying to figure out how many had been found."

"You think they are going to try to take the tablets?"

"No. I think they are going to try to stop the Wild Hunt from being cast this year. I had heard a few of them talking about it where they were holding me captive."

The Second Chosen hummed and looked off to the side. "Normally, I'd ask for a report to be made, but from what I'm seeing it'll be best if I file it for all of you." She pursed her lips to one side while thinking. "Was there any information on when they would try to attack outside of that?"

Raven shook her head. "Not that I heard of. But it is best to let the people know not to venture away from the city. It isn't safe."

"And let the Council know that extra measures will need to be arranged around the lake during the spring solstice," Winona added. She drew in a deep breath. "Right. I have a lot of unexpected work that just came my way. Focus on yourselves. I'll take it from here."

The Dark Elf gave a slight bow of her head. "Thank you."

The connection winked out, and everyone stared down at Raven as they let what they had just heard sink in. But it was clearly scrolled all over their faces that they didn't want to believe what they had heard.

"They are going to try to stop the ritual?" Vanessa asked, finally.

Raven nodded slowly.

"Why would they do such a thing?" Bobo questioned.

"From what I heard, they are more powerful now than they ever were. Because of the tablets slowly soaking up all of the magic on Raen, black magic is more powerful. And because souls that pass on don't get judged and move on to the afterlife, they are stuck in the spiritual realm. Their grief calls to the first vengeful souls. They come and take these souls with them. They corrupt them until they become one with the rest of the vengeful spirits. With all these bitter, vengeful souls I'm afraid …"

"The blood mages are more powerful than any standard magic caster," Leon finished for her.

Raven nodded grimly. "Exactly."

"Double-dip a candlestick," Vanessa expressed under her breath. "They don't want the spell to be performed because that will restore the balance and take their power away!" Her hands formed into fists at her side. They planned to use all of those spirits that just wanted to move on.

Malachi whistled. "Well, I sure know how to pick them. You are just a bag of trouble, missy," he said with a wink.

"You've no idea," Bobo mumbled.

Lyx broke the conversation with, "Are you feeling any better?"

"Yeah. I'm just starving," Raven admitted.

"Well, my dear. You are in luck because, tonight, I am making shepherd's pie," Bobo announced. "Come, come, gentleman. Aid me in the kitchen while these ladies tend to the wounded."

With that, they all dispersed, and Vanessa and Lyx helped Raven to the bathroom to wash up.

That night after dinner, Raven glossed over the happenings and how she came by all that she knew. The blood mages had been keeping her magically bound by putting vervain in her drinking water that had been spelled by dark nymphs, and they had been poisoning her food. It wasn't killing her, but it sure felt like it. After realizing that these were the cause, she stopped eating and drinking until she had enough magic regained to perform a long-distance teleportation spell.

"You pushed yourself too hard," Lyx said with a pout.

"I did what I had to in order to escape," Raven replied.

Vanessa squirmed about on the couch as she gently snuggled into her aunt. "Lyx is right. You pushed yourself too hard. Going that long without food and water was really risky."

"It sure beat being tortured and poisoned," Raven expressed.

There was no denying that. Vanessa could only sigh as she tried not to imagine what the Dark Elf had to endure while she had been locked up. "I'm just glad that you're here and that you are okay." She then snuggled closer. A realization dawned on her as soon as she was comfortable. "Oh! I forgot to tell you!" Shooting up from the couch, Vanessa then gingerly grabbed Raven's hands and pulled her aunt to her feet. "Come with me," she said with a bright smile.

Leading her through the living room and down the hall, Vanessa brought her to the room she had painstakingly spent so much time in aiding the construction of. She turned the handle and swung open the door to reveal the room that had mirrored so much of the home the young witch had remembered from back in the Black Forest. Raven looked it all over in quiet amazement.

"Better tell her how much you love it before she explodes," Bobo advised from the living room.

Raven turned to face the Spellweaver. "You did this for me?"

Vanessa nodded in reply.

The light glistened over the forming of her tears. "This is the nicest thing I've ever had done for me. Thank you, little shadow." She couldn't move as fast as she wanted to, but the Dark Elf took the girl into her arms and hugged her as tightly as her battered body would allow. "*X'iera eh*, little shadow. Thank you."

"Recovery will be better spent in here, rather than on the couch," Vanessa whispered.

Raven only nodded in reply. "It sure will."

Chapter 34:

Before bed that night, Vanessa and Leon performed one more healing spell for Raven. The potion Vanessa had made would do most of its healing as Raven slept. Having food and fresh water in her system would help as well. The Dark Elf was already feeling more like her old self. She admitted that a night of decent sleep on a soft bed would have her 'fit as an enchanted fiddle' come morning.

They all rested soundly that night. The next morning, however, they were all awoken by the crystal balls, compacts, wall mirrors, and placid pools of water in the house jingling with the emergency broadcast alarm. With a piercing scream, Vanessa sat straight up in bed, immediately looked around the room, and scrambled for her crystal ball. Once her magic connected with the orb, the transmission sounded through the apartment.

"This is the High Priest Council urging all beings to remain within city limits. Due to dangerous conditions outside Tolvade's borders, we advise any and all beings to remain inside the city until the Wild Hunt ritual is completed at the end of the month. If you need assistance with something outside the borders that cannot be put off until the given time, seek an audience with a Hunter status member to file a request report. Thank you, and have a good day."

Lyx rubbed sleep from her eyes as she peered over to the young witch. The crystal ball then had a scroll float over its surface. Vanessa tapped on the message and it unfurled.

All Coven members are on light duty and information retrieval scrolls until further notice. Three hours of minimum magical training are to be conducted daily, and spell usage is to be reported to headquarters until the day of the Wild Hunt ritual. The city and the inhabitants are our top priorities. We are to prepare for the event as usual with added precautions. Report any suspicious behavior and events that seem out of the ordinary as soon as they transpire to the Coven.

Blessed be,
The High Priest Council

The connection winked out, and Lyx and Vanessa shared a look. "Well, that happened faster than expected," the succubus mumbled.

But they both knew that this was the proper response to the threat that was growing outside the city. The only thing that nagged at Vanessa was that these beings had years to prepare for this. Years to calculate, build, form, and plan while the Coven only had a handful of weeks. Were they going to be okay, or was this doom knocking on their front door?

The next two weeks were spent in some strange limbo where they were enjoying their confinement and cracking jokes or playing games with each other or practicing spells. All the while, the threat that loomed outside the city wasn't forgotten. They expected an attack any moment but tried to carry on like they were free of danger.

Vanessa had obtained a clearer understanding of what was listed in her grimoire with the help of Raven. But it was the moments that weren't filled with laughter and fun that set everyone on edge. It was the moments when they were left sitting in quiet contemplation of the growing dangers that rested along the Black Forest. The ticking of the clock was an annoying reminder of the troubles that they were to soon face. Each day that brought them closer to the ritual's date played with their nerves.

"I don't like this," Vanessa admitted as she pushed a boiled carrot around on her plate. "We're waiting around like bumps on logs while those cursed beings and blood mages are setting some dark plan in motion."

"Meeting them head-on is a death wish, little shadow. It would put us in their hands. We have no idea what their line of defense is or how great their numbers are. Going just by ourselves is suicide and taking any number of able bodies from the Coven isn't much better," Raven explained. "Remaining here where we know the layout of our battlefield is the best course of action. Resting up, practicing spells, expanding our knowledge, these things help in the middle of a fight just as much as a well thought out plan."

Bobo started to gather up the dishes from the table as he added, "Indeed. The city will be protected by the barrier when the Wild Hunt ritual is performed," he reminded.

"But it can only hold back so much. Not an entire army! From what we know, this has been in the making for years, and everything has seemed to go according to their plans," Vanessa said.

Malachi shook his head and sniffed. "Nah. They didn't calculate you, Bobo, or not obtaining the tablets. Just with you two as a variable in this whole equation, you tear apart any flawless plan they thought they had concocted."

"Don't forget, they don't have the advantage. They have numbers, but that doesn't mean that they have great fighting skills. Have you ever seen blood mages attack? Yeah, they are strong and powerful and scary ... but they are sloppy. There is no unity to them. They collect with the same goal, but their approach is nothing short of chaos," Leon informed.

Vanessa leveled her gaze on the Summoner as she said, "Chaos still takes lives, Leon." It was a truth that made the whole room go silent.

"Chaos also leaves room for mistakes, and that's all that you need to win a battle, Vanessa. Winning a battle can stop the senseless killing. You only need your opponent to make one mistake, and they lose everything." Raven's words held a warrior's wisdom.

Nodding, Vanessa sighed and replied, "Let's hope they make a mistake at the start. The less lives taken, the better."

No one disagreed.

"A rested soul is a prepared soul. I suggest we all turn in for the night. Tomorrow is the ritual, and we have no idea what the enemy plans to do or when they plan to do it. Let us retire early and hopefully gain an upper hand on them," Bobo suggested.

"Agreed. Let's clean everything up and head to bed," Lyx stated softly.

Sirens gave their eerie cry to the dawn-kissed morning. The rays of the sun had barely peeked over Tolvade's rooftops when the first wave of the unnerving sound rolled through the city. It was louder than the emergency broadcast, and it carried out through every district and street with the sound of its warning.

Frantic knocking pounded on her bedroom door.

Raven's voice could be heard through the barrier. "Move out of the way."

The door opened wide and Leon stood behind the Dark Elf, his face toward the hall, as he spoke to the young witch. "Zaraltrac has had a prison break. The inner city is being flooded with feral demons and anything else that's been cooped up behind spelled bars."

Swinging her feet over the side of the bed, she rushed over to her wardrobe and rummaged through for her clothes. Lyx was on the other side of the room doing the same thing. "How long ago?" Vanessa snapped as she pulled up a set of cloth pants, a pair that had never done her wrong when she did hand-to-hand combat training on Coven grounds.

As she slipped into a tight-fit tunic, Leon answered with, "Less than thirty minutes ago. They are still battling most of the inmates inside the building."

She sucked at her teeth and grabbed her spell-belt. "Any instructions from the Coven?"

Raven tapped Leon and gave him a thumbs-up, indicating he could turn around. Vanessa started to put her hair into a sloppy, tightly woven braid.

With the young witch now properly dressed, Leon walked further into the room. "Nothing yet. It's pure chaos. They were preparing reagents to take to Lorvo Lake for the ritual when the prison break started."

"Double-dip a candlestick," she snarled and swiped her staff from the wall near the door and pushed past everyone in her rush. Raven and Leon quickly followed. Lyx was fastening her whip to her hip as she hurried out of the room behind Vanessa.

Out in the hall, they were each greeted with a bottled smoothie from Malachi and Bobo as they handed them out. "I fear it's breakfast on the run today, everyone. Eat up. Battle on an empty stomach never helped anyone." The gentleman-beast cheered them with his own container and then downed the contents. They all followed suit as they headed for the stairs. As they hurriedly rushed through the halls, Vanessa yelled to those looking alarmed and confused, "Stay indoors, and don't leave your homes unless you have to!" She didn't explain why. That would only feed the panic. Give an order and keep moving.

They barreled down the steps and continued to yell at any being that was lining the streets to go home or to a friend's house and stay there until further notice. Just as she was instructing a group of centaurs, a great golden orb of light lifted from out of the Coven rooftop. It screamed as it pierced through the air, higher and higher until it exploded. Glittering lights spread out further and further until a small orb of golden illumination hovered over a respective spot. From the light, a voice boomed.

It was the Celestial.

"Code Pandora. This is not a drill. All residents of Tolvade are to seek shelter. If you cannot stay at your own home or fear it is too dangerous, go to a friend or relative's home. There are shelters near the town square and within the Coven for those to seek shelter in as well. All homes, businesses, and hospitals are to accept wayward souls inside for safety. Code Pandora. If you live along the edge of the city, be advised, you are to IMMEDIATELY move further into the city. Code Pandora. Seek shelter now. This is not a drill."

The message started to repeat as the sirens sung through the morning air. The centaurs and surrounding beings all turned and ran to what they deemed as a safe place. Vanessa and the others stopped as their orbs started to jingle.

Struggling to gain her breath, the Spellweaver huffed and puffed as she dug out the orb and answered the call. "All Coven members not already assigned a role, go to the town square now."

Again, the connection winked out after the message repeated for a final time. They didn't waste any time. As they rushed for the town square, they pocketed their devices and weaved through the crowded streets as beings hurried off to their destinations. No one was screaming or yelling, but they were far from calm as they quickly closed up shop and dashed off to wherever they considered safe.

Up ahead, they could see a multitude of Coven members collecting in the town square. High-ranked Summoners were gathering and calling over various members into smaller groups. As they neared, she caught sight of Riker's fiery hair and his vampiress pet. They were speaking with another couple of Coven members. One with short, black hair and the other with honey brown curls. Beside each of them were water-based demons. One was very apparently a rusalka while the other dripping wet demoness came across as a kelpie. Seeing Vanessa and the others fast-approaching, Riker pointed to her and Leon before he hooked it toward himself suggestively.

"Looks like we are paired up with Riker," Leon remarked between pants.

She nodded but said nothing. It seemed that the Coven was going to split up into teams and tackle separate missions. This had Vanessa worried. With the unexpected prison break on the morning of the ritual, she was worried that they wouldn't be able to handle an onslaught of beings attacking them in hopes to destroy any prospect of the Wild Hunt being cast correctly. She pushed these thoughts to the back of her mind, and they all came to stand with the other members and their respective pets.

"Thea and Rafe, say hello to your team members for the day, Vanessa and Leon." He then motioned to the pets. "This is their pets, Namara and Mokana, and this is Lyx and Bobo," he stated pointing to each of them.

"Yo, I'm Malachi," the Sleekit added.

"Raven," the Dark Elf added.

"You're not Coven members," Rafe stated with a suspecting glare to the extra beings present.

"Raven is my last living relative and can aid in magic casting." She then turned to the azbanonite and tried not to cringe as she looked back to Riker. "I've made an oath to protect Malachi," Vanessa stated quickly.

That earned a very angry look from Riker. "You and I will have a chat after we survive this mess, Spellweaver Peterson. As for you, Malachi, I suggest you follow one of our escorts to a safer place until everything settles down."

"He can go back to my place. I contacted my family on the way over here. They can meet up with the escort on the way toward my mansion," Leon informed.

"Good. The last thing I need to be is a sitting golden goose. Good luck out there." Malachi paused and looked at Vanessa. His features twisted with worries. "Be safe, Vanessa."

She nodded in reply, and Malachi was quickly escorted with a few others.

"What are our orders?" Thea asked.

"We're instructed to head to the northern borders of Tolvade to reinforce our weak point," Riker informed.

"Just us?" Vanessa screeched.

"This is what the Coven has ordered," Aurora replied.

"It would appear we are the smallest team," Bobo added.

Riker looked at them all with a brow raised. "Take a second look as we prepare a teleportation spell, Peterson. This team is the strongest the Coven has to offer."

As Thea and Rafe set up a teleportation circle to send them to the northern border as quickly as possible, Riker's orb jingled. "Keep working on that spell, you two. Aurora, assist them." He pulled out the device and answered it.

"Riker speaking."

"They … attacking our southern … and the Great Orb …" The connection fizzed for a moment.

When the connection was re-established, Riker angrily inquired, "What's going on?"

"We don't have long. The enemy ... already launched two separate attacks on our south side. Now, they ... attacking the Great Orb. We'll lose connection indefinitely, and teleportation circles back to HQ—or anywhere within the city limits—will be implemented until ... get it back online," overseer Colleen explained.

"Don't waste the resources and manpower on it. Keep a few members on the Great Orb to get it back online as soon as you can and then send out all magic-wielders to Lorvo Lake."

"Yes, sir!"

The crystal ball went still and black.

Pocketing the orb, Riker addressed everyone present. "I'm sure I don't need to repeat what she said. Once the orb is down, we'll lose our ability to communicate and teleport freely throughout the city. These cunning creatures are up to something, and I don't like it. If we have to travel back here from the north side, it will be on foot. Be prepared for anything, and have your weapons drawn and defensive spells ready."

"We're ready!" Rafe called out.

"We don't have time to waste, let's go," Riker ordered.

From the Borlimane district, a massive explosion was heard, and the Summoner seemed unaffected by it. "Move out before we get locked down in battle." His cold gaze drifted and landed on Vanessa as she wondered if they could save anyone before teleporting. Riker's hand reached out and snatched Vanessa by the cloak and quickly pulled her dangerously close. "That's an order."

Vanessa blanched, and her eyes grew in fear.

Raven snatched her out of his grasp and pulled her toward the circle. "This is war, little shadow."

Vanessa gave her a sad, questioning look as she asked, "I don't know why you're telling me—"

Raven's starlit orbs held Vanessa in place as she whispered in a tone that held hints of ice, "In war, you can't save everyone. No matter how hard you try."

Those words cut deeper than any forged metal or powerful spell ever could. Vanessa felt her heart break. She didn't want to believe those words. Not for a single moment.

Bobo, Lyx, Aurora, and Leon entered the circle with the others. And, after doing a quick headcount of everyone present, Riker entered as well. There were electric crackles and a loud *zap* before they all disappeared from the town square.

 *Chapter 35:*

They had landed on the other side of the dam. Farm fields with new, neon green grass and freshly tilled soil stretched for as far as the eyes could see. In the distance, beyond the haze of gray clouds, the Red Tipped Mountains could be seen rising up angrily from the ground. The homes and market places around them were quiet. The inhabitants had wasted no time in taking the Code Pandora to heart and fled to safer dwellings deeper in the heart of Tolvade.

Lyx swayed her tail languidly behind her and sighed. "It's quiet," she whispered.

"That isn't always a good thing," Aurora stated, suspiciously eyeing the horizon.

"It's too quiet," Riker mumbled.

Leon asked, "We are to combine our power and strengthen the northern defense?"

Nodding, Riker replied with, "Yes. Once the High Priest Council has enacted the protective barrier around the city, we will reinforce this side before going to aid them on the southern side."

Bobo glared off into the distance and took a step forward.

"What's wrong, Bobo?" Vanessa asked.

Aurora answered while her blood-red eyes were fixed on the stretch of rolling farmland, "Something isn't right."

A low hum of magic sounded off, the source coming from beyond the inner city. The High Priest Council had begun the ritual process at Lorvo Lake, and they were activating the protective forcefield for the city. It was a power that was felt more than it was seen. Within seconds, a milky forcefield fell down a few feet away. The blue cloaks were sure to be setting up to start the Wild Hunt spell.

"Once the ritual is completed, all the magic that had been drained from the world these past couple hundred years will return," Raven whispered.

"That's the kind of thing I want to hear. I could use a little more juice," Leon said with a smirk and rolled his shoulders.

"Let's get on with the spell," Riker ordered.

"Rafe and I have already prepared the chalk lines, sir," Thea informed.

He nodded and motioned for the others to come and stand alongside him. Each and every being lined up on either side. One by one, they raised their hands and started to whisper the incantation.

"What was made, strengthen, from foes of our nation, keep them back, keep us safe, may the wards know your grace. Goddess reach down, touch that which is spelled, and ensure the enemy is repelled."

They repeated it. Over and over. All the while, the chalk lines underneath them pulsed with power. Slowly, a wall rose up and started to stretch out. Bit by bit, and inch by inch, it was slowly taking over and making the entirety of the ward stronger. It was the furthest point of the city from Lorvo Lake on the far southern side of Tolvade. Which made it the weakest point in the spell. If they were attacked from that front now, they would have no hopes of keeping the city safe.

As this thought crossed Vanessa's mind, she saw something in the distance. A black mass, the edges smoky. The size of it looked like a ghost, and as its dusky arms stretched out, Vanessa's eyes widened.

It couldn't be!

Oh, but it was. Another rose up from the ground, and another, and another. Their arms all outstretching. It was banshees. They craned their heads back just as Thea cursed under her breath.

"Hold the line!" Riker ordered.

"Keep your masters protected!" Namara screamed.

Every pet obeyed the order and put both hands on their master's shoulders. They firmly planted their feet on the ground in preparation.

The banshees, in a number of twenty or more, opened their mouths. Their cry rose up. It was a sound that shot through the air like arrows. The murky beings pulled something dark from the depths of the ground. As if invisible hands were yanking something forgotten and dangerous from underneath the surface. As the cry rose in pitch, the magical backblast hit the small platoon of witches and wizards. The forcefield ate up most of it, but it was still powerful enough to send everyone's hair and capes fluttering behind them.

They shielded their eyes by closing them and turning their heads away from the explosion. But their concentration of the spell never wavered. As they turned back, to their horror, they saw it.

Inky black wisps of haze rose from the ground. It rose up and grew as if the horizon was ablaze and all that could be seen was the blackened smoke of destruction. And as the tendrils of abyss-colored clouds ebbed, they saw an army of blood mages, cursed creatures, and wolves from the Black Forest lining the horizon.

"By the goddess, no," Rafe gasped.

"Blasted conniving crows!" Aurora barked.

"It's an illusion. It has to be," Mokona blurted out hopelessly.

Riker narrowed his eyes and snarled. "No. This was planned. They fooled us."

Bobo looked upset. "Spineless scoundrels, their plan worked."

Leon's face twisted in anger. "We should have known!"

Vanessa, the least aware out of the group because of her lack of battles, turned down each line and asked, "What? What is happening?"

Raven's features hardened as she replied with, "The prison break was a diversion. I suspect those enemies attacking the southern borders were all illusions. They planned to attack from here all along."

Thea spoke next, "It's our weakest line of defense both magically and in numbers. They caused chaos to distract us and then divided us before attacking our only source of fast teleportation and communications!"

Lyx's tail slammed against the ground. Rubble erupted from beneath the blow. "Venomous snakes!" Her wings started to outspread.

"Hold your position!" Riker commanded. His icy gaze bore down on every being present. "We'll hold them off here as best we can. The spell won't hold back a number that large. Disconnect from the spell. We fortified it enough."

"What are we going to do?" Vanessa asked.

"We are going to step out and fight them off," he answered.

Namara gasped. "That's suicide."

"Letting them breach the city is more suicidal, and the repercussions will cause calamity to the entirety of Tolvade's inhabitants," Aurora reminded.

Thea looked at Riker and something registered in her. "The defense system!"

Riker smiled at her. "Indeed. I'll need you to activate it. Take Rafe with you. You'll need help with battling your way through the city. Activate the defense system, and then report to Lorvo Lake. No matter what, we need that ritual to be completed."

Namara nodded and took a few steps back from everyone. Water that was once dripping from her form and had collected into a pool around her feet followed her. The kelpie closed her eyes and released a slow breath. The droplets started to rise up from the ground. Collecting, stretching, and creating a thin sheet of water around the being. Slowly, that form changed shape into that of a horse. Rising up on her hind legs, she whinnied and slammed her hooves on the street below.

"I'll be as swift as I can," Thea informed everyone.

"Don't let me down," Riker ordered.

"Hurry. Go. We'll hold them off as long as we are able," Lyx urged.

Thea leaped up onto the kelpie's back and helped hoist Rafe up behind her. It seemed Mokona would be fine on foot. They all took a final nod to each other. Nothing more needed to be said. With a short whinny, the kelpie galloped out of sight.

Turning back to face the approaching army, they all stepped through the barrier and took a defensive stance. "Leon, you and I will work on a volley of air attacks. Lyx and Aurora, you two take prepared potions and drop them over the enemy. Bobo and Vanessa," he paused as they faced Riker, waiting. "I want you two to advance and give them hell."

Leon paled to the words. "You can't be serious—"

"I assure you I'm nothing short of serious. Out of all of us, they are the strongest. Out of all of us, they can hold the line back before we, too, must advance. This isn't just for the citizens of Tolvade and for the sake of the Coven. This is to ensure that the Wild Hunt spell is completed and all of Raen can be saved. If you have a problem with me putting countless lives before my own, I suggest you speak up now before your wavering confidence and personal emotions destroy any hope of the High Priest Council finalizing the ritual and you get us all killed!"

There was a long stretch of silence. Leon didn't say anything. He didn't need to. The emotions were scrolled all over his face. It was a swarm of anger and hurt and everything in between.

"Now, if you are finished with questioning my orders, then get prepared. We don't exactly have much time, Summoner Zvěrokruh."

Any warmth that Vanessa had grown to see in the older wizard died. It was replaced with a soldier. Someone that knew of all the risks of war and was prepared to take each and every one of them. His chilling gaze rested on Vanessa and Bobo. "We are the last line of defense. We just have to hold them back long enough for Spellweaver Bauer and Summoner MacBain to get the defense system up and running."

"That could take hours," Lyx said with a sorrowful look.

Aurora sighed, "Let's hope that they don't take that long."

Riker puffed out his chest and nodded once. "If we last long enough, we can hobble through the forcefield and be safe. There, we will mend and head over to assist those in the inner city."

The more that they all talked, the more Vanessa realized that the chances of them surviving all of this were ... they were slim to none. Her heart plummeted. She felt like she was in a sinking ship amidst a relentless storm. The ground vibrated with the thundering advance of the army. She felt sick to her stomach. But when she looked at the scourge in the far distance, she knew that they were going to wreak havoc on the city if they prevailed. Her brow bent with determination.

Turning to face Riker and the others again, the young witch said, "I'll do everything I can to keep them from nearing you and Leon."

"Vanessa," Lyx whispered, but Bobo held up a hand to stop the succubus, and he shook his head.

"I know that I can trust you with this task, Vanessa," Riker admitted. An old glimmer of the warmth returned, but when his slate eyes fixed on the approaching army behind them, it froze over once more.

"I'm going with her," Raven informed.

Riker nodded to her. "Very well. Keep her safe and keep that army at bay."

"As long as I have breath in me, they will not advance a single step further," she growled.

Lyx looked at the army and frowned hard. "Leon, get as many Oil and Fire spells as you can prepared. We might be able to funnel the forces."

Leon nodded. "Right. They'll be too confident about their numbers and will avoid the fire. They won't bother with putting out the flames."

"I can muster up a few curses," Lyx added.

"Sir, Lyx and I can handle the aerial attacks and ensure that the forces deal with their own problems within their ranks." Aurora turned and waited for her master's response.

Riker, pleased with all the growing tactics, nodded to the group. "Good. Good. All of this might be enough to slow them down and let us keep our hides alive for another day. Now, let's hurry up."

"Yes, sir," they all barked out in unison.

Turning to face the vampiress, Riker said, "Work with Lyx on creating curses and potions to drop on the enemy."

Before going with Riker and Lyx, Leon ran over to the Spellweaver and crashed into her with a hug that was almost constricting. She let out a breath of air and laughed. Though, the sound was more nervous than happy. His hands went to the sides of her face as he pulled away just enough to look her in the eyes.

"Promise me you'll come back," he whispered as he searched her hazel hues.

She nodded, her hands cupping his. "I will," she softly replied. "Wait for me."

Diving forward, Leon kissed her. He kissed her like he was begging with his lips what he feared to say. It tasted like "I love you," and it felt like a quiet goodbye. They pulled away, breathless. "I'll be waiting," he said, his voice shaky and his lower lip trembling. He didn't trust himself to say more.

She nodded, untrusting of her voice.

"Zvěrokruh!" Riker snapped.

Reluctantly, Leon stared at Vanessa and slowly slipped away until he turned and ran over to his fellow Summoner.

Vanessa took in an uneven breath of air and let it out gradually as she tried to slow her out of control heartbeat.

"We best head out. We can talk tactics on the way," Raven suggested.

"Right," Vanessa whispered. "Let's cloak ourselves first. Not like three of us are going to be very intimidating when uncloaked, but we can at least be less of a target along the way."

No one disagreed. They applied the cloaking spell and headed deep into the fields. In moments, the army would be on the wall. With luck, between the airstrike and the Oil and Fire spell Lyx would be blasting at the army, and Leon and Riker's summoned attacks, they might be able to hold the forces at bay. It would have to be enough. It may not save their lives but it would buy everyone else time. Sometimes, in war, that is the best tactic that you have. Self-sacrifice. You give your all in the hope that the ones you are trying to save get that moment, that split second, which they need to perform the miracle that will turn the tide.

While they trotted along, Vanessa reached into one of her personal pouches and pulled out the hag stone. It could save a life. It could stop a spell. She looked at her amulet. She already had something like that. It needed to be activated, but she had it. She looked at her battle-ready aunt, black eyes fixed on the foes dead ahead. She chewed on her lips and let her eyes wandered over to Bobo and the memory flashed before her eyes. *Smoke spiraling up from his chest. Blood covering the floor. The mighty Botobolbilian lying motionless on the ground.* On more than one occasion, he had suffered from blows that would kill an average demon or being. She couldn't imagine walking away from all of this without either of them. She had to make a choice and, in her heart, she already had.

"Bobo," she said and waited for him to look at her. She stuffed the hag stone in his pocket. Raven silently watched. "You be careful. I can't bear to lose you. I've already lost too much."

"My dear …"

"On all of Raen, I wouldn't trust anyone more at my side than I do you. Don't let me walk away from this alone." Vanessa's eyes welled with tears. "I've spent enough of my life alone. I have things I want to do, and I want you all there with me. That is what I'm fighting for today. I'm fighting for our better tomorrow."

Bobo's eyes soften. "As you wish," he whispered and pulled out his ax.

She looked at Raven and grabbed her aunt's hands in her own. "I—"

But Raven stopped her by laying the tips of her fingers over the young witch's lips. "Even if you tried to give it to me, I wouldn't have let you. I think you made the right choice. All I've known is battles, little shadow. Today, this is nothing different."

Vanessa hugged the Dark Elf. "Thank you for understanding that it wasn't because I didn't love you."

"I never would think that."

Silence stretched for a moment, and then Raven smirked at the threat beyond. "They'll regret thinking that this was going to be easy."

The vibrations underfoot became numbing, the growing line of enemies became more daunting as each foe's body became more defined. The howls and screeching of the cursed creatures and wolves filled the morning air. The sounds were enough to send Vanessa's heartbeat to a maddening rhythm.

A shadow passed overhead and then another. A piercing cry filled the sky. Lyx looked like she had ripped open a portal to Hell and was pouring lava from her hands. It rained down one side. Immediately, any advancing forces on that side were met with a blaze that engulfed them. It trailed for a distance before the succubus rose up in the sky, barrel-rolled, and then changed direction. The magma-like flow halted as she sped through the air. Faster and faster, the demoness flew until she reached a spot just beyond the first wall of flames, and she started to pour again. Her screech rattled Vanessa's eardrums. Walls of fire erupted from the ground below, and the painful wails of those unlucky enough to hit the spell rose and mingled with the marching of endless feet. Heat washed over them as the fires raged on.

Vanessa stopped between the flames and watched as Lyx flapped away before rounding once more, her flight aiming for the more distant shadow of Aurora. The vampiress had already tossed a curse. Its green, smog-like cloud consumed everything in its wake while screams and hollers poured out of the noxious gas cloud in the midst of the army. It looked as though the curses were going to be dropped on the rear of the army where most of the blood mages were.

"Get ready!" Raven barked.

The cloaking spell was still activated, but Vanessa felt like every evil being could see right through her magic. It felt like they could see her just as they could see the fields and the sky. Bobo's hand went to his side, and he took hold of her own. "Trust that Leon and Riker won't abandon us," he assured softly.

Her crazed heartbeat slowed a tick or two as she looked up to the mammoth-sized being at her side. "And I won't abandon you." She turned toward Raven and held her aunt's hand. As she spoke the next statement, her voice cracked, "I love you. I love you both." She locked eyes with each of them, squeezed their hands, drew in an uneasy breath, and slowly let go of them before she removed her staff from her back.

The banshees swirled overhead with their haunting cries as they fought with Lyx and Aurora in an attempt to stop them from tossing curses. Occasionally, the crisp sound of a whip cracking overrode the thundering noise surrounding them. But the mass of beings ready for bloodshed kept marching.

"Wait for it," Vanessa whispered.

Bobo put both hands on his ax, gripping it tight enough that the young witch could hear his skin rub over the grip. Raven hunched down, twin bone-blades in hand, eyes narrowed at the enemy, and her cape thrown back. She looked like a hellcat ready to pounce.

Vanessa lifted the staff and prepared the first spell as she whispered again, "Wait for it."

The army started to merge and come for the only opening. Each step drew them closer to the group. Further into the narrow passage the army came. Their chaotic stomping feet matched the tune her heart was singing.

Closer.

… Closer.

"NOW!" Vanessa belted out and let the first spell shoot out from the staff.

The cloaking spell fell away. A volley of spirit arrows blotted out the sun overhead as a summoning circle appeared. Countless beings fell as the arrows plowed through the first line. Vanessa's spell sent a massive troll, with oozing boils and gnarled features, rolling through the throng of malicious beings.

"Next wave!" she bellowed and prepared the next spell. She could feel Bobo and Raven at her side twitch with anticipation to attack. "Ground me!" she ordered.

From within the marching army, they saw towering catapults. She watched as they paused and started to fill the cradles. Lyx flew overhead, and the Spellweaver screamed up to her, "Aim for the catapults!" The succubus looked down, noted the newfound trouble, and flew past toward her target. The banshees were zipping by in hot pursuit and behind them was Aurora.

The tip of the staff glowed. The spell was ready. Vanessa shot out another monstrous wave of magic, and the next line went down. The summoning circle over the army started to pulse. Leon and Riker were preparing to let loose another volley of spirit arrows. "Let the next line come to us," she said and took a few steps back. They all fell back to let the army reform and advance.

Her palms were sweaty. Her heartbeat thudded painfully against her chest. The cracking sound of logs snapping in twain broke through the army as she watched one of the catapults crumble. But the other went off successfully. It slung a boulder doused in oil and fire toward Tolvade. It hammered into the dome of the forcefield and rolled off the side, but bits of fire still rained down through the disrupted barrier. Crackles of energy popped and exploded from the barricade. Sparks of magic flew all around the boulder as it fell down and landed with a ground-shattering *thud!*

"Come on, *Thea*," Vanessa said under her breath as she looked at the city.

Focus now on the army, the next line was about to come through the opening. The witch sucked at her teeth as her mind raced for a spell.

"Bobo, with me?" Raven asked.

"Aye," the ogre growled, and he rushed into the battle alongside the Dark Elf.

Vanessa held her position and started to chant. "They advance without mercy, they wield weapons of iron and stone, they come to take my life, they come to destroy my home. I combine my efforts with my fellow man and ask his next spell to grow, make it double, make it painful, and be a killing blow!"

She held her staff over her head, yelled, and then pointed it toward the summoning circle. The force of the spell sent a shock through her arms. She felt her feet sink slightly into the soil. A bolt of bright, yellow magic shot out from her staff like a lightning bolt and struck the circle over the army. The summoning circle grew double in size. The once baby blue outlines of the spell bled into a threatening red, and the light of it illuminated the ground in its menacing glow. Spirit arrows shot out from the spell and consumed twice as many creatures as the first spell. The summoning circle then sputtered, popped with small electric zaps, and disappeared. It would take a while for the next one to be prepared and summoned. For now, they were on their own. That truth struck home as Lyx zoomed by and made way for Riker and Leon, most likely to prepare more curses. The banshees followed after. A few of them slammed into Aurora's back as the two demonesses attempted to make their getaway. Any real help from the others would be most likely be halted by battling their unwelcomed guests.

"We're on our own for a while," Vanessa warned.

"Noticed," Raven said with a snarl as she kicked away a lifeless body.

Bobo grunted and watched as the sea of beings kept pushing forward. For the amount of damage they had done, it seemed to matter little. The lines reformed. The army didn't stop their march. They pushed on like an emotionless void of beings and trampled over their fallen comrades.

Nothing was said. The group took a short moment to catch their breath. They planted their feet, picked a target, and prepared for the next wave.

And it came within seconds.

Leon yelled to Riker, "We are going to need more citrine and essence of belladonna for Lyx's curse potions."

"I've got them. Give me your spare bag of will powder. I'm going to be focusing on building the next circle," Riker answered.

A screech gained Leon's attention. His eyes grew in fear at the sound, but the look melted into comfort as he realized it was Lyx fast-approaching. That comfort was short-lived when he saw the banshees gaining speed behind the succubus. Their wailing grew louder as they neared them.

"Uh, Riker, we've got a problem," he informed while frantically dipping his hands into various pouches.

Riker looked up just in time to see a banshee hurling at him. The Summoner dodged the attack and rolled on the ground and then pushed with his hands to send him hopping back to his feet. His wand was unhooked and withdrawn. Pointing it, he prepared to fling a spell, but the object was knocked out of his grasp by a speeding banshee as it flew by. Another came from the opposite direction and slammed into him, sending him flying back and landing on the ground with far less grace.

"Riker!" Leon shouted.

When the wizard looked in the direction of the distressed Leon, he saw that the Summoner was holding a banshee off of him, the spiritual being weighing down on him and screaming in his face.

Dodging another attack, Riker yelled back, "A little busy!" His eyes searched the ground. *Where was it? Where was ... there!* His wand was feet away. Overhead, Lyx and Aurora hissed and screeched as they battled mid-air with three or more banshees. "Hang in there!" Riker told Leon as he turned for the weapon. As he turned, a banshee screamed and locked onto Riker. It raced for him with a wailing cry.

The wizard ran toward the wand, pushing himself to outrun the banshee hot on his tail. He dove forward, snagged the weapon, and rolled out of the way as the banshee clawed at the open air where the Summoner had been just a second before.

Pointing the wand, he began to hurl spell after spell. It didn't necessarily knock the beings out of the sky, but it did slow their attacks and cause them to have to fly away before attempting to hit or claw at them. Already, the Summoner had his hand pulling out of the gold dust pouch. Once he was within range, he pointed his hand and yelled, "Force push!"

Immediately, the female spirit screamed and was sent flipping through the air. Rushing over to Leon's side, Riker helped him to his feet. "We need to hurry up and take care of them. Vanessa and the others can't hold them off forever."

Leon watched the sky swarming with night-shaded banshees. "Every moment we spend with these beings is putting them at risk!" He spared a quick glance to the open fields dancing with wall-high flames. Snapping his vision back to Riker and then overhead to make sure they wouldn't be attacked again, Leon asked, "Do you have any enhancement and ice runes?"

"I like the way you think, Zvěrokruh," the wizard said with a smirk and got ready to pull out the runes.

Wailing cries grew uncomfortably close as the banshees headed straight for them. They were speeding at the two men with reckless abandon.

"Watch out!" Leon bellowed while pushing the wizard out of the way.

The demonic beings darted through the space between them. Their sorrowful cries rattled the Summoner's eardrums. They took to the sky and pulled up before turning upside down and turning back toward them. Riker slapped the runes into Leon's hand. "Hurry the hex up with that spell. I'll cover you!"

Without a word, Leon crouched down and started to dump out the ingredients on the ground. Meanwhile, Riker started to hurl spell after spell without relent to the circling band of wailing spirits. Aurora dashed through the cloud of banshees and hissed as she slashed her claws wildly. Like a flock of frightened crows, the beings dispersed and then recollected. An angry scream shot out of them and they started to fly after the vampiress. From above them, the attack came. Lyx dove straight down and grabbed one of the banshees and flung them into the flying group. They were sent every way and whirled about the air. A massive hiss escaped as Riker took notice of his pet being assaulted by a few of the creatures. A banshee clung to her back and raked its claws over until red, ugly lines formed.

"Aurora!" Riker yelled and pointed his weapon at them, shooting one spell after the other at the collected group. A few darted away while the one on her back screamed and scratched at the vampiress's wings. A sick sound, like leather tearing, filled the sky, and it was followed by a cry of anguish. The banshee responsible was met in the face with a bolt from Riker's wand, but the vampiress plummeted from the sky as she attempted to flap helplessly with one wing.

Crash!

Aurora was down. That was one less to aid with the aerial attacks. The Summoner wanted to run to his pet, but he couldn't leave Leon defenseless. "What is the status?" Riker demanded with anger dripping from each and every word.

"Done!" Leon announced victoriously.

Just as he jumped to his feet, he saw a black mass of banshees flying straight for the ground. In their clutches, poised to hit the ground, was Lyx. She snarled, slapped at them with her tail, and swiped at them with her claws. But it was no use. The succubus was pummeled into the ground, and the night-shaded ball of banshees darted away from the dust clouds, leaving the battered succubus behind.

"Lyx!" Leon cried.

The demoness lay unnaturally still. Her vision was fixed on him and Riker. There was a determined look filling her drooping eyes. Blood trailed from the side of her mouth. A faint corner smile formed. "I'm fine," she rasped. "Finish … the … spell." Slowly, her tired eyes closed.

Leon got ready to cast the spell, but the banshees had all started to return to the army. Upon seeing this, the Summoner seethed with rage. "*Raaaa!*" Leon pointed his wand toward them and shot out a few spells, but the bolts couldn't reach that far. Before long, they sputtered out into nothing but glittering dust.

Riker grabbed a hold of the wand-wielding hand and shook his head at the distressed wizard. "It's no use, they are out of range."

Limping over, Aurora held her side. Her one wing dragged over the ground while the other was folded on her back. "I'll tend to your pet. You two finish the spell."

"Give me those runes, Leon," Riker commanded with his hand outstretched.

"Why?"

"I'm going to combine them with the spirit arrows and the summoning circle," Riker said with a twisted smile.

"It's going to take longer to conjure up the spell, but it could give them more time to prepare a larger long-ranged spell." He knew that Vanessa and the others were limited with short-ranged spells and hand-to-hand combat on the frontlines. If the spell was properly conducted, they would not only eliminate the enemy the spirit arrows made contact with, but they could also freeze a chunk of their forces. Granted, it may not be much. But it would buy them time. And that was all that they could do, buy each other time. They could only hope that they could finish it before it was too late. Once the army forces defeated the others, they would push through, and nothing would be able to stop them. Without the forcefield enacted, the city would be defenseless against the attack, and any help was hours away and hindered by the feral demons and beings that had managed to escape the prison. Lorvo Lake couldn't be left defenseless, but the point that the army had chosen would fall within seconds of them reaching the forcefield. Everything was riding on Thea and Rafe, and they had to keep holding back the army. They had to slow their assault. Victory or defeat depended on how long they all could keep the cursed creatures and blood mages from advancing.

"Focus on making the summoning circle, Zvěrokruh," Riker ordered the Summoner. "I'll fuse the runes."

Vanessa slammed her staff into the head of a blood mage and stabbed the other end into the gut of a naga. Bobo came over and grabbed the blood mage by the neck and hurled it into the crowd. The bodies that the blood mage connected with fell over like bowling pins. Raven pulled her ax out of the chest of one cursed creature and threw it into the back of one that tried to run past them.

They were all panting, and sweat was dripping down their faces. The metallic-tinged perfume from the puddles of blood rose to mingle with the smoke clouds. War was a mix of blood and ash. It tasted bitter. It smelled like destruction. It looked like chaos.

The Dark Elf ran and retrieved her ax. Turning, she sneered at the next wave rushing for them. "We can't keep this up forever!" she screamed. But it wasn't to anyone in particular. It was yelled at the sky like an angry prayer. They were reaching their limits. Vanessa clung to her staff to steady her weight as she wavered on her feet for a moment.

Bobo watched them and furrowed his brow. Without thinking twice, the ogre faced the endless marching army and ran for the oncoming enemy.

"Bobo!" Vanessa screamed.

"Stick with us!" Raven called. But the ogre stormed with fury toward the yelling crowd of cursed beings.

Vanessa cried out, "What are you doing?"

"I'm giving you hope!" he snarled back and let the power overtake him. Green fire fluttered over his arms, it grew into lapping flames, and engulfed his upper body. With a roar, the demon pulled back and swiped, with all his might, through the first being. The blade went clean through, and, erupting from either side, a wave of green flames shot out. The blast of the hellfire leveled the crowd and cast a sick, green glow over the next. Countless beings flailed and hit the ground, trying desperately to put out the flames.

Bobo turned around and yelled to his master, "Get up and fight! This isn't over yet!"

It was visible. The waning strength that the witch felt died away. New vigor filled her. She straightened up and nodded once to her pet. Raven grinned at the destruction Bobo had caused.

Swiftly, the Dark Elf raced over and beyond the ogre. Her blades crunched through the skin and bone of her opponent, and she kicked off of the body. The lifeless corpse was sent spiraling back to the frontlines.

It happened so fast, Vanessa had felt like they really had a chance, and then she saw the firebomb hurling toward them. The army didn't care that their own men were in range of the blast.

"Bobo! Raven!" she screamed. It was too late. She needed to move faster. There was too much space between them. "Please, goddess, help me!" she whispered as tears filled her eyes. She was almost close enough. The amulet was grasped and tugged from around her neck. The sound of crackling flames filled the air. Vanessa held out her arm in front of her like her charm was a weapon. She prayed she was close enough. She leaped forward and activated the talisman.

The explosion was unmerciful.

Even though Vanessa has seen the firebomb coming straight for them, she couldn't brace herself for the impact. The amulet went off successfully, but the blast from the firebomb was so monumental that Vanessa blacked out upon impact within her talisman's barrier.

There was silence for a moment. Then there was only the unyielding sound of ringing resonating in her ears. She couldn't hear the marching of the army or the creaking of the approaching catapults' wheels, but she could feel it. She couldn't hear the fires surrounding her crackle and pop as they ate away at grass and twigs, but she could smell it and felt its blistering heat. Slowly, her dulled vision became crisper with detail. Smoke surrounded them and was caught up in a passing breeze. The flames danced with the wind. The ringing ebbed until the sounds were only muffled, but slowly becoming less muddled.

She blinked and saw Bobo. He was on all fours, shaking off the confusion the blast had caused. His hand reached for the ax on the ground and limply dragged the weapon toward himself. Raven was pulling herself to her feet, though she looked shaken. A straggler pushed past, and the Dark Elf turned, hurled a throwing knife from her thigh strap, and screamed, "I still have breath in me!" The enemy fell to his knees and flopped over, lifeless, onto his side. Raven turned and glowered at the enemy. Her eyes snapped to Vanessa. "Get up! Get up and fight! There is life in you still! Fight! *Verrbina!*"

Bobo was on his feet. He swayed only for a second before he took a defensive stance and roared out to the enemy.

There were too many. They were too tired. The waves of beings never stopped. They didn't have time to recollect or mend. Her body ached, her mind raced, her magic was waning, and her dust was running out. Overhead, she saw the velvet black of racing banshees as they screamed their way back over to their forces. Her stomach knotted as she looked behind her. There wasn't a single demoness in the sky. Her heart sank and worry wrapped her up in an unwanted hug. Despair snuck in.

"Don't give up!" Bobo yelled to her.

She looked at her pet. The worry that had been growing was quickly turning into fear. He could see it, and he was going to stomp the life out of it. "I am still with you. We will not die here. Do you hear me? This is not our end. This is. NOT. OUR. END! You *are* strong. You *are* merciless. You *are* powerful. And this is nothing to you. If I've learned one thing as your partner, it is that you will not stop. You will fight and lay down your life to defeat the enemy. Give them hell, my dear. Give them hell, and I will give you every ounce of power that I have."

Her mind shattered through the growing doubt. Bobo was right. He usually was. And she was not weak. She never was. She believed more in herself now than she did months ago.

Raven ran over to Vanessa's side. "Do you have another major spell in you? We can't keep up with short-ranged attacks. We'll be overrun before long."

The Spellweaver thought about it for a moment. She nodded. "I think I can muster up a spell. I'll need you two to buy me time."

"Get started on it then." Raven ran over to Bobo. "Let's buy her some time."

"Gladly," the ogre growled.

Vanessa dug through her pouches, her mind mentally scanning through spells and incantations. Something. Anything. That's when she thought of it. A blinding spell. She could try for a massive blinding spell. It would slow the enemy, cause them confusion, and would give them a chance to mow down more enemies before they could reach the opening. By then, hopefully, Leon and Riker would have completed another summoning circle for the spirit arrows. If they were still alive, and she was praying to the goddess that they were.

Gold dust, runes … they were all hastily pulled out and combined.

While she worked on the spell, Raven and Bobo rushed toward the first batch of enemy beings. A lamia and a chimera darted for the duo. Clashing into one another, Raven blocked the blow from the lamia and kicked it away. Both of her axes came down. One missed, but the other grazed over the creature's shoulder. It shrieked and pulled back before lunging forward with claws scrapping through the air. Sweeping up, Raven slammed her bone ax into the lamia's stomach and pulled up. The being snarled and then went quiet. Pushing the creature away, Raven looked up to see who the next foe would be. A volley of blasts were heading right for them. She held up her arms and yelled. *"Gra'thena!"* A forcefield shot up, blocking the spells, and then instantly went away.

As the defense spell faded from her and Bobo, her black eyes fixed in horror as she saw the wolves fast-approaching. The one leading the pack leaped over the next wave of creatures and headed right for them.

"Bobo!" she called out to the ogre.

He had seen them coming. Preparing hellfire, the demon ran for the wolf. He struck at it before it could jump. The ax bit into the front paw. Reaching out, Bobo punched with a green-flamed hand at the beast's chest. It slammed into the ground on its side with a whimper and shook it off. The flame ate away a patch of fur and then died out.

The yellow eyes of the wolf narrowed at Bobo and Raven, then flicked over to Vanessa as she was about to begin her incantation. If a wolf could smile, it did. The evil intent was plain for all to see. It was etched deeply into its wolfish features. Two more beings ran into the mouth of the passage. Bobo was instantly on them. With a snarl and a howl, the wolf bounded straight for Vanessa.

Raven looked at Vanessa and then Bobo. She remembered the hag stone. He was safe ... but Vanessa. She had used her amulet already. "No," The Dark Elf whispered and ran after the wolf. "*Zvakhasta!*" Her feet glowed orange, dust kicked up behind her. The wolf opened its jaws. Raven pushed herself as fast as she could. Tears filled her eyes. "No!" she roared.

Her body slammed into Vanessa's, sending the young witch rolling away. The wolf bit down. Raven's axes sliced at its throat. Both of them fell over. Vanessa screamed out in horror.

Half-crawling and half-running, Vanessa rushed over to her aunt's side. "No. No. No. Please ..." She rolled the Dark Elf over. Bobo's hellfire went off behind her in rapid succession as he tried, with all his might, to hold off the horde.

Countless punctures from the wolf's bite covered Raven's shoulder and stomach. Vanessa clamped a shaking hand over her mouth and quieted a wailing cry. Tears welled up and spilled over as they ran down her cheeks. Raven's starry eyes drifted open, and she smiled at the young witch. "You're safe," she whispered breathily.

"Don't ... don't talk ... Let me heal you," she said, but she knew that healing spells weren't going to fix this.

Already, Raven's skin had paled. Her motion was sluggish, and the life in her dark, starry eyes was dulling. "Listen to me. I don't have much time." She convulsed with a dreadful, gurgling cough, and winced in pain. As Vanessa watched, she saw black veins were webbing from the puncture wounds. With every second, their reach laid claim over a new portion of skin. Vanessa shook her head and cried. She hiccupped and tried to hold it in.

Raven went still again, her breath rattling as she drew in a lungful. Her hand rose up and touched the side of her niece's cheek. "Little shadow," she said softly. She waited for those hazel eyes to lock with her black hues. "I'm so proud of you." She paused, shut her eyes, and drew in another ragged breath before opening them again and saying, "You're not alone, Vanessa. You never will be. Even if all on Raen perishes ... you're *not* alone." She smiled, but when she inhaled, she looked like she was in unfathomable pain. "I'll be watching."

Vanessa cried and held her aunt's hand against the side of her cheek and whispered, "Please stay. Stay with me."

"I'll always be watching."

"I don't want to lose you. *Please!*"

"I love you, little shadow."

Vanessa hiccupped and sniffled. She didn't want to say goodbye. She didn't want this to be the last moments they ever shared. But death doesn't care what you want. It never would. If she didn't say anything now, it would haunt her forever. She faught past the pain. "I love you, auntie," she croaked.

The Dark Elf smiled one last time, and then slowly closed her eyes.

As her hand fell away, Vanessa felt something leave her body and go with Raven. It wasn't real. Any moment, she would save her. A spell would bring her back to life. Her power would activate and ... something would happen. Any minute now. Raven was just exhausted. She wasn't dead. She wasn't. But every time she tried to convince herself that it wasn't true, and the Dark Elf didn't breathe or move, Vanessa felt a fresh wave of pain.

Finally, she pulled her aunt's body up in her lap and screamed at the sky. As if she were begging heaven to open up and destroy everything that took her happiness away, she screamed. Until her throat hurt, she shouted. As if she were summoning storm clouds and rain, she wailed up to the heavens. It was a long, wordless cry that said everything her heart couldn't say.

Bobo let another wave of fire out and rushed over to her side, panting. "Is she ...?" He looked and his eyes widened. "No ..." he whispered. The ogre frowned hard and then looked over to the numerous cursed creatures. "My dear ... they are coming," he reminded. "We have to keep going. We have to fight." He hated having to say each word. There was nothing he wanted more than to let her mourn and have her moment. But he couldn't do that.

The Spellweaver hung her head. For a fraction of a moment, a small second, she wept. Then she gently laid Raven on the ground. In that short amount of time, something changed in the witch. Her ashen smeared face fixed on the army, and she felt the angry tears flowing.

Bobo grabbed at her robe's sleeve and asked, "What are you about to do?"

There was heat in her voice as she said, "I'm going to make them pay."

"Then I will ground you. She mattered to me as well. Until the end, I'm by your side, Vanessa. As long as I'm here, you won't be alone."

As soon as he said it, her heart was hit with pain.

Alone.

Raven's voice filled her mind. *"You're not alone, little shadow. You never will be. Even if all on Raen perishes … you're not alone."*

Fresh tears spilled from her eyes. "Thank you, Botobolbilian. You are the best thing that happened to my life."

The gentleman-beast smiled then. "Of course I am. I mean, look at me."

They both gave a short laugh, and he helped her to her feet. She watched the army come for them as she focused inward. That door, the quiet place where her power resided, she mentally reached for the knob. "Bobo, hug me. Hug me and summon your hellfire," she commanded in a soft voice. It was far too sweet-sounding for the devastating spell she was about to unleash. It was far too kind for the overbearing pain that consumed her being.

"As you wish," he whispered, coming closer to her.

Thundering footfalls drummed against the soles of her feet as the army pushed toward them. In numbers that would drown them within seconds, they rushed for the pair. A line of black ate at the horizon. Seven people couldn't hold off an army forever, but they did it for just under an hour. Most wouldn't survive for five minutes, and they had managed to do it for almost an hour. Now, she had to use every bit of her power to push back one more time.

The battle-ax dropped to the ground. She shut her eyes and steadied her breathing, but she couldn't stop the tears that fell. Bobo's arms were warm as they wrapped around her. The prickle of her magic danced over Vanessa's skin. The heat intensified as Bobo summoned his hellfire. In her mind, she pulled the door open. And it was like something snapped inside her. The door shattered, the room concealing her power rushed through and overtook her. She focused on her spell while the magic thrummed over every inch of her being. They lifted from the ground, and the ogre hugged her tighter. His chin rested on her shoulder. Her arms rose out to the side, and her voice echoed as she recited the incantation.

"Wicked they come, in droves, in hordes, ready to strike me down without remorse, lift me up in prayer and light, give me the strength to continue the fight, let my power be like a stream, that carries away my enemy with screams."

She was like a star, an eerie star that was rising up from the bloodstained fields. Green flames lapped around them as if a small, jade sun had appeared in the smoke-riddled sky. The ends of the lime-colored fire curled and twisted violently as it grew in size. It consumed the young witch and ogre until their blackened silhouette disappeared within the blinding viridescent light.

Clouds stretched over the veil of the sky and covered the face of the sun, hiding from it the atrocities that were about to befall the battlefield. Vanessa's voice boomed across the land below as the army pushed through the opening of the wall. It looked like a black flood was rushing out and rolling over the fields. "Be consumed by hellfire!"

Three, loud booms pounded through the air and were followed by three rings of hellfire that pulsed out of the blazing green orb. It traveled down, down, down to the field and slammed into the army. Though the spell was massive, it hardly touched a third of the army. But it did enough damage to stop them, momentarily, from advancing. Blood mages formed a line as rock trolls lined up to defend the main army. Multiple arcane blasts slammed into Vanessa and Bobo's hovering form.

An in-range catapult's arm was drawn back and hitched before a cyclopes loaded the cradle. A group of hobgoblins jumped around and poured buckets of oil while a nearby blood mage cast a fire spell to ignite the boulder. Creaking could be heard as they pivoted the enormous structure and aimed it for the Spellweaver.

"Bobo," she whispered, her hair whipping about her face inside the ball of fire that her magic and the ogre had created.

"Yes?" he whispered back.

Her arms draped around his own, and she squeezed while closing her eyes. The taught rope holding the arm of the catapult could be heard being cut, and it slung the boulder at them. She felt fresh tears stream down her face.

"I love you."

"And I love you, my dear."

As the boulder whirled toward them, a summoning circle opened up just over Vanessa and Bobo. Shards of glowing ice rained down from the portal. The boulder slowed and then stopped inches from reaching the pair. Then it quickly plummeted and crashed down on enemy forces that had begun to push through the opening in the wall of flames.

The spell she had cast started to wane. The flames flickered like a candle dying in the wind. She headed for the ground before she magically exhausted herself. Her vision faded in and out. "Bobo, I'm losing control," she informed.

She could feel him at the edge of his own abilities yet still pushing what little remaining power he could into her and the spell she was casting. If she kept this up until they got back to the ground, they both may not make it. She couldn't risk both of them passing out, or worse.

"Hold on!" she advised and abruptly ended the spell several feet from the field below. They landed and rolled, grunting in pain as they came to a jarring stop.

Bobo called out to his master, "Vanessa?"

"I'm okay. I'm over here," she groaned. Though she was alive, she felt like she couldn't move. Everything in her hurt. Her body felt like it was on fire, her mind felt like it was consumed by a sleepy fog, her limbs throbbed with pain from the impact, and her eyes struggled to say open. Blinking, Vanessa tried to un-blur her vision. Through the blotted scenery, she could vaguely make out that Bobo didn't look much better than her. He was hunched over and trying to get to his feet, but he fell as he tried to take a few steps in her direction. "Bobo," she croaked and reached out. Digging her fingers into the burnt soil, she dragged her body over the ground. Both of them were clawing and crawling their way to each other.

Already the horde was swarming through the opening of the oil flame's spell. They did everything they could. Once reaching one another, Bobo drew the young witch into his arms protectively. Their backs faced the oncoming army. Their eyes were fixed on the city. The forcefield hadn't been activated yet. One had to wonder if Thea, Rafe, and their pets were even still alive. Vanessa felt utterly defeated. They had tried so hard.

"We didn't fail," Bobo whispered as he hugged her.

She nodded and gripped his arm. "We did something pretty amazing today," she rasped in a tired voice.

He nodded. "Indeed, we did. Dare I say, it was legendary?"

She laughed. "Riker better watch out, he's got some competition." Even as she made the joke, the tears started again. It was hard not to cry when you knew that you were moments away from dying. Her chest tightened while the ground trembled as the enemy neared. She knew that they wouldn't be spared. They clung to each other like driftwood in the middle of an unforgiving sea. She could hear an approaching roar of a lone soldier. Everything in her wanted to fight back, but everything hurt too much to even try. Screwing her eyes shut, the witch awaited the killing blow.

A burst of light flashed next to her. As she opened her eyes, she saw the enemy on the ground, motionless, as green flames ate away at the body. She blinked, confused. "Bobo, did you?"

"No, my dear. I've got nothing left in me," he admitted.

They both turned their attention to the rip in the space nearby. A vortex swirled just a few feet away. To their amazement, within the growing vortex was Ma. She fussed with her snowy bangs and brushed off her dress. Smiling, as if she hadn't murdered a cursed creature, she waved at the two. "Hey, babies! Sorry I'm a little late. I had ta call in a fava to my Uncle Vinny," she informed and fully stepped out of the portal. She saw the fast-approaching army and made a face. "Well … looks like I got here just in time." The imp turned and whistled into the portal. Within seconds, countless imps came rushing through the opening. Ma focused on her nails while imp after imp came pouring out.

With a sniff, the old imp stepped forward and yelled to the line of demons. "All right, ya brimstone bathers! I want you ta put everything ya got in focusing hellfire on tha frontlines of dose guys. Anything strong enough ta come through will be dealt with by tha Coven memba's."

"How?" Vanessa asked. But the question was so vast. How did Ma know where they were? How did she know to bring help? How would the Coven members deal with whatever came through the hellfire? All of her questions were answered when Winona stepped through the portal.

The woman's cool eyes fixed on the female imp as the Second Chosen attempted to flatten her hair that had been mangled by the portal spell. "That was, by far, the most unpleasant thing I've ever had to deal with."

Leslie pushed past with little regard for the Coven member. "Whateva ya say, toots. Dat was nuttin'." He ignored the glower the Second Chosen was giving him and motioned to the rest that seemed to be still coming through the portal. "Ova 'ere!"

"Come on. Come on. I can't keep dis open all day, ya know?" Ma complained.

Healers and a handful of Hunters came rushing out of the portal. Leslie pointed to Bobo and Vanessa. "Get dem outta 'ere."

"No," Vanessa barked. Everyone gave her a look.

She tried to stand and failed, while on all fours she begged the nearest Healer, "Mend me. Just enough so I can walk."

"Ma'am, I really should—"

"I won't fight. I need to get her body!" she yelled.

It was Winona that picked up on what had transpired before anyone else. "Where are they?"

Vanessa gave her a look. The Second Chosen spoke a bit softer, a tone that the Spellweaver would have never expected from the older woman. "We need to get you all out of harm's way and closer to the forcefield. We don't have much time, and we don't have many members that came with us. We still have to hold them off a little while longer. I need you to trust me with the task of gathering the body."

Her heart was breaking all over again. She wanted to do it. But she would be wasting resources to do so. As much as she didn't want to accept it, Vanessa needed to trust Winona. Nodding her head, she held back any plea to let her be the one to get her aunt's body and lifted her aching arm to point at the mass covered in a red cape a few yards away.

Winona looked and then made eye contact with the young witch again. "I'll bring her to you." Standing, the Second Chosen ordered a few of the men to escort Vanessa and Bobo over to where Leon and Riker were. They barely made it halfway across the field before they saw a galloping gang of centaurs running out of the city and onto the battlefield. A collective war cry clung to their lips as they sped across the field.

After noticing Vanessa and Bobo staggering their way over, Leon dashed across the field to meet with them. He slid to a stop and looked her over before kissing her. It felt so good. For a single moment, she lived in the press of their lips. It was a beautiful way to forget about everything for just a few seconds. Pulling away, the Summoner let out a breathy laugh. "I thought I was going to lose you," he admitted.

She tried to smile, but her lips kept trying to betray her and frown. No matter how hard she tried, she couldn't stop the action. Her lower lip quivered as she spoke, "You've no idea how many times you almost did."

He hugged her then. "I'm so sorry."

She shook her head and gripped the Summoner like he would fly away and she had to keep him there with her. "She's gone," she cried. "Goddess, help me, Leon, she's gone." She felt her chest tighten and the dreaded clouds of sorrow creep in. A fresh burst of wetness washed over her face.

"What ... who ..." but he stopped, and she felt him look around. "No. No ... oh, goddess, no ... Vanessa." He didn't know what to say. She couldn't blame him. Outside of wailing and crying and feeling like she was dying, she didn't know what to say either. The only family that she had—that she had known— was gone.

As the war ensued behind them and countless beings combined to keep the enemy at bay, it didn't seem to matter. The distance had helped to give the slight feeling of comfort, but it was more so because sadness was stronger than any fear. It consumed her like a hungry beast. It claimed every part and piece of her and didn't let go. Fear has nothing on sorrow. Sorrow could swallow you up until there was nothing left. Not even fear. And she felt it course through her like a thousand shards of glass.

 *Chapter 36:*

Once they were over by Riker, the Healers went to work on mending the demonesses. Bobo stayed behind with the doctors to look over Lyx. After being informed that the demoness would be fine, the young witch wobbled over to a more quiet area and practically crumpled on the ground near the city wall. It felt so good to just sit down and not be on high alert. Her body couldn't fully relax, but she could rest for a moment. That was better than nothing. Vanessa chugged from a lamb-skin spelled pouch. It wouldn't be much, but it could help her regain a fraction of her magic and tide her over until rest and proper mending from a doctor came to pass.

The image of Winona with a body draped on her back was silhouetted in the distance. She watched it and lied to herself. Raven was acting like a kid and managed to trick the stone-cold Second Chosen into giving her a piggyback ride. She wanted to smile and would have if the ugly truth wasn't so raw and real. When the witch got closer to them, Vanessa turned away and focused on the ground under her feet.

Winona came over to the young witch, but the Spellweaver couldn't help but fix her gaze on the cloak-covered body now lying on the ground mere feet away. The Second Chosen held a hand out. Within her grasp were Raven's twin bone-axes. As the young witch let her eyes roll over every dent and blood splatter on the weapons, she felt new knots form in her chest. When she went to retrieve them, her hands were shaking.

"I figured you'd want them," Winona said softly.

Vanessa curled her lips into her mouth and bit down as she felt the stinging promise of fresh tears assault her vision. She wordlessly nodded and took the blades from Winona slowly. They felt heavy in her grasp. But some of that weight had little to do with the physical weapons themselves.

"Thank you," Vanessa managed to squeeze out.

Winona said nothing. She turned and focused her attention on preparing a spell before she would rush into the fray with the rest of them. Within minutes, the Second Chosen was running out into the field, leaving the distraught and quiet Spellweaver behind.

Vanessa had a hag stone from her mother and bone-axes from her aunt. But she'd trade them both and all the magic in her body to just have her family back. It rose like a storm in her. The tears and pain she had silenced back in the face of battle pounded against her chest with a vengeance. Deep down, in her innermost being, she wanted to fall apart right then and there. It wasn't the countless strangers or fear of being judged that made her keep her grief in check. It was the fact that she wanted to see the army fall before she gave in to the sadness.

Leon came running over and kneeled next to her side with a potion uncorked. "Here," he said slightly out of breath.

"What is it?" she asked. Could someone ever hand you food, drink, or potion without you asking such a crucial question? If you must ingest it, it was only proper to inquire what the hex was about to be put in your mouth, right? But she didn't really wait for him to reply. She tilted the bottle up and drank. Mainly because she didn't think Leon would try to poison her.

"It's mugwort, peppermint extract, and ... uh ... a hint of basilisk's blood," he informed reluctantly.

She felt like she was turning green. The urge to throw up was strong enough to chase away her sorrow for a moment. "You gave me a Blood and Peppermint potion?"

"Ah, and they say you didn't pay attention during your brewing classes!" he countered with a grin.

"How could you?"

"It's the fastest way to give you a magical boost. We aren't out of the dark yet."

"It's an archaic practice. I'd prefer to sleep on the battlefield, thank you," she grumbled and wiped her lips.

"It doesn't taste so bad. The peppermint helps."

"I wish you wouldn't have told me. I drank ... blood." As she said it, she cringed, shivered, and swallowed hard.

Leon laughed at the expression. "Come on, ya big baby. We need to prepare to aid them in the next assault."

"What's the status?" she groaned out the question while pushing herself to stand on her own two feet without assistance.

"Not good," he admitted grimly.

She shot him a look. "Still?"

"You should know better than everyone present that we aren't a match for an army that size. We aren't killing as much as we are injuring them. But, to be honest, we aren't doing much more than stalling them. They are going to break through soon."

Vanessa growled and looked for something to kick, but she found nothing and settled for stubbing her toes into the soil. "Double-dip a candlestick!"

"Pretty much."

"Any word from Thea and her team?"

He shook his head.

She frowned and sighed, exasperated.

The next question was if they tried to contact them with an older and far more complicated means of communication was there anyone that would answer? She didn't want to believe that Thea and the others had met their end. They seemed so in sync with each other. Their teamwork was something to aspire to accomplish herself. But if Thea's team had been compromised, then they had to come up with a plan to finish the job and save them.

Leon pressed on with the matter. "If we don't figure something out soon, we might have to retreat further into the city and try to hold them off there."

Vanessa didn't like the sound of that, and it was evident by the expression she wore. "No, that would leave the sanctuaries unprotected and put the inhabitants of Tolvade at risk. There is a high risk of the forcefield being jeopardized."

"It would give us more forces."

"But the cost of the action would be too great. We'd have to use every bit of our manpower just to push them back out of the city."

"Staying here for too much longer is suicide!"

He was right.

She bit at her thumb while thinking. Did she have all the reagents to perform the old, and almost forgotten, communication spell? Would they just be wasting time trying to contact them? Her head spun while she attempted to come up with a decent plan.

Just then, there was a massive explosion but, this time, it wasn't from flaming boulders slamming into the barrier or one of the many thunderous eruptions from within the city or even on the battlefield. However, it did come from within the city. The initial sound was followed by a massive wave of air that crashed into everyone. Vanessa, Leon, and everyone on the fields were all sent flying as the magical backblast whipped through every being without restraint.

After tumbling to the ground, Vanessa scrambled to her feet and watched as a thin wave of magic enveloped the city. Her wide-eyed expression was replaced with a victorious smile, and she yelled to the reinforcements, "The forcefield is up. Fall back! Fall back!"

Being after being called out over and over the order. Leon grabbed Vanessa and motioned toward the city. "I'll go get Riker. You go, you've done enough. Get to the safety of the city."

"What about Bo—" her question was cut short as Bobo came to her side with a very happy Lyx in his arms. Vanessa was sure she heard the succubus purring.

"Let us not waste another moment." Bobo led the way with Vanessa following after.

Everyone came rushing through the double-magical barrier. With the forcefield enacted and strengthened by the spell performed by the blue cloaks, there was nothing on Raen that would come through the walls if it meant the city or its people harm. As they fell back into the safety of the city, the imps, Coven members, and centaurs did their best to push back the enemy forces. As they all ran and fell through the magical wall, the counting of casualties and injuries began.

"How are you feeling, Lyx?" Leon asked.

She didn't respond. She only dreamily gazed up to the ogre that cradled her in his arms. Poor Bobo looked everywhere but into those amber orbs of hers, and his cheeks bloomed a bright red as he surveyed the surrounding empty buildings and streets.

Vanessa cleared her throat. "Lyx?"

"Hmmm?" the succubus hummed happily.

"Are you feeling okay?" Leon asked again.

The demoness nodded slowly. "Oh, yes," she purred, her eyes still fixed on Bobo.

A medic walked by and addressed Vanessa. "Both of the demonesses have stable pulses and have had proper mending. We urge them to only fly for short periods of time, no heavy lifting, and to stay grounded if having dizzy spells."

"I understand. We'll follow up with a proper visit to the clinic after all of —" Vanessa's words were interrupted by a massive explosion coming from the center city.

"Banish a banshee. They're tearing the city apart!" Leon growled.

The last of the reinforcements came flooding through the barrier. A couple of imps carried a weak-looking Ma on their shoulders. A sea of bodies started to circle around the older imp. They called for her son repeatedly as they limped away from the barrier. Leslie shoved any being between him and his mother out of the way. His ears drooped, and his eyes misted. Closing the remaining distance, he collapsed on the ground next to the worn-out imp right as the two carrying her laid her down on the street.

"Ma, Ma. Are you okay? It's me. It's ya baby boy, Leslie. Speak ta me." He spoke frantically as his shaking hands slowly reached out to her and pulled the older imp onto his lap.

Ma opened her eyes and took in a slow, steady breath. Her smoked-smudged features made the lines on her face more visible. She had seemed to age a hundred years in such a small amount of time.

Ma limply grabbed her son's hand, "I … need ya ta listen ta me, Leslie."

"What, Ma. Whada ya need? Anything ya want. I'll get it for ya."

"I need ..." she whispered ever so softly.

"Anything. Say it and I'll get it!" He turned to look behind him and yelled, his voice cracking. "Can I get some help ova 'ere?!"

"Don't fuss ova me," she rasped. The old imp coughed off to the side, every movement seeming sluggish and slow. When she turned back to her son, she smiled wearily and said, "I ... need ..." she paused to draw in air, the very act looking painful.

"Whateva you need, Ma."

"I need ... *grandbabies*."

Instantly, he dropped Ma from his loving arms. "She's fine," he mumbled.

"What an ungrateful son. Droppin' your *own* injured motha. I thought I raised you better, Leslie!"

Relief washed over Vanessa as she saw that they weren't going to lose someone else. She was happy for Leslie. Part of that happiness hurt.

"You're not alone, little shadow."

She felt herself stuffing the pain away to deal with it later. She would focus and process it all when their lives weren't on the line. She felt light-headed and sick to her stomach, but she managed to snuff out the urge to cry. It couldn't have happened at a better time as Riker came rushing over with Aurora.

"Second Chosen Winona has instructed us with a verbal order from the High Priest Council," he paused and drank a magic replenishing potion like it was nothing. Vanessa's face twisted in repulse as she remembered the ingredients. It wasn't surprising that he had one. It was typical of battle veterans and those that often found themselves in situations where magic was your only option to carry them, but they were expensive and took a week to brew.

"What are the orders?" Vanessa asked.

"We are to remain in the northern district until the Wild Hunt ritual is completed."

"Stay?" she gasped.

"What about the chaos in the inner city?" Leon questioned.

"I'm not sure they will need the extra manpower," Bobo answered.

"Why wouldn't they?" Vanessa asked.

"He's right," Riker replied. "I've received news that along with various retired Coven members, many civilians have risen up to aid in corralling those that had broken out of the prison. And the most surprising is that the Skrittish have emerged from beneath the city to help in the task."

"The Skrittish emerged?" Lyx had broken her view from Bobo to blink, baffled, at Riker.

The Summoner nodded. "Yes. It seems that this whole ordeal has stirred many inhabitants of Aeristria. Between the tablets and the cursed creatures gathering, everyone seems to have noticed that something big has been coming for a while. Everyone is helping turn the tide as best they can. "

"We can't let the people of Tolvade fight!" Vanessa shouted.

"My dear, they feel strongly about protecting their home as you feel strongly about protecting them. You can't make that call for those beings," Bobo informed softly.

"He's right. Besides, the more we have to fight on our side, the better," Aurora added.

"They aren't equipped to fend off feral demons and blood mages," Vanessa countered.

"No, they aren't. But they do know this city like nobody else, and with the help of other Coven members, they can help without dying," Riker informed.

"But they are still at risk." The young witch didn't seem happy no matter how Riker spun the details.

Riker took a step forward. He was practically toe-to-toe with Vanessa, and he looked down at her with his usual icy gaze. "Then I suggest if you want them to stop risking their lives, you help follow orders so they aren't in more jeopardy. Thea and Rafe will be staying in the inner city. We have to hold the northern border."

She stared right into his cold, gray eyes and drew in a slow, calming breath. Her eyes flicked to the barrier just as a wave of dark creatures bashed against it. Magic popped and the enemy was flung to the ground. Everyone inside the forcefield felt a blast of air rush through the city from the impact.

"This is the weakest point," she muttered.

"That's why we are needed here most. If they get through this last line of defense, Tolvade is lost," Riker reminded.

"We just have to make sure that the barriers hold up until the Wild Hunt spell is cast?' she asked.

"By the goddess ... I hope so," Bobo grumbled.

"Yes," Riker replied.

Leon sighed. "Well, the good news is after the ritual is completed, the High Priest Council can focus more on defensive magic."

Vanessa frowned as she watched a troll bash against the barrier and roar at everyone present. "What if they don't stop even after the spell is cast?"

Riker focused on the army as they assaulted the barrier. "Then, we prepare for war."

 *Chapter 37:*

They had all replenished their dust pouches before the Coven members, imps, and the other reinforcements went to comb through the city for stray demons on their way toward the center city. The blood mages had started to line up along the barrier. From the looks of the catapults being loaded and the blood mages starting their chanting, they were getting ready to launch an attack that was going to shake the protective wall. They couldn't break it, but they would be able to disrupt it long enough to let their forces leak through.

Vanessa hovered her hands over the barrier. She could feel magic, pure magic, hum over her palms. Her skin felt like it could soak up the vibrations and turn it into her own power. Warmth wafted off of the barrier. Although there was comfort in its ability to keep the enemy at bay, it was still unnerving to have less than a foot of space between her and a massive, bloodthirsty army. She looked into a set of eyes surrounded by coal-colored streaks, and a chill crawled up the back of her thighs and over her spine like a hundred frozen slugs were slithering over her body. There was nothing in the eyes of her opponents but a hunger for power and the desire to stop at nothing to obtain it. Fires grew in the distance as the boulders, covered in oil, were lit. The orange glow of the flames didn't make any of the faces in front of her that were twisted with malice look any friendlier.

"They're about to release the catapults!" Vanessa warned. She pushed her palms against the barrier and the magic vibrated through her. Slowly, she started to recite the chant to keep the forcefield strong. They wouldn't have to hold on much longer. At least she hoped that they wouldn't.

"Don't rush me," Leon grumbled behind her.

"Normally, I'd agree to not rush perfection, my good man. However, time is of the essence here," Bobo reminded.

"Done!" Riker yelled. "Take formation!" he ordered, and he and Leon took to each side of Vanessa. Both of the men's hands grasped ahold of each of her wrists. Their own palms slammed into the barrier, and there was a massive ripple that raced over the face of the shield as the spell added to the defenses. "Form the chain!" Riker commanded. Aurora took a hold of his wrist and placed her hand on the barrier. Lyx took hold of Leon's wrist and placed her hand against the forcefield. "Concentrate," Riker growled. Silence passed and they all closed their eyes. Another moment passed. Vanessa could hear the catapults release. "Now! Ground us!" He barked.

Instantly, Bobo slammed his hands into Vanessa's back. Power surged through her. She felt it break through her like a furious, rampaging unicorn. She cried out as the power ate through her limbs and body, latched onto her magic, and coursed through her being. She could feel it racing through to the two men at her side. Connected like this, they were all opening up and sharing their magic, becoming one force to fight back against the army. Bobo pushed more power out, and Vanessa felt tears falling down her face, but her vision was eaten by light and her mind was swallowed by static. She couldn't form a single word or proper chant. She knew only power, and that power flowed through them all, but then she felt it recoil.

A pulse. Quiet and quick.

Thadump …

The magic zipped through them all and it was like they were replenished, but it was more than that. Vanessa could feel the power changing course. As if it had a mind of its own.

Thadump …

… *Daughter of Saellah, we hear you.*

Every bit of power and magic collected and changed course. Her ears could hear them crying out beside her, but she couldn't see anything. The door, the one she envisioned so many times within the innermost parts of her, was gone. It was just wide open space with blinding golden light pouring out. It felt warm. Like a summer afternoon was washing over her, and the scents of warm vanilla and

Bobo's tea steeping in the teapot filled her nostrils. She felt hands. She felt hands all over her. They were cold and didn't belong to any of the casters present. But they didn't induce fear. It was like she had known them before. She couldn't see bodies or faces. But she felt these gentle hands guiding her deeper into that source of power.

"We will break this barrier and then we will break you!" A malicious voice spat from the other side of the forcefield.

Her vision came to with blinding clarity. She blinked and focused on the twisted visage hidden under the shaded cloak. Her eyes narrowed at the enemy. "You'll never touch me," she said and then felt it. A snap. A click. As if years of practice and knowledge all slammed into place. A key was turned, and something in her unlocked.

"You'll be the first to die!" Another blood mage promised.

Her mind assaulted her with visions of everything she had fought over the past several months and then all the visions came to a sudden halt as she remembered holding Raven in her arms. She felt warm and real. Then she was gone. Her heart torn asunder.

"Everyone in that city will die. We will reign supreme!" another promised with a vile grin.

Vanessa never wanted anyone to feel her pain. Having family one moment and then it ripped away the next. Having a life that was theirs and then it being altered by the hands of death and destruction, she didn't want that for anyone.

"Get back!" she yelled.

The words left her, and much like back in Sylas' office, she felt her words leave and take with them a portion of her magic. It hit the forcefield, melted into it, and sent a shockwave through it, making the army lining the barrier all take a step back and others fall over.

Bobo grunted in pain behind her. "I can't hold on much longer," he yelled. Vanessa could feel him sway in place for a moment.

"Keep going! Giving up isn't an option," Riker roared.

Another assault was cascading through the sky, the flames chasing the boulders like they were falling stars aimed right at the barrier. When had the first wave struck? The power must have overtaken her that badly. All she could think was *fortify* as she looked at where the boulders would hit. She felt the magic weave and mend, making that portion of the forcefield stronger. There wasn't much else she could do aside from feeding her power into the barrier. It had to remain up.

It had to.

Prickles of energy skittered across her skin. The air felt charged. Feeling a spiritual shove, Vanessa gasped and saw the most glorious site overhead. The boulders slammed into the forcefield, embers and raining flames scattered all around. And, up in the sky, the clouds were forming and swirling. A storm was coming. A storm that had the thundering hooves of horses and unicorns, it had the rolling cry of wolves and hounds, it had the raining tears of spirits that had watched countless lifetimes of cruelty and pain. And it formed over the city and was carried on the face of graying clouds.

"*You. Shall. Be. Judged!*" A booming voice rumbled overhead.

Lightning illuminated the growing clouds as beasts and beings formed and took shape.

"The Wild Hunt!" Lyx cried. Bloody tears streamed down her battered face. "They did it! They did it! It's the Wild Hunt!"

A great quake shook the ground beneath their feet. In the distance, Vanessa could hear a building collapse. Dust clouds ran through the streets and filled the air. As the clouds lifted, Vanessa could see a portion of the Wild Hunt split from the sky and fall like a tornado funnel over the Black Forest. A moment later, it rose up and charged over the treetops and crashed into the ground. Like a flood of angry spirits, the Wild Hunt raced as rolling gray clouds at speeds that Vanessa couldn't keep up with and zipped through the army. Immediately, the clouds dissipated, and in their wake stood the elves!

"For Aeristria!" The Allatari bellowed with pride. His people all roared in compliance and ripped through the cursed creatures. A pain in her chest lifted. As if she had grown accustomed to some heavy weight and now felt the chains fall away, her chest rose and fell with a thankful, unburdened breath. Her promise had been kept.

Exploding out from the ground far out in the fields were nature-garbed creatures with hunched backs and bird-bone masks. The Crix had joined the fight. With the soldiers of the center army compromised, the enemy was forced to withdraw from the frontlines that were surrounding the city.

"Fall back. Retreat! RETREAT!" the blood mages snarled.

Bobo collapsed behind Vanessa. The Spellweaver heard him hit the ground before she could turn around. "Bobo!" she cried after watching the front lines scatter. She broke formation and knelt next to him.

Lyx looked like she had been run-through by a blade as she cried out, "Booboo!"

Blade and spells could be heard colliding outside the safety of Tolvade's double-barrier. Riker was in the distance on his crystal ball. Vanessa could hardly make out the image on the surface as the reception sputtered over the glass orb. She ignored it further as she shook Bobo. "Hey. Don't do this to me, okay?" she whispered. She didn't know if it was to him or herself. It was selfish, but she didn't want to lose anyone else. "Bobo?" she shook him again.

"Can't an ogre get a moment's rest?" he rasped, his lids reluctantly opening.

She laughed and crashed into the demon's chest. "Don't scare me like that."

He limply embraced her. His whole body was tired and sluggish. "I was just taking a moment to collect myself," he lied. "You're so dramatic," he declared with a lazy smirk.

She sniffled past happy tears and rolled her eyes. "I think you're dramatic enough for the both of us," she exclaimed while laughing.

The ogre winced, and she looked him over, "Are you okay?" Her hands dipped into a dust pouch before they started to glow, and she held them over his body.

Reaching up, Bobo closed his massive paws over her palms and shook his head. "I'm quite … all right, my dear."

"I can give you some of my magic," she said with worry scrolled over her features.

"You'll push yourself too far trying to help me."

"Step aside," Riker stated and knelt down beside the demon. "It's my last one. Let's split it so we both aren't out of commission."

The magic replenishing potion was split between Summoner and demon without another word spoken. It would be enough for a few protective spells as best, but, most importantly, it would keep them from passing out from being magically fatigued. The effects would only last a few more hours. Vanessa wondered if they could get everything in the city under control in that amount of time. From the looks outside, the Crix and elves were sending the dark creatures packing. The ones that could escape death, that was. There were still feral demons and blood mages and deadly crooks and murderers within the city to deal with.

"The inner city is protected. Spellweaver Bauer and Summoner MacBain managed to work together with Coven members and others to handle the situation," Aurora informed.

The young witch was baffled for a moment. So much chaos was handled by them? They had to be an amazing team! She had been holding off an entire army, but they were on the frontlines battling the escaped inhabitants of Zaraltrac prison! After taking a moment to process the news, Vanessa asked, "What does that leave for us?"

"We're to report to HQ for treatment. After that, we help clean up any stragglers," Riker stated while helping Leon get Bobo to his feet.

It was nice to know that they wouldn't need to rush into battle right away. They could heal up a bit first. Though, she didn't know if the treatment would be as thorough as it normally would be. There was no telling the devastation the escaped prisoners had released on everyone, and how many beings had been harmed by them until they got back to the Coven. She could only hope that number was small, but she knew realistically that wouldn't be the case.

As she had presumed, there were a lot of injured beings. A lot. The main lobby was covered in cots that hardly had enough space to walk through between them. Imps and fairies darted around with herbal teas and medicine while gnomes tended to the injured and made sure the healing incenses kept burning. Savannah Snow was dead center as she looked over charts and conversed with fellow medics before sending them on their way.

The doctor brushed her icy blonde hair over her shoulders and gave a tired smile to the group as they hobbled their way through the main entrance. "Well, well. I was surprised I hadn't seen you yet."

"The day isn't over. She still had time to come hobbling in with fresh wounds for you to tend to," Bobo stated.

"Says the ogre that had to drink a potion to stop his magical exertion," Vanessa snapped.

"Hopefully, you were wise and didn't overdose on them. They are great pick-me-ups in the middle of battle, but too many of them can have an adverse effect. We have rooms dedicated for those that did that already," Savannah informed.

Vanessa gulped with wide eyes. "H-how many is too many, exactly?"

Savannah signed off on a prescription and replied with, "For the typical caster around two or three. However, the stronger ones can endure up to four or five."

Any unease quickly died off.

"Where should we sign in?" Riker asked.

"I don't see a spare bed in the place," Leon grumbled to Lyx.

Savannah knelt down and tapped a red imp on the shoulder. She pointed to a sheet of paper and then to the medical wing. The imp nodded too much too fast and grinned with a wild giggle. "Yes ma'am doctor ma'am!" it shouted and then sprinted down the halls.

"No time for signing in. Step forward," Doctor Snow instructed while dipping her fingers into her spell pouch. "I'll assess your symptoms here, and, according to your condition, we'll see what to do from there."

Vanessa tugged on Leon's shirt and gave Riker a look as she said, "Let the demonesses go first. They were hurt more than us."

Everyone looked over to the succubus and vampiress, but it was Bobo that motioned with a sweep of his hand toward the doctor. "Ladies, please. You're in far more need than I or anyone present. I implore that you be seen first."

"At least someone here has manners," Aurora stated with a faint smile as she looked Bobo over curiously.

Lyx was quick to say, "He's taken," earning a generous bout of laughter from the rest of the group.

One by one, they were seen. Lyx and Aurora were told that their injuries would need multiple sessions and lots of rest. Doctor Snow had recited the same thing that the field medics had told them. No long-term flying or heavy lifting and to stay grounded if they had any dizzy spells. Vanessa, Leon, Riker, and Bobo were lightly mended. They all had abrasions and various cuts and bruises. For most of the injuries the doctor found, the group wasn't even aware that they had gotten. They were warned to not take any more potions unless it was a dire situation.

Doctor Snow then prescribed them each a minimum of three hours of spelled sleep in another location of the Coven to aid in regaining lost magic. They all took the doctor up on that and were informed that the Coven library had made accommodations for those needing rest more than healing treatments.

On the way downstairs, they passed by multiple Coven members keeping a calming barrier up to help those in the lower level to rest without worries gnawing away at them. Slowly, they each took a bed.

A few sandmen floated over. Their tiny, red umbrellas were open and propped on their shoulders. The beings wore powdery blue and creamy white tunics. Their free hands opened a deep, blue velvet pouch hanging on their hips. The one hovering near Vanessa smiled. It wasn't the type of smile she'd expect from a stranger. It made her feel at ease, consoled. The beings were well-known to bring comfort and sleep and were even used to put patients under for everything from prescribed sleep to conking them out in a deep coma-like slumber before they'd have surgery. The dust was grasped in the being's hand, and it looked like ordinary, plain, magicless sand. And, in fact, it was. But once the sandman blew over the grains, it glowed. It is the breath of the beings that made the sand into a sleep aid. Such was their power. As the sand drifted over to Vanessa's bed, the being turned the red umbrella on his shoulder. She could see in it, as it spun faster and faster, the sun setting, and the underside of it turned from red to a midnight blue. Stars twinkled and moved over the material. Eventually, the scene turned black. She saw Raven smiling at her. She heard her parent's voices. Her eyes grew heavy as the dream played out over the fabric of the umbrella. Before long, the Spellweaver and the rest of the group were all fast asleep.

Three hours had come and gone faster than they would have liked. Such was the repercussion for magically exerting yourself. It was better than going into comas or dream paralysis after using too much magic though.

Vanessa heard the soft flapping of wings and a voice that sounded like it was woven with tiny, ringing bells. "Miss. You're prescribed time is up," the miniature fairy informed.

Vanessa groaned and went to roll over, thinking she was home in her own bed, and flopped right onto the floor. "*Ugh!*"

"As graceful as ever, I see," Bobo's tired, snarky voice found her wounded pride first.

"Give her a break. We all feel like the walking dead," Leon said, though the Spellweaver could hear him trying to hide the hints of laughter in his voice.

"Don't remind me of those cursed days. Took weeks to get the smell of the lych off of me," Riker grumbled.

"Not to mention the state of the streets after it all was over," Aurora stated with a wrinkle of her nose.

Fluffing her hair with a yawn, Lyx added, "Could have been worse. There could have been *two* angry priestesses."

Everyone shuddered at the thought.

"I don't feel as lethargic anymore," Vanessa admitted.

Bobo explained by saying, "That's because the Wild Hunt had been successfully performed. Magic that has been kept locked away has finally been released and is slowly returning to its rightful place."

Vanessa stared at her hands, having remembered what Raven had told them back at the Black Forest about the magic returning to not only the beings of Raen but the land itself. It would make healing over the next few days a lot easier, that was for sure. She placed a hand over her chest. It felt lighter despite the heaviness that resided within her heart. "The spelled promises," she whispered to herself.

"Your promise to the elves was fulfilled the moment the Wild Hunt was summoned," Leon reminded.

Bobo nodded with a hum of agreement. "And that Sleekit fellow—"

"Malachi," Lyx corrected.

"Yes. He is safe and free to do as he pleases now that the culprits for his assassination attempts have been properly whooped right out of Tolvade," the ogre finished.

Leon thought for a moment and sighed. "That reminds me, I'm going to have to send a messenger pixie to inform my parents and to let the guy finally leave the house."

"He'll see it as a blessing, I'm sure," Bobo assured.

Riker stretched, and his back cracked with the effort. "Time to get moving, everyone. Those demons and blood mages won't put themselves back in their cells."

A slightly larger fairy flying by halted and turned to face them. His shaggy brown hair tickled his brows, and his green eyes darted about the group members. His voice was soft and raspy as he asked, "Are you talking about aiding the cleanup crew?"

Riker turned to face the flying being as he spoke. "Why do you ask?"

The moment the Summoner's eyes fell on the fairy, the being stopped flapping its wings for a moment and almost fell from the air. Catching itself only after a short plummet, the being cleared its throat and nodded with a nervous smile. "I-I-I didn't realize it was you, Summoner ..."

Seeming bored, Riker rolled his wrist as he wordlessly urged the fairy to explain.

"Right," the fairy said. It lost some of the fear and spoke to the team saying, "A Summoner and Spellweaver team managed to create a massive de-summoning spell in the town square. They combined forces with members of Tolvade, the Coven, and even the Skrittish. It was very heroic, indeed."

"Are you saying that there isn't much to do in the city?" Leon asked.

The fairy nodded his head. "What didn't manage to flee from the city was captured, imprisoned, or de-summoned. Those that escaped made a break for the northern border. If they managed to make it past the elves, they fled toward the Red Tipped Mountains with the rest of the straggling cursed army."

"You know that won't be the end of them," Bobo muttered.

"A task for another day. They'll be licking their wounds for a long time. I doubt they'll be able to plan anything anytime soon." Vanessa seemed sure of her reply.

"Nothing we can't counter with a Summoner team and topped off spell pouches," Riker added.

Lyx pursed her lips to the side, "I suppose the only thing we need to do now is to get ready for the event."

Vanessa shifted and hugged herself. "I think I'm going to help with repairing some of the damage to the city and go home to rest."

Leon turned to face her fully. His brow was bent in confusion. "Don't you want to make an offer to the temple?"

"I can do it tomorrow. The ritual lasts three days. I just want to heal up more, take a potion-filled bubble bath, and call it a day. I've had enough excitement."

"But—" Leon started.

Riker held out his arm to stop anything the Summoner was about to say. "Go on, then. You and Bobo help everyone out topside, and I'll see if we can get a clean connection to get further instruction from the Council."

"Thanks," Vanessa replied, but her voice sounded empty. "Come on, Bobo," she whispered to her partner.

The two trudged out of sight, and Leon looked amazed and half-angry at Riker. "Why did you do that?"

"Because she wouldn't be able to focus on making a proper offer at the temple even if you did convince her to go," Riker informed.

Aurora looked Leon over. "You smell like her. She must be important to you. How can you not see what she is going through? I didn't even need to tap into my otherworldly strengths in order to tell that the girl is suffering quietly. She is busying herself with work."

Leon watched Vanessa disappear up the nearest stairwell. "You're saying she's avoiding going to the temple because of what happened today?"

Lyx touched her master's arm lightly. "Think about it, darling. She lost someone close to her today. That temple is where you say your final goodbyes to the dead. Her heart isn't ready for that just yet. Give her a day."

He understood. It was scrolled all over his face. Vanessa had always been like that. She escaped truths she didn't want to deal with by burying herself in work. She was dedicated to the Coven because of what it represented but also because it gave her a way to flee from the loneliness and pain. He sighed to himself.

Leon and the others said nothing. They just looked at the murky staircase dimly illuminated in the usual torch glow. The battle had been all over the place, and it was like the trauma of losing Raven had been blotted out from their memories. But it wasn't forgotten by Vanessa. Every breath was a reminder that she was living and Raven wasn't. A pain like that can be hidden but never forgotten.

 *Chapter 38:*

For the rest of that afternoon until dusk, Vanessa, Bobo, and the others all combined their efforts with the Coven members still strong enough to produce a spell, in order to clean up damaged parts of the city. However, it was like putting a bandage on a sword wound. The real clean up and reconstruction of buildings and streets were going to take weeks if not months. But it was enough patchwork that the beings of Tolvade could enjoy the festivities of the spring ball that took place on Lorvo Lake alongside the ritual without too much worry.

That night, as promised, Vanessa soaked in a healing potion bath infused with lavender oil and a hefty amount of salt. The potions had been brewed by alchemists that had paired with the Skrittish. They had made enough for everyone, and anyone that had taken part in the battle could take one as they left the Coven building. Bobo could be heard down the hall groaning in pleasure as he enjoyed both the bath and his new, spacious tub. Vanessa, however, was silent. She watched the ripples in the bath and seemed lost in the blank reflection of the water. Part of her hoped that she would see Raven's dark eyes and white hair staring back at her. But she never did.

She sunk deep into the warmth of the bath and listened to a drop of water fall into the tub. Her eyes misted. Her mind wandered. Would she even be able to sleep tonight? The ghosts of her past actions seemed to be haunting her, and they didn't care one way or the other the torment they were wrecking on her heart.

She soaked until her skin had become pale and full of wrinkles. Her aches and pains felt soothed, but there was a dull soreness in her chest, a strain on her lungs, and a lump in her throat. They were things that would not dissipate with time but would become another piece of her. It would become something fashioned to her soul and be carried with her everywhere she went. She sighed, dried off, and then got dressed.

When she opened her bathroom door, Bobo was seated in a plush armchair settled in the corner next to her bedroom window. He had an open book poised to block her from his vision. "Are you decent?" he asked.

She looked down at her pajamas and quirked her lips to the side. "Yeah."

The book slowly fell away, and the ogre crossed his leg over the other with a sniff. "It was far too stuffy in my room," he lied.

She laughed through her nose and shook her head. "I don't believe it. That room is ten times what it was."

"Hardly. Nine times the size, at best."

She giggled then, and he chuckled softly.

"I find it cozy in here," he said after a short pause.

She sighed and went to her bed and noted the cup of tea on her nightstand. "Calming tea?"

He hummed, "Mhmm."

She smiled softly and took the cup in her hands. She sipped and felt the hot liquid warm her from the inside out. Hints of peppermint danced on her tongue. "I always loved this after our missions," she whispered.

"It has always been a fond ritual of mine, to enjoy a cup of tea with you after a hard day."

She felt it rise up in her, the urge to fall apart. She didn't look at him, fearing the welling tears would fall and cause the demon distress. Instead, she bit down on her cheeks to try and chase the sadness away. Even between her teeth, her lips quivered. She blew over the rim of the mug, and the steam was chased away. Even her breath sounded like it was shaking. After drinking half the cup, she put it back on the nightstand, turned down the covers, and crawled into bed.

Silence stretched out to claim every inch of the room. It was a quiet that would feel homey if there was a soft ticking of a clock or if it were accompanied by the pops and crackles of a lazy fire. But it was plain, endless silence.

From beside her, the frame and mattress creaked as she felt Bobo sit on the bed, kick off his slippers, and slowly lay down next to her. She still didn't cry. She held it together even as she felt her throat tighten and eyes burn.

"We'll go to the ritual tomorrow and make an offering." She had meant to say it louder, but her voice couldn't rise up beyond a quiet murmur.

"Yes," Bobo replied in a careful voice.

She nodded. "I'm tired," she whispered and closed her eyes. But sleep didn't want her. Memories of that day did. She screwed her eyes shut and tried to imagine anything other than flaming boulders being catapulted and dodging spells meant to claim their lives. She tried to hush the echo of battle cries and attempted to snuff out the scent of burning flesh from her nose. She tried. She tried so hard. With everything in her, she avoided seeing that one painful memory that relentlessly banged on the doors of her mind.

The warmth of Bobo's embrace brought every wall and defense crashing down mercilessly as he wrapped her up in his arms. Her voice cracked as she accepted the voice inside that she had tried to silence all day. "I miss her. I miss her so much, Bobo!"

"I know," he whispered. She could hear it in his voice too. Sadness blanketed them both. "You're not alone," he said softly.

Alone.

That dreaded word holding the weight of every curse that Aeristria had to offer was uttered, and it crashed into her with the vibrant memory of Raven taking in one, final breath. She couldn't hold it in anymore. Her mouth opened, and she wailed. She cried. Tears consumed anything the young witch could have said. It drenched her soul in grief. She let go and wept her heart out. She let the tears consume her until she couldn't shed another tear. And she was still sniffling when sleep claimed her.

 *Chapter 39:*

The next morning, Vanessa woke up feeling like she was hungover. Her limbs didn't want to comply with her, and her head throbbed from spending the night sobbing herself to sleep. She tried to eat the breakfast Bobo had prepared, but she lacked any real appetite. She felt numb, but she pressed on with her day.

She was huddled over her third cup of tea her pet had prepared for her and leaned next to the bay windows that overlooked the center city. She could see the Gentle Titan river sparkle under the sunlight like diamonds had been thrown over the face of the water. Overhead, the continuous swirling of the Wild Hunt could be seen. Every so often, a wisp would break away with a collection of beasts, animals, and beings and race through the sky before merging with the great cloud once more. At nightfall, during the ball, the cloud would descend with all the spirits that wished to come and greet the living.

She sighed for what felt like the thousandth time. Her eyes were sore and looking at the bright light of the day wasn't helping. Breaking her vision from the outside world, Vanessa turned away from the window and went to sit on the couch.

"Have you put any thought into your attire for this evening?" Bobo asked.

She twitched her lips and groaned before replying. "No."

"Hmmm … no surprise there," he muttered.

She gaped at him and then scowled. "I don't want to dress up for it."

"Wear your boots under the ball gown. It'll make you feel like you aren't betraying your true masculine self."

"Th—" she stopped and thought about it for a moment. "That's not a bad idea, actually."

The book fell away from the ogre's face. "I was joking. Please tell me you are as well."

She stood from the couch with a grin. "Nope. I'll wear my boots to the ball. Heels pinch my toes."

"That's because you have fat feet," the demon mumbled and put his book away with a sigh.

"You wear them then."

"I'd wear them with more grace than you shall ever acquire, my dear. And then, how would you face your peers? I'll save yourself the embarrassment and go with my dress loafers."

"All of your loafers are dress loafers."

"And so begins my tough choice for the day. Which set shall I wear?"

She rolled her eyes and went to her room.

"There isn't a gown in there, Vanessa. You're wasting your time."

He wasn't wrong. She always rented her ball gowns every year. So there wouldn't be anything but her usual garbs in her wardrobe and dressers. Unless, that is, Sara managed to sneak one of her dresses in when they moved things over.

"I'm getting my crystal ball!" she snapped.

"Oh?"

Her muffled voice trailed from down the hall. "Yeah. I was thinking of using my spring bonus to pay for a new, tailored suit for you and a custom-made ball gown for me."

"Who on Raen were you thinking of asking to pull off the job in a single afternoon?"

"Akane, the tailor yokai that runs that small shop down by the bar and grill."

Bobo contemplated her words for a moment. "Are you talking about The Looking Glass bar and grill?"

"Yes."

"I didn't know that there was a tailor over there."

She looked exasperated. "Spiritual Threads. It's right next door!"

"Oh, yes. I remember now. Quaint little shop."

"They are a bit pricey but can manifest the clothing within a couple of hours. They just have to get a spiritual reading and ask some basic questions."

"I'm always up for a new suit," Bobo muttered with his chin up.

"I know," she replied with a smile and made the crystal ball call.

"Spiritual Threads, Akane speaking." A woman with wavy black hair appeared on the orb. A peach and silver robe that overlapped in the front was covered in a pattern of pale green and blue flowers. On one side, a lily hairpin with dangling gold beads was fixed to her night-shaded locks. Her narrow eyes glossed over the face of the orb as she took into account every visible being present.

"Yes, I need one ball gown and one suit made for this evening."

"Occasion?" the pale woman asked, pulling out a large pad.

"The Wild Hunt Ball."

"The dress size?"

"Ten."

"Favorite color?"

"Red."

"Attitude?"

"Rude," Bobo mumbled.

"Shy," she stated awkwardly.

Akane paused and eyed the Spellweaver over. "Hmmm ..." She scribbled something down on her pad and said, "Please send a magical imprint through the call."

Vanessa concentrated on her magic and felt it ball up in her stomach. After a moment, she released it into the hand holding the orb. Akane closed her eyes as the magic connected with her. "I have it," she stated and then pointed a long, thin nail to the ogre looking over the Spellweaver's shoulder. "Is the suit for the gentleman I see in the crystal ball?"

Vanessa nodded as she said, "Yes."

"Very well," she rasped and flipped to a new page. "Same occasion?"

Bobo practically threw Vanessa to the floor as he took over the call, but her hand remained holding the orb. "And you call me rude," she hissed under her breath.

"Suit size?"

As she listened to Bobo give his answers, she sat in an uncomfortable position and sighed, letting her lips trill as she did so. Bobo gave her a look, but he was too occupied with the call to make a comment about her sounding like a horse.

She thanked the goddess for that.

Within hours, they had their new clothes ready for pick up. Bobo went to gather them while Vanessa stayed behind to let the excitement of the upcoming events eat away at her nerves. She wasn't fond of the anxious feelings that were sending her emotions into a wild frenzy. It was so bad that she gave a short scream when Bobo burst excitedly through the front door.

"Vanessa!" he boomed, features aglow with his elation.

"Aah!" She held a hand over her heart and stared at the ceiling. "By the goddess, Bobo ... my heart almost exploded."

"Mine too!" he proclaimed with a wide grin and a bright sparkle in his eyes.

"What?" She gasped and ran over to the garment bags. "Let me see!"

He happily let her take her order, and he unzipped the protective casing to his suit and pulled out a navy blue, black, and silver three-piece suit. Silver buttons and trimming lined the breast and sleeves and a patch of black made up the shoulders and followed the hem of the suit. The vest was all silver with eight-pointed stars all over the fabric. Around the neck of the hanger was a red tie that gave the suit a splash of color. "Absolutely perfect," Bobo stated while looking the clothing over.

Meanwhile, Vanessa had darted for her room and hung the garment bag on the clothing bar before unveiling the dress underneath. As the plastic covering fell away, Vanessa clamped a soft cry under both of her hands. It took visible effort to take in a breath and not cry all over again like she had last night.

The dress was apple red and decorated in black, brilliant rhinestones in a swirling pattern. The sleeves were long and formfitting before belling out and the edges of the cuffs could easily tickle the top of the floor when worn. Though it was elegant and beautiful, it was the cape that took her heart. It was sheer, shimmering in the dusky glow trickling in through the bedroom window. And golden stars and moons and swirling silver galaxies covered the entirety of it. It made her think of Raven's eyes full of the night sky. She would have loved to see Vanessa wear the dress. She reached out and traced the line of the gown with the pads of her fingers with a sad yet happy look.

A soft rapping on her open door brought her attention to Bobo. "Do you find it suitable?" he asked.

She smiled, but it kept trying to turn into a frown. She finally settled with a nod. "I do," she admitted softly.

"Well then, my dear. I suggest we get dressed. It's almost time we departed for the party."

 *Chapter 40:*

The lake was lit up with thousands of lights. A grand crystal and candle chandelier was suspended over the center of the outdoor dance floor with a magical glow. Floating, yellow-tinted orbs of light were scattered across the lakeside like stars. They shed brilliant light across the bank that was decorated in white, sheer curtains and golden, silk bows. Hundreds of tables were spread out over the lawn, and their white, linen tablecloths waved gently in the spring breeze. Following the giant stones that made a path to a large, dome-shaped building, one would come upon the main ritual grounds for the yearly Wild Hunt spell, the Domus Mortuorum.

The Domus Mortuorum was both where the ritual altar for the Wild Hunt was and where the beings of Tolvade could mourn the dead. It was a graveyard. Where headstones were not visible, but the dead resided there like it was a second home. With proper prayer, offerings, and magic given at the base-level altar, the spirits of the dead could visit for extremely small periods of time. During the casting of the Wild Hunt, the inhabitants of Tolvade were required to give an offering to aid in the given magic for the spell. It was that very act that Vanessa dreaded because this offering was a goodbye to those that you've lost. It was something that she really didn't want to do, yet, there she was.

Just a few more offerings and the Wild Hunt would descend. Bobo had made his offering earlier and told Vanessa that he'd be waiting for her across the lake. She wanted to be one of the last groupings to make an offering that night for many reasons.

Standing in front of the altar, she felt pangs of pain shoot through her body. There were no more beings to hide behind. No more lines to stand in. Vanessa lit an incense stick and stuck it in the white sand of a massive stone bowl in front of the altar. Its smoke married with the hazy trails from hundreds of other sticks and rose up through the building, climbing over the various paintings on the stone walls. From what Vanessa remembered, the stone came from the Red Tipped Mountains and held magical properties. Paired with the water from Lorvo Lake, the ritual grounds practically hummed with magic. However, Vanessa felt numb to it all as she knelt in front of the altar.

"I can only offer my magic, auntie. I hope you can forgive my lack of gifts," she whispered and bowed her head. She lifted up and faced the stone slab. Her mind searched inward. Her arms stretched out to either side. "May the goddess bless your passing from this world to the next!" Goddess ... words had never hurt so much until that moment.

She felt like her heart was breaking all over again. She drew in a deep lungful and willed herself to hold her emotions together. Slowly, she released the air from her lungs and imagined a river of magic following her breath. Outside, over the top of the building, trumpets could be heard bellowing out through the twilight sky.

> "It's descending!"
> "The Wild Hunt is coming!"
> "It's happening!"
> "It's so beautiful!"

Many that had been giving an offering finished up their prayer and raced outside. After years of performing the offering and running outside to see a family that never came, Vanessa felt conflicted. Would this year be any different? Even though she knew that the spell had been done correctly, she still doubted that things would change for her. Maybe she just didn't want anything to change for her because it would mean Raven was really gone, and that was a reality she didn't want to accept just yet.

Vanessa bowed to the altar again, stood, and headed out of the building. Crickets chirped a soft song. The breeze wove through reeds by the banks of the lake. Frogs croaked, adding to the melody of the night. Vanessa watched as the thick fog that the Wild Hunt had left behind skittered across the water and drifted by the island. She could see and hear the spiritual beings uniting with their long-lost friends and family. The festivities started, the enchanted band played the first waltz of the night, and Vanessa watched from the quiet, lonely island.

From behind her, there was an echoic voice that called out. It sounded both detached and close by all at the same time. "Vanessa."

... *Was that?*

Her gaze drifted up to the stars, and she tried to emotionally prepare for what she would see when she turned around. It was going to be bittersweet. That much was certain.

She turned, the vision of the dance floor, the band, the beings ... it all faded away. And as she fully came around, her heart stopped beating for a moment. She held her breath. The world all around her slowed.

Her starry gaze seemed less illustrious as she was washed in a milky glow. Her white hair was whiter. And the sadness in her eyes was more than anything Vanessa could have remembered the Dark Elf had when she was alive. Was being dead that bad?

"Hello, little shadow."

Any strength the Spellweaver had started to break under that pet name. But she looked around, batted her eyes, and fought the urge to cry again. She chose to fix her eyes on the ball across the lake.

"How are you?" Raven asked, taking a step forward. But no sound followed. It was only the illusion of walking. Raven was no longer a part of this world. This was just her spirit.

"I'm okay," Vanessa lied, refusing to look at her aunt.

"Are you mad at me?"

"No?" she sounded angry and confused when she answered. But when her astonished gaze snapped back to the Dark Elf, the first tear spilled down her face. Her brow bent and her mouth frowned. The truth hit her with a force that no spell on Raen could rival. "Yes," she quickly whispered. "Yes, I'm mad at you!" she announced louder.

"Vanessa—"

"You were supposed to come *home* with me," she yelled, her lip quivering.

"Vanessa," Raven tried again.

The young witch pointed behind her, to the north and in the direction of the now empty battlefield. "There were so many things that we could have done to stop that wolf!"

Raven stayed still and silent as her niece yelled. She waited for the young witch to be done and then asked, "Like what?"

Vanessa felt her heart sink. Words dried up, and she floundered for a reply. "I—I don't know. *Something!*"

"I did what I had to in order to keep the promise I made to your parents. That I would keep you safe from harm. I'll do it again. Given the chance, I would die a thousand times just to get to this same moment."

Vanessa shook her head and let more tears fall.

Raven closed the distance and placed her cold spiritual hand against the young witch's cheek. "My death is payment for your life that I would never think twice about paying."

The Spellweaver wanted to tear away from the touch but, instead, she leaned more into it as her voice cracked. "I want you here. I want you back. It isn't fair. I'm not strong enough for all of this. Not without you … *Please?*"

The Dark Elf smiled softly, and she pulled the girl into her arms. "Oh, little shadow. If I could take this pain from you I would."

Vanessa sniffled. "Please come back? Please? I just … I want you back." She could hardly see past her tears as she said, "I finally had my family. I finally had my place. I finally belonged somewhere."

"*Shh* … There, there. I know. I know." The weeping grew and Raven had to just hold the young witch while she fell apart. When the sobbing had slowed, Raven pulled away from the embrace and smiled sweetly as she gave a pointed look behind the Spellweaver.

Leon. Lyx. Bobo. They were all there. And, across the lake — at the end of the path—was Riker. Vanessa's lip quivered. She knew what her aunt was going to say before she opened her mouth.

"You are not alone. You never were. I was a part of your life, and I love you. Nothing will ever change that. Not even death. But they love you too." Raven turned Vanessa around and held her face in her icy palms. "That's family, little shadow. The people that have a love for you that transcends all the curses and torments of this world, of this life, they *are* your family. They always will be. You are so strong. You are so loved."

Vanessa couldn't talk. She could only nod between sobs.

"Now, I need you to wipe those tears. I ran into a few beings that want to meet you."

The Spellweaver's breathing hitched, and she hastily wiped her face. "What?" she breathed, confusion scrolled over her features. But that look melted away as Raven stood off to the side, and Vanessa gasped. New tears spilled. Happier ones.

"… Mom? … Dad?"

"We're here, baby girl. We are finally here," Charles answered.

"Oh, baby. It's so good to see you," Larissanna cried, opening her ghostly arms and running toward her daughter.

Vanessa never ran toward a pair of ghosts so fast.

Larissanna was fussing with her daughter's hair as Vanessa told the story of how she summoned Bobo. Raven interjected with comments on how brave and valiantly the ogre could fight, leaving the father to feel as though his daughter was in good hands. Larissanna kept asking questions about Leon and his family, and Raven excitedly spoke Elvish, and Larissanna and Charles all laughed with the aunt. Even if it was for a short period of time, Vanessa felt happy.

"How do you fair on the dance floor?" Charles asked.

"If you're asking if she knows how to dance, she does," Bobo replied.

Vanessa's mother and father looked proud.

"She can two-step all over my feet perfectly," he added.

Everyone laughed while Vanessa turned a bright red.

Raven quickly changed the topic. "Where did you get this cape? I'm in love!"

"I agree. This is a beautiful outfit, Vanessa," her mother gushed.

Vanessa went from burning a hole with her eyes into the ogre's new suit to lighting up at her mother's and aunt's words. "I ordered it from Spiritual Threads. It's one of a kind!"

Larissanna pouted. "My child, your feet must be killing you. Why don't you sit for a while before you have to take to the floor for your dance?"

A mischievous grin slid over the girl's lips, and she pulled her dress up enough to show off her boots. "No worries, mom. I'm comfortable," she exclaimed with a burst of giggles.

"Ha ha! That's my girl," Charles bellowed and slapped Leon on the back as the Summoner was sipping out of his champagne flute.

While Charles and the others surrounded Vanessa and chattered away, Leon tried to catch his breath. Bobo saved him with a handkerchief, a pat on the back, and a gentlemanly smile. Lyx watched them all (ignoring her master's plight) and swished her tail happily behind her.

The band music slowed.

Leon spoke up with a look of detest. "Looks like the Hunters' waltz is over."

"Aren't you from an upper-class family? You should know how to dance," Bobo said.

"Eh … I mean, I wouldn't go signing me up for any contests, big guy. I'm okay at best. There's a reason I joined the Coven, and it isn't for their yearly balls."

"Careful, if your dad hears you, you'll never hear the end of it," Vanessa warned.

Lyx laughed lightly. "Isn't that the truth?"

The music had stopped, and the Celestial spoke to everyone present. "It is time for our Summoners' and Spellweavers' waltz! All Coven members with this ranking, please, come to the floor."

"Goddess, help me," Leon groaned.

"I'm going to just hide under the table," Vanessa muttered and tried to walk away. Lyx and Bobo were quick to capture her and shove her onto the dance floor.

"Look at our angel, Charles. She's so grown up," Larissanna whispered.

"I couldn't be prouder," he replied.

Raven watched Vanessa nervously take her place in line with the women and smiled as she watched her niece stand a little taller, a little more sure of herself. "I couldn't be prouder of her, either."

All of the respectful demon pets lined the outskirts of the floor and watched their masters all bow to one another as the music softly started to play.

Vanessa and Leon were paired first. He kept wincing and Vanessa kept apologizing. But the Summoner couldn't stop chuckling.

"I'm sorry, I've got two left feet," she whispered.

"You're fine, Vanessa. It doesn't help that I keep messing up the dance moves myself," he assured and softly kissed her forehead.

Oddly enough, the action dissipated most of the young witch's worries. For a few steps, she didn't mess up and they looked graceful.

"Time to change partners," Leon warned.

Vanessa cringed and forced a smile. "Okay."

He spun her and she almost tripped over her feet and landed in the unsuspecting arms of a tall (*much* taller than her) man with short, black hair. She blinked up at the male. "Rafe ... was it?" she asked, feeling a tinge bit better having known the person she had been paired with next.

"Yeah. Va-nessa, right?"

"Yeah," she answered with nervous laughter. He didn't say anything about her past achievements or failures, and she was thankful for it. Suddenly, Rafe winced in pain, and she sucked in air sharply. "I'm sorry. I'm not the best," she admitted. As quickly as she had said it, her toes throbbed as the man stepped on her own feet. Looking up to his flushed features, she tried not to laugh.

"I'm honestly not so great myself," he whispered.

They both laughed and turned to the music. As the band played, the two of them tried their best to keep up with the proper footwork needed for the dance and laughed whenever they stepped on each other's toes. Again, it was time to change partners.

"Good luck," Vanessa whispered.

"Same to you," Rafe whispered back and spun her.

She almost slammed into her next dance partner, but he had more grace than her and caught her with ease before moving into the waltz like the blunder never took place. Blinking, she looked up to see Riker. Normally, he would appear stiffer than a golem and as scary as a blood mage, but when he looked down at her, his gray eyes softened.

His voice was hardly audible as he spoke to her, "Forward, side, close. Down, side, close. One, two, three. One, two, three ..." She looked at her feet, and he let go of her waist in order to lift her chin. "Don't look down. Trust me and follow my lead."

She nodded and mentally repeated the steps in her mind, and it helped. "I'm doing it. I'm dancing!" she exclaimed hoarsely.

"You've got this," Riker said while spinning her and releasing her to the next partner.

As she danced with her next partner, she noticed Leon and the other Spellweaver, Thea, dancing with one another. They looked like a match. Their steps were graceful and all eyes were on them. They flowed from one step to the next and turned with style. Honestly, Vanessa was worried because the more she thought about it, the more she realized that Thea was the witch she had been hearing about over the past several months. She was smart, witty, came from a wealthy family, and was strong. And she could dance? What if Leon thought the two of them were a better match after just one dance? She frowned at the notion.

When the dance was over, Vanessa was sipping on a drink over by the punch bowl with the others when Leon came over.

"She started off pretty sloppy but I'm sure, with lessons, the next ball won't be a complete disaster," Bobo said.

"I got my feet stepped on too!" she barked defensively.

"I'm sure your feet are fine in those boots, my dear."

"You're wearing boots?" Leon whispered heatedly.

"Heels pinch my feet," she snapped back.

"Could you imagine her in heels stepping on your toes when you two had taken to the dance floor, Leon?" Bobo inquired.

Leon cringed.

Vanessa puffed up her chest proudly and said, "That is exactly why I wore boots instead of heels, Bobo."

"No dear, that's exactly why no one will dance with you," he corrected.

SMOKE, LIES, AND GRIMOIRES

Lyx sputtered over the rim of her drink with a half-cough sprinkled with undertones of laughter. Gaining her breath, she shot back to Bobo, "Be nice!"

"Where's your parents and Raven?" Leon asked, changing the subject.

"They went to talk to Ell," Vanessa stated with a mix of emotions.

"Oh. I see."

"You looked rather grand and proper out on the dance floor with that Spellweaver Thea, my good man. I'm surprised," Bobo stated after dabbing his face clean of any crumbs.

Leon scratched the back of his head with a pink hue to his cheeks. "Yeah, I'm not the best."

"Could have fooled me," Vanessa grumbled. Her words sounded a touch more peppery than she intended, and it gained the Summoner's attention.

"Are you jealous?"

"I'm just saying you two seemed to have a lot of chemistry out on the dance floor."

He chuckled then. "Dancing for people like me and her is nothing more than business at best. There's no emotion to it at all."

"It appeared like you two were quite a match, that's all I'm saying."

"Vanessa, you don't have anything to worry about. That's Thea. *The* Thea Bauer. Even if I managed to have some half-baked affection for her, did you see the guy she's with? That's Summoner Rafe MacBain. It took me a while to realize who they were, but I can't compete with him. And she, though not magically as strong as you, is widely known for her ability to hold her own in any sort of battle or situation. Besides," he grabbed her around the waist and pulled her closer, "you're the only witch for me. In and out of the Coven, it doesn't matter. I want *you* by my side."

She blushed then and lightly slapped his shoulder. "I was only teasing you," she muttered. But it was nice to hear him say it. "You know, I'm kind of glad I got stuck with you a couple of months ago," she said with giddy laughter.

He shook his head with a light chuckle. "Me too."

"Me three!" Lyx chirped while latching onto Bobo's arm.

The ogre looked at all the expecting faces and groaned. "I suppose it isn't the worst thing that has happened to us."

Leon squeezed the Spellweaver a little harder and dropped his voice down to a tone that was all for her. "Vanessa, you remember the elves from the Black Forest?"

She nodded. "I do. That staff was such a great parting gift!"

He smiled nervously.

"That reminds me, I never asked you … What did they give you?" she asked.

His hand reached into a small pouch and withdrew two silver bands woven like vines and covered in carved flowers. "They gave me future-gazing rings."

When she looked up from the rings at Leon, she saw it scrolled all over his face. "I never want to give up on you, Vanessa. I never want you to give up on me either. We've been through a lot together. And I've got to admit that I love you more than I ever thought I could love someone. If I can face all the dangers of Aeristria at your side I'll be a happy wizard. I want nothing more than to go through every adventure, heartache, and mission with you. Vanessa, will you accept a fate tied with me?"

She opened her mouth and felt words fail her. "I—I mean …" Stopping to think, she locked eyes with the Summoner and really thought about his words. They had been through so much. She always felt respected, understood, and—most importantly—loved by him. And she loved him. She was more worried that he wouldn't love her or that he would change his mind. Never once did the young witch doubt her affection for him. From the start, she tried to deny it because she didn't think she deserved it. But when she glanced down to the rings and back up into his bright blue eyes, she knew the answer.

She laughed. "Yes. Yes, of course. A thousand times, yes!"

He slipped the future-gazing ring on her finger and held her hands in his with a grand smile. Before he could kiss her or even hug her, Bobo cleared his throat.

"So much for taking it slow," Bobo muttered to the young witch.

She prodded him lightly in the stomach with her elbow. "Be happy for me," she hissed with a smirk.

"Oh, I am, my dear. I now have a capable man to look after your troublesome self." She scoffed and turned away from her demon. The ogre pulled her away from Leon and scooped her up in a tight bear-hug. "Congratulations, Vanessa," he whispered into her ear with a faint sniffle.

"Vanessa, Leon, Bobo, Lyx!" Ell was waving frantically at them. Her eyes were red and puffy, but she had the brightest smile on her face.

From across the punch bowl, Vanessa heard another familiar voice. "Why isn't there any good meat dishes at these posh events?" Malachi asked as he sniffed over the treats, crackers, and cheeses that were laid out on the table.

"I didn't know you came to these sorts of events," Vanessa said.

He shrugged his shoulders. "I come for the food," he said, scratching at his chest.

Lyx shooed him away from the table. "Don't do that next to the food. You'll get fur all over it."

"I'm not hurtin' nothin'."

"Is there a problem?" Riker asked standing behind the Sleekit.

Malachi paled.

Vanessa giggled and watched as Ell, Raven, her mom, and her dad walked over to them. She looked all around her and felt her heart swell. She finally felt at peace. It pained her that she would always miss her blood family. But she knew that Raven carried with her a sadness and guilt that even spending a lifetime with Vanessa wouldn't free her of. Even dead, there was more happiness to the Dark Elf. There was brightness in her eyes that couldn't be dimmed or denied. As for Vanessa? She still had a family. She had people she loved and cherished and a whole life full of adventures waiting for her. This was where she belonged. And it felt so good to finally realize that and embrace it.

The whole group was circled around and chatting away or laughing at jokes and stories. It was like something out of a dream.

She smiled. She laughed to herself. She let every ounce of happiness stir and build up inside her.

"I love you guys," she proclaimed.

They all stopped, turned, and replied in a unified collision of voices, *"I love you, too."*

The love and joy she felt in that moment was the most beautiful magic of all.

Tonight, they would dance, eat, drink, and talk. At sunrise, the Wild Hunt would take the spirits back into the sky. There would be one more night to spend with them before she had to wait another year. But she knew then that the next coming year would be full of missions and outings and a million things to keep her busy. Life was such a grand adventure on its own. There was no telling what the future would hold. But she knew she wouldn't face it alone.

Because she would never be alone ever again.

She realized now that she never truly had been.

The End

From the Author:

This is the end of Vanessa and Bobo's tale, but don't worry! Book #6 will be out this fall, and you can have one more dance with the dangers of Aeristria with Thea. If you could take a moment to leave an honest review, it would mean so much to me and Octavia. They help us small authors in so many ways, and they can aid fellow readers on their next book journey.

I have so many novels in store for years to come, and nothing makes me happier than to share my countless stories, worlds, and characters with you.

May your books be blessings to you and bring you comfort in your time of need. They are some of the greatest friends and treasures this world has to offer. Be joyful and walk in love and light, readers.

~Nia Rose

www.ingramcontent.com/pod-product-compliance
Lightning Source LLC
Chambersburg PA
CBHW051600100726
47898CB00001B/165